SURPRISE ATTACK

"To arms! To arms! We're under attack!"

Driving into camp on a blown horse, helmet and lance missing, blood streaming down one arm, came a Scorpion of the Red Century. Dark hair flying, she reined the horse to a halt, jumped from the saddle, steadied herself, panted at Gull and his officers.

"General, we're under attack! Demons, shades—long black cats with wings! We've lost twenty—in the first wave—"

Before Gull could answer, a pair of Gold centaurs pounded into camp from the opposite direction. One had an arrow in his upper arm. "General! Captain Holleb asks you come! War mammoths and blue barbarians and archers come from west! All hell breaks!"

Greensleeves called from a treehouse balcony high above. "Brother! The wizards are loose! They've slipped their leashes!"

Look for
MAGIC: The Gathering

Arena
Whispering Woods
Shattered Chains
Final Sacrifice

From HarperPrism

MAGIC
The Gathering ™

FINAL SACRIFICE

Clayton Emery

HarperPrism
An Imprint of HarperPaperbacks

Dedicated to Ron Albury and Vic Cecere,
Adventurers All

HarperPaperbacks   *A Division of* HarperCollins*Publishers*
10 East 53rd Street, New York, N.Y. 10022

Copyright © 1995 by Wizards of the Coast, Inc.
All rights reserved. No part of this book may be used or reproduced in any manner whatsoever without written permission of the publisher, except in the case of brief quotations embodied in critical articles and reviews. For information address HarperCollins*Publishers*,
10 East 53rd Street, New York, N.Y. 10022.

Cover illustration by Kevin Murphy

First printing: May 1995

Printed in the United States of America

HarperPrism is an imprint of HarperPaperbacks.
HarperPaperbacks, HarperPrism, and colophon are trademarks of HarperCollins*Publishers*

❖ 10 9 8 7 6 5 4 3 2 1

CHAPTER

1

"MORE WINE, AND QUICKLY, YOU BAG OF snot! I'm thirsty!"

The innkeeper hurried to the cellar and returned with an amphora of his best stock: dark red wine carried over the mountains and aged more than five years. Slowly, so as not to spill it or antagonize the young wizard, the innkeeper poured a mug full and handed it over.

Gurias of Tolaria lifted a hand off a girl's shoulder, accepted the wine, sipped. It was excellent, better than anything the wizard had ever tasted. But it wouldn't do to show the locals any mercy. He dashed the contents in the innkeeper's face, laughing as the man sputtered, then threw the heavy mug at his forehead as the man rubbed his eyes. Gurias laughed again, touched an amulet at his breast, and sent a small bolt of lightning crackling down his finger. Since the innkeeper was standing in a puddle of wine, the electricity sizzled down his wet clothes and charred his feet. The innkeeper yelped, turned to run, and Gurias shot another bolt that crackled against his rump.

"Oh, my!" the wizard crowed. "What a life!"

He pushed the two farm girls away, rose, stretched, took a pace around the small inn. He had the place to himself. The villagers, he knew, stood outside in the cold and drizzle and awaited his orders. He'd kept them waiting, the whole village, since noon, enjoying their misery. Perhaps he should send them to bed, so they'd be fresh for his orders tomorrow.

For Gurias had plans. He'd been kind so far. Two days ago he'd strode into town, bowled over the reeve with his lightning spells and magic cudgel. When a dozen men and women had come at him with grain flails and pitchforks, he'd frozen the lot, shoved them over into the mud, then pounded them savagely with his magic-dancing cudgel. He'd issued a few orders, then taken over the inn and tasted the best the town had to offer. He'd plucked two girls from the crowd for company, used his cudgel to wallop them into obedience as they stood paralyzed.

"But I want more," he muttered. Hiding their anger and shame behind blank bruised faces, the farm girls watched the boy pace the room, thinking, hands behind his back. Gurias was a lad of average height and face, with strawberry-blond curls and a limp mustache. He wore good clothes, red hose, and a doublet of brocaded blue, with a blue hat and red feather; he dressed the way a wizard should dress, he supposed. At his belt hung a long knife. His magic cudgel stood by itself near the bar. The low-beamed smoke-stained room was heavy with heat and the smell of spilled wine and the girls' loathing.

"I want more," he repeated. "I started out as nothing but a wizard's apprentice, you know. An old fart up in the hills, Tobias, took me on because I was so clever—I'd worked out a way to call the stock from the hills without leaving the back stoop. But Tobias had no concept of what magic-using can be. Study and study and more study—it's stupid! Once I'd learned everything he knew, and more besides, I left to begin my career.

"And I've started here. You're lucky!" He pointed a finger and the girls flinched. "Treat me right and you'll go far! Once the rest of the valley brings in their silver and best horses—or else I turn up the heat under the reeve and the elders locked in the smokehouse—we'll be ready to move down to Bywater. And don't you girls fret. I won't harm your families. Some slaves to help with the horses, then we sell them—horses and slaves, I suppose—and we can buy a tent, maybe a wagon. You can be my maids and I'll dress you in lace! Ha! Eh?"

He turned as the door opened quietly. In came a woman, alone, in garb that said she was not of this valley.

The woman presented an odd contrast and yet a strong serenity. She was not tall, but slim, with lustrous brown hair that fell in unruly waves around her shoulders. Her face was tanned from a lifetime outdoors. She wore no jewelry, and her gown was very plain, of a pale green like lichens that grew on tree bark. Her sleeves, Gurias noted, were darker green, the rich deep summer color of good grass. A plain belt of braided grass adorned her waist.

But her cloak was what first arrested his attention.

It hung softly around her shoulders past her hips. Originally of a tight-woven green wool, the cloak had been embroidered with more details than could be noted in a hour, or a day. Like some fabled tapestry on a castle wall, the cloak sported scene after scene drawn with bright threads. Along the hem, a satyr chased a nymph past a marble plinth that was cracked as if from an earthquake, and atop the plinth danced leprechauns. Around the base coiled a huge snake with an elvish arrow clenched in its jaws, the steel head crumbling with rust. Past the snake was a glimpse of a rocky harbor, and in the water rowed a curious carved canoe paddled by dark-skinned folk with kinky hair and bright feathers. They traveled oblivious to a monstrous wave rearing above the sea. At the crest of the wave danced a flaming horse with a tail of fire that streamed across the sky, until it crossed a shaft of sunlight that burned into a yellow field where stood a giant horse of wood and sheet iron. And on and on went the strange designs, one leading to another, passing out of sight around the mysterious woman's curves.

Gurias tore his eyes off the bold images stitched into the cloak and met the woman's mild green eyes. He tried to sneer. "Give me that cloak, woman! I want it!"

The woman's voice was equally mild. "My cloak? This poor rag? Why I should give it to you? Are you some"—she hesitated—"formidable wizard?"

Gurias smiled. This one was astute, not like the rest of the stupid cattle that dragged themselves around this mudhole. "Yes, I'm glad you can see it! I am Gurias of Tolaria—that's a place I found on a map. I've got more spells than you can count. I've decided to become squire of this village and all the lands hereabouts."

"I see." The woman glanced at the farm girls, who watched warily for a chance to escape. The woman stepped over broken crockery, made to lean against the bar, found it sticky. She reached a hand toward the magic cudgel, which stood upright by itself as if driven into the floorboards.

"Don't touch that!" Gurias barked. "It's magic! It'll hurt you!"

But the woman reached anyway. For a second, Gurias stopped thinking about himself to wonder who she was. She wasn't from this valley, for surely that cloak was a noblewoman's garb, though her gown was plain as if straight off the loom. Was she traveling through in a coach or sedan? Why hadn't he heard of her approach? (And why wasn't she wet if it were still raining outside?) Perhaps she was from some mansion down near Bywater, the lady of the manor. It might be worthwhile to capture her and gain entry to the home. Imagine the riches—

She was still reaching for his cudgel, but Gurias hung back, waiting. It would be jolly to see the cudgel teach her a lesson. He'd trained the club to soundly thrash anyone who touched it except him. He chuckled, "All right, pick up it. You'll be sor—"

Gurias gawked as the noblewoman picked the stick up easily, turned it in her hands, examining it. "Hey! It's not supposed to—"

Idly, the lady propped the stick back upright, but it fell over, lifeless. What . . . ?

"What have you done?" Gurias demanded. He strode toward the bar. Enough was enough. He'd treat her the way he had the farm girls, lay her over the bar and thump her backside—

But as the boy wizard reached for his fallen stick, he stopped. Rippling in earth colors—green then brown then blue then yellow—popping up from the floor, twinkled a quartet of little folk in green.

Pop-eyed, Gurias stared. The creatures wore neat clothes all in green, tidy as dolls. They had green knit caps and brown pointed beards, but one was clean-shaven, and Gurias realized it was female. She smiled brightly from near the floor, for she was no taller than a squirrel, and made a small curtsy with the tails of her tunic. Gurias would have laughed if he hadn't been so surprised.

For at that moment, the tiny troupe grabbed up the fallen cudgel and took off running. The tiny female—a leprechaun, Gurias realized—put her thumb to her nose and waggled her fingers while sticking out her tongue.

"Hey!" yelled the wizard. He kicked at the female leprechaun and somehow missed her. He ran after the four and his stick. With an agile leap, he jumped clear over them, planted his back against the wall, and yelled, "Got you!"

The tiny quartet laughed, a tinkling sound like wind chimes, ran straight between his legs, smack into the wall—and through it.

Gurias stared stupidly at the boards where they'd disappeared and rubbed the wooden wall.

Then he snapped his head up at the noblewoman, who'd parked her rump on a high stool. "You're a wizard!"

"Druid," she confirmed with a nod. For the first time, Gurias noted she was young, not much over twenty: no more than four years older than he.

"Oh, a druid." He dismissed that with a wave of his hand and craftily sauntered her way. "I know them. They make rain and help crops grow and—heal trees or something."

At arm's reach, he suddenly snatched her brown wavy hair and yanked her head askew. He whipped out his long knife, showed her the blade. "Well, *I'm* no tree-coddler! I'm a *real* wizard—"

He didn't notice the woman curl a finger around the edge of her cloak and touch a picture of an arrowhead crumbling red.

What Gurias noticed was his knife blade. He'd had it cleaned and sharpened just today, had ordered the blacksmith to do so, but the blade was already rusty. Must be the damp air, he thought, but no. The rust spread across the blade, pitting it deeply. In seconds, the sharp point dissolved. The destruction continued until Gurias was holding a brass hilt and red flakes lay on the woman's thigh.

Gurias still held her hair and head at a sharp angle. Gingerly he let go. "Who . . . exactly are you?"

"Your nemesis," said the woman easily. She shook back her hair and caught a fold of her cloak, where a winter storm hurled sleet.

Instantly Gurias was engulfed in an icy blast from the farthest reaches of the northlands. Biting cold seared him like fire, until his skin went white and numb and frostbitten. Teeth chattering, he shook uncontrollably, shivered so hard he almost fell. He tottered to the fire, but found no heat there, even when he plunged both hands into the flames. He looked down at his legs, found his feet encased in ice and frost licking up his legs. He might have been buried in a snowbank, or frozen into a glacier such as he'd seen glinting in the mountain crevices. He reached for the amulet around his neck with its lightning bolt. He'd kill this druid if he could summon the mana, but his hand couldn't grasp the charm. Even his breath was icy, and he wondered if his guts would freeze solid.

With a spasm, he keeled over backward. Ice shattered off his lower limbs, but he was too numb to move. He gazed at the smoke-stained ceiling and beams. Gwendlyn's Groin, he was too young to die, especially from a magic blast! *He* was the wizard! *He'd* been born to control others, not be controlled—

Shuddering, through eyes glazed with ice, Gurias saw looming over him the two farm girls he'd forced to sate his sexual lusts. They smiled with glee. Both raised clog-shod feet.

"Oh, n-n-n-n-no!" Gurias had time for one whine before a wooden shoe smashed his nose flat.

The girls kicked him for a long time, taking turns, aiming their blows well, avoiding his head so he didn't black out. They were farm girls, and strong, and kicked hard enough to break down a door.

At some point, the winter-blast spell dissipated. The kicking made Gurias warmer, but that was small consolation.

Gurias came to when someone dashed water in his face.

He lay across a beer-stained table with his arms trussed by his head. Straining, he found his magic cudgel lashed across his shoulders and his wrists tied to it. Sitting along the cudgel, like sparrows on a

fence, were the four leprechauns. As Gurias stared
from the corners of his eyes, the small round-cheeked
female walked across the hill of his shoulder, reached
out for his mustache, and with a mischievous grin,
yanked a hair from its few companions. Gurias
yelped and snorted, which started his smashed nose
bleeding again. He could feel blood crusted on his
face, stinging his cracked lips. In fact, all of him was
cracked, mashed, split, and scraped. Funny, he
thought with a groan, he'd never read of this happening to wizards in those old dusty books of Tobias's.
Maybe he should have paid closer attention. . . .

Voices droned all around. Most of the village
packed the tiny inn. The reeve, reeking like a smoked
ham from his imprisonment, addressed the druid.
"We can't thank you enough, milady. You've saved
us from ruin. He was just warming up, this one, just
feeling his oats. He'd have turned mean soon, started
turning us into beasts or skinnin' us alive or something, milady. . . . "

The woman's voice was like a spring balm in the hot
room. "You needn't call me 'Ômilady,' good reeve. I
am Greensleeves, as called by my family and friends,
and I consider you all friends. I'm only sorry I couldn't
come stop him earlier, but we were detained—"

"*Greensleeves!*" bleated several people. The villagers babbled, and the reeve spoke for them.
"Greensleeves the Archdruid? Who's got the wal-
lopin' great army with Gull the Woodcutter? Well,
what are you doing *here* in this backwater, milady?
Uh, Greensleeves. We're nothing for highborn folk to
bother with!"

"On the contrary, good sir," corrected the druid.
"It's exactly the common folk we wish to help, for
both my brother and I were common folk made
homeless by wizardry."

The crowd buzzed. Gurias groaned. This was not
good news.

Greensleeves resumed her seat on the stool. "I see you are confused. Please let me explain.

"Have any of you heard of the Whispering Woods, far to the south of here? Ah, you have. Well, on the eastern edge of the woods there was once a village called White Ridge. My brother, yes, Gull the General, was a woodcutter while I was the village idiot, yes, since birth, with no more mind than a baby bird. Gull took me to the woods for company. It was a humble life, our village small but content, like this one—and how I envy your quiet, productive lives here.

"The gods had other plans for us. One day a pair of wizards appeared in our valley, and they dueled, with soldiers and clockwork beasts and blue-skinned barbarians and walls of briars and Uthden trolls, and more. We villagers were caught in the middle of chaos. An earthquake split the valley and drained our precious river. A spell of strength-draining and then a rain of stones felled many, including our mother and father and siblings. All our family was wiped out, save our brother Sparrow Hawk, who was captured and lost. And when the battle was over, the survivors faced looters and vampires and ghouls come to the slaughter, and rats that brought plague. Most fled, until only Gull and I were left, and we took to the woods.

"But I prattle. To make a long story less long, we fell in with a wizard who pretended to befriend us—a fiend named Towser, mark his evil name. Working for him, we left the Whispering Woods, and I came into my mind. We learned later that the magic of the woods had so saturated my being that I had the powers of wizardry: vast powers. When Towser tried to sacrifice me—to suck the mana from my soul—I managed to fight back. By then, my brother had the beginnings of his army, and we defeated Towser and drove him away.

"But once rolling, like a snowball down a hill, we couldn't stop, nor do we intend to. Gull and I found that many villages had been savaged by wizards vying for power, foraging after goods and magic, using people and discarding them. Once they come into power, wizards think themselves gods. My brother and I are out to persuade them otherwise."

Lying trussed on the table, Gurias gave an audible groan. *This* was the "noblewoman and druid" he'd tried to force?

Greensleeves finished. "So we've mustered a campaign, a crusade, if you like, to stop wizards in their depredations and bring them to heel. Stop them, capture them, correct them, kill them if necessary. But to make the world safe for common folk to live their lives without fear and bullying."

Someone raised a shout, and in moments, everyone was cheering loud enough to raise the roof. The archdruid, one of the most powerful wizards in the Domains, blushed at the fuss.

People had questions: How they might help, what came next, could they volunteer? Folks took a renewed interest in Gurias and jabbed his wounds to see him jump.

Greensleeves finally waved her hands. Silence fell. "I'll answer some of your queries, and then I must go. We learn of magic in many ways: my students of magic have a device that learns of magic disturbing the ether, and we send scouts to scour the countryside. When I heard there was a small wizard being obnoxious here"— people hissed at Gurias, and jabbed harder—"I thought of my lost home and came to help. I'm only sorry it took so long to arrive, and for that, my sincere apologies."

The crowd wouldn't hear any apologies, but praised her and toasted and cheered and offered gory and obscene suggestions as to what to do to Gurias. The battered wizard went both ice-cold and sweltering-hot to hear them. He'd only come to the village and done what anyone would have done. Why should they resent that he could lord power over peasants?

But mostly he worried about what would happen to him *after* Greensleeves left.

But in the end, Greensleeves bid them good-bye and came to Gurias's side. Gently as a falling leaf, she laid a hand on his chest. She looked at him with round, green eyes and sadly shook her head. Why? Because she pitied him? Was he to die now?

Then the world rippled with color: green, brown, blue, yellow. . . .

One moment Gurias was lying on a table in a steamy, smoky room, and the next he was lying on a plank floor in a small round hut lit by dozens of candles.

The walls were lined with tables crammed with magic paraphenalia: crocks, retorts, pots, jars, skulls, cocoons, tin clockwork animals, statues, crowns, and much more. Above the tables were shelves crammed with books of all sizes and colors, and more geegaws hung from the rafters.

Working at the table were a tall dark-clad man, and a shorter man with a huge nose and side-whiskers who could have been half-elf. He was dressed like a clown in every color.

"Welcome back," said the dark man. Greensleeves smiled and stood on tiptoe to kiss him. The big-nosed man discreetly looked away.

The archdruid pointed to Gurias, lying trussed and half-stupefied. "This is our offender, as your palantir identified. He has a lightning spell, and can paralyze; a few others, and the cudgel can beat someone on its own."

Big Nose nodded. "That'll be fun to experiment with."

"Remember what happened with one of your experiments, Tybalt," Greensleeves warned.

Tybalt shuddered. "I remember. Shall we slap the helmet on him?"

Greensleeves nodded. "As you need. He was the village bully. You can see how they resented him."

She addressed the wretch on the floor. "If you would learn magic, young wizard, learn this. Many will master you until you learn to master yourself."

"Lucky he's alive to hear it," Tybalt muttered. He kept his back turned as Greensleeves kissed the tall man again, then left. She swept out the door and sharply around the corner to the right. The night was black outside, but there was no rain.

Tybalt nodded at the big man, yet hid a grin. "Cut him loose, will you, Kwam?"

The magic student also hid a grin as he used a table knife to slice Gurias's bonds.

The battered wizard sat up slowly, massaging his wrists, gauging the distance to the door. Slowly he gathered his strength. Neither of the students seemed to notice. Kwam and Tybalt fiddled with his magic cudgel.

Without a sound, Gurias leaped to his feet like a cat and bolted for the door. He'd been the champion runner of his village once, and if he could get a head start—

He flew out the door, stepped onto the tiny wooden stoop outside, and leaped for the invisible ground in the dark.

And realized he was high up in some giant tree.

Branches whipped his face, leaves caught in his fingers as he fell and fell and fell, screaming all the way—

—until he suddenly splatted into a net strung between trunks thirty feet down. One leg splayed through a hole, and one arm, so he landed on his face in the rough hemp. His heart started beating again, erratic and slow. He was alive!

And humiliated.

Thirty feet above, Tybalt and Kwam laughed and whooped and cried real tears. Gurias's face flamed under its bruises as he bounced gently in the net.

Tybalt howled, "I *love* when they do that!"

CHAPTER
2

IMMUGIO STRODE THROUGH THE ARMY like the mountains that had spawned him. The earth shook under his huge feet, and he sank a full six inches into the churned dirt and offal and rubbish and ashes that ringed the walled city. He carried a whip woven of an entire ox hide with nine long lashes. He had originally fashioned the whip with iron hooks at the tip, but had beaten to death the first four soldiers he'd punished. Immugio needed soldiers to do his dirty work, and to whip. A warlord needed someone to order about.

He'd been ordering for a week now, and enjoying it. He whipped his troops as he bawled orders and liked to see them writhe and work faster—for his success.

The army numbered in the hundreds, mostly orcs and goblins he'd scrounged from the hills, but also a large contingent of renegade men he'd enslaved. This filthy band of thirty cutthroats he'd found skulking as highwaymen and robbers, eager to waylay a merchant train or raid an isolated homestead, scum who enjoyed torture, rape, looting, and arson. He hit these men just as much as he whipped his orcs. Immugio didn't care if they hated him, as long as they obeyed.

And soon he'd rule an entire city. On this highland plain, in the center of these ruined fields, oppressed by the dark autumn sky, lay Myrion, a small walled city well defended by its inhabitants. They fought valiantly and had pushed back Immugio's ragtag army four times in six days. But Immugio was wearing down their forces bit by bit, as rain wears down a mountain. Soon starvation and fatigue would take their toll, and then the orcs and renegades would breach the walls and gate, and rejoice in defiling the city.

So he whipped his hordes of orcs to work the hastily built catapults and trebuchets and ballistae. At the rear, the renegades labored in the chill air and mud to build a siege tower with a battering ram in its belly. That war machine would turn the trick and put Immugio's army inside by noon tomorrow.

But they wouldn't destroy the city, not entirely, for Immugio planned to enslave some survivors, to rule over them and be respected.

Born to an ogress of the Short Hand tribe, Immugio was himself the product of rape, for the ogre tribe had sustained a raid by stone giants from farther west. Immugio showed his mixed heritage. He had the height of a giant, but the hunched back of an ogre. He had long black hair as coarse as a horse's tail and a thick beard, but the snaggly tusks of an ogre. He wore only a pair of raw bearskins around his hips, but suspended from his thick neck, hanging down his chest, was the death mask of his giant father, the rapist who'd spawned him. Immugio had tracked the giant down and felled him from ambush, peeled his face from his skull as he died, and dried it over a slow fire, so there appeared not one but two glowering visages when the ogre-giant bastard stomped across the filthy field.

Immugio plied his whip and his wits and his magic to make others submit, and suffer, for he knew nothing else. Never in his life had he known peace or a kind word. A half-breed growing up amidst his mother's tribe, his giant features had earned him ridicule and stonings and burns and broken bones. When he'd come into his own giant size, he'd broken many heads in return and been forced to flee his home. Finding his father's tribe upcountry, he'd met with the same abuse for his ogreness. So, having slain his father as a parting gesture, Immugio went south.

And discovered something new.

Whether fanned by hatred, or spawned by the odd mixing of two bloods, Immugio found he could move the earth around him and the sky above. With a gesture and a thought, the ogre-giant could bring rocks tumbling from the high peaks, pull clouds over the horizon and make them shed rain and snow. He could uproot trees and collapse caves, divert rivers, smell out gold and silver and copper and lead.

And that was when he'd decided to get back at the world for his pains. He'd begun in the south, the highlands, where humans dwelt, weak and puny beings who put their faith in the soil. Immugio would become their king—how hard could it be?—and from a new kingdom, return to north with new weapons and new powers, and he'll slay all of the Tall Folk. Then he would be the only giant there was, and men would not know he was a half-breed bastard, but think him mighty and godlike.

And this city was to be the first stepping-stone. Yet humans, he had learned, while small and helpless singly and in pairs, could be damnably stubborn and feisty in groups. And they were clever enough to send arrows and stones against a giant, as he'd learned when he led the first assault on the walls, which was why he led from the rear now, and drove men and orcs forward with his whip. Greed drove them also, and the renegade men lusted for vengeance, for many were criminals driven from the city. They laughed as they plotted which houses to visit and whom to torture first of the citizens.

It wouldn't be long now, Immugio gloated. One more day and they'd leave the brassy stink of their own wastes, charge into the city—

Immugio turned. Men who should have been fashioning the siege tower shouted at the rear. Screamed in fright.

The half-giant saw why.

Suddenly, from nothingness, strung along a low ridge a half-mile behind his army, stood a line of soldiers and cavalry.

The line was as long as the giant serpent of the legends: men and women and horses and centaurs and a huge wooden construct and even a two-headed giant. And at their center, surrounded by a ring of lancers, rode a tall man who carried a double-headed axe on his shoulder.

Immugio swore, stuck his whip in his belt, rubbed his eyes with both hands, but the apparition did not fade away. His orcs and renegades had seen the opposing army now, and howled in fright. These were not helpless citizens and a few city guards and soldiers—this was an army like theirs, only a hundred times more potent. As one, Immugio's army broke and ran for the hills and caves and crevices that ringed the highland plain.

The big man at the center of the army raised his two-headed axe high, and trumpets rang out. Drums rumbled, and the soldiers sent up a mighty shout. And charged.

The chase was on, like war dogs after crippled rabbits. As the first terrified wave of gray-green orcs reached the edge of the plateau, a long, rippling line of archers, all human females clad in black, hoisted fluted bows into the air and loosed a line of sizzling death. At the opposite point of the compass, more archers arose, these black-haired, solemn-faced elves in shiny green tunics like snakeskins. Pale tattooed arms drew arrows to nocks, and more orcs died.

At the rear, the renegades so thirsty for innocent blood fled toward Immugio. Hard at their heels marched phalanxes of infantry with red or black or white or blue plumes in their helmets. Their feet shook the earth as they tramped steadily onward, sure as a glacier, sure as death.

Immugio had no time to worry about his panicked soldiers. A large contingent of the army was aimed straight for him.

The big man, general of the army, mounted on a dapple-gray horse, surrounded by mounted lancers, bellowed. His force moved out at the gallop, wide, around the tramping soldiers. Before them, in an undulating wave, thundered fifty centaurs in painted armor with long, feathered lances. Behind the general's entourage came another fifty horse-folk.

Trapped on three sides, with the city on the fourth, Immugio decided to stand his ground. He could move the earth and sky, after all, and would.

Raising arms as long as trees, he waved his hands and howled a garbled mixture of ogre and giant. And the sky above responded. The overcast roiled, clouds thickened. Thunderheads dropped lower, and lightning crackled between them. Cold, thought Immugio, he'd send cold upward and turn the cloud mist into snow. And fetch a blizzard to bury the city and hide his escape. He laughed as the first flakes shimmered above, felt one and then many dot his face.

Then no more.

Shaking his head, Immugio frowned at the sky. The clouds rolled again, but back to their normal state, the thunderheads flattening along the bottom, the rifts between widening. Before many more seconds, Immugio could see clear sky. The sun would come out next. Who . . . ?

He peered around, but his eyesight was bad, so he couldn't discern the small figure in the embroidered cloak who stood at the rear of the army and pointed slim fingers upward. Immugio knew some wizard was there, for never before had he failed to move the sky.

Turning, seeking a way out, alarmed for the first time, he unthinkingly grabbed the frozen rictus, the dried face of his father at his chest. The death's head seemed drawn into a grin, as if it knew revenge was not far off.

But the ogre-giant was too slow. Almost before he could blink, a double ring of armored centaurs surrounded him. They whirled like autumn leaves, two rings trotting in opposite directions, passing at lance-length, tripping lightly as deer amidst flowers, watching the giant and their comrades at the same time. Immugio raged at the two-tiered ring of pointed steel. He could smell them, a sweet odor of hay and alfalfa and woodsmoke and leather polish and metal. It made him sick to feel threatened by such puny things.

Raging, the giant raised his oxhide whip and lashed out. His long reach aided him, for he got past a centaur's lance and tangled her head and torso with long cords sticky with dried flesh and blood.

But his death grip only lasted a second. Even as the centaur jigged out of formation so as not to slow the line, a dozen sharp blades were plied. Broad heads of polished steel pinked at the cords, severing them in a trice, and Immugio was left with a leather stump as long as his arm.

He roared as something pinked the back of his knee. At a whistle from some commander—they all looked alike, gaudy as bluebirds and robins and cardinals, their only similarity their rose-colored armbands that fluttered in their breeze—a centaur stepped into the circle and scored a slice on the giant's skin. He

turned, raging, only to take another pink in the side of
the knee. And another, and another.

For the first time, his red-eyed rage was tempered
by panic. He would be flayed to ribbons before long.

Howling, cursing, Immugio stooped and slapped
hands on the ground. Growling, he caught up handfuls of soil and ash and willed the layers of earth
below to shake. He felt it respond, for these mountains moved all the time and needed only the proper
insertion of a lever to set them quivering. The first
tremor touched his fingertips, as if the earth itself
feared him, and he ignored the jabs at his rump as he
splayed his great bare feet and waited for the shock
that would send these centaurs tumbling—

But the quivers only jumped once, barely rattling
pebbles, and quit. Far off at the edge of the plateau,
the small wizard woman had calmed the earth, stilled
the tremors, sent the energy rippling far away.

Immugio was shocked. His best spell, undone!
Fear gave the giant pause, and it cost him. A score of
nicks and cuts dinged his forearms, legs, heels. These
puny ants, these horse-folk, would cut his very legs
from under him.

"Enough!" Bounding to his feet, Immugio lowered
his head and, roaring, charged full at the circle of
lancers. He'd crush a few, bull past them, splinter
their bones and pulp their meat before he ran far, far
off into the hills—

But another damned whistle sounded, and there
were no centaurs to stomp. Seeing him charge, they'd
flitted aside like a flock of sparrows. Immugio
laughed to see himself in the clear. Only ruined crops
and smoldering campfires and trash were between
him and the hills. He'd—

Take more pinks in the backside.

The centaurs reformed and matched his clumsy running easily. From behind, on both sides, they took turns
lunging close, stabbing as deeply as they might without

losing their weapons, then sheering aside as their companions rattled up behind. Jab, thrust, cut, swipe, slash; Immugio lost blood as if to monster mosquitoes.

He howled in rage and frustration and fear. He could die out here. They'd make a throne of his skull. His father's dead face, slapping on his hairy chest, seemed to be pushing him back while laughing at him.

It wasn't supposed to happen this way. But the ogre-giant could see no solution but blind running, and hoped he could reach the hills.

Yet the cuts lessened, only every other centaur scoring. He must be pulling away from them.

What he couldn't see were the lassos being unslung, whirled overhead, and flung with uncanny aim by eyes more keen than any human's.

Something hooked Immugio's toe.

He stumbled and crashed full out. Mud speckled with rye chaff plugged his nose and he snorted.

Immediately four, then eight, then twelve and sixteen iron-shod hooves danced on his back. The massive weight of the armored horse-folk pinned even the giant. Immugio thrashed his arms to prop himself up, but four lassos snarled his hands, almost snapped his fingers as the centaurs jerked backward with all their weight. Thunder ringing in his ears, Immugio felt the centaurs leap clear over his body, wrench his arms around and pin them at his side.

In seconds, he was helpless. He closed his eyes, waiting for the thousand cuts that would flay his flesh from his bones. Or the single telling blow he would never feel as his spine was cleft.

His dead father's face, ground into the mud under his traitor son, yet managed to gag Immugio's throat.

After a while, when nothing happened, the giant opened his eyes. All fifty centaurs ringed him. They coiled ropes or touched up their lance blades with whetstones. They waited.

A gentle thudding of hooves announced for whom

they waited. Not a centaur this time, but a horse and rider trailed by thirty lancers with green armbands. The army's general, the big man with the double-headed axe. The ring of centaurs gave way, and the man rode forward and dismounted.

Toting his axe, he strode toward the giant's immobile head. The general wore a plain helmet of black-painted steel with a leather visor. Long brown hair spilled from under it around his tanned face. He wore a shirt of simple undyed wool, a leather tunic, a plain black cuirass, and a leather kilt with tall laced boots. At his belt hung a braided mulewhip. Of all the soldiers on the field, his garb was the plainest. His left hand lacked three fingers, yet he easily toted that long-handled woodcutting axe.

The man strode forward calmly, crouched to look into the giant's bloodshot eyes, found him awake and alive. Casually, he raised a boot and propped it against the bridge of Immugio's nose, square between the thick eyebrows. The long axe dangled in his hand, not two feet from the giant's eyes.

The big man said, "I am Gull the Woodcutter. Do you yield?"

Immugio nodded as best he could and growled, "Yield."

In the distance, the city gates cracked open, and out spilled a shrieking, singing, crying, laughing, joyous multitude—the staunch defenders of the city. Gull smiled to see them.

Somewhere far off, Immugio's dead father crowed with laughter.

The giant had been rolled and lashed with thirty ropes held by thirty brawny centaurs when Greensleeves walked up. She had her own entourage, four armed female bodyguards with spears and swords and shields, who shuffled between her and the captive giant, and her bevy of magic students, including the big-nosed Tybalt and her lover Kwam.

For a while the officers of the army watched the mop-up. All the orcs and renegades left on the field had been butchered, first by waves of Gull and Greensleeves's soldiers, then by the avenging citizens come to the field. Scouts and archers beat the bushes to find stragglers. One by one, various captains rode up to report no survivors, until only Immugio was left of his army.

"And what do we do with him?" Gull asked. "He's too big to wear that stone helm of submission or whatever you call it, unless you stick it on his nose."

Tybalt answered for his mistress. In his hands he held a helmet of green stone, the most powerful of artifacts. Tybalt had charge of the helmet, for he'd first fathomed its purpose, though he'd almost lost his sanity doing so.

"Size is no matter to magic," he told Gull. "Watch."

Gently, he approached the recumbent giant, who tried to stare around and not at the sky. Tybalt set the helmet on the giant's sloping forehead, as if balancing a bowl of soup on a lopsided table.

Immediately Immugio hissed, strained at his bonds, jarred the centaurs. He thrashed his head, but Tybalt hung on doggedly.

What the ogre-giant heard was a howling in his brain.

The helmet was a bondage device stronger than any chains and manacles. It had been fashioned, Greensleeves and the others knew, centuries ago during the Brothers' War. The Sages of Lat-Nam, the most powerful college of wizards ever convened, had crafted the helmet, then poured their collective wills into it. Immugio, the helmet's latest victim, heard hundreds of wizardly voices demanding, commanding, ordering that he submit, obey, and cease all wizardry.

Immugio rocked, cursed, fought, but in vain. He was no match for dozens of dead wizards. Finally, after long brain-wrenching moments, the giant croaked, "I will desist. I will submit. Yes, masters."

"That's that." Greensleeves nodded. She dusted her hands, looked over the plain, and brushed back her hair. "Can we do anything for these poor folk who've had their crops ruined and have lost so many lives?"

Her big brother nodded. A half-dozen officers awaited Gull's orders, and under them waited hundreds of soldiers. The erstwhile woodcutter should have been used to such command by now, but it still gave him an eerie feeling. "It's too late to replant. We'll have to dredge up food somewhere, bargain it from the southlands. And I want to scout the hills, make sure no more thugs like Man-Mountain here lurk about. We'll set up a wagon train, help the militia secure the roads, rebuild the walls, get these corpses on the pyres—" He broke off to begin issuing orders.

Greensleeves nodded absentmindedly, concerned with her own details. She studied the giant and wrinkled her nose. She was used to foul odors, but this giant was as rank as a cesspit, crawling with fleas. She wondered whose death mask he wore on his muddy chest. Idly, she asked her students, "A giant wizard is new. Though he's actually some ogre-giant cross, isn't he? So we've now seen a troll wizard and a goblin wizard besides. And one of Helki's centaurs shows wizardry skills, I hear, but she won't say who. . . . "

Led by a capering band of musicians and three fluttering banners, a party of citizen elders marched toward them to offer official thanks to the conquering heroes. Gull and Greensleeves paused in their deliberations to await them.

Greensleeves mused, "They're going to sing legends about us, you know."

Gull squinted at her, tapped his big axe on the giant's hairline. "You think so?"

CHAPTER
3

IGNORING THE GROANS AROUND HER,
Chundachynnowyth scuttled about her tower room.
Her feet scuffed in grooves worn into the granite,
grooves she herself had laid down in centuries of bustle. She stopped at an alcove, brought a candle closer
to see the progress of her experiment.

A man hung in chains from the wall. His face was
ashen, his body limp. He would have died long ago
but for Chundachynnowyth's magic. The skin of his
chest had been peeled back, the muscles sliced off,
the ribs sawn through. He hung, alive and suffering,
so that Chundachynnowyth might study the beating
of his heart. Fastened with copper rivets to his ribs
above the gaping hole was a small beaker filled with
vile chemicals. Tubes from the beaker just touched
the heart. As Chundachynnowyth shuffled close, the
man whimpered, anticipating still more pain. The
wizard ignored him, talked to herself instead. Most
chilling, she rattled on like a batty dame tending her
roses.

"Here we are. Now to add antimony. A poison, to

be sure, but in small doses it's a tonic. Then we'll see if it speeds up or slows down—ah!"

She'd sprinkled a pinch of the poison into the beaker. The prisoner, the living experiment, writhed as the poison jolted his heart. The man groaned, "Please! Please!" Pain made him writhe in his bonds, but Chundachynnowyth touched his lips with a withered hand and froze him momentarily. She hated to do it, for she already expended a great deal of mana just keeping these wretches alive, and introducing more might skew the experiment. The heart beat wildly, pulsing as if to explode, then gradually slowed down, resumed its erratic rhythm.

Chundachynnowyth made a note on a wax tablet with a hardwood stylus. "Well, well. Faster. Good to know, good to know."

She shuffled away, past more prisoners, each with some grisly experiment attached to their hearts or livers or lungs or brains. There were eight prisoners all told, each captured while traveling the edges of the fen wherein lay Chundachynnowyth's small castle and tower. Some were humans, some elves, one an orc. Some were more dead than alive and hung quietly, but most knew what was happening to them and lived in a unending nightmare they could not escape. On tables around the room, and on other floors, were cages of animals, also victims of cruel experiments.

Chundachynnowyth wore rags and a tattered apron, for clothes were not important. Neither was food, or love, or companionship. She was stooped and gray-haired, an oddity for one of her race, for she was old, had been old for centuries.

The wizard was of full elven blood, but no longer considered herself elven. Chundachynnowyth had moved beyond everything, beyond magic and planeswalking, she thought, to stand poised on the edge of life itself, to capture its essence. There was only one thing she wanted nowadays, and she pursued it and nothing else.

As old as she was, she wanted to live longer. Forever, in fact. If she'd ever had other goals, they were long forgotten. Once, centuries ago, she'd stumbled across a secret that appeared to prolong life, and now it was all she worked on, all she sought. To live forever, to grow older than mountains and the sea and even the moons above, that was her goal. So she'd gathered stories and legends and recipes and potions and cures and artifacts, and had come here, and worked.

That she experimented on living, suffering beings meant not a thing. They were nothing to her, so she should be nothing to them. The prisoners were to be used, to further her experiments. If they died, it simply meant the experiment had failed, and she must try again. She must never stop trying, for that might mean her own death, the only real tragedy.

She laid down her wax tablet neatly and picked up another. Ah yes, time to turn up the heat under that small elven girl, the one she was depriving of sleep. Even with a low fire to char her skin, the girl kept nodding off. Chundachynnowyth would try painting sulfur dissolved in mineral oil to the charring, see if that level of pain could rouse her. To do without sleep, Chundachynnowyth had concluded long ago, would be a coup. It would give her more time to experiment. . . .

A flutter at the window was all the noise they made.

Greensleeves touched a toe to the wide stone windowsill and grabbed a cornice to make sure her sister-in-law had also landed safely before the flying spell dissipated.

Lily had barely touched down before she put both hands to her mouth. She'd seen the prisoners ranged along the walls, smelled the deathly reek that permeated the tower. Without a word, she whirled and vomited out the window.

Greensleeves prayed, "Oh, Spirit of the Forest, help us and these poor souls."

Lily, wife to Gull the Woodcutter, had to sit on the windowsill to regain her strength. She wore white from head to toe: white shoes and hose, white gown, a short jacket such as a dancing girl might wear, and a white scarf over her head. The clothes were brightly stitched with flowers, not just yellow lilies, but red roses and purple violets, along the hems and seams. Yet her gown hung away from her a good foot, for she was well into her second pregnancy. She had an excuse for being weak-stomached.

Greensleeves wished she had one. Having seen and heard many awful things, she was still woozy at the horrific sight. On tiptoe, she crossed the room, approached a woman with her head bolted into a framework that kept her shaven skull—and open cranium—immobile. The woman gave no sign Greensleeves was there, but her entire body shuddered at regular intervals.

Barely able to look, peering in the fitful light of a few candles, the wizard forced herself to study the magic here, for it hummed all around like a swarm of mosquitoes.

"Oh, no!" she whispered. "Magic keeps them alive! But Caleria's Ears, *why*?"

Biting her knuckle, Greensleeves tried to think what to do. For a moment, she was ashamed of herself for even trafficking in magic, if this was one of its uses. A tear squeezed out of her eyes. But she steeled herself. Magic was a force and could be used for good or ill, or not at all.

Yet the druid could see no way to save these tormented souls. Except one.

Laying her hand on the tortured woman as gently as she could—the prisoner shuddered once more—

Greensleeves whispered a simple spell, the most simple in some ways. Quickly, like a clean cut, she withdrew the mana sustaining the woman, drew it into herself, even though it was twisted, corrupted mana that made her feel polluted. She steeled herself against the pain as the mana, lacking an outlet, burned through every nerve in her body.

When she removed her hand, the woman gave one final shudder. Her heart failed, and she died, at peace at last. Greensleeves sent a prayer winging after her and moved to the next victim.

At the windowsill, Lily hugged her aching stomach and wished she were home. She'd agreed to come on this raid because she, of all their company, was the only wizard who could fly. A scout, one of the Pradesh gypsies, tracking rumors, had wormed into this dismal swamp and found this island, peeked inside and seen the missing travelers and hideous experiments, sniffed the magic being used and abused, and glimpsed the aged crone scuttling about. Greensleeves, knowing they faced an ancient, experienced mage, had opted to shift to the far side of the swamp, then fly silently to the uppermost window. Although she was already carrying a child, Lily had agreed to help immediately. Gull's wife didn't consider herself a proper wizard, for her only consistent spell was flying. But she'd been eager to be of help in the army's great crusade. Yet Lily wished her mouth didn't taste so sour and they could leave quickly. She peeked out the tower window and wondered how her husband fared.

Greensleeves had stilled another ravaged heart, brought someone else peace, all while hating herself because she couldn't do more. But a screech from the doorway made her jump a foot.

"What are you doing?"

Before Greensleeves could react, a slithering horror loomed above her. An overpowering stench roiled from the thing, a stink of the slaughterhouse and sewer that made her gag.

Tall, the horror was covered with leathery skin, but with features so scrambled Greensleeves could barely understand what she looked upon. All she could think was someone or something had been turned inside out.

A mouth gaped at her from the back of a neck. An eye peered from between shoulder blades. Fingers wiggled on a chin. Bones erupted from the leathery skin, chased their way around ribs and between tufts of hair, and cut back inside. Blood vessels pulsed everywhere. A gland seeped bile that leaked down a leg.

Greensleeves shrilled and backed away from this horror, banging into a table and upsetting crockery. All spells were forgotten. She only wanted to get away, instantly, before the thing *touched* her.

Even now, the monster reached out a crooked arm that erupted from a misplaced shoulder blade. Backward-growing claws dappled with horny toes and warts clasped for her face.

At the doorway to the tower room, Chundachynnowyth shrilled. "Get out! Get out! You'll disrupt my experiments! You'll spoil everything!" Consumed with trepidation, the crone was barely aware she'd conjured up this horror of horrors, a thing she'd forgotten existed.

Lily pushed herself erect from the windowsill and almost fainted at the horror. But she wasn't directly threatened and so could react. She had neither weapons nor spells and could only move awkwardly with her swollen belly. For lack of anything better, she tottered to a table, grabbed a pot of some clear liquid, and hurled it at the horror. The fluid pinwheeled across the room, dappling Greensleeves and the horror both. Lily hurled another, and another, the pots bouncing off the monster, crashing and smashing against the walls and floor, then an oil lamp, which sputtered and ran fire down the stone. "Fly, Greensleeves, fly!" Lily meant "shift," but couldn't think of the word. If Greensleeves could conjure herself away, Lily could fly out the window. But where were Gull and the rest?

A twisted, deformed hand tore at Greensleeves's hair, another at her cloak. Riven by terror, the druid couldn't even think to shift. She only wanted to be away, to be safe.

The wizard Chundachynnowyth was recalling that she, too, long ago, knew how to conjure beings and animals. She had tagged many creatures in her younger days. Now if she could just remember—ah!

Licking dry lips, the old elf raised her hands, pictured a beast-man she'd known of massive bone-crushing strength, a creature from fable. Uttering snatches of ancient spells, for she disremembered them exactly, she peaked the tips of the fingers together and called forth—

—a heap of dry bones.

Backing from the horror, Greensleeves tripped over the huge bones with a clatter and landed on her rump on the cold, filthy stone floor. The horror took a faltering step, for its two legs and half a third were oddly sized. It opened a fang-toothed mouth in its chest, lolled a red forked tongue at her. The druid screamed. She was ashamed of herself for panicking so, but couldn't help it. This was worse than any nightmare. She'd picture this thing for decades to come in the dark recesses of the night. If she survived.

She scrambled up, scattering bones, fell again.

Lily searched for another weapon, yanked a stool from under a table, and hurled it, staggering the monster. It twisted and stamped toward her. Bones crunched under its mangled feet. They were human bones, Lily noted absently, but the skull was a bull's with truncated horns. Why had the old elven wizard conjured that?

Chundachynnowyth was wondering that, too. Why had the minotaur failed her? Oh. Had it died of old age some time past? Had she not summoned it in that long? But thoughts of dying, especially of old age, distracted her momentarily. She had to get back to her experiments to ward off death. No, first, she had to banish these interlopers. With what? Muttering, she pictured a cave under a volcano. Or was it a grotto under a sea cliff . . . ?

Then the elf remembered. Peaking her fingers, she conjured a white cloud before her. A swirling chittering jittering cloud that swooped and spun like chimney ashes. Bats, they seemed at first. But they had twin sideways-hooking jaws like praying mantises, and multifaceted eyes like flies.

The instant the white horde materialized, they continued their eternal quest for food, for insects, and for heat. In seconds, they were skimming and swirling around the two women, flitting through their hair in search of ticks or lice or fleas.

Lily screamed as the things engulfed her like a cloud of mosquitoes. She plucked at her jacket to yank it over her head, but it fit too tightly with her swollen bosom. Slapping at the bat-things, she blundered into a table and upset it with a crash.

Greensleeves was not very distracted by the insect-bats, for they were just normal animals, if strange. But the horror still snatched at her, and the bats blurred her vision. Fear was giving way to anger, and she swore with her brother's oaths, but then she slipped in a pool of oil and fell again.

Spirit of the Forest, she only wanted to be away. Far away. In the Whispering Woods she loved, near her favorite tree, a quiet spot where she could luxuriate in its shade, listen to the twitter of the birds and chatter of squirrels in its branches, relax in a place of peace. . . .

Chundachynnowyth saw an advantage. The woman in white was distracted by the bats. The snippet in green was trapped against the table, about to be shredded. What else could she throw at them? And where were her guards? They should have come running at the screams. Chundachynnowyth peaked her fingers together. Why hadn't she thought of simply freezing these two earlier? She was getting fuddled. . . .

Yet Greensleeves was equally fuddled, and conjuring without knowing it. She wanted to be away, by her favorite tree, but had to remain here, waiting for her brother, so she couldn't flee and leave Lily stranded, yet if she were near her favorite tree. . . .

As these jumbled thoughts surged with her power and deepest wishes—

—the tree came to Greensleeves.

A massive red oak, one hundred fifty feet tall, it had towered over the forest, lord of its domain. Its crown had a spread of hundreds of feet filled with tens of thousands of leaves. It weighed tons and tons.

But, unthinkingly, Greensleeves had conjured it to the top floor of a castle tower in a swamp.

She saw only a ripple, green then brown then blue and yellow, but the ripple was as big around as the girth of the tree, larger than most houses. There was only time for a glimpse as tons of wood and bark appeared in the room. Then, as the ripples vanished and the tree came fully into being, its weight and size bore down on the small stone tower.

Shoved outward by the tree, the whole corner of the tower cascaded into the swamp. The floor collapsed in stone slabs that belched dust from between cracks. The outer wall crumbled, roof slates crashed and splintered. Tree roots dropped tons of earth into the lower sections of the tower, half-buried the wreckage.

Having brushed away the tower's corner, the massive tree lingered only a second. Then it toppled.

It dropped, straight down, crushing granite blocks and tables and errant guards and trapped prisoners, finally smashing against the very ground of the swampy island itself. Greensleeves had unwittingly conjured the tree at hand's reach. Now she jumped back and covered her ears as the tree wreaked its havoc then, tilted by the remnants of the tower, toppled sideways. The archdruid had a glimpse of night air, fireflies flickering above fetid water, cypresses hung with moss shaking gently at the tremor. Then the tree struck the swamp.

Everyone in the room was thrown off their feet by the shock. Black water parted as if by a miracle, gushed away to obliterate grass, cattails, and small trees. Mud roiled in waves, welling up in a nauseating stench, then slapping all around with percussive noises. The top of the tree, as big as the tower itself, snapped off like thunder booming, and the breaking of branches sounded like a hurricane. Night birds screamed and frogs croaked for miles around.

The horror was gone. The tree had come between it and the druid, and the monster was first crushed to pulp against the outside wall, then scraped away by sliding stone blocks and roof slates.

So, Greensleeves noted in panic, had been a handful of the prisoners they'd come to save—or put out of their misery.

As she staggered to her feet, the building continued to fracture along the edges. But the tower had been crafted long ago by masters, each huge block fitted by oxen and magic, and the remnants of the tower and rest of the tiny castle could stand with even one corner ripped away. Mosquitoes, kept at bay by a simple magic spell, now swarmed into the room. Lily clambered to her feet, hissed at a gash in her hand from broken crockery. Two half-dead prisoners moaned in their chains against the sundered wall. It was hard to see, for most of the candles and lamps had been upset or extinguished. Out the open corner, by starlight, Greensleeves stared at the ruins of her favorite tree, ripped from its home and dropped into a stinking swamp.

Then whirled as Chundachynnowyth screeched, "My tower! My experiments! You've ruined them!" The elvish woman's long face and pointed chin and tall curl-tipped ears were a mottled blue. "You've—you've—"

Greensleeves backed and almost fell off the edge of the broken floor. A floor slab tilted, dropped, slid along a mound of fresh dirt. The druid checked quickly for Lily, found her clutching her wrist while cowering behind an overturned table. Where was her brother and guards?

And what could she do to stop this mad elven witch?

If she had to . . .

Chundachynnowyth had stopped screeching to clutch at her chest. She gasped in pain, her breath a wheeze and whistle. Slowly, like a dying tree, she sank to her knees, then slumped on her face, contorted in agony. Finally she twitched and lay still. Her lips were still murmuring, "My exper-i-ments. . . . "

Past the dying wizard was the stairwell and single door to the room. A clashing sounded without, and light flickered as bodies surged back and forth before the torches ensconced on the walls. A growl sounded, and a roar, and a final smash.

A guard flew sideways into the room. He wore black scale armor like an insect's shell, a long yellow gypon marked with a red sun, and a closed leather coif that showed only his eyes. Punctured in the chest by some huge blade, the man tripped over the dying witch, crashed into a table, and slumped to the floor.

Into the room stepped Gull the Woodcutter, his great double-headed axe dripping blood, his clothes spattered. He shoved back his helmet, wiped his brow. "Whew! These bastards are *tough—*"

His voice trailed off as he surveyed the dark room, the dying crone at his feet, his sister pale as ivory, his wife bleeding from a hand wound, the destroyed wall. But mostly, he saw the chained prisoners with gaping holes surgically cut into their bodies: living, suffering experiments. When Gull found his voice, it was a croak. "We should have come sooner. . . . "

Behind him stepped some of his Green Lancer bodyguards. "Muley" was their leader, a stocky woman with a hard-bitten mouth and twin short swords. Other Greens came behind: a woman with red pigtails below her helmet, a former fisherman who looked fat but was not. Muley kicked the fallen guard, found him not dead, and finished the job with a jab to his throat. She spat, "Akron Legionnaires! Pah!"

Gull caught his breath, nudged the unmoving crone with his foot. "Heart failure. I've seen it enough in horses to know."

"She wanted to live forever," said Greensleeves. Then she was crying. The doomed and tortured prisoners she'd had to extinguish with her own hands, that horror coming for her, the hideous callousness of the ancient wizard, her fear for Lily and Gull, the ruin of her beautiful tree—all threatened to smother her. Wary of the unstable floor, Lily and Gull came and put arms around her.

Gull said, "Stop now, Greenie. It's all right. We're safe."

Lily cooed, "We've saved these people. Well, not really, but we've ended their suffering. Or will."

Her brother added, "We're doing good. We're making a real difference here, accomplishing something."

Greensleeves sniffed and sobbed. "I know, I know. But sometimes it's so—we work so hard—there's no one else to do it—but, oh, sometimes I wish I'd never heard of magic!"

CHAPTER
4

"OH, KWAM, I'M *SO* TIRED OF *FIGHTING*!"

"*We* never fight," her lover tried to joke.

Greensleeves and Kwam strolled hand in hand through the summer woods. The druid enjoyed the sun on her face and breeze in her hair, the smell of rich earth, breathing its perfume, the *chip-chip-chip* of cardinals and the caw of crows. Yet the two went quietly, for they had snuck away from camp, stealing a bit of freedom. And Greensleeves's heart was heavy.

Even though she and Kwam had been lovers for three years and had grown comfortable with each other, at times like this Greensleeves felt it strange not to be alone. She'd spent most of her life alone, wandering these woods. To be sure, she'd been an idiot back then, but a happy one. Intelligence could be a curse. But she certainly loved Kwam and his quiet, reassuring company. She needed him, for he brought her peace, as did the Whispering Woods themselves.

Yet when they stopped at a gaping hole in the

ground, she found it hard not to cry. She said aloud, "I'm sorry. I didn't mean for it to happen."

The hole was irregular, a hundred feet across and thirty feet deep. Tips of roots stuck up like worms testing the air. Around the hole was nothing but last year's fallen leaves and acorns turning to mulch.

Here her favorite tree had stood. Hers and Kwam's, for they'd often lain against it and made love in its deep green shade. But Greensleeves had killed it. She'd screamed for protection from a slithering horror, called up something, anything, while wanting to run and hide in the deep woods, and had gotten her tree. And lost it. The huge red oak had saved her life—and soul, probably—but now lay in a distant swamp next to a charred ruin, for the adventurers had burned the haunted castle and tower. Greensleeves could have conjured the tree's carcass back, but woodcutters and foragers would only cut it up for firewood, and she didn't want that.

"And even that," she said, "is selfish and wasteful. For they'll have to fell other living trees."

Kwam said nothing, only listened patiently while she brooded.

"I can't stand all this fighting. I just can't. I haven't had a moment's peace since I learned magic. We go out and we 'thump wizards' as my brother puts it, and we come home here, and there are dozens of petitioners asking—no, demanding!—that we go out and do it again! If there were three of me, a hundred, I could thump wizards day and night for the rest of my life. And that last wizard, that elven witch, the things she conjured—ugh!"

She shuddered, and Kwam put both arms around her. Sleeping with her, Kwam knew her dreams dissolved to horror-filled nightmares every dawn. The tall man said, "Would it help to say you saved a half-dozen lives?"

"But we didn't save them!" the druid murmured

against his black shirt, feeling like a little girl again. "We didn't save them. I only killed them, snuffed them out like guttering candles. Oh, it was horrible! I hate having all this responsibility, hate having to answer to everyone! I don't have a minute's peace!"

Kwam kissed the top of her head. "You've got a few minutes now. You should make the best of it and not fret."

Greensleeves shrugged out of his arms and stepped away from him. "You don't understand! I wish I could just go off somewhere into the depths of the Whispering Woods and just *live* there alone with you, and study nature and find cures and talk to my animal friends and live quietly!" When he didn't answer, she puffed, "Well?"

Reluctantly, he shook his head. "There are no simple answers in life. Some would say if you get a few minutes' peace in a day that's enough, for many toil night and day and suffer besides, barely surviving. You wish to live alone but with me: two contradictory ideas. And you want to find cures. For whom? Animals? People? You'd find a steady stream of invalids at your door asking for help."

"I have that now!"

"Exactly. Because you have the power to help, people come to you. The only time they didn't was when you were a—"

"A simpleton. A dunce. A dolt. Go ahead, say it. I know what I was!"

"You were blessed. Touched by the gods. Gifted with second sight. If you deny that, throw it away, you shirk your responsibility, ignore your gift."

Greensleeves turned away and regarded the woods with tears filming her eyes. That she had responsibilities and could not shirk them was *not* what she wanted to hear. She wanted sympathy, not sense. Yet she knew she was whining, and hated herself for it.

She felt like one of Kwam's clockwork toys, over-wound and ready to explode.

The dark man looked chagrined at having chastised his lover, but he was truthful. "I don't wish to upset you, honey, but when you have immense power, people naturally expect things of you. If you were a queen, they'd ask you to settle feuds and border disputes. If you were a surgeon, they'd beg you to heal them. And if you were a windmill, they'd hook you to a saw or fulling engine or a grindstone."

"So I'm a machine that produces miracles."

Kwam only spread his hands. "Even the gods are badgered for help. Every prayer has a request tucked into it. Sailors pray for calm seas, farmers pray for rain, gamblers for luck. It shouldn't surprise you that common folk ask for succor and solutions to their problems."

"But I'm a commoner just like them!" the woman wailed.

Kwam shook his head. "No, love, that's not true. It hasn't been true since the first time you conjured a—what was it? a badger?—to save your life. You're a wizard, one person out of ten thousand who can work magic."

And his voice reflected bitterness, for Kwam was a student and lover of magic, but could not himself manipulate magic. It was in the hope that someday he, and Tybalt and Ertha and Daru, might someday learn how to conjure that they studied artifacts and spells and scrolls and gadgets.

Greensleeves sighed. "It's done me precious little good. I couldn't use it to save my family. I can't find Sparrow Hawk, who's lost forever. . . . " She was even tired of her own whining. "All this talk, and I'm no closer to a solution."

Kwam came close, enfolded her in his arms, and this time would not let go. "It would help to have a clear goal. What do you want from life?"

"I want—I don't know what I want."

"More time to yourself? To be left alone? More time with me? Fewer responsibilities?"

"Yes, all those. And something else. I want peace inside myself."

Kwam kissed the top of her head and stroked her brown lustrous hair. "I don't know much, but I know peace can only come from inside."

Greensleeves sighed. "So it's even my fault I can't find peace?"

Kwam had no answer, only hugged her tight.

"There she is!" came a cry, and both lovers jumped.

Four stalwart bodyguards tramped up, harness and weapons jingling. These were Greensleeves's bodyguards, who called themselves the Guardians of the Grove, their leader Petalia, a dark-haired woman with wide blue eyes and a chiding manner.

As Kwam stepped back, Greensleeves almost smiled, for she could predict word for word what Petalia would say.

"Milady! *Please* don't wander off like that! You *know* there are enemies *aplenty* who seek to harm you! *Please* keep us by your side!"

The druid nodded meekly. She could not condemn her bodyguards' instrusion, for they were so devoted she felt ashamed at having deceived them and slipped away.

Each Guardian wore her hair long, flowing from under a helmet down her back. Each carried an iron-rimmed kite shield of rowan wood, a long sword at hip, and a short heavy boar spear, the tip a foot long and wickedly sharp, with a crossbar below the head. At Petalia's command, the Guardians dressed alike, with green shirts and skirts, and quilted breastplates and helmets of white ox hide. Painted on each shield was a white sleeve with green cuffs. Their uniforms, Greensleeves knew, mimicked her own clothing, which amused her secretly.

What was less amusing was that her bodyguards dogged her constantly, so she could not even visit the privy or go walking or make love without at least two guards present. There were six altogether, the two "night owls" currently sleeping. The bodyguards clung to Greensleeves at Gull's insistence, for three times in the past two years assassins had tried to stab, poison, or kidnap her. Only luck had carried her through these attempts, and Gull had finally canvassed the army and handpicked Petalia, who had handpicked other Guardians from the toughest women in the army. So fierce were they in guarding their mistress, they were often called the "Bulldog Bitches" behind their backs.

Greensleeves loved her bodyguards, was glad for their devotion, but sad that she needed protection. They were one more sign the world was too much with her.

And she knew her captain, Petalia, had a hard task. According to the hierarchy of the army, she was Greensleeves's "inferior," and so couldn't chastise her mistress openly; she could only "remind" that Greensleeves needed protection. Even her phrasing was quaint. The druid had not "wandered off," she'd used a camouflage spell to sneak away. Greensleeves promised not to do it again, only because it upset her protectors so.

But the archdruid thought it ironic that, as a simpleton, she'd roamed the forest amidst bears and wolves and elves, and never been harmed. But once she acquired magical abilities, she'd become a target of hatred and envy and dark plots.

As the party started toward camp, an ominous feeling washed over Greensleeves so suddenly she looked to see if clouds had rolled in. But the sky was clear.

She hoped the future stayed the same. For her sake and all her followers.

As the two lovers flanked by four stern bodyguards

strolled through the summer woods, Kwam tried to distract his ladylove with news of magic study.

As always, there were dozens of geegaws and artifacts to study: bottles and tools and clothing and books and scrolls and jars and helmets and other oddments. Some were booty captured from wizards, some fetched by travelers, some bought outright from jewelers and peddlers and artisans.

"We're still sorting the pile we took in our last, uh, raid," Kwam was saying. He hesitated because they'd looted much from the castle of the villainous Chundachynnowyth before torching it.

He went on, animated in talking about his other main love, magic. His eyes shone in a way Greensleeves loved as he counted on his long supple fingers.

"We've got some sort of cocoon that looks like an insect's spinning, but Daru aimed the tin dog at it, and the dog barked, so we know there's magic inside. Perhaps a jeweled dragonfly, or a crystal one. The librarians have stories about them, but not what they do.

"We cracked open an old oilskin bundle sealed with wax and found a clockwork fish! You wind a key and it flaps around the room, flying as if swimming in the air!

"We've also got a metal sphere that a peasant dug up in a field. He fetched it here in a barrow, for it's too heavy for four men to lift. It's so hard we can't cut it with any steel tools, or even scratch it with a diamond.

"And we've a helm made of coral, from the southern oceans, too big to fit on a normal man's head. It might be the helmet of a sea god. . . . "

If Greensleeves was worried about the future, at least she could take pleasure in the homey comfort of Greensleeves's Grove, as the army's headquarters was called. Despite the many people milling there, it was still a sacred spot that brought her joy.

They followed a stream, a rushing freshet from the depths of the Whispering Woods, that gurgled and chuckled and clucked, babbling inanely yet comfortingly, like the coo of a baby. They reached a stretch of rocks like giant stair steps and skipped along them like children till they came to a drop. A natural rock pool spread out below, big enough for children to wade and chase minnows and crayfish. Then came the trees—giant oaks old and mossy and wise.

And high amidst the tree branches, a village.

Greensleeves stopped on a rocky outcrop, holding Kwam's hand, thrilled, as always, by the view.

The houses were mostly small huts anywhere from five to fifty feet off the ground. There were dozens of them wedged among the branches like giant bird nests. Some stood alone on posts, while others could be reached by stairs. Still others, higher up, were connected by rope and plank bridges, and finally ladders.

One of the higher huts, slung between bobbing branches, belonged to Greensleeves and Kwam: their sanctum. Around it, above and below, were smaller huts where slept and watched her bodyguards. Off in another tree, supported on long beams and occupying a full fork, was the home of Gull and Lily, with its beehive huts for Gull's lancers. Highest of all, by itself, was a single hut, the lair of the magic students, far up in case a spell went awry. And there were other huts for cooks, the families of the bodyguards, supplies, and more. Carved from wood and shingled with bark, they looked like knobs grown from the trees themselves. And well they might be, for Greensleeves had overseen their painstaking construction: not a single iron nail was fixed in any hut or tree, but all were fitted with pegs and bark ropes and cleverly carved braces.

This treehouse town was the center, the heart, of Gull and Greensleeves's army. The other factions of

the army were spread over the forest and surrounding lands, the farthest contingent, the Red Century,
actually camped outside of the Whispering Woods
altogether, three hours' ride away. With so many
people, the army could not cluster for fear of harm-
ing the land and spreading disease, so they kept their
distance. If need be, of course, Greensleeves could
summon hundreds with a wave of one hand. She had
power enough, she supposed, to uproot this entire
forest and fly it to the Mist Moon, if she'd known
how to fly.

And there were times she wondered if she
shouldn't. For the whispering in the woods was dying
out.

Well could she remember how, when she was
younger and alone out here, the woods had hissed and
burbled with a never-ending sursurrus like a thousand
people speaking too low to be heard, as if the trees
themselves talked and shared secrets. Or the wind
clung amidst the branches, bearing news. The noise
had frightened normal folk, so that only a simpleton
and hammer-headed woodcutter would venture here.
Yet in the past three years, the whispering had
reduced to a mere trill high up, no louder than the
cicadas' song in late summer. Why the whispering had
faded, Greensleeves did not know. Or whether it
would return when they left the forest someday. Or if
it would die altogether, and something mysterious and
wonderful go out of the world. . . .

And that, too, was her fault.

For Greensleeves knew they had damaged the forest in other ways. This many people, no matter how
lightly they walked, impacted the woods. In tune
with the nature of things, the druid could feel the
compacting of the earth, smell sewage seeping into
ground water, feel axes and saws bite into the trees
as if it were her own flesh. Some of the harm she
staved off with magic, conjuring earthworms and

healing bark and encouraging plants, but she couldn't stop all the damage.

They couldn't live in these woods forever, she knew. Not and have them remain the same woods.

"And if I don't speak for the trees, who will?"

"What's that, honey?" Kwam had been waiting patiently, as had her guards, while she was lost in reverie. She was embarrassed at lamenting aloud.

Kwam clutched her small, callused hand. "You can give up crusading any time you like, you know. We could live apart, just us two. Or you could live alone, if you prefer, and I come visit you. You can do whatever you want, because you deserve happiness, because you're precious and sweet and wonderful."

The archdruid, one of the most powerful wizards ever to walk the Domains, sniffled like a little girl as she hugged him close. "Oh, Kwam . . . I wish I knew what I wanted. . . . "

A shout and laugh and squealing caught Greensleeves's attention.

A baby, barely two, clad in a short dress, waddled barefoot through the grove, chasing something around a tree trunk. She squealed when her father hopped out with a "Boo!" The baby warbled, ready to cry, but Gull scooped her up to elicit more piglet shrills.

Hyacinth, named for a flower, like many women of lost White Ridge and her mother in her dancing-girl days, was fair-skinned and pink-cheeked, as both Gull and Greensleeves had been. Yet her hair was as black as a raven's wing, like Lily's.

As Gull plunked the child down and ran off again with his daughter in pursuit, Lily held her lower back with one hand and followed her daughter's explorations. Gull had dictated his children should be fiercely independent and allowed to roam at will— within the limits of safety. There were, after all, twenty or more Green Lancers nearby at all times.

Kwam kissed Greensleeves and excused himself, venturing back to work. Trailed by her Guardians, the druid arrived in time to hear Hyacinth squeal again. She'd discovered her father's hiding spot and, as he tried to run off, grabbed his kilt. At the tiny tug, Gull *oof*ed and crashed to the forest floor, and his daughter danced on his stomach in delight. Lily excused herself to nap, smiling at her sister-in-law as she passed. Greensleeves had to react quickly when Gull lobbed his shrilling daughter at her. "Catch, Auntie!"

"Gull!" Yet the druid managed not to drop the squirming bundle, who begged to be tossed again. Greensleeves held her upside down instead, until her face went red, then righted her and set her loose to chase sparrows.

Gull, who knew his sister better than anyone in the world, reached out and tousled her hair. "Why the long face, sourpuss?"

The druid combed her hair with her fingers. "Does it show? I was trying to put up a brave front. . . . " The two spoke as if they were alone, for they'd learned to ignore the omnipresent bodyguards; they must, or they'd never say anything. "Gull, do you ever get tired of fighting?"

The woodcutter's brown face turned down in a frown, then he shrugged it away. He stuck both hands in his wide brown belt. Greensleeves noted again his maimed left hand, missing the three last fingers. She could have regenerated them easily, as old Chaney had regenerated Gull's crippled knee. But her brother had never asked, and she hadn't intruded by offering. She wondered if he refrained because of his innate distaste for magic, or if he kept the missing fingers as a symbol of when he'd been a simple woodcutter, far from magic and the worries of the world.

"Sometimes I do," he told his sister. "Tracking wizards and bashing their thralls and monsters and storms can be a burden. Sometimes I feel as if we're shoveling water against the tide. But it's what the gods have dealt us. Once I felled trees, now I fell wizards. At least I'm good at it. Though I'd have been happy to grow old in White Ridge, taking over the family from Mother and Father, teaching Sparrow Hawk and the others our stories and trade. . . . Except I never would have met Lily." He shrugged again. Gull was not one to worry about the meaning of life.

"But how long can we do this, Gull? How long before—we can't."

"I don't know. Until I'm too old to bash monsters, I suppose. Then someone else will take over. General Hyacinth, perhaps." He grinned at the thought of his toddler in a steel plumed helmet. "Or until I'm killed, which is more likely. But I could get killed cutting trees, too. All the more reason to play with my daughter today. But we have an officers' meeting."

The army's general plucked his hands from his belt, accepted his axe from a lancer, and caught his sister's elbow.

"Aye." Greensleeves sighed. She didn't resist. "We always do this time of day."

Sleep eluded her, so Greensleeves slid from under Kwam's arm and out of bed. Sky-clad, she wandered out of their tiny hut onto the platform that encircled it, leaned against the balcony railing, stared up through leaves at the whirling stars. Two Guardians, at opposite sides of the tree, pointedly ignored her.

Both jumped when a faint voice asked, "Why so glum, child?"

Greensleeves saw the ghost of a woman sitting higher up in the branches of the giant red oak. "Hello, Chaney." Her guards tried not to notice the ghost.

Since Greensleeves was pale and naked, looking

across at the ghost was like looking in a mirror. Chaney resembled Greensleeves now, or the other way around.

Chaney had been a powerful archdruid who'd taken Greensleeves under her wing, taught her everything she knew: many years' worth in the magically collapsed space of a few months. Chaney had then been a ruin, one side withered by strokes, dying by inches like a tree, yet she'd staved off death with magic until her student had been ready. Breathing her last gasp into Greensleeves's lungs, she'd passed on her mortal energy, charging Greensleeves with power beyond measure.

Chaney had died a withered husk. She'd returned a young beauty.

As a "shade"—not ghost or spirit—Chaney was slim, with a heart-shaped face and long shining hair the color of beech leaves in autumn. She wore, as always, a plain gown of wool bleached white, and went barefoot. Greensleeves wondered at times whether shades actually touched the ghostly ground they walked on.

The dead druid spoke to the living one. "You've been worrying how you and your friends affect these woods. Fret not, dear. Nature is stronger than she looks. A tree falls and dies, yet her bark and bones become soil for a thousand such trees in later years. The forest will endure the tramp of a few feet, and bear it till they are gone. Yet I sense other matters concern you, also."

Greensleeves pouted. Was she so transparent, as thin as this shade, that everyone could discern her thoughts? Still, she asked for advice. "What . . . are our responsibilities to one another, mistress? How . . . ? Must I address every grievance brought before me? Must I solve every problem? Must we seek out and punish every evil-doing wizard? A cat wouldn't have enough lives to punish a hundredth of them, if the stories be true."

The dead druid smiled in a vacant way. "You complain that people come to you with their problems, then you run to me with your problems?"

"Oh. Uh . . . " Greensleeves could have kicked herself. That was exactly what she was doing.

"Responsibilities . . . " Chaney's shade wasn't entirely listening; she was distracted by something in the ether. "It's hard to remember . . . to concentrate on the doings of mortals. Their troubles seem so trivial . . . But I seem to recall, you are responsible for those responsibilities you accept. . . . It's a question of sacrifice, surely. We must all be prepared to make the final sacrifice. . . . "

Greensleeves stifled a sigh. A circular answer was useless. Chaney had appeared many times since dying, hinting of secrets and ideas that were incomprehensible, as if rendered in another language. It was hard to commune with the dead, she'd learned, because the dead were so unconcerned with the living.

But Chaney startled Greensleeves by saying, "Others speak of you, child, and intend you harm."

"Again, or still?" asked Greensleeves. "We've made so many enemies in the past years I can scarcely count them. Yet I have them under control, as near as I know."

Strange though, that Petalia had carped about people out to harm her. Chaney spoke from beyond the veil, yet used the same words. A shiver ran down her back, and she hugged her waist.

Chaney looked off into the distance. "I hope to see you again, daughter. I may soon pass into the arms of Gaea's Liege, the collector of souls of the green woods. . . . But for your responsibilities, you must ever be ready to make the final sacrifice. . . . "

With that whisper from the afterworld, the druid faded away.

Greensleeves was left with an empty space on a branch, like some hole in her life, and the word "sacrifice." But hadn't she sacrificed enough already? She had almost no time to herself, hadn't had for years now.

Greensleeves glanced at the sky and saw that clouds covered the stars. She'd known that without looking, of course, in tune with the weather and world as she was, but it was an old habit.

"The world is too much with us." Then she yawned and turned for bed. "And I conjure questions from questions. Good night, Bly, Doris."

"Good night, milady," chimed the guards.

Wriggling under Kwam's arm, yanking the blankets around her, Greensleeves lay in bed, listening. The night was cool and still and peaceful, the magical whispering only a hush. Her heartbeat matched the pulse of the forest.

But something told her storm clouds boiled just over the horizon.

CHAPTER

5

A WISP OF GRAY ASH WINKED ON BRIGHT
white sand.

Though the brilliant sun made it hard to see, the
ashes grew, swirling as if stirred by a dust devil, spun
upward, finally outlined the figure of a huge armored
man. His armor was patchwork, some of it fine silver
with red chasing, the rest common steel rusted in
spots. A closed helmet had wide cattle horns splintered at the tips. The wizard tugged off the huge helmet. Revealed, he was fat, balding, jowly, none too
clean. He had but one eye. This was Haakon the
First, self-styled King of the Badlands.

"About time you got here!" snarled a woman in
brown robes with yellow jets. Drunk, she slurred her
words. Her long black hair, once glossy and full,
hung lank and dead around her shoulders and half in
her face. "We started without you!"

"Without me, you're nothing!" growled Haakon.
"Gad! It's hotter than the hinges of Hell! Why must
we meet on this infernal island?"

He moved from the scalding sun into the shade of

a pavilion thatched with fresh-cut leaves as big as elephant ears. The canopy was connected by thatched walkways to a variety of huts like beehives: a manor house of bamboo and palm leaves. Beyond the pavilion was a beach of white sand that glittered like diamonds and a tropical sea as deep as a sapphire. Small tufts of islands dotted the horizon. The pavilion faced a jungle full of thick leaves that rustled in the sea breeze.

Scattered in the shade of the pavilion were nine odd figures with little in common except magic and hatred.

Roasting in the tropical heat despite the breeze, Haakon shucked more armor. Two wizards moved away from his body stink. As he crashed down in a chair of lashed bamboo, a slim brown man hurried forward with a tray. On it were mugs carved from coconuts, spilling over with a yeasty brew. Haakon took two mugs and drank greedily, though he complained in gasps, "Ugh! You call this beer? Pah! I'd sooner drink horse piss!"

Dacian, the dark-haired woman, burped and signaled for another cup. "I'll drink to that, by the Rocks of Ragnar! May the gods send us a rain of real wine!" She drained a mug, then threw it at the servant, who scuttled backward, head bowed.

"Don't abuse my help, Dacian." Their host waved a hand to send the servant away; he trudged toward a thatched village that could just be seen down the beach and around a curve of jungle. Ornate fishing boats were pulled up in the surf, but there was no sign of anyone moving about. The villagers had learned to stay out of sight.

Towser wore robes of rainbow stripes, blue at the hem leading to yellow at his waist, with jutting red wings at the shoulders. His hair was blond and combed straight back from his head. Once he'd combed in limewash to stiffen it, but he had none here, so used manatee grease, which gave off a rank smell no amount of perfume could cover. He looked young, no more than twenty, but there were fine wrinkles around his eyes and mouth, and his eyes were old. "I've only just gotten these natives obedient. I had to kill their king and queen and half a dozen more before they'd submit. They're hardheaded but tractable."

"I don't care about your godsforsaken domestic help!" sneered Dacian. "Teach them to grow grapes and they'll be useful!"

"You've had enough juice of the grape!" retorted another woman. "And it's filled your mouth with prattle that makes our ears ache while distracting us from our true purpose!" The speaker was gorgeous, as regal as a queen, with blond hair teased around her head and a filmy robe of the richest red. She toyed with a long staff that sported a knob carved to resemble herself in gold. She was Fabia of the Golden Throat, Priestess of the Cult of the Unseen. Fabia had vast powers of persuasion and had once built herself a closed colony with followers to worship her. Then she'd taken to "winning" converts by raiding seaports and kidnapping from merchant trains. Once the rumors reached Gull and Greensleeves, they and a handful of others had rowed one night to the island, gotten close to Fabia with a camouflage spell, and trussed her in a sack. Stripped of her followers and possessions and turned loose, she'd found that without worshipers, she was bad company even to herself.

"Stop hissing!" hissed a short woman who lounged in a chair. She had curly red hair and wore an goldembroidered tunic of blue with a wide studded belt and tall boots. An ocean wizard, she carried a spear with a long tapering blade. It looked ancient and ornate, but was a fake. Greensleeves had taken from her the real Lance of the Sea, which she'd used to stir the seas and make life hell for fisherfolk until they paid tribute. She was Dwen of the White Isle. "You lot make me sick! You squabble like cats tied in a bag!"

"We might as well be trapped in a bag. And blinded and hamstrung besides." Immugio, the ogregiant crossbreed, was too big for a chair, so he sprawled on the cool sand, careless that his bearskin breechclout hung askew. The death mask he'd ripped from his father's face was less intimidating these days; muddied, smoke-blackened, and grease-stained, it had curled into a sardonic leer. The giant growled, "I hope some of your help does prove recalcitrant, for t'would give me a excuse to eat them. I'm so hungry from this gruel and fish I could rip a man apart like a lobster and feast on his guts."

Dacian made a face at the thought, then belched. Fabia looked out to sea as if the giant hadn't spoken. She only associated with "perfect" humans. Anyone else, speaking or not, was an animal. Dwen rapped her spear against a peeled post, as if eager to be off.

Thunderhead, the Goblin Queen, sipped coconut beer and giggled: even that little bit had her addled brain drunk. She wore a tattered boar's hide crawling with lice and fleas, and a ratty cape that had once been drapes in a castle. Her skin was gray-green, her hair gray, and around her brow was a crown made of bent nails. She was no more than belt high. The mug in her hands looked like a cask. "Yes, yes! I could fancy a liver with no worms in it! Bring a young one here, Towser, and make her mad so we can chop her legs off!"

Some groaned. The only one who stayed quiet was Gurias, who claimed to be of Tolaria, though he'd never visited the place. With his red-blond curls and limp mustache, red hose and brocaded blue doublet, he felt itchy and hot. The red feather in his blue hat drooped into the corner of his eye. Gurias had his grudges, too, for despite his lightning and strength-draining spells and his magic cudgel, he was a slave. He disliked these dangerous wizards and wished to be elsewhere, but Towser had conjured him and so he remained: he had no shifting powers of his own.

The only one not complaining was Karli of the Singing Moon, a desert wizard of dark, almost black, skin and bright white hair. She wore a flowing shirt and trousers, red slippers that gave her flight, and a jacket stitched with many buttons—her grimoire, each a marker for a spell. She enjoyed the wizards' discomfit and mocked them with her sparkling black eyes, the only one on equal footing with Towser. The two sat close together and often discussed in whispers; haltingly, for Karli had only recently learned their language.

There were two others not present. Off by himself, down the beach, stood an older man with flowing hair and leather headband, an ermine cape and goat hide tunic despite the heat, his tunic painted with the symbol of a red eagle. In his belt he carried a magic mace. He whistled and raised his arm, and from the sky dropped a red-brown eagle all aflame. The flames winked out as it alighted on the man's forearm. Behind him in the shade slept a huge shaggy wolf. Ludoc was a mountain wizard.

Somewhere in the jungle lurked a gray-green sedge troll, warty and lank-haired. He was a wizard, too, but could conjure no better name than Leechnip.

Towser had convened this meeting by commanding the wizards come, or else conjuring them himself. Karli aided in this, for she and Towser were different from the other nine souls.

The nine grouses—the armored Haakon, the ogre Immugio, the drunken Dacian, young Gurias, gorgeous Fabia, Queen Thunderhead the goblin, impatient Dwen of the ocean, Ludoc of the mountains, and the troll Leechnip—were all enslaved, but not by

Towser. Each had fought Gull and Greensleeves's army and lost, each been crowned by the stone helmet of submission, each bound to Greensleeves as a "parolee" by invisible tags: the archdruid of the Whispering Woods could summon them anytime and call them to account. Nowadays each was a slave as they themselves had enslaved "pawns," common folk. And each burned with a smoldering resentment.

And each, by a quirk of the magical stone helmet, could contact the other bound wizards, though Greensleeves was unaware of this fact. Initially, Dacian and Haakon had come together to convene a congress of wizards to oppose Greensleeves and Gull. They had then contacted Karli, the desert wizard, who'd once handled the helmet. Then they'd contacted Towser.

And found themselves Towser's slaves.

Towser and Karli were the only two "free" wizards of the congress. They'd fought the brother and sister to a standstill and gotten away. With their advantage—they could hide from Greensleeves indefinitely—they'd assumed control of the congress.

And over time, they contacted other enthralled wizards and finally, today, brought them here.

For a purpose yet to be revealed. . . .

The squabbling went on as the beer flowed, but finally Towser pitched his coconut shell behind him. He stripped foam from his mustache, called loudly, "Enough! I didn't conjure you fools to drink yourselves blind or gorge on my servants. It's time we talked. Where's that fool Ludoc?" Towser whistled, and reluctantly the grizzled mountain wizard plodded toward the congress, his wolf trailing after him with tongue lolling. "I guess we don't need to summon Leechnip. He'll do as he's told or suffer."

Towser plucked a cup from the trembling hands of Dacian and lobbed it out of the pavilion. Deprived of her precious liquor, she protested, but Towser silenced her with the back of his hand.

"Enough bellyaching. We—Karli and I—are ready to begin. We'll have our say; you'll get orders. Then you can crawl back to your caves or swamps or ale bars."

Towser stared around the circle of angry and bleak stares, but no one objected, so he went on. "That's better. Do as I say and we'll get along. I've decided it's time to start our campaign. We go on the attack!"

Now they objected.

Dacian wailed, "We can't oppose Greensleeves! She's got ten times the power of all of us together! She's like a goddess! She should have gone planeswalking long ago! The gods know why she stays in this vale of tears! I could planeswalk once, but that damned helm binds me to this plane!"

Ludoc, who listed under the weight of his eagle, grumbled, "And Gull's army is more capable every day. And every soldier more loyal than a war dog. They even call one century the 'Black Dogs.'"

"And the artifacts!" piped Fabia. She brushed her hair into its proper wave. "They've got grimoires stacked to the ceilings, it's said, and enough magic weapons to outfit a company!"

"True enough," Towser agreed. "I've seen them."

"*What?*" asked a half dozen. "You've *seen* Greensleeves's treasures?"

"Have they still got my lance?" demanded Dwen. "It's worth a hundred trashy geegaws! I need it back! It can stir the seas like a stick in a puddle! It can part them to the ocean bed, or call down the rain and the lightning—"

"You bore us," growled Immugio without moving. He was propped on his elbows and sleepy in the heat. "I can bring down lightning with a snap of my fingers."

"Stick your fingers up your nose!" Dwen retorted. "I could send the sea chasing you uphill and drown you like a rat! Or a fat boar!"

"We'll see who's fat, midget!" The giant made to

rise, but suddenly stopped at the sound of Towser's voice.

Towser told him, "Sit down and shut up! We're here to improve our lot, not prattle like children!"

The giant growled and continued to rise, taller than Towser even half-reclined. "I'm sick of you telling me what to do! I don't see any scars on you! You lurk here in the shadows, so far away from Gull's army the people are a different color and the ocean's warm! What kind of coward—"

Casually, Towser plucked a silver wand from his belt and brushed it against the giant's knee.

The giant howled as his leg jerked so hard it almost broke . He grabbed for it, hissing with pain, but his hands twisted into claws until the fingers looked as if they would snap. Immugio raised his hands, but his back spasmed. He wet himself as his spine twisted like a sapling in the wind. His jaw clacked shut so hard he broke a tooth. The wracking agony went on and on, one muscle fighting another, shearing and twisting, none under his control. Gradually the spell passed, his tortured muscles eased, and he lay panting and hissing.

The other wizards stopped bickering and paid attention. They'd learned the lesson.

"As I was saying," Towser returned the Disrupting Scepter to his belt, "follow my orders and we'll succeed. You'll be free of Greensleeves's thrall, both she and her brother will be dead, their army scattered. We'll loot their artifacts, divide them up, and you can return to your homelands and resume your miserable lives. Now stay put while I fetch something."

Nothing moved except thatch in the lilting sea breeze, and Ludoc's eagle, which shivered and fluffed up, waggling its tail feathers down the back of her master's ermine cape.

Towser came back from a hut with a wooden box as long and wide as a child's coffin.

The wizards craned their heads to see inside as he tilted back the lid. Perhaps their only common trait was an addiction to magic, and this box seemed to sparkle with it.

"In here," Towser told them, "are tools to set us free. Or start us on the road to freedom, for you'll need wits and courage and cooperation besides." He added under his breath, "The gods help us."

He put his hand in the box and drew out an artifact. "Behold! Our salvation!"

Hanging from Towser's hand, on a silver chain, was a curious pentacle. The arms of the star were of yellow wood bound with a ring of cold iron. Inside that was another ring of red gemstone and, centermost, an ant frozen in amber.

"What is it?" asked Dwen cautiously, respectfully. No one wanted to taste that Disrupting Scepter. Immugio could only now sit up, still quivering.

"Something old," Towser told them. "Older than anything living. This pentacle binds the wearer to the earth, binds him to the soil. It also binds yourself to yourself, in a manner of speaking, so you can push yourself farther, accomplish more. But that's by the by. It's the binding-to-earth properties we want."

"I don't . . ." began Fabia. Then she got it. "*Binds?* You mean, if one of us dons that, we can stay where we *are*, where we *wish* to be?"

Most of the other wizards caught on, and then clamored for the pentacle. Towser silenced them by raising a hand. "True. Since it binds you in place, you can't planeswalk, but you also can't be summoned—by anyone. Greensleeves could turn blue trying to fetch you, but you'd stay rooted like an ash tree on a mountainside."

"But there's only the one!" growled Ludoc, sweating in his furs. "We can't all use it!"

For answer, Towser put his other hand in the box and drew out half a dozen pentacles. "Not anymore!

With an invisibility spell, and a good degree of luck, I slipped into Greensleeves's magic hut and stole the first one. She needed it once, so the story goes, but no more, so she turned it over to her students. By searching far and wide, and laying out more money than you lot will ever see, I had copies crafted and imbued with the magic of the original pentacle."

"Then . . . we're free!" screamed Dwen.

And all of them were laughing, chortling, howling, rubbing their hands, and shrieking, even Immugio.

Towser let them run on, then raised his hand for silence. He got it, and their rapt attention. "And this is not all. I've many facets to my plan, more than any diamond. We'll be free and triumphant in short order. Let me conjure something else, and you'll see the second part of our salvation. But," he added, "be careful how you tread, for this is no artifact. . . . "

Towser opened his grimoire, a brass-bound book that hung from his belt, thumbed to a page, stepped away from the crowd that the other wizards might not hear, and muttered a spell.

Out on the shimmering sands of the beach there appeared a tiny glinting point of light that grew within seconds to the height of a man, then taller.

The wizards gasped.

The man was over seven feet tall and so heavily muscled he looked like a skinned bear. He wore a black, red-striped kilt, leather war harness, and tall boots, with armbands of red leather. Red for blood. On his head was a fantastic iron helmet. Thin ruby plates made his eyes glow a dull red, and intricate fangs in the lower half gave him the snarl of a saber-tooth. Curved horns, stylized after a reindeer's, curled around the helm to jut forward past his brow and jaw. Hanging from a thick studded baldric, so long it brushed the ground, was a fearsome two-handed sword.

The warrior folded his arms across his chest, muscles rippling like a nest of pythons, and frowned at the assembled wizards. He showed no surprise at being conjured, some noted, so must have been awaiting Towser's summons.

Fabia, priestess of "perfect people," was transported by all that brooding maleness. "Who *is* he?"

"A Keldon warlord," Towser announced with a smile. "From the Kelds' bleak land in the north, where the strong survive by consuming the weak. Totally in my service. *He* and his special training cost even more than these pentacles."

"What 'special training'?" Everyone looked. Gurias, the youngest of them, had spoken for the first time.

Towser frowned. "Never mind exactly what. Suffice it to say, this warlord will prove the better of Gull the Woodcutter."

"Has he troops?" asked Immugio. The ogre-giant was over his shaking-up. "A warlord's no good without soldiers to command."

"We'll get troops," Towser answered easily. The sea breeze had picked up and tossed his greased hair about his face. "You have orcs—"

"They were all killed."

The striped wizard sighed. "We'll get more. Fabia has some followers still, a few. Dwen has her cave-folk. Karli can summon more warriors than the desert has grains of sand. Troops are not a problem. *And* they'll be reliable this time. No breaking from battle, no running."

"Why not?" asked Ludoc. "How will you instill battle rage in them? Sufficient to beat Gull's volunteers, that is."

Towser signaled with a nod that the warlord should reply.

The giant man turned away from the pavilion toward the village of brown-skinned natives. He cupped his hands around his mouth and bellowed, "Attend me!"

The wizards scuffled to see, as from around a stand of jungle there appeared a dozen, then two dozen, and finally all the natives of the island, from the oldest grandmother to the smallest child being carried in a parent's arms.

The warlord raised a mighty hand and waved them on. Uneasily, but irresistibly, the natives crept forward. They were all good-looking people, free of disease, well-fed, brown and strong from a lifetime of fishing and swimming. When they'd advanced like one giant animal to within a dozen feet of the warlord, he clapped his hands.

"Fight!"

Immediately, the natives' placid faces twisted, ugly and hateful. A man belted his neighbor alongside the head with a closed fist. A boy lowered his head and bashed his mother in the stomach. A woman dropped her child to be trampled underfoot as she grabbed a man's hair and wrenched away handfuls. Another man, knocked sprawling, latched onto her leg and bit until blood flowed. Two men above him kicked him with bare feet until he was unconscious or dying, then fell to kicking one another. A mother clawed at her daughter's eyes, bit one of her ears.

The wizards stood stunned at the butchery. Within a few minutes, only the strongest and quickest were alive, covered in their own and others' blood, still fighting. When the last pair fell, from exhaustion or blood loss, only a few villagers twitched. The rest, horribly maimed, lay still forever.

Towser turned from the spectacle and waved toward the warlord. The smell of blood was rank, but the sea breeze pushed it inland. Gulls and other seabirds began to circle, to peck at the dead and dying.

"There's your answer. A Keldon warlord inspires others to fight as well and viciously as he—any troops become fanatic suicides. Do you believe Gull

and Greensleeves's starry-eyed volunteers can withstand a larger force charged to wreak such havoc?"

Numb, the wizards shook their heads. Meekly, they
accepted the pentacles Towser doled out and hung
them around their necks.

"Now, while Greensleeves fails to summon you—
and it's been months since she bothered—you'll
gather forces, wait for my word to spring the trap.
It's only a matter of days before we're free once and
for all!"

Ludoc and Immugio, harder and more bloodthirsty
than the rest, cheered. But the others wizards were
quiet. They sorted through this new information and
opportunity, tried to figure how to turn it to their
own advantage. No one trusted Towser as a slave-
master; if he could hand out artifacts, he could take
them back. So each wizard fell to figuring how to
save his or her own skin, to get free, to use the others
and come out on top.

Fabia of the Golden Throat saw one way. Flicking
back her golden hair, she sashayed over to the
Keldon warlord and touched his brawny arm with
her soft one. Light as her caress, she worked a spell
to read his thoughts, but found them cloudy and confused. The man's thinking was as simple as a child's.

Very useful, she thought. Summoning another spell
first crafted by Gwendlyn Di Corci, the great seduc-
tress, she purred, "My, but you're strong. Masterful.
Tell me, when your service to Towser is finished,
would you be master of yourself?"

The warlord's rumble was a long time coming.
"Towser would have me kill Gull the Woodcutter,
and so I shall. There is no other goal."

"But surely," Fabia pressed alongside the giant
man, ran her toe playfully along the back of his naked
calf. "When that's done, you'll want another goal.
Have you thought . . . to be king somewhere, with a
queen by your side—"

"Kill Gull the Woodcutter!" shouted the warlord suddenly. He flung out both arms, raised mighty fists. Fabia was dumped onto her rump in the sand. "Death to Gull and Greensleeves!"

Fabia rose, smoothing her clothes and her dignity. She turned, flaring, when Towser laughed. "The warlord is mine, Fabia. Body and soul, till I'm done with him. Find another playmate." The rainbow-striped wizard hooked a thumb at the field of dead villagers. "Him, perhaps."

Towering over the corpses, Immugio rubbed his hands and smacked his lips. "We'll eat hearty tonight!"

CHAPTER
6

"SO," SAID GULL, "THE BIG QUESTION BEFORE us remains: What do we do next?"

A clamor of voices answered him, for everyone had strong opinions and had argued the point for days.

No one noticed as Greensleeves arrived, folded her embroidered cloak around her, and sat down on a long bench. There was a meeting every noon, over dinner, of all the army "officers." The meeting took place under a pavilion, really just an arbor tied across four posts in Greensleeves's Grove. Most of the officers were there, including some the druid barely knew. There were so many new faces in the army these days, she often felt like a stranger. Gull's bodyguards, the Green Lancers, surrounded the pavilion, standing at ease with slanted spears. Down the grove where the brook widened, hostlers and aides minded the officers' horses.

At the head of the table sat her brother Gull, looking every inch the warlord, though—the standard joke—he would only admit to being a woodcutter. His dignity, never high, was compromised by his daughter Hyacinth perched on his shoulders. The toddler hung onto her father's hair and ears and kicked her fat legs so they drummed on his leather jerkin.

Greensleeves's sister-in-law, Lily, was here too, leaning on pillows to support an aching back and protruding stomach. Lily had "temporarily" assumed the post of quartermaster one morning when old Donahue died quietly in his sleep. Trained in business as well as the courtesan's arts, she had filled in to keep supplies and weapons and clothing and food flowing smoothly into and through the camp. To everyone's surprise, including Lily's, she proved superlative at it and was permanently assigned the post. She'd continue to fill it as long as pregnancy allowed.

What Lily did *not* fulfill, Greensleeves knew, were magic functions. Barring emergencies, Lily (and Gull) thought it too dangerous to handle mana while bearing or caring for a child; it could be too much a strain on body and mind. Sometimes, Greensleeves thought, she admired Lily her simpler life.

Varrius, bronzed and black-bearded, commander of the army, reported on his "centuries": companies of one hundred soldiers, a term he'd brought from his seaside city of mercenaries. There were four full centuries named for colors and, lately, animals: the Red Scorpions, the Blue Seals, the White Bears, and, queerly, the Black Dogs.

Helki was there, the female centaur in her fluted painted armor and feathers and armbands. She captained the Rose Cavalry, a mixed company of humans and centaurs, and her mate, currently in the field, commanded the Yellow or Gold Cavalry. A special peak had been lifted in the roof of the pavilion so the centaur might stand upright. Greensleeves liked Helki for her boldness and fierce loyalty, but also for her sentimentality: centaurs would break out singing about home, and cry, in an instant.

"Jingling" Jayne was there in somber colors of the woods: gray, brown, and moss green. Her only decoration was a black-feather sigil stitched to each shoulder, emblem of the Ravens, the scouts that were the eyes of the army, able to kill or kidnap a guard from a picket line and not disturb a leaf. These days, the scouts attracted some truly dangerous people: frontier folk who'd fought every day of their lives, with no qualms about slipping into enemy territory with a knife and garrote. Lately, a troupe of Pradesh gypsies had enrolled as scouts. They had dubbed their captain "Jingling" when they'd surprised *her* on a scouting trial because her knife rattled. So stealthy were they, the rest of the army considered them ghosts.

Also in attendance was Hermine, sloe-eyed leader of the all-female company of D'Avenant archers, who dressed in black like so many crows. Greensleeves had often wondered what drove these women so that they dedicated themselves to the bow and each other.

And, too, there was Uxmal, who stood on a stool, for he was scarcely belt-high to Gull. In an army of oddballs and misfits, Uxmal and his crew were among the strangest. Thirty had stumped into camp one morning. They spoke with a queer inflection, came "from de south, ov'r de hills and wader." Either gnomes or dwarves, they were very dark, with black beards teased into tufts and clamped with gold rings. (They all had beards, yet bets circulated some were female.) They wore coarse smocks of bright stripes, pointed hats, but no shoes, for the bottoms of their feet were as hard as flint. Each dwarf led one or two strange pack animals: gray-brown shaggy creatures called llamas. They had come far, Uxmal explained slowly, very far to join the army of "Guh und Grenslavs." They wished to help and needed no pay: their god would reward them, they insisted, without stating how. When Gull asked what they could do, they broke out shovels and spades and picks and threw up an earthworks before supper. Gull welcomed them like old friends and dubbed them the sappers. Greensleeves liked their bubbling musical talk and easy grunting laughter.

Finally, there was a smoke-eyed fanatic, Nazarius, who led a pack calling themselves the Martyrs of Korlis (whoever that was). They lived to die in battle and hurled themselves into the fore of any fray. They also refused to go away. Gull and the other officers agreed they were useful: they fought like mad dogs, terrified the enemy, absorbed arrows, and broke lines time and again. Besides, they'd all be dead soon. There were only sixteen left out of the original fifty-four.

The so-called martyrs weren't the only stragglers to drift into the army. Word of the crusade against wizards had spread far and wide to lands they'd never heard of, and people flowed from all points of the compass to join up. Cripples came dragging themselves on their hands. Runaway farm boys came with pitchforks and pigs. A blacksmith had walked in with two mules and set to repairing Stiggur's clockwork beast without being asked. A blond woman called herself a Verduran enchantress, though no one had seen her enchant anything yet. A Muronian holy dervish preached doom from the back of a cart, though only the Martyrs of Korlis listened. A company of cartographers, headed by the elder Kamee at Gull's right hand, mapped the territories the army crossed and interviewed everyone who could speak, trying to fill the holes in their maps. A covey of librarians recorded legends and rumors and histories. There were leatherworkers, cobblers, armorers, cooks and helpers, freightmasters, woodcutters, nurses, and schoolteachers.

And, of course, Greensleeves's own contingent of magic students, who spent their time collecting and deciphering arcane objects and scrolls.

The druid had still more allies tucked in the back of her mind. Never far away was the tag to her friends of the deep forest, elven archers led by a scarred female with an eyepatch. Another tag led to a tropical volcano swarming with hundreds of ant-folk, ancient creations left over from the Brothers' War, smelling of formic acid like a bat cave; when conjured, they fought with mindless fury and no fear. And Greensleeves could summon many more creatures to fight, from scads of squabbling goblins to fleet timber wolves to elementals from lost planes in the upper ether.

So many things and people to keep track of, Greensleeves thought wearily. She plucked up a handful of grapes and ate a few absently, discovering she wasn't hungry. Her mind and soul were too full. So many considerations to juggle. The elves, for instance, would battle, yes, but never linger, plus they'd kill orcs or goblins immediately, no matter who they sided with. And the ant-soldiers couldn't fight in the cold, and for no known reason disliked the sound of drums and attacked musicians. As for using her friends of the forest, people were always suggesting she call up wolves and bears to battle, while Greensleeves was forever explaining that animals did not battle to the death in nature, they only tussled for rank and then submitted or ran away, therefore were no more than a diversion in a fight.

And she was so tired of fighting.

Today, as usual, the officers' table was heaped with bread and meat and fruit and surrounded by waving hands and wagging chins. Presiding over them was Gull, who listened to everyone, argued when necessary, then made decisions based in fairness and sense generally accepted without question.

There was talk of many issues. A shortage of iron, trouble with polluted water in the Golden Vale, a knife fight among the Reds, a pack of orphans gone wild, new fighting tactics developed by the centaurs, and much, much more. Preoccupied, Greensleeves only half-listened.

Something ripped the grapes from her lax fingers. "What . . . ?"

Behind her, Doris stabbed a strong hand under the table, yanked out a bundle that squirmed and spat and kicked. Greensleeves *tsk*ed. "Oh, it's you."

The squirmer was a goblin, the only one in their army, a rude little thief named Egg Sucker. He had gray-green skin, gray hair with a skunk stripe, and was dressed in filthy rags from a mangy rabbit. And had a mouthful of grapes that he spluttered onto Doris's white leather armor. "Lemme down, lemme go! I didn't take nothing!"

"Yes, you did!" Doris shook him. He weighed no more than a dog. "You stole milady's grapes right from her own hand!"

"Did not! And I wanted a chicken wing anyways, but no one will gimme one!"

Doris shook the goblin hard enough to rattle his teeth, but Greensleeves stopped her and saw the goblin set safely down. The druid tore off a drumstick and handed it over. "There? Will that satisfy you?"

Egg Sucker eyed the offering as if it were poisoned, then snatched it away. "Not very meaty. I always get the slops nobody else wants. And no biscuit?"

Rolling her eyes, Greensleeves gave him a biscuit. Grabbing, he made to run off, crashed full into Doris's legs, made to duck through. But the brawny bodyguard trapped his head between her knees. "What do you say to milady?"

"Let go, that's what I says!" His voice was muffled. "Why are people always picking on me? I didn't do nothing!"

Greensleeves was laughing. "Egg, why do you always steal food when we're willing to give it to you? Oh, let him go, Doris. You'll get fleas."

Released, Egg Sucker took off like a shot. Out of belting range, he turned to jeer, "Ha! I always steals you blind, you great boobies! You fat sloths can't catch Egg—"

Running backward, he forgot the stream, tripped over a rock and made a great splash. Spluttering, "I hates water!" he saw his biscuit dissolve in his hand. A fat trout flashed off with the chicken leg. Howling, he dove after it.

By now, half the table was laughing, but the serious Kamee, who'd lost quills and ink bottles and whole maps to the little wretch, asked, "General, why do you tolerate that pest? He's worse than useless! He steals, he starts fights—"

Gull shrugged, which jostled his daughter so she giggled. "Egg is a mascot, sort of. He was left over from the first raid on—the first raid." He meant the battle that destroyed White Ridge. "I've never understood myself why he stays with us: he could have easily run off with other goblins we've fought. But I don't mind him. He's our good-luck charm."

"More like bad-luck charm," muttered Varrius, who'd also lost items from his tent.

"Well, any luck's better than none, my father used to say. Now." He held up two hands, showing seven fingers. "We come back to the question of what is next. But before we flog this horse again, I want you to attend Kamee. She's got some news that may give us direction."

The solemn-faced chief of the cartographers and librarians calmly unrolled a large, freshly inked map. As people weighted the corners with stones, she pronounced, "According to what we can deduce, this army has pacified and explored most of the northern end of this continent. . . ."

"It has?" Gull asked. "*We* did that?"

"For the most part," Kamee hedged. She ran a gnarled ink-stained hand over the map. "Here, south and east of us, is where White Ridge once lay. We used that as a starting point. The Whispering Woods, we now know, extend some twenty leagues west, then trend into a common forest where lies the star crater. West is a swamp, then foothills, then the Ice Rime Hills, and finally the ocean at a port called Concord. Moving north some twelve leagues, we find where the basalt monolith once stood, and not far beyond the northernmost peninsula of that coast . . . "

She went on, sketching with her hand as people watched the continent unfold, fascinated. "North and east are the Smoke Mountains, where we defeated Gurias of Tolaria and the half-giant Immugio. Our scouts continued through the mountains, found no evidence of wizards preying on common folk, so trended eastward and struck another sea. Locals call it the Sea of Whales, after huge gams that pass by every winter. The western sea is generally called the Sea of Fire after the glorious sunsets. Along the north is a strait called the Rip, shunned by sailors because of its fast currents."

"We've written down the names of surrounding continents. To the north lies Icehaven. To the west, archipelagos called the Spice Islands. To the east, Stonehaven, after the looming mountains along its shore. But mind you, these are what our local seafarers call them: the natives no doubt have different names." She added that the continent they stood on was most often called Aerona, for an ancient goddess of fertility who sacrificed herself that people might plant crops in her body.

"Aerona," said Gull in wonderment. "Yes! I've heard it called that by old Wolftooth and Morven, a sailor. But to think we're naming seas we've never seen. . . . "

As the officers pored over the map, Kamee called down the table, "How fare your tags, Greensleeves, your captive wizards?"

"Eh? I beg your pardon?" The druid shook her head: it was cluttered with odds and ends. "Oh, they fare well, I suppose . . . "

"'Well?'" asked Gull. "We don't want them to 'fare well,' Greenie. We want them stone-cold miserable."

Greensleeves frowned, irritated with her brother and herself. She had to admit it had been—a month or more?—since she'd summoned her "parolees." Greensleeves had but to tug the invisible tag strung along the ether and fetch them hither, reasoning that if called to task once a month or so, they couldn't get up much mischief. But . . . "I'm sorry, I've been neglectful, but I've been busy. And—"

Gull, solicitous of his little sister, asked patiently, "And what, Greenie?"

"I—" She stopped, gathered her wits. "I must confess I'm not happy with this arrangement. I'm a druid, after all, charged with protecting the forest and those who cannot speak for themselves, balancing the needs of thinking creatures against the unthinking. . . . I'm not a jailer," she finished, "and there are simply too many wizards for me to keep track. I could spend days just conjuring them and seeing they behave."

Immediately the never-ending argument bubbled up around the table—what, exactly, should the army *do* with a captured wizard?—but Gull raised his hands to forestall it. "Wait, wait. I'll be the first to admit that Greenie's been unfairly charged with guarding our captives, but I'm confused. Exactly how many *have* we shackled with these mystical chains?"

Greensleeves shrugged. "I've lost count. All the fighting's become a blur."

Lily, as quartermaster, cleared her throat, dug through a stack of papers and parchments, and pulled one out. "We have battled . . . oh, my. Greenie's right, too many. Under our thrall are, let's see, Haakon, Dacian the drunkard, Dwen of White

Isle, the goblin queen Thunderhead, that filthy sedge troll Leechnip, old Ludoc with his flaming eagle, Fabia the Priestess, that young snot Gurias, and Immugio the ogre-giant. . . . We know others not enthralled. Let's see . . . We compromised with the Leprechaun Queen. Garth One-Eye of House Oor-Tael in Kush retired to his vineyards, but will help if needed. That fraudulent 'Son of Adun Oakenshield' hanged himself. That horrid elven witch, Chunda-something, died. And . . . a few wizards wriggled off the hook. That dark desert woman with the white hair, Karli of the Singing Moon. That woman in the buffalo robe who called down the birds on us. The one in the ram horns who threw stones. The twins in green silk . . . That red girl who could run so fast . . . and that's it."

"And Towser," growled Gull, "who destroyed our village, killed our family, and let our brother Sparrow Hawk be enslaved."

Lily nodded. "Yes, him." Whom Gull had served as horse wrangler, and she as a dancing girl, until both were betrayed.

"That many," Gull muttered. "Who'd have thought we'd be burdened by success? But Greenie's right. It's too much for one person to track. We *must* find some simpler way to curb these bastards—"

Out rolled the old controversy. Varrius, the soldier, waved both hands. "These wizards (begging your pardon, Lady Greensleeves) are like vampires! The best thing for 'em is to chop off their heads, fill their mouths with garlic, and bury 'em deep! That'll curb 'em—"

Kamee shot back, "We can't be taking lives in cold blood! And we need these wizards! If we could convert them to the right, they could heal the sick, teach us potions—"

Uxmal gargled around a mouthful of grapes, "Put to worg dig ditches and privies. Whip if slow—"

Helki shook her maned head and rustled leaves in the canopy overhead. "Better we lock them in one place, some remote castle, jailed tight—"

Hermine, of D'Avenant's archers, shook her bow. "Target practice! That's all they're good for—"

As the wrangling ran on and on, Greensleeves gathered her embroidered cloak around her and slipped away from the table, passing through the sun-dappled glade. Four bodyguards trailed after.

Holding her skirts, Greensleeves mounted the stairs that circled the great red oak. One of her guards went before, one followed, and two stayed at the bottom.

At the top, the druid found the round wooden chamber where the magic students poked and prodded their precious artifacts. Daru was there, a stocky woman with cornshuck hair, and the tall dark Kwam. At Greensleeves's entrance, Daru excused herself, slipping by a bodyguard.

Greensleeves thought, A whole forest to roam, and I spend my days stepping around people.

"Kwam, I don't know what to do."

The student put down a grimoire he'd been studying by the window, leaned back with folded arms to give his full attention. "Don't know about what, love?" They spoke intimately, as if Doris weren't standing with her back to them in the small doorway.

"Myself, my responsibilities. I'm supposed to track these wizards we've leashed, and I've neglected my duty."

Kwam nodded, which could have meant anything. "I know it's hard, Greensleeves." (Why did she get such a thrill from his saying her name? Even mental exhaustion couldn't dull the charge that ran down her spine.) "It's true the burden falls on you and is unfair. A temporary solution has become a perma-nent problem. But who dreamed we'd gather a herd of recalcitrant wizards like stray cattle?"

The druid went to a small, irregular window in the plank wall. She stared out at the forest. From this view, there were no human works evident. "I just wish they'd go away."

Kwam took her shoulders from behind, hugged her gently. "But if we could turn them around somehow, there's so much we could learn—"

Greensleeve whirled, "Oh, Kwam! Not you too!"

He stepped back, hurt and ashamed. "Well—no, you're right. I'd use them in my own fashion if I could, and so use you, and that's selfish. I'm sorry."

Greensleeves crept into his arms, hid against his dark-clad chest. "I'm sorry, too. You're not selfish. If anyone is, it's me. But I don't want to be a jailer!"

Kwam patted her head and kissed her glossy brown hair. "I understand. Nor should you be."

She hugged him again, enjoying his warmth, then turned away. "But I must. For now. I've been slack when everyone else in the army works so hard. And maybe if we conjure them, a solution to their parole will present itself. . . . And better late than never, Mother used to say. Here, I'll summon Haakon. Doris can guard and you can badger him with questions. Ask him how he summoned demons without being torn to pieces. All right?" She smiled bravely, and Kwam smiled back.

Stepping to the center of the small room, Greensleeves closed her eyes. Kwam stepped back, and her two bodyguards flexed grips on their spears.

Concentrating, Greensleeves sorted through the myriad tags that lurked in her mind. She had many images for the mental sorting: she was a spider at the center of her web, and the tags touched people and objects; she hovered on a cloud, and by peering through a telescope, could see and touch her charges far below; she held in her hand a deck of cards, and by shuffling, could find the image of each. All these images were valid, yet didn't tell the whole story. For even as Greensleeves held each wizard in thrall, so too they touched her, and oddly enough, she felt responsible for and protective of them.

Even Haakon, King of the Badlands. She touched a tiny stone spire embroidered on her cloak, felt the tag to the man, a fat, smelly bully, but one burdened by sadness at his own inadequacy. She disliked Haakon, brash and unapologetic and profane, yet he'd suffered under their thrall, for in conjuring demons to escape he'd had an eye gouged out. His own fault, most said. But Greensleeves knew the siren song of magic, how it could backfire and burn the spellcaster. . . .

Why . . . ?

Casting her mind, her spirit, across the ether, tugging the invisible tag, Greensleeves found Haakon—and yet didn't. He was there, in a hollow roundabout fashion, as if she'd found his armor but not the man. And yet he was close by, too. Too close.

But she couldn't summon him.

Shaking her head, she made sure to touch the embroidered spire. No, something anchored the man—a binding spell. Queerly familiar. Where had she felt that sensation before?

"Kwam!" She snapped her eyes open, found three people staring, puzzled at the delay. "Where's my nova pentacle?"

"What?" The student turned, shuffled papers and geegaws, and opened a small wooden box—empty. "It's gone!"

"Oh, my!" Greensleeves touched a redbird stitched on her cloak. The sigil for Dacian the Red, now usually drunk and harmless. Surely she could be fetched. . . .

No. The tag was there, but something kept Dacian rooted.

Blinking, Greensleeves stared through her bodyguard. The Guardian asked, "Milady, are you all right?"

"I—can't—conjure the wizards. . . . "

A thunder of hooves drowned out her last words. A voice lifted through the treeborne windows and door.

"To arms! To arms! We're under attack!"

Driving into camp on a blown horse, helmet and lance missing, blood streaming down one arm, came a Scorpion of the Red Century. Dark hair flying, she reined the horse to a halt, jumped from the saddle, steadied herself, panted at Gull and his officers.

"Captain Dionne's compliments, General—but we're under attack! Demons, shades—long black cats with wings! We've lost twenty—in the first wave—"

Before Gull could answer, a pair of Gold centaurs pounded into camp from the opposite direction. One had an arrow in his upper arm. "General! Captain Holleb asks you come! War mammoths and blue barbarians and archers come from west! All hell breaks!"

Greensleeves startled Gull by calling from a treehouse balcony high above. "Brother! The wizards are loose! They've slipped their leashes!"

And it was her fault.

Officers and attendants scrambled every which way, mounted horses, shouted orders. Gull let the captains go. First they needed information.

He barked at his sister, who scurried down the stairs with skirts hiked high. "Greenie, go east! You can fight demons and shades! I'll go west and take war mammoths! Then we'll—"

He paused, stunned. They had to split their forces. Always before they'd met and made attacks together: teamwork was their strength. Now that advantage was gone. A sure sign of larger danger.

Gull could only add, "I'll send a messenger if we need help, or sound the trumpets all at once! Be careful!" he added lamely. Then he vaulted to the saddle of his dapple-gray Ribbons. His thirty Green Lancers, ten of them roused from sleep, had mounted, and the force thundered off after the twin centaurs with yellow armbands.

Greensleeves descended to find her horse Goldenrod saddled and waiting, her Guardians of the Grove mounted and ready, all six, for even the baggy-eyed night watch had been roused. Her hands shook as she grabbed the reins. She had a sudden premonition all their careful preparations were about to be smashed.

But she wouldn't tell anyone that.

"Hang on, sisters! We'll see where we can best help!"

She spun a hand in the air, seemed to catch a handful of it. Horses whickered as a shimmer of magic rose around them, brown at the bottom to represent the earth, green for grass and life, blue for the sky, sun-yellow encompassing their heads like a cloud of halos.

But as she winked away, Greensleeves couldn't help saying, "Spirit of the Forest, another battle!"

CHAPTER
7

LAID OUT BEFORE THEM, LIKE A CHILD'S
game gone mad, raged a furious battle.

Greensleeves and her six bodyguards had rippled
into existence on a low hill just at the edge of the
Whispering Woods.

Her bodyguards whirled instantly to check behind
and found the camp followers huddled within the
woods: the husbands and wives and children of the
soldiers. They awaited the outcome of the battle,
helped as they could ferrying weapons and water,
nursing the wounded, looting the dead. Already some
of the stronger folk were toting wounded to the shel-
tering forest.

Gull's captains were allowed to set up camp as
they liked, as long as rules of order and sanitation
were observed. The camps of the Red and Blue
Centuries, captained by professional soldiers, had
tents laid out arrow-straight in a long line parallel to
the woods, with guard posts at the four points of the
compass and the officers' tents in the center.

The edge of the Whispering Woods ran north-south

here. Greensleeves knew the landscape well, for ten leagues south lay the ruins of the village where she'd been born. The terrain rolled down from the edge of the woods, dropped off a granite shelf to a twisted riverbed: an easily defendable position with a clear escape route into the woods. North and east, the land rose slowly toward blue hills in the distance. Too stony for farming, too remote for shepherding, these were unplowed meadows bright with the small buds of yellow and blue and red wildflowers.

Those flowers would grow brighter next year, for they'd be watered with blood.

Out a half-mile, perched atop a hummock, the eastern divisions of Gull's army had gone forth to meet the foe. The three units had formed a wedge to protect their flanks and keep open a retreat, if necessary, across the twisted river. One side of the wedge was the Red Century, the Scorpions, in scale mail and red kilts and red plumes on steel helmets, led by Captain Dionne, an olive-skinned woman with curly black hair. The other side was the Blue Century, the Seals, blue tunics and scale mail and blue plumes, under Captain Neith, bronzed with a black beard. The rear wall of the wedge and floating force was the Rose Cavalry; half centaurs, half mounted humans under Captain Helki. The centaurs were gaudy in painted fluted armor and feathers and pink armbands. Other cavalry soldiers wore only pink armbands as their uniform. They were a mixed lot, including blue-robed desert riders once under the thrall of Karli, a former Black Knight of Jerges, a trio of sisters all in fur on shaggy ponies from the far north, and others with only their sterling horsemanship in common. Scattered about the field, in hollows and high grass, were somber scouts in gray and brown and their raven feather sigil, longbows rising and falling as they shot again and again to pick off outriders and their officers. Over the troops, upright lances bore ribbons of red, blue, and rose that snapped bravely in the summer breeze.

They'd need bravery today, for an awesome force was arrayed against them.

When Greensleeves saw who led it, she gasped with shock. "By the Spires of Pendlehaven, no!"

In the distance, on another hillock, directing the attack, Greensleeves saw Haakon, King of the Badlands; Ludoc, with his wolf and flaming eagle; and Leechnip, a sedge troll wizard.

Three magicians, each conquered by Gull and Greensleeves's army. Defeated separately. Yet arrayed here, together.

"*How?*" Greensleeves spoke aloud in her shock. "How did they get in contact with one another? They were hundreds of leagues apart! And they lived to compete, not cooperate! How—oh, no!"

Now she understood. There was only thing these wizards had in common.

Greensleeves herself.

"Milady?" asked Petalia, chief of bodyguards. "Shall we attack?"

"What?" Greensleeves shook her head, touched her brow. "My fault! This is my fault somehow! But I don't know how!"

"Milady?" The bodyguards looked at one another in confusion.

Greensleeves cast off her self-damning. The least she could do was throw herself into the attack, undo the damage she'd wrought. She slapped Goldenrod's reins. "Come on!"

The ranks of Gull and Greensleeves's army were being devastated.

With armored arms in the air, Haakon had summoned a horde of demons: waist-high dried-leather monsters with glowing red eyes and long white fangs. Hundreds of them swarmed onto Greensleeves's charges, yet stacks of demon bodies lay knee-deep along the front lines. Red or Blue soldiers worked in pairs, as they'd been trained by their old commander, Rakel of Benalia. One partner would spit demons through their dry guts with a long lance. His or her partner would fence with a sword or axe to drive back more demons, alternately killing and keeping from being killed. But many of their spears had broken or fetched up in the sheer numbers of demons, and most partners were reduced to hacking with hand weapons. From the back of her galloping horse, Greensleeves glimpsed demons with their heads split or lopped off, grasping arms sheared away. Yet many soldiers took damage, bitten to the bone on their arms and thighs and calves by long white teeth, raked in the face by filthy claws like daggers. Demons were so thick they looked like a black wave out to engulf the troops, and monsters at the back climbed over their comrades to punish the humans.

Amidst the demons wafted bundles of tattered rags, misty in the bright sunlight. These, Greensleeves guessed, were shades that derived nourishment from rampant fear. Though they caused little physical damage other than to chill someone to the bone, they were a terrifying distraction that made the ranks squirm and duck as if from giant mosquitoes. Fear was the shades' weapon, and even the stoutest troops might run if terror broke the line.

At the back of the wedge and among other spots on the hillock, cavalry diced with a dozen winged cats, huge, long-bodied, tufted-eared things dark and glistening as new-dug coal. The cats would leap as if pouncing for mice, then suddenly flap their wings and soar straight at a rider's chest. When they got past a lance point or sword swipe, they bit and clawed and latched hold of a collar, rent flesh and crushed bones. Their sleek black hides turned most blades, and even the mighty centaurs had to swing two-handed at them with bronze swords to draw black-boiling blood. Three centaurs were down already as were two cavalry soldiers, one beheaded by a single bite. As Greensleeves watched helplessly, a devil-cat wrapped two claws around the back of a centaur's torso and kicked with back legs under her ribs. The centaur was disemboweled from ribs to groin.

Amidst the wizards' conclave, at the extreme rear of the fighting, old Ludoc swirled both hands. Dressed in goat skin and an ermine cape, he was a mountain wizard, Greensleeves knew. Now he conjured dust devils tall as apple trees and steered them at the ranks of Greensleeves's army. Four miniature tornadoes spun crazily, penetrated the cavalry's flanks, and knocked centaurs and horses sprawling.

Greensleeves lost sight of the wizards as Petalia steered their plunging mounts down the limestone slope and across the gurgling riverbed. Water drops flew about them, sketching rainbows overhead. As the horses labored up the opposite slope to within bowshot of the battle, Greensleeves combed damp hair from her face. Had she seen . . . ?

Yes. She swore with her brother's choicest oaths. Closer now, she saw a golden circle bobbing on Ludoc's chest. The nova pentacle. Hers, given her by Chaney years ago, that Greensleeves might conquer her fears of madness and inadequacy and learn to finally shift through the planes of the world.

So Ludoc had stolen her . . . No.

Greensleeves blinked, stood in the stirrups to better see. That filthy troll, Leechnip, hunkering behind a boulder, *also* wore a nova pentacle! And so did Haakon, though it was hard to see against his gold-and-red chased armor.

Three pentacles? What, by Chatzuk's Curse, was afoot here?

"Never mind!" she shouted aloud. "I'll solve that later!"

"Milady, look out!"

Petalia raised her shield to protect them both, swerved her mount in front of Greensleeves. The captain grunted as something smashed her shield with a bright flash. Greensleeves smelled burnt paint and wood.

Up on the hillock, Haakon had fired a rocket from his fingertips. He shot more in Greensleeves's direction, the small comets arcing, almost invisible in the summer sky, exploding to shower dirt and grass and rocks and wildflowers nearby. Petalia shouted over the clash of battle for the bodyguards to ring Greensleeves, and in seconds she saw only women's backs in quilted white armor and their hair snapping in the breeze.

Cursing her guards' efficiency, Greensleeves strained to see the enemy. Ludoc conjured a brace of cave bears, but the big bruins shied from the noise and alien smells of the winged cats and raging centaurs and bowled off across the meadow. Not far from the Red Century stamped a raging red bull, hooking its horns in anger. It blinked at a sudden pall of bluish fog that stank and made soldiers retch.

So many spells and creatures came so fast, Greensleeves wasn't sure who'd conjured what. Not that she cared. She hopped off her horse and swatted it out of the way, as did her bodyguards. She couldn't conjure from horseback: she needed the earth under her feet.

Tugging her cloak by its leading edge, the druid glanced down and found an embroidered decoration, a bridge over which tripped a coach drawn by four white horses. Under the bridge was not blue water but black mud. Touching her fingertip to the spot, she pictured the actual place, a fen far to the west of the Whispering Woods. With her free hand, she drew an imaginary circle around the distant wizards and mouthed a simple spell.

Instantly, the heavily armored Haakon and the grizzled Ludoc balked and staggered at the knees. The hillock they stood on opened in the middle, turning to liquid, like a cup of dark tea. Haakon sank to his knees, then hips, in seconds. Ludoc, understanding the danger, flipped his eagle aloft, where it caught flame, then threw himself flat on his face. Black, evil mud splattered around them both.

Both men howled in sudden pain, for Greensleeves had not only conjured a quagmire but one where hot springs boiled into black mud. Ludoc cursed and tried to swim out of the scalding gunk soaking his clothes. Haakon just floundered, sunk to his armpits and still sinking. Greensleeves would need to shift him elsewhere soon, lest he drown.

Then she recalled she *couldn't* shift Haakon as she'd done in the past, for his nova pentacle anchored him in place as surely as the quagmire sucked him down.

But Greensleeves didn't need big magic. Letting her mind flit over the forest, she pictured a fresh-fallen branch: a widowmaker, her brother would call it. Touching the branch in her mind's eye, Greensleeves plucked it from *there* and dropped it *there*. Flailing, Haakon suddenly found a huge branch in front of his chin. Desperately he clutched it, hung on, pulled himself up. Ludoc had almost swum out of the quagmire, and Leechnip had run off somewhere.

With more conjurings stalled, Greensleeves turned to the existing threats. The demons still tore into her soldiers, the black cats raged amidst the cavalry. Down went her hand to touch a tree embroidered along the left edge of her cloak to find a red-brown ant crawling on its bark. She whispered a spell.

Rippling upward from the ground, brown to green to brown this time, in amongst the rampaging demons popped up five, then ten, then fifty, then a hundred of the most curious soldiers.

They were five feet tall, reddish brown dotted with stiff hair, covered in what looked like armor but was in fact their carapaces. On necks as thin as a finger were supported heads made of plates with round segmented eyes. Stuck to the tops of their heads by some brownish stuff were tropical leaves that mimicked plumes. Each soldier carried a short-hafted triangular-bladed weapon, half shovel, half spear.

Without prompting, they plied their awkward weapons against demons. Yotian soldiers, they were, ant-soldiers, sexless workers fashioned, according to legend, by either Urza or Mishra as a militia, a home guard, to protect their allies' cities while the real soldiers were away. No one knew if the Yotians had been mutated from ants or men, or both. But Yotians were fearsome fighters, for they existed to attack enemies, especially nonhuman enemies striking at humans.

All of the ant-men fought the same, with a curious thrust and twist, as if digging holes in a dirt wall with shovels. Identical, they worked like cogs in a big machine, or birds feeding from the same dish. Their blunt spade-spears snagged demons in the throat, ripped leathery skin and splintered bone. And the Yotians took no damage, for the demons couldn't chomp through their tough hides any more than a turtle's shell. Slowly, but steadily, a hole opened around each Yotian, with a dike of dead demons encircling them.

Greensleeves cast a glance at the evil wizards. Haakon had clambered to dry ground, plastered with hot black mud up to the eyeholes of his helmet. Ludoc was gone. Where?

"*Hist!*" A bodyguard, Doris, leveled her spear. Off to their right appeared three heavy-shouldered mountain goats, all white and shaggy, with horns as long as pitchfork tines. A fourth goat twinkled into existence, still with snow from some distant sierra sparkling on its coat. The mark of Ludoc of the mountains.

The foremost goat lowered its head and charged.
Doris leaped in its way, jabbed her spear point in the
ground, held tight to the shaft. Head down, the goat
spanked its nose and horns on the spear handle and
angled away. Doris yelled as the second goat began
its run.

"Deal with it, please!" Greensleeves couldn't
bother with normal creatures. She needed to stop
those devil-cats. "Don't harm them if you—"

She yelped as someone bumped her sprawling with
a brawny backside. Petalia shunted her mistress aside
to plunge her spear under a goat's ribs, piercing its
heart as the brawny animal stampeded by. Red blood
stained white fur as the goat charged on another
thirty paces, then suddenly dropped its head and
somersaulted over its own horns.

Dusting skinned palms, Greensleeves scrambled up
and tried to look everywhere at once. Fire from the
rockets crackled through the coarse grass and weeds
and wildflowers. Enchanted, the flames crawled with
many jagged fingers toward Greensleeves's party, but
the wizard only waggled her fingers, lifted water
from the river, and dropped it hissing in a fan before
her. This was foolishness, she thought. If three wizards couldn't conjure more dangerous things than
goats and fire—

But this was only one of two attacks, she remembered, for war mammoths and blue barbarians struck
from the west against Gull's centuries.

She hadn't had time to consider it before, but now
the thought stunned her as if she'd struck a stone
wall.

How many wizards were arrayed against them?

Even more disturbingly, Greensleeves recalled the
last time she'd seen "blue-painted barbarians." Such
warriors had been summoned by the wizard Towser,
who'd destroyed their village and betrayed both Gull
and Greensleeves. The druid wondered if her brother

had recalled that already. More than once in the last
three years, he'd wished to get hands on Towser's
throat.

Was *Towser* nearby? Was *he* part of this devil's
pact that conspired against them? Had he fashioned
the multiple nova pentacles?

Unconsciously, Greensleeves waved her hands, dis-
missing the worries. There was much to do here. Too
much. She had to scotch three wizards and their minions, then journey elsewhere and try to protect the
rest of her army.

Her bodyguards had driven off the mountain goats,
fended off the questing red bull. Yotian ant-soldiers
had reduced the demons by a third. Just as mind-
lessly, the demons had turned on the ant-soldiers,
until the main battle was small burnt-black bodies
swarming over red-brown ant-men. Greensleeves's
human soldiers, with a moment to regroup, grabbed
up fallen lances and spears and converged on the
winged cats. Menaced by dozens of long steel points
whether they flew low or soared high, the cats fell
back snarling. Many soldiers pegged arrows at
Haakon only to see them bounce off his invisible
shield. Helki, the centaur captain, shouted to collect
a detail to charge the hillock where Haakon reigned.

Yet the soldiers were stopped once again.

Between them and Haakon swirled what looked
like ashes from a campfire. The ashes hardened,
froze, and formed an irregular wall like snaggly teeth.
Many of the soldiers froze and backed away involun-
tarily. Even Helki blanched and backstepped.

The objects were tombstones, Greensleeves made
out: gray slate, white granite, reddish sandstone.
Dozens of tombstones etched with winged death's-
heads, angels, monsters, glyphs, runes, curses. All tip-
ping one way and another, as if the graveyard from
which they'd been pillaged was tumbledown and overgrown. Ivy vines still wrapped many stones. The army

recoiled, loath to cross that tilted line, fearful the souls of the robbed dead might come hunting them.

Captains yelled, sergeants bellowed and shrilled, soldiers fell back from the tombstone wall and the retreating winged cats. Shuffling over their own dead and heaps of demons, they dressed their lines, mopped sweat, drank from canteens, wiped blades, consoled the dying, and readied for the next attack.

Yet Haakon had retreated behind the hillock still marked by the quagmire, and Ludoc and Leechnip were out of sight. Some demons tussled with Yotians, but the humans and centaurs had a breathing spell. Greensleeves wondered what to do next. Keep the high ground? Or pull back to the woods? She wished her brother were here to tell her. She must ask Dionne or Neith. And should they try to capture the errant wizards—again? She should—

"Hell's Caretaker!" shouted Petalia. Greensleeves turned only to find herself surrounded by a wall of female flesh and blood. Her bodyguards had dropped into ranks of two to defend her. From what?

Then she saw. A sneak attack.

Rushing them came a behemoth the likes of which Greensleeves had never imagined.

Minotaur! was her first thought. Yet it wasn't.

The giant walked upright, half again as tall as a man. It was composed, she guessed quickly, of living rocks polished like sea stones. Yet behind a curved steel mask—once gilt and elegant, now pitted with rust—with a single slit for eyes and an iron grill for a mouth, it sported a neck thick and brown as a horse's complete with snowy mane. Horns curved from its face, or the mask, to tower above its shaggy head. Its body was girded with straps of rusted armor and nothing else. Its hands and feet ended in pincer claws like a scorpion's.

"Ur-Drago!" bleated Bly. "Ur-Drago, Scourge of the Swamp!"

A legend, Greensleeves knew, something to

frighten children. Yet here and alive. From a swamp: that would be Leechnip's contribution. As if in confirmation, the naked gray troll capered fifty feet behind its slave, shrilling with evil laughter, the nova pentacle slapping its skinny chest.

These thoughts flickered through Greensleeves's head for a second, then the thing hit them.

The monster crashed into the Guardians of the Grove like a falling tree, yet the women refused to give ground. Greensleeves was rammed backward. She heard bones break, a woman hiss in pain, a spear shaft snap as it struck the creature's rocky hide. Sunlight glared in her eyes as she tumbled to the meadow ground. A flower, a blue bachelor's button, tickled her nose.

Ur-Drago trod on the corpse of Bly, his rocky foot having smashed her to jelly. Bly's dead eyes were wide open in horror, staring at the sky, as if a childhood fear had finally caught her after all these years. Another guard, Alina, was dying, her neck snapped in a rocky claw like a vice. Yet the survivors plied spears and swords valiantly. Petalia leaned on her spear and shoved hard enough to strip skin from her callused palms. She jammed her blade into the monster's armpit, trying to pierce its heart.

Yet Greensleeves could tell this was no redblooded creature of the land, but a construct cobbled of pure magic. Petalia's spear shaft snapped from the strain, the blade lodged deep in the thing's body, having done no harm whatsoever. Ur-Drago—was it some dragon construct, with that name?—clawed for Petalia and almost knocked her head off, taking no notice of her assault.

Forward, stepping on two fresh bleeding bodies, stalked the thing. For Greensleeves.

She couldn't fight it, the archdruid knew. She had no spells to immobilize it, at least none she could remember right now. A quagmire would mean noth-

ing to it, for it lived in swamps. A wall of brambles or
stone spears or earth it would simply shatter. Any
creature put up against this killing machine would be
crushed. It had to be sent away, so far no human or
living thing would ever suffer it again.

Greensleeves knew such a place, a dark hole full of
fear she'd found in her dreams. She knew it well, for
she steered clear of it.

Yet to send the behemoth away, she must touch it.

Stumbling backward, Greensleeves saw Caltha
smashed down, her collarbone crushed, Kuni
knocked sprawling from a head wound. There were
only two guards left to oppose it, and they simply
clung trying to keep it away. Petalia screamed for
Greensleeves to run, quickly. Behind her, the archdruid heard a thunder of hooves, centaurs or cavalry
running to her rescue, probably with lowered lances.
Yet nothing earthly would stop the behemoth.

So she muttered her spell, an unsummoning spell
combined with a distant reaching, a reaching for
somewhere so far away she went cold inside to consider it.

She kept the spell balled in her hand, tightly, but it
fought to get out. Her fingers cramped; her arm
trembled.

If she muffed this spell, became hypnotized by the
vastness of it, she'd be the one to fall forever.

Petalia screamed as the monster trod on her ankle
and snapped it like a stick. Still the woman clung to
it, as did two others. Greensleeves barked, "Let it go!
Let go! Please!"

Startled, the two struggling guards obeyed. Yet
Petalia, their leader, could countermand orders, and
did now. "Run, milady!"

Greensleeves grit her teeth, held the spell from
engulfing them, grabbed for Petalia's arm with her
free hand. But all her strength went to keep her fist
closed. Thunder roared in her skull.

She had no choice. Before others died, she had to loose the unsummoning spell.

Hopping forward, she touched her fist to one of the Ur-Drago's claws and opened her hand. The monster nipped at her, but she scuttled back and fell. "Petalia! Please—"

Too late.

Nothingness rushed upon them like a tidal wave.

Around Ur-Drago's claw there spun a well, a vortex of blackness so deep it hurt to look upon. In a heartbeat, the blackness spiraled around its arm, torso, head and crooked knees, his waist. And around the clinging Petalia.

A howling sounded, a roar to suck all sound from the ears and the world. The black cyclone engulfed Ur-Drago and the bodyguard. With a snap, both were sucked into a rapid circle, a hole gaping in the sky like a misplaced mineshaft.

Yet this was no mere hole. This was the abyss, an infinite well of darkness that lay—Greensleeves knew not where. Between worlds? Between planes? Between life and death? Between reality and dream?

There was no way to tell. Only in her darkest haunted dreams had Greensleeves glimpsed the abyss, and always she'd recoiled from it as if from a great height, and survived to wake the next morning shivering.

And here was the vacancy before her, sucking away this monster. And her most faithful follower.

Greensleeves shouted, reached out a hand to grab Petalia, even if she were dragged with her.

Yet the bodyguard knew what was happening, saw the danger to her mistress, and refused to reach out, lest she drag Greensleeves in.

Through tears, Greensleeves saw the two disappear down a long, long tunnel of darkness, spinning, both staring up, losing color until they were ghosts, souls of the damned, sent to death too soon.

Then the abyss slammed shut with a deafening boom.

CHAPTER
8

CENTAURS AND CAVALRY AND FOOT SOL-diers clustered around the archdruid. Healers tended Caltha's smashed collarbone and Kuni's creased skull, but could do nothing for Bly and Alina. Down in the field, soldiers and campfollowers mopped up after the Yotian ant-soldiers, slitting the throats of wounded demons. The winged cats were gone, running and flapping jerkily for the distant hills.

None of the three renegade wizards was to be seen.

Surrounded by weary and bloodstained fighters, Greensleeves sat in a crumpled heap and wept. "Oh, Petalia!"

The Guardian captain had been so kind, so patient, fussing like a mother, harrying the other guards to do their best, to protect Greensleeves at all costs, even to their lives. Now two guards were dead, and Petalia had lost her life, or worse, was still alive in some infernal pit, trapped forever because she'd loved Greensleeves and done her duty.

Greensleeves wept at the sorrow and the pain and

shame of it, for she'd never considered her life worth any of her followers'.

Yet even now she couldn't vent her grief, for there was still much to be done.

Too much, she thought. She felt like a willow in a hurricane: supple, bending, patient, but pushed too far and ready to snap.

Still weeping, she crawled on her hands and knees to the bodies of her two dead bodyguards. One thing, at least, she could salvage. One thing to help make amends.

Soldiers had pulled the two women's mangled bodies straight and covered them with their cloaks, but Greensleeves tugged the cloth aside and laid hands on their unflinching faces.

Still warm. There was hope.

"Spirit of the Forest. Bones and roots of my ancestors. Life everlasting in the deep green, hear my plea. Bring back life to these who fought so valiantly, who loved so much. Let them live and feel the sun on their backs again. Spirits, I implore you—"

She rattled on, calling on the mana of the forest: all the stretches of forest, from the dappled glades like cathedrals, to the stippled brambles at the forest's edge, to the deep quiet glens where nothing moved in the shadows of the great trees. She called the mana, bent it to her will, channeled it to her dead charges who had not yet departed.

Soldiers gasped and fell away. Greensleeves kept her eyes closed, feeling, drawing on power, channeling.

Under her hands, the warm corpses changed. Bloodstained skin gave way to feathers and fur. The warmth lingering within them grew, spread, even as the bodies contracted in size.

Then, at a wriggle under each hand, Greensleeves let go.

A hare, long-legged and soft-furred in gray, galloped from under her hand. From the other, in a furious beating of feathers, a ring-necked pheasant flapped squawking into the sky.

All that was left of Bly and Alina were some empty clothes and discarded weapons.

Weary unto death, Greensleeves accepted help at either elbow to rise. Then she took a deep breath of summer air and sun, wiped her face, dusted her hands. She cast about and saw the battlefield was under control. Scouts reported the wizards were long gone, conjured away.

Greensleeves smoothed her skirts while her mare Goldenrod was fetched. She tried to think of praise for her bodyguards, something like Gull would say. He'd gotten good at speeches. But her native shyness won out, and she said only, "Thank you for your bravery. I am sorry for your dead companions . . . Caltha, you're hurt. You must stay here."

"Milady, no! Please!" The dark woman, barely out of girlhood, gestured with her makeshift sling and winced, tears on her cheeks. "I can ride with you!"

Before Greensleeves could answer, Kuni, with her brown face and straight black hair and a bloodstained bandage for a cap, took over. "No, Caltha. Rest for now. Milady, I'm assuming captaincy. We need more Guardians, and I'm drafting Micka there. She's brave and will do."

Greensleeves sputtered, "No! Don't bring anyone else into your fold! I just killed Petalia, or worse, and we lost Bly and Alina!—" She was crying: she didn't want anyone else hurt on her account.

But the Guardians of the Grove were a stronger force than Greensleeves herself. Nodding, Kuni ordered a big farm girl, Micka, to step out of the Red Century and don the garments and armor of the dead Alina. Doris gathered up the clothes of the smaller Bly. "We'll pick up another—"

They were interrupted by a clatter of hooves. A bloodstained messenger of the White Century rode up. "Please, milady Greensleeves, we're attacked by magic in the south!"

"I forgot," said the archdruid. "The battles are not over yet. They've barely begun."

Despite the messenger's disheveled condition, the forces to the south had not suffered as badly as their eastern brethren.

Greensleeves and her four bodyguards rippled into being behind birch trees in the southern stretches of the Whispering Woods. In this spot, because the soil was sandy and dry, the trees grew farther apart and not so tall. Single oaks spread their branches wide. Birches made brilliant white patches like skyrockets taking off. The grass was coarse and tough, but a stream provided water before sinking in a ravine and disappearing.

There was only one century camped in this spot, the White Bears, commanded by a towering woman with a thick shock of yellow hair named Cerise. Being inside the forest itself, Cerise had set up camp on different lines. Officer's tents were clustered in a beech grove near the center. Radiating outward, the sparse trees had been trimmed back somewhat and tents erected in concentric circles. At the outer edge of camp was a neat breastworks of dirt surrounded by a ditch, for Uxmal's dwarven sappers resided here. Past the ditch, all trees had been cut back for three hundred feet, a decision Greensleeves had allowed with some pain. Thus the soldiers and sappers had a cozy shaded retreat within and clear line of sight without.

This small force was stationed here less than a mile south of Greensleeves's Grove, where the officers met and planned. They were the "back door" emergency force to help defend the grove if attacked. A wide trail wound from the rear of the encampment back toward the grove, and strung along it were many of the camp's "idlers": artisans, cooks, nurses, the healer's hospital, Lily's quartermaster corps, and

other remnants and oddballs of the army. Stiggur and
Dela, the army's "heavy infantry," made camp near
here with the clockwork beast. As did Liko, the two-
headed giant, now with two good arms, thanks to
Greensleeves's regeneration spells. The so-called
Martyrs of Korlis kept company here, keeping folk
awake with their weird chanting, as did the copper-
skinned dwarves who dressed in bright stripes and
pointed hats, and who often sang the night away. All
these workers and soldiers were now inside the
breastworks, many watching with weapons at hand,
others carrying on normal tasks.

As Greensleeves steered her horse down the trail
and into the rear of the encampment, she saw a pile
of bodies heaped before the breastworks: greenish
bald-headed rag-clad orcs, mostly, and their smaller
cousins, gray-green goblins with thatches of gray
hair, all stippled with arrows. Farther down the campaign ground, toward the tree line, was an inter-
locked sprawl of human bodies, some in short red
robes that Greensleeves recognized, some wholly
naked.

The only living thing in sight outside the breastworks was the clockwork beast with Liko alongside.
Steered by Dela, Stiggur's "assistant engineer," it
paced with a rhythmic *clump clump clump clump*
back and forth before the tree line. Stiggur, as
scrawny as ever, stood atop the beast's back and
watched the woods. Thumping, swaying, jingling,
clanking, whirring, the clockwork beast looked like
four trees carrying a blacksmith's shop.

The ancient beast was constructed of thick dark
oak and slabs of sheet iron, with guts like a mill-
works, a maze of wooden gears with cogged teeth
and leather pulleys and tilting cantilevers, and no
power source except magic, folks guessed. The boy
Stiggur, who'd adopted the beast, over the last three
years had added to its structure until it looked like a

walking fort. Low walls along its spine were roofed
and sheeted with copper. Mounted on its rump was a
ballista with spare arrows racked along the beast's
iron flanks. A small crane was mounted up front, for
hauling up goods, and rope handles and railings ran
all around, while rope ladders climbed its sides. The
driver's seat, protected by small detachable walls,
was slung in a harness, and other compartments and
gadgets were fitted here and there. And then there
were the decorations. The sheet iron flanks had been
scraped and painted with brown and white blotches,
like a real horse's hide, and the head decorated with
an artificial mane made of unraveled rope. Still, the
beast was an ungainly and ugly thing. But useful.
Stomping onto a battlefield, with a two-headed giant
alongside, it could rout whole squads of cavalry or
infantry, who feared to be trampled under those huge
clumping feet. Besides, the giant crossbow shot six-
foot arrows that could penetrate both sides of a barn
at half a mile—when they hit.

When Stiggur caught sight of Greensleeves and his
entourage, he grabbed the end of the crane rope and
leaped into space: a clattering ratchet eased him
swinging to the ground.

The picket called out Greensleeves's arrival, and
Captain Cerise climbed down from a wooden obser-
vation platform at the center of camp. Leaving her
officers behind, she trotted to report. Stiggur pelted
up to add his observations.

"Greensleeves!" the boy shouted. "We drove 'em
back! They didn't have a chance! We slaughtered
'em!"

The archdruid waved a hand to silence the boy:
young man, really, for he was sixteen or so now,
dressed in deerhide like his hero Gull. Turning to
Cerise, staying in the saddle that she might see over
the breastworks, she listened to the report.

"The war dogs started barking, milady," began the

captain. (Sometime back someone had addressed Greensleeves as "milady," and now the druid couldn't break the army of the habit.) "Ravens came runnin', reported a giant out there. That big bastard Immugio: we knew him from the Battle of Myrion. He conjured orcs 'n, goblins thicker 'n fleas to come at us out of the woods. Not at a trot, I can tell you. Their captains wore out whips drivin' 'em from the shelter of the trees. Finally Immugio must 'a put the fear of something into 'em, for they come at a rush. But we just dusted 'em back and they retreated. Two of ours wounded, none seriously. Stiggur there took a shot at Immugio with his monster ballista, split a birch next to 'im—"

"The bastard *ducked* or I would split his gullet!" the boy supplied.

"Then, screamin' like furies, came those red-robed idiots—"

"Fabia's Cult of the Unseen." Greensleeves stifled a sigh. "Before your time."

"Ah, thank 'ee, milady. Well, our own idiots, the Martyrs of Korlis, took that as a personal challenge, and before I could stop 'em, they shucked their tunics like they was on a honeymoon and charged over the breastworks. You can see they're still out there."

"Indeed," said Greensleeves, peering from the saddle. The martyrs had gone to gory glory, into the arms of Korlis, whoever that was.

Greensleeves shaded her eyes. "Oh, my . . . Immugio and Fabia of the Golden Throat." Two more wizards who'd lived half a continent apart. Neither had known the other, yet somehow they'd become linked.

And Greensleeves knew the link was herself.

Shaking her head, she asked, "The goblins. Did the giant bring them? I know Fabia didn't: she despises anything but 'perfect' humans."

Cerise shook her head: proud of her lion's-mane hair, she disdained a helmet. "No, milady. There's a goblin in charge. A female wearing a crown like a ring of horseshoe nails. She—"

Greensleeves rubbed her forehead. As she'd feared, it was the goblin queen, Thunderhead. Another of her "parolees" slipped off the leash.

"Madness," she muttered to herself. "Madness to think we could harness those wizards and their consummate evil."

"Milady?" Cerise asked. "Do you have any orders? Shall we maintain position here or fall back toward the grove—"

"Hare dey gome!" bellowed Uxmal the dwarf. Instantly everyone shifted grip on their weapons, drew half-nocks on bows. Not one of her soldiers or campfollowers was afraid, Greensleeves thought, or at least didn't show it.

But she was terrified. Not by the current menace, but by the overall horror it implied. Every wizard they had ever conquered, it seemed, had joined to attack them en masse. Could even their army, strong and dedicated as it was, withstand such a force?

A squawl and clatter resounded from the trees. Orcs crept forth, slapping iron swords on leather shields and bellowing, making noise but little progress. Salted among them were shorter goblins with flint-edged clubs or stabbing spears. A few of Fabia's red-robed fanatics formed the flanks. Behind, looming like a mountain, walked Immugio. He shouted and hollered, but kept thick tree trunks between himself and the clockwork beast.

From the left flank of the defenders' army, Stiggur gave a "Hyah!" A rope *tunged*, and an arrow as long as a canoe ripped into the birches, banked, and killed three orcs, who fell, spinning sideways. Beside Stiggur arose a small scrawny figure: Egg Sucker. The goblin stuck his thumbs in his ears, jeered at his own kind under the birches, turned and flipped up his ragged skins to flaunt his bony backside.

Greensleeves noted that over the dried death mask on Immugio's chest hung a nova pentacle. She craned this way and that, even stood on her saddle, but saw neither Fabia nor the goblin queen, Thunderhead. She tried to think what to do.

Cerise shouted for archers to nock and stand ready to pour forth a withering rain of arrows, but Greensleeves shushed her and concentrated. The army was spoiling for a fight, could easily defeat this orc-goblin horde, but the archdruid wanted to spare any lives she could. There'd be many more battles before the day was over.

"Hold your archers, please, Cerise. Have the sappers stand by with ropes and mallets, and cut long stakes. An armspan or more."

Disciplined, the captain didn't ask, though she did wonder as she trotted to Uxmal and relayed the strange orders.

Greensleeves slid off her horse and pushed between her steadfast bodyguards. The orcish army, unopposed, had turned up the noise and crept closer, though still outside bowshot. Orcs hurled curses and obscene gestures. Goblins hopped up and down like children. Fabia's fanatics stalked at the outskirts of the mob, bronze swords flashing overhead. The snaggle-toothed, bull-necked Immugio raised gnarled hairy hands and roared a battle challenge his army echoed.

Greensleeves's army hung poised, waiting to see what its leader would do.

The archdruid tugged her embroidered cloak across her front, touched a spot that depicted a long-haired man lying rapt under a tree. Then she waggled her fingers at the howling army.

Instantly many orcs and goblins fell silent, choking on their war cries. Most of Fabia's fanatics halted in their tracks. Dazed, they peered around at their sur-

roundings as if seeing the forest for the first time.
One touched the bark of a birch tree, discovered a
fuzzy caterpillar, and summoned others to see it.
Another pointed at clouds and imaginary pictures.
Others joined in, until someone picked a wildflower
and sniffed it, after which many followed suit.

Half-mesmerized, the army stalled. Unentranced
humans and orcs lashed out angrily at their dazed
companions, striking them when they gave gentle or
dreamy answers.

"What spell is *that*?" asked Micka, against discipline. Kuni snapped at her to belt up.

"Serenity," the druid told them. "And here's
another." She touched another picture on her
embroidered cloak and made a shooing motion with
both hands.

In the half-dazed milling mob, a droning caught
the attention of the wary. The sound thrummed,
became a buzz, then a high whine.

From the bushes and bracken and leaves underfoot, there arose yellow-and-black shapes.

Bees as big as fists.

Screaming, orcs lashed out at the killer bees and
were stung. They couldn't know the bees would only
attack if attacked, and so infuriated the insects.

The serenity-entranced humans and orcs watched
curiously as their angry compatriots were overwhelmed by the enormous bees. Within seconds,
scores of orcs were yelping, swatting, then fleeing.
They dragged a yellow-black whirlwind after them.

Their leader, Immugio, ignored the bees drilling his
thick hide. He screamed abuse at his splintering
army, slapped at them, kicked out and killed some
with his big bare feet. Then he ducked as another
huge arrow chopped the leaves over his head. Stiggur
had held his fire, but attacked now that he saw the
bees attacking.

As the orcs bolted to the woods, soldiers near

Greensleeves gasped, then yelled, and finally laughed. Cerise smirked and shook her tawny head. "Hell of a way to win a battle! But what're—"

"The ropes and stakes for?" asked Greensleeves. "Watch."

Stooping, she caught up a small twig at her feet. Squinting, the druid lined up the twig in her hand with a tall oak standing next to the giant. Then she broke the twig.

A loud crack warned Immugio, who looked up as the treetop shattered. He howled, once, before the crown toppled onto him, mashing him to the ground with its entangling branches and green-oak weight. Leaves thrashed as the giant tried to bull free of the deadfall trap.

Greensleeves nodded downfield, but the dwarven sappers had already spilled over the breastworks, laughing and singing in their strange guttural language. Cerise shouted two companies of White Bears after them and ordered the rest to stay put.

"Oh, wait!" But it was too late. Before Greensleeves could stop them, some soldiers rushed amidst the dazed humans and orcs, who were still entranced by the serenity spell, and butchered them. By the time she'd called to Cerise, there were no enemies alive on the field.

But the sturdy dwarves performed well. Scrambling over and around the deadfall, they flipped ropes over the trapped giant, cinching his legs and arms. Others swung mauls to pound in the fresh-cut stakes, and Immugio was staked down tight.

Greensleeves shook her head at the needlessly shed blood, but there was nothing for it now. She debated whether to interrogate Immugio, learn who else was in this attack, but decided that, without torture, the giant would only berate her.

Wiping her brow, Greensleeves found she was suddenly peaked: all this magic-making took its toll. But there were still battles to the west, and maybe more elsewhere. Someone offered her a flagon of wine, but she asked for water instead and got it. Drinking deeply, she gasped out the story of events in the east and west. Cerise nodded her shaggy head and awaited further orders.

Greensleeves could only say, "There aren't any. I mean, uh, just see no one gets past you to the grove. Keep messengers moving between the other factions so you're informed. Uh . . ."

Lily, Gull's wife, had waddled over from the rear of the encampment. A nurse carried her daughter, for the pregnant Lily had enough trouble walking just on her own. She laid a hand on Greensleeves's arm, and the archdruid covered it, glad for the human contact.

"I hate to intrude, Greenie, but there was an awful commotion to the west. I fear Gull's troops have met something—something hard to handle."

The archdruid nodded. "I'll do what I can, sister. Thank you."

She mounted Goldenrod and found she had not three bodyguards but four. A small quick woman with slanted eyes named Miko was introduced: Kuni had drafted her from the Bears. In a small precise voice, Miko said she was honored to join the Guardians.

"Oh, yes, thank you, but . . ." The druid looked at the small woman's tunic and skirt and white oxhide armor. They had been Bly's and were still wet with her blood. But Miko didn't seem to mind. The druid only shook her head and caught the wrists of her new bodyguards. "Miko and Micka. Thank you again. I'll try to keep you straight."

And alive, she prayed. Amidst all this destruction and waste. Which was all her fault.

The battle in the west was so different, when Greensleeves rippled into being, that she could scarce believe the two fights were but a few miles apart.

Remaining mounted, Greensleeves peered past the surrounding trunks of red oaks and huge golden birches. At first she couldn't make out what was happening.

The forest was thick here, too thick for fighting, her brother would say. Nor was it the proper camp of the Black Century, for that was almost a mile farther west. Gull's army must have fallen back to this stretch of woods. Greensleeves had tried to shift as close to her brother as possible, but couldn't even see him. The battle was chaos.

Besides the thick tree trunks, patches of impassable mountain laurel, and tall rocks, there was billowing smoke in three or four spots, and no wind to drive it off. For a moment, Greensleeves worried, because the forest was dry these days. Reading the sky, she knew a breeze was building, but no hint of rain. She'd have to make some when she could.

Meanwhile, Greensleeves saw only the vaguest blurred shapes dashing between tree boles. Black Dogs, with black plumes and black trousers and armbands, trotted by, jingling, in two directions. A company of black-clad female D'Avenant archers jogged past, faced south, and knelt as their commander barked. Then she countermanded, ordered them to unnock and rise and jog on. A file of Gold cavalry, soldiers and centaurs, threaded through the trees just at the edge of vision. Screams sounded at their destination. A bestial trumpeting shook the air, making leaves shiver: a mammoth's cry. Yet Greensleeves couldn't see the giant beast anywhere. And where was her brother?

Most arresting was a single still figure not twenty feet away. The dead barbarian lay curled, as if asleep, with a gaping bloody wound in her side. Her hair was white, drawn up in a tuft at the top. Her skin was tattooed in whorls and lines, then dyed blue with woad, an extract from a plant root. She wore leather armor and laced sandals. Her weapons were gone. Her face was peaceful, despite white tusks that protruded from her lower jaw.

Greensleeves stared. These blue barbarians she had seen only once, long ago, when her adventures had first begun. They were thralls of Towser, he of the brushy hair and rainbow stripes and easy lying treachery.

He had to be close.

"Milady, there." Kuni pointed. As smoke wafted clear, through the trees they glimpsed lancers in green: Gull's personal bodyguards. Nudging her mare with her knees, Greensleeves aimed in that direction, four bodyguards spaced around her mount.

But before they'd gone a dozen yards, Micka, the big farm girl, wrenched her horse's head around and almost snapped its neck.

"Hola! For Greensleeves!"

Riding at them full tilt from the smoke came a trio of wild-looking men waving cutlasses.

CHAPTER
9

THE RAIDERS WORE THE RAGGED SHIRTS
and baggy pants of sailors, in faded but wildly mismatched colors, sashes, earrings, and with kerchiefs on their heads. Two were swarthy, tanned black by years at sea, and the third black-skinned to begin with, a man from the far south.

Greensleeves knew what they were: pirates. They were either in the pay or under the thrall of Dwen, an ocean wizard who'd wielded the fabled Lance of the Sea—until Gull and Greensleeves took it away. The horses they rode had traces picked out in yellow and blood on the animals' flanks. Obviously the pirates had ambushed some Gold cavalry.

Of her four remaining bodyguards, Kuni, with the bandaged head, was slowest. She barked orders at the others. Micka, Miko, and Doris shouted, lowered their lances, and charged. Kuni leveled her lance, yanked her shield around, and placed herself before the druid.

The pirates split, shouted to frighten their foe and bolster their own courage, and swung rusty, bloody cutlasses wildly overhead. But stealing and riding a horse was not the same as fighting mounted, as they quickly learned.

Micka, big and blue-eyed and golden-haired, couched her lance in her armpit, hunkered low, and aimed well. The long leaf-shaped blade caught a pirate square in the belly and slashed out his back. At the same time, she raised her shield high, deflecting the dying pirate's final, weak cutlass stroke. Then she dropped the lance so she wouldn't be carried away. The dying man drooped in the saddle, the lance butt jabbing the ground. Micka hauled out her sword and kicked her mount toward a second attacker. ·

Doris's opponent, the black pirate, saw his friend split almost in half, and learned, but not enough. As the bodyguard lunged with her lance, he twisted sideways, half out of the saddle, to save his belly from the steel. But Doris could follow him there, too. She swiped the lance sideways, whapping him in the ribs with the haft, then drove her mount into his. Off balance already, the shock and Doris's push toppled him from the saddle. He screeched when his ankle, trapped in the stirrup, snapped as he hit the ground with his shoulder. He didn't suffer long, for Doris spun her horse almost in midair, rearing fully upright, and punched down with the long lance, the weight of the horse adding to the strength of the blow. The lance ripped through the man's chest, slicing his lungs and heart, and buried itself so deeply in the soft forest loam it jammed in the roots below and the bodyguard had to leave it behind.

Whipping his head around, finding himself alone, the third pirate kicked his horse mercilessly and aimed for the biggest space between trees he could find. But little Miko, hot to prove her worth, turned her horse and plunged alongside him. As they dashed between the trunks, her lance tangled in leaves overhead and was snatched from her hand, so she had to claw out her sword. The escaping pirate turned to see if he was pursued—a mistake. When its bridle twisted to one side, his horse faltered. The pirate saw a brown horse and a raging armored female fighter almost upon him. He tried to dive free of the saddle, but Micka's sword neatly cleft his spine. Dying, the pirate sailed from the saddle, crashed into a tree trunk, and lay still.

Doris, Miko, and Micka glanced around to make sure their foes were unmoving, then retrieved their lances, trotted to bracket Greensleeves again, faces flushed, puffing, but happy. Kuni gestured in the direction they'd been going. "Milady?"

Numbly, Greensleeves nodded toward the distant Green Lancers. She hadn't had time to cast a spell. Or even think of one.

She hoped to be as quick as the bodyguards when she was *really* needed.

In a small clearing was a hastily constructed two-sided barricade made of four trees which had been toppled and hacked, their broken branches thrown back to form a roof of sorts. Added to the barricade were Gull's Green Lancers, a shoulder-to-shoulder circle of outthrust steel. That they faced all directions confirmed what Greensleeves had already seen: this was a running battle scattered throughout the forest. But there weren't thirty lancers anymore, only twenty, who were mostly blood-spattered and bandaged, gashed and bruised. Ten Black Dogs had been drafted into the ranks to achieve their full numbers again.

As the mounted party trotted closer, Greensleeves saw bodies lying amidst the trees everywhere. Green Lancers and Black Dogs with wounds, pirates and blue barbarians riven by spears and pierced with black arrows, and some pale-skinned folk dressed in skins. Some enemy corpses had been hurled up onto the barricade, or had died trying to cross it.

In the summer heat, Gull had shucked his shirt to stand bare-armed in his deer-hide jerkin, his massive double-headed axe dragging his belt down on one side. He was smeared with blood, both his own and others', but never paused in his work. He barked at messengers, sending them running to the different centuries and his wife, the quartermaster. He questioned dun-clad scouts. He ordered soldiers too badly wounded to fall to the rear. He even swung his great axe to lop off branches that got in his way. Greensleeves felt a flush of pride for her big brother, who'd only wanted to be a woodcutter and live in White Ridge forever, yet was thrust by fate into battles and generalship, the most reluctant of warriors doing a fine job of running a war.

All the while, Black Dogs came stumbling to the barricade from the woods, winded and wounded. Gull gave them little rest, ordered their sergeants to form them up. Greensleeves couldn't help but be alarmed at their condition and reduced numbers. There were fewer than sixty Black Dogs left of the original hundred, less than eighty cavalry, a score of D'Avenant archers, twenty Green Lancers, and a handful of scouts. The fighting had been fiercest over here, she guessed.

Gull saw his lines begin to assemble, then turned to his sister, who had stayed on her mount. "Greenie! It's a hell of a mess! They've hit us in waves and picked at us while we fell back! Twice! We've got Dacian out there and Dwen, that ocean wizard. And Towser, that infernal son of the devil, must be here somewhere, for we've his blue barbarians to kill. And war mammoths with little houses atop, with archers in them. I've sent for Stiggur's clockwork beast and Liko. How goes it elsewhere?" He glanced at the four blood-smeared bodyguards, guessed the fate of the others, but said nothing. He'd seen too many die this morning—but he worried about his "little sister's" safety.

His sister told him, quickly, of the battle in the east, the rout in the south, and of the other wizards. "It's like the end of the world, Gull! Every wizard we ever fought is here today."

Gull shook his head. "But it makes no sense. They've attacked us on three fronts, but the attacks are so piddling! Not that my soldiers aren't fighting and dying like heroes, but I think we're just being softened up. There must be more lurking out there. A trap waiting to snap shut."

Greensleeves nodded. Her brother's worry echoed her own. "I agree. Our victories have been too easy. It's as if these are the first spatters of rain, and there's a hurricane brewing."

"Aye." Preoccupied, Gull unconsciously dug in a pouch, pulled out a whetstone to hone his axe, as if this were just another break in woodcutting long ago. "And *why*? What's their goal, other than to thump us? *Why* call all this magic just to chase us through the woods? And how the *hell* did all these wizards get together? Dacian and Dwen are from two separate realms! How did—"

"That's my fault," Greensleeves interrupted.

"*Yours?*"

"I enslaved them with the stone helmet!" In her agitation, Greensleeves flapped her hands as she had when a simpleton. Goldenrod shied, and Gull grabbed the mare's bridle. "The only thing they have in common is me! Somehow, I don't know how, they've become linked to one another. Perhaps it's some function of the helmet the Artificers intended to use in order to track their thralls. We still don't know how the cursed thing works!"

"Magic," spat Gull. "The old bugaboo. You can't trust it. Never could."

Greensleeves didn't rise to the bait: she'd heard the argument too many times. Gull hated magic because it had destroyed his homeland, and that was that. To him it would always be a force for evil and little good.

As if to emphasize Gull's pronouncement, the earth sent a thrill through their feet. At the same time, a pelting and whapping sounded all around them. "Earthquake!" shouted a woman. "Stone rain! Cover your heads!" shouted a man.

All Gull said was, "Again?"

Greensleeves was whisked from the saddle so quickly she bleated in surprise. Doris had grabbed her. Kuni yelled. In seconds, Greensleeves was pinned under four bodyguards holding overlapping shields overhead.

The pace of falling rocks picked up, thudding and bouncing all around them like deadly hail. The noise of stones—sea stones, Greensleeves noted, polished round—clattering on the wood and iron was deafening. Pounding, plinking, ringing, the stones piled up around them. A screaming horse crumpled as its skull was smashed. Another broke its reins from a tree and ran blindly. Someone yelled as a stone banged through their defense. Now Greensleeves knew why the lancers had bruised faces. She tried to think of a defense, drew a blank. Poor Goldenrod . . .

Pressed to the earth, Greensleeves felt it tremble underfoot. But this wasn't an earthquake, she realized, rather tunnels being bored under their position. Dimly, for she'd been an idiot back then, she recalled how Dacian had undershot the village of White Ridge with tunnels that spouted Uthden trolls, tiny scavengers after coins and metal. But why tunnel now? To get behind Gull's army? Why bother, when the army was scattered hither and yon?

Gull was shouting to his troops above the pounding and plinking. "They did this before to cover an attack! As soon as it lets up, be ready to fight!"

More fighting, Greensleeves thought, maybe the worst yet. More people would die, their faithful followers. Like Bly and Alina and poor lost Petalia. So much death, all for their crusade to force wizards not to force others. Was it worth it? Hadn't they saved countless villages, even a whole city from rape and plunder? Yet why couldn't they find a better way than fighting?

With a rap, clink, the odd ping, the stone rain let up.

Instantly, Gull sprang to his feet. "Let's go! Up, everyone! They'll be coming! Man the barricades!"

Greensleeves's bodyguards unfolded. The first thing she saw was her gentle yellow mare, Goldenrod, dead on her side, half-covered with stones.

A forward scout roared, "It's the big attack!"

Gull braced his hands on two Greens' shoulders, hoisted himself up to see over the barricade, and landed in a clatter of rocks. "Lord of the Pit! We're in for it now! *Sound the trumpets!*"

The raiders came at a run.

War mammoths, skin-clad drivers behind their heads, trotted stiff-legged betwixt the giant tree boles toward Gull's thin line. The great shaggy beasts were so tall Greensleeves's brother could barely have reached their bellies by raising a hand. Their pounding feet shook the forest floor. Strapped around and over their rust-brown shaggy fur, swaying precariously, were war platforms lined with kneeling archers. Like the drivers, the archers were men and women as pale as vampires, with shaggy blond hair, clad in reindeer skins or furs of arctic fox and timber wolf. Their bows were almost flat, barely curved, drawn to shoot stone-tipped arrows. Beside the mammoths ran more bandy-legged cave people, waving clubs and short stabbing spears. With them came the blue-dyed tusked barbarians, howling just as wildly. Mixed among them were more pirates just as battle-mad.

And leading them . . .

Gull's soldiers lined the barricade and spilled beyond it, spears up, arrows nocked, swords and axes at hand, shields in place. Gull had placed himself at the center, and his lancers clustered around him. The general spit on his hands and took a hefty swing with his axe. "The big bastard's mine!"

Greensleeves felt a catch in her throat at the boast. For leading the charge was the biggest man she'd ever seen.

He was huge, this one, and frightening.

Layered in muscle, he was taller than Gull and probably twice his weight. He wore a red kilt and leather harness and a ghastly ruby-eyed fang-mouthed iron helm. In his hands he swung a massive two-handed sword, and he bore no shield. No foe, it was clear, would live long enough to return a blow from him.

The warlord howled loudest of all, his voice a gravel roar like rock splitting. "Gull! I come for you! I'll kill you!"

"Not without a fight!" the woodcutter roared back. Shouts on both sides were louder than thunder. "Stand fast, soldiers! Cavalry, go!"

With a scream, cavalry and centaurs tore away from both sides of the barricade, swung wide of the oncoming horde, and charged heedless of danger straight for the six oncoming mammoths. The archers atop the war platforms on the beasts' backs hollered their own challenge. Bows snapped and arrows rained among the Gold Cavalry.

Huddled behind the lines and barricade, surrounded by her four bodyguards, Greensleeves despaired. Some four or five hundred madmen charged them, a half-dozen war mammoths, and the monstrously large warlord, a mammoth among humans. Gull's force was less than half theirs. And her brother was in the lead.

The warlord halted in his tracks fifty feet from the

line. He waved the cave folk on around him, howling, "Fight! Fight! Fight!"

The first wave hit the barricade.

Blue and white skin met green-ribboned lances and hard-swung black-hilted swords. Greensleeves had to peer over the shoulders of her bodyguards, but she saw the chaos as the two lines smashed like a tidal wave on a granite shore. She was close enough to smell blood, hear the scrape of steel on bones, the clash of weapons. Cave folk, women and men, howled like wolves as they dashed at Gull's line. They hurled themselves onto the long line of leveled spears. A cavewoman died, blood spurting, as a lance ripped open her throat. A brute ducked past a lance only to run his guts onto another. A woman leaped with both feet onto the dying bodies and swung overhand, flailed with her obsidian-studded club, then died. Cave folk died up and down the line on cold steel. Yet even as the Black Dogs stabbed and clubbed with spearpoint and butt, they were forced back a hair by the sheer weight of numbers, buried under an avalanche of flesh.

At the forefront of the battle, yet hampered by protective bodyguards, Gull knocked down any cave folk that came near, all while hollering at his forces to stand fast, keep shoulder-to-shoulder, watch their backs.

Careless of lives, the warlord had only one command. "Fight!"

Dazed by the ferocity before her, Greensleeves joined the fray. Despite the suicidal charges of the cavalry and centaurs, who stabbed and slashed and fought to turn the beasts, the mammoths were pounding toward the line, so close the skin-clad archers on their backs let fly arrows into Blacks and Greens around Gull. No one could stop the behemoths—except a magic user.

Touching her cloak where an embroidered orange

figure flitted above a campfire, Greensleeves wiggled her fingers as if shooing flies.

Instantly, around the faces of the six mammoths, there winked into being tiny flaming creatures: fire sprites no bigger than hummingbirds. And like all sprites, these creatures had a mischievous streak. Such big targets they couldn't resist.

Flickering, trailing black smoke as they singed the air, the fire sprites whisked into the fur under the mammoths' eyes. Dry, greasy, shaggy, it instantly caught fire, crisping and curling, filling the animals' eyes with smoke.

The giant elephants went berserk.

One stabbed down its four feet so hard and fast the cinch holding the platform on its back snapped. Archers were pitched bodily from twenty feet up in the air. Another mammoth, its hair ignited on one side, turned violently, trampled pirates, and banged its neighbor, jolting both to a stop, flinging archers like fleas. A third mammoth closed its eyes and slammed headlong into a giant red oak, braining itself and half-uprooting the tree.

The last beast plunged straight ahead. Greensleeves shrilled as cave folk, blue barbarians, Greens, and Blacks were crushed like eggs under the massive pounding feet. The barricade was smashed wide open. Gull shouted to his Blacks to fill the gap with spears.

The warlord took advantage of the chaos. He waved on the second line, the blue barbarians. "Fight! Fight!"

More canny, trained in war, the barbarians roared and raged and stamped their feet and spat in their anger, but they kept their heads. Working in teams, they smashed lances aside with their curved bronze swords or long lead-filled clubs and rawhide shields. Yet they were battle-mad, too. Climbing the bodies of dead cave folk, the barbarians swung right and left and forced a gap between the lances. Crowding close, swinging savagely, even as D'Avenant arrows slammed into them, they forced the Black Dogs and Green Lancers to adopt their secondary defense: swords. Quickly, stubbornly, Gull's line fractured in a dozen spots. And still hundreds of barbarians and surviving cave folk pressed the line, battered at its edges, shrieked and howled and died.

Within seconds, it seemed, Gull's line was brushed aside, torn open like an ant's nest by a bear.

Before Greensleeves could conjure anything, the forest was a swirling melee of swinging, slashing grapplers. Her bodyguards pushed her backward and stabbed at foes who had spotted Greensleeves. But Greensleeves was too absorbed in her brother's plight.

Having caused scores of deaths, the warlord had finally entered the battle. Swinging his huge two-handed sword, he carved through allies and enemies alike.

Straight for her brother.

Incredibly, Gull was hampered by his own Green Lancers, for his dedicated bodyguards pressed to keep between him and the warlord, as with any threat. While a hundred smaller battles raged around them, Greens scrambled, some forward, some trying to get around Gull to stab with lance and sword. Gull tried to order them back, only to see them hewn down like wheat by that massive two-handed sword. Their blood splashed both men.

Finally Gull himself knocked Greens aside in order to meet his foe: a single duel on a field of honor.

The warlord roared, "Die today, Gull the Coward!" He slung his sword behind him, slashed waist-high to cut Gull in half, killing more Greens. Roaring, Gull leaped over their bodies, fighting mad himself.

The brawny woodcutter swung his great eight-pound axe. "Take *this*"—with a hideous skull-piercing *clang*, he deflected the awful blade—"*bastard!*"

Yet the force of the warlord's blow spun him half around. He barely got his feet under him as the massive sword swung over his head. A Green Lancer reached over Gull to stab at the enemy from underneath and was kicked aside. Muscles bulged in the warlord's arms, and he slashed straight down.

Gull was too winded to shout more threats. He sidestepped the blow, saw it chop into a tree trunk at his side. In that second, Gull hopped in close and swung the haft of his axe at the warlord's throat—a killing blow, if he could land it.

But the warlord had anticipated him.

The warlord shrugged, dropped his shoulder, and the hickory haft bounced off his iron-hard muscle.

Striving to pull back his axe, Gull realized he was too close. Green Lancers, who had leapt forward, had to check their thrusts.

A brawny arm drove an elbow like an anvil down onto Gull's shoulder, smashing his collarbone.

Hissing with pain, Gull ducked to the left to get out from under. But the warlord swung his other hand, which clutched the sword, fast and hard.

Gull had his head belted around, almost snapping his neck. The warlord smashed him in the breast and throat, savage blows that would have felled a tree, and kicked hard enough to shatter Gull's kneecap. The woodcutter was knocked back into his clustered lancers, pitifully few of them now standing.

"Like you pain, Gull?" the warlord sneered, panting. He slashed with his sword to drive lancers away from the supine Gull. "I've plenty more to deal out!" He kicked, cracking ribs, rolling Gull half over. Muley, captain of the Greens, already streaming red from a head wound, leapt forward to protect Gull, but the warlord flicked her away with his bloody sword.

Greensleeves bleated aloud. The warlord was playing with Gull, *enjoying* the punishment, making him suffer before killing him.

"Why?" she asked the air. "Why hate my brother so? They've never even *met* before!"

Dazed to his core, Gull crawled to his knees, tried to gain his feet, yet he was too weak and confused even to lift his axe. Another lancer died trying to grab his wrists.

Rearing back, howling with glee, the warlord smashed the pommel of his awful sword on Gull's head.

The woodcutter slammed facedown, out cold or dead.

Yet even now the warlord didn't finish him. Protecting his prize, prolonging the victory, the fiend kicked Gull to rouse him. "You're mine now, Gull! Mine to slice the flesh from your bones! Mine to carve out your heart and eat it! Mine to make a drinking cup of your skull, to quaff deep and slake my thirst for vengeance!"

Why? rang Greensleeves's mind. Why such hatred from a stranger? What vengeance?

By now, even the Green Lancers, reduced to a handful, held back, for they believed their beloved leader dead. And they were mostly alone. As the duel had raged, Gull's army had fragmented. Clusters of Black Dogs, desperate to stay alive, had unwillingly retreated in the face of superior numbers, pushed back by a blue-and-white tidal wave.

Now the first clutch broke and backed, deflecting blows, but retreating nonetheless. More soldiers fled even as the cavalry disengaged. Men and women moaned and cried, a collective grief mourning their loss and the death of their leader. There were scarcely a hundred of Gull's followers still standing or mounted. All delayed, though, reluctant to flee, hoping their leader might still be alive.

Greensleeves was moved bodily, chivvied backward by her bodyguards. She was stunned by the ferocity of the battle, the horror visited on her brother. She cursed herself, for she hadn't conjured a single spell to protect him. The savage attack had come too fast.

And now it was too late, for the warlord kicked Gull once more and got no response. He could play cat-and-mouse no longer, so raised his sword with two hands, pointed straight down, ready to plunge it through Gull's chest.

"Milady, please!" begged Kuni. They all but picked Greensleeves up by the elbows to move her. Kuni flashed her sword in great sweeping arcs to keep back blue barbarians, who were eager for more killing. A handful of Blacks and the Greens, cursing through their tears, clattered in Greensleeves's direction, eager to protect the other leader of the army, for their general was surely dead. Kuni barked, *"Milady, you must—"*

"No!" yelled the druid. She shot her arms out and shoved people aside, unconsciously loosing a shield spell around herself. *"Not without my brother!"*

CHAPTER
10

THE WARLORD'S SWORD STABBED DOWN
at Gull.

Greensleeves slapped a hand to her cloak, where two embroidered foxes studied a golden field. Her other hand crossed two fingers and pointed at the warlord.

The great sword stabbed—dirt.

Where the warlord had loomed over Gull stood two confused barbarians.

Thirty feet away, the warlord cast about for his prey.

Greensleeves had switched the warlord in space, juxtaposed him with two barbarians, for it took two normal folk to equal his massive weight.

Surviving Black Dogs and Green Lancers bulled the barbarians aside and stooped over their fallen leader.

But the warlord howled, "Fight! There!" and every soldier on his side raised weapons and screamed— battle-mad once more. Even the wounded and dying sought a weapon, or else crawled with bare bleeding hands to the attack. The warlord slung his sword over his shoulder and led them.

Greensleeves chivvied her bodyguards forward. A dozen feet from Gull, the druid shot back her sleeves, tossed long brown hair from her face, and touched a sun dog outlining a fat-cheeked sun embroidered on her shoulder. Her fingertips sparkled.

Soldiers on both sides howled.

Rippling before their eyes, blinding, was a many-colored wall of light. Lights flashed and popped in midair, hundreds of them, like giant flickering candle flames. For thirty feet in either direction, high as the trees, touching the ground, lights blazed and shimmered and winked and exploded. As the warlord's force staggered back, his half-naked body singed by the heat, blue barbarians and cave folk just stared in awe at the display.

Every inch of the wall was achingly beautiful, impossible not to watch, yet the light seared the eyes and made folk blink and shield their vision. A giant red light pulsed as rapidly as a beating heart at head height. Alongside it, as sinuous as a snake, a twisting chain of green lights rippled in rhythm. A blue light winked into being, grew to the size of a cartwheel in seconds, and exploded in a shower of sparks. Up and down, back and forth, winked and pulsed and throbbed the lights, until almost everyone in both armies stopped to stare at it.

Then the spell disappeared, leaving only blue spots in the eyes of the beholders.

Greensleeves hollered to the bedazzled Blacks and Greens, "Fetch my brother!"

After a stunned moment, they obeyed, hurtling forward to where Gull lay prone. Doris and Micka and Kuni and Miko yelled as the druid then rushed up, too, holding the fluttering edges of her cloak.

But the warlord acted faster. The giant man howled, "Think not! Charge!" His soldiers squinted for the enemy and rushed to attack. They were half-blind, but hundreds of them opposed some fifty of Greensleeves's, who clustered around Gull or else straggled through the woods.

She needed something else.

Threading among bodies and weapons, Greens and Blacks latched onto Gull's arms. His right, wrenched out of its socket, tilted sickeningly, yet Gull never stirred, and for a moment Greensleeves feared he was dead. But a worm of red blood crept from under his hairline, and she knew dead men don't bleed.

Now that she'd rescued Gull . . .

Touching an embroidered mountainside with a vast crack in its face, Greensleeves squatted and laid her palms on the damp churned dirt. This spell would be quick because she knew the land under the Whispering Woods. She had only to send an impulse down, down to bedrock, find a channel for the energy, drive in a wedge.

The earth jumped.

People tumbled off their feet, flipped into the air like dry peas in a jar. Weapons spilled from hands, men and women stumbled and sprawled, leaves tumbled from overhead, dirt spurted from cracks and fell like brown rain. Only Greensleeves kept her place, hands on the earth. Doris reared back and tumbled over her with a clatter of armor. Even the Keldon warlord slipped and fell heavily, leaving an imprint in the soil a handspan deep.

Then, as people struggled to roll over, grab their weapons and helmets and rise, came an aftershock. The trembling, jiggling, shuddering force rattled teeth, wobbled eyeballs, churned fluid in ears, and made folks nauseated. Most fell to their knees again, or stayed as flat as turtles and clutched the quivering earth.

Greensleeves yelled once more, and stumbling soldiers grabbed Gull again and dragged him onto the shoulders of two brawny lancers. Pushing, as clumsy as children, the soldiers clambered to their feet with Gull hoisted high. Shakily they jogged toward Greensleeves and her sphere of protection.

Not twenty feet off, the fallen warlord was the first to shake off leaves and dirt, as a dog shakes off water, and rise. Light glistened on his sweaty bronzed skin despite the detritus clinging to him. The muscles in his upper arms were as thick as Greensleeves's waist. She could hear him breathe like a bellows, sucking wind to power the massive body. How could anyone be so large? she wondered. He must be enchanted, charged with mana, both to give him total control over his thralls and to make him so big and strong.

Oddly, for a brief moment, she wondered who he was, and why he'd surrendered himself to the magicmakers who'd perverted him so. But she knew the answer. He'd lusted for power and gotten it, for a price.

Magic always demanded a price.

The bodyguards toting Gull passed her party, and Kuni snorted, for they were now the only thing opposing the warlord. As the warlord swayed on his feet and leveled his huge broadsword, Greensleeves found herself staring, fascinated. Even the man's cheeks were layered with muscle. He had good white teeth behind the iron fangs and a reddish stubble along his elongated jaw. In the sudden quiet, he steamed like a blacksmith's forge, radiating energy. Raising his sword, he began a battle cry—

—and was replaced by a birch tree.

Using the juxtapose spell again, Greensleeves replaced him with an equal weight of wood. The warlord was a hundred fifty feet away now, standing in a hole where the birch had stood, surrounded by upright trunks like white prison bars. With a frustrated roar, he shoved two trees aside, snapping them off like twigs.

"Call the rest close!" Greensleeves ordered, and the stragglers in the forest came running into rough formation.

The barbarian army and pirates cast about, dazed and confused. Greensleeves could see fatigue in their eyes and knew the charm of battle madness was a two-edged sword: its victims would fight like furies for a while, but be wracked by exhaustion when the spell wore off. Like race horses run too hard, they slumped and wearily awaited orders. Blacks and Greens, tired but whole, carried Gull on their shoulders while reforming a ring of outthrust steel. Greensleeves's guards clustered around, so she had to peer past armored shoulders.

"Time to go!" she called. "Stand still!"

Raising a hand like a claw to the sky, she touched a cloud on her cloak and ripped downward as if tearing the air.

Rain smashed down.

Rain so hard, so thick, so intense, no one could see more than a foot. Water beat on everything and everyone, a blinding downpour loud as a waterfall. The world was a gray wall. The temperature plummeted and folks shivered. Soil underfoot turned instantly to mud, and people stumbled as feet stuck.

Return to the grove, she thought, three miles distant. Reform. Call in the White Bears. Surrender command to Varrius and let him lead the fight. Round up stragglers, reestablish communications. Prepare to flee if necessary. Greensleeves had power enough to move the army to another continent. Get solace for her brother. Get a chance to think. And see Kwam.

She could have done more here, she chided herself. Destroy the warlord's entire army somehow. Open a chasm in the earth to swallow them. Burn them with hellfire. Drop an ocean on their heads. Open the abyss. People had died out here, good friends, and she might have prevented those deaths with a wave of her hand.

Yet fighting went against all her teaching. As archdruid, she was charged with maintaining balances, weighing equal force against force, using as little mana and resources as possible. If she unleashed her power, lashed out blindly, wiped out lives and disrupted the balance, she'd be no better than the greedy grasping wizards they strove to stop. Yet looking at the dead around her, it was small comfort to know she'd upheld her principles.

As the deluge drummed on her bare head, streamed down her face and collar, Greensleeves was wracked by doubt. What would Chaney have done? she wondered. What would she do next time? What to do with all this power?

The captain and most sergeants of the Black Dogs were dead, and soldiers were confused as to who had command. Finally a wounded sergeant yelled over the pounding rain that everyone was accounted for.

Dully, waving a hand, Greensleeves summoned a ripple of brown at the ground, then green higher, then blue, and finally yellow.

Through a rain-shot yellow haze she saw the warlord's hideous iron mask bear down on her.

Then they were gone, back to the grove.

And smack into disaster.

Greensleeves's sacred grove had been overrun.

She'd dropped her reduced and ravaged force right into the midst of the enemy.

Enemies bright as birds and deadly as eagles. The men and women wore blue flowing trousers and rainbow-colored shirts. Their heads were wrapped with iridescent turbans studded with jewels, and gilt-edged cloaks fluttered around their shoulders. Curved scimitars winked and flashed. There were hundreds of these folk, desert warriors, Greensleeves knew, ranged in concentric circles all around the

grove, even along the edge of the babbling brook.
Arrayed in ranks in the lower grove were a hundred
more desert riders on glossy black horses.

Stunned, soaked, and half-drowned, Greensleeves
and her battered fellows cast about themselves. High
up, framed in the door of the magic hut, was Karli of
the Singing Moon, dark-skinned and white-haired, in
rich clothes and a jacket studded with buttons and
medallions, her grimoire, much the same as
Greensleeves's embroidered cloak. Beside her was
that young snot Gurias, who'd terrorized a village
with his petty lust. He, too, wore a nova pentacle
over his doublet, while Karli, having never been
enslaved by the stone helmet, had none.

Evidently the two wizards had looted the magic
hut, ransacking scrolls and artifacts. Fear fluttered in
Greensleeves's stomach. Where was Kwam? And the
others?

The pavilion was wrecked, pulled down and kicked
apart. The council table was flat, food and bottles
crushed underfoot. Many huts and lower treehouses
had been vandalized, their doors smashed in, fires
kindled inside. Rope bridges and nets had been
slashed to tatters. A handful of White Bears, sent by
Cerise as a rear guard and messengers, lay hacked to
pieces where they'd been surrounded.

Greensleeves had been foxed, tricked, gulled.

As her brother had feared, the piddling assaults on
three sides had been feints to splinter the army. Then
had come the main assault, from the west, led by the
warlord. But that attack, too, was to wear them
down, make them retreat.

Back here, to the sacred grove, the heart of the
army.

The tunnels, she recalled. During the warlord's
first wave, she'd felt tunnels ripple underfoot. Dacian
must have conjured them for these desert warriors to
pass through. At a glance, Greensleeves saw the tun-

nel mouths, like giant molehills, in the north. They'd toppled trees that lay with roots exposed.

The enemy had tunneled underneath because, if they'd shifted, Greensleeves would have sensed the disruption in the forest mana. She'd wondered about the tunnels at the time, then forgotten them in the heat of battle.

And now she'd pay the price. A fresh force waited in ambush here, outnumbering her pitiful wounded troop ten to one. Gull was unconscious, perhaps dying. And two or more wizards opposed her.

Greensleeves grasped all this in a flash. Around them rose a hum, a growl, an angry mutter, like war dogs eager to slip their leashes.

"Spirit of the Forest, lend me strength!"

From the balcony of the magic hut, Karli called down, *"Kill them! Destroy Greensleeves!"*

Gurias was first to act, as if he'd waited a long time for the chance to avenge his humiliation.

Banging his hands together, fingers pointed, he loosed a bolt of lightning that scorched the air and lashed down at the archdruid.

A mighty bolt, Greensleeves saw. He'd learned from the experienced wizards. Yet even as he began his spell, she hurled up a shield spell to deflect the lightning easily. The invisible wall wrapped around herself and the foremost soldiers and bodyguards. Perhaps she could even—

Unaware of her mistress's shield spell, Doris, her bright blond curls now wet and pressed flat, leapt into the path of the lightning bolt.

"No!" shouted the druid.

The green-clad Guardian raised her only weapons, sword and shield—the worst possible defense, for the sword was steel and the shield rimmed with iron.

The bolt struck both, flashed through Doris's body,

exploded her heart, boiled the blood in her veins, and cooked her in a second. A charred wreck flopped against Greensleeves's skirts.

"Oh, Doris! Oh, no!"

For a moment, time froze. Gurias was laughing above, cheering himself. Karli was shrieking orders. Desert warriors were closing on the battered party. Yet Greensleeves heard none of it.

Why? Another soul lost, another death by loyalty. *Why* did people keep dying to save *her*? And why couldn't she better protect them?

And *why* did these wizards keep attacking her?

Greensleeves's mind reeled with the day's events. She'd been hounded, chased, pursued from tree to tree, seen her brother struck down, her bodyguard friends killed and sucked into limbo, her soldiers intimidated and chivvied and wounded and wiped out at every hand, all for love and loyalty. The sorrow of it all, the waste, threatened to overwhelm the druid, to strangle and subdue her.

But it was these wizards' doing. . . .

Greensleeves was shocked as her sorrow was suddenly scoured away. Anger, cold and deadly, uncoiled like a snake in her belly.

She raised a hand to the sky as if to pull down a cloud and pointed the other like a long arrow at Gurias and Karli on the balcony. "I'll give you *lightning*!"

The clouded sky exploded as a bolt of lightning crashed down into the grove. The flash blinded everyone, the stink of burned air made them recoil, heat made them jump.

The sizzling bolt thrummed into the druid, all the energy of the heavens caught in Greensleeves's arm. Then she shouted an ancient and dangerous spell, and the energy gathered into a flaming ball at her fingertips.

Then leaped into the air and blazed toward the magic hut.

Karli barely had time to dive into the sky, catching a breeze with her pink flying slippers with the turned-up toes.

The young arrogant Gurias had no chance at all.

The lightning struck the young wizard and blew him apart in a cloud of red steam. Clothing, jewelry, hair, shoes, the nova pentacle, all were reduced to flinders in an eyeblink. Only his skull stayed intact, and it pinwheeled across the sky to thump on churned moss.

The bolt traveled on and struck the giant red oak.

Incalculable energy bored deep into the tree, scorching the bark, driving through heartwood, boiling sap to steam in a second. Hissing steam, trapped beneath the bark, blew the tree to smithereens with an earsplitting bang.

Splinters, branches, leaves, slabs of wood and bark as big as coffins spun through the air. A contingent of desert warriors at the base of the tree were smashed into red jelly by hurtling fragments. Other scimitar-wielders were hurled back by the exploding fragments, knocked sprawling, some with bruises, other with huge splinters driven into their bodies. A branch as big as a dragon, shot as if from a ballista, spun amidst the cavalry in the lower grove and killed riders and horses by the dozen. One stretch of tree, dozens of feet tall and weighing tons, toppled on a score of infantry. Roots exploding from the ground filled the air with dirt and rocks as big as skulls, raining in the faces and eyes of more desert warriors. Fragments of leaves, blown into wet scraps like oatmeal, buried half the foe.

Greensleeves stood erect, having sketched a shield spell over her threescore followers and wounded brother. Shouting over the noise and screams and ringing in their ears, the sergeant of the Black Dogs, the only surviving field officer, ordered weapons raised and pointed outward, for he knew an attack

would follow once the enemy pulled themselves
together.

But Greensleeves combed wet hair from her face
and hollered. "No! I'll handle them! *All* of them!"

Farthest away from the destruction, the riders on
black horses in the lower grove were first to recover,
and they thirsted for revenge for their comrades'
deaths. With yips like desert jackals, they put spurs to
their glossy mounts and bore down on Greensleeves
and the ring of steel around her.

They didn't get far.

Clapping her hands, the druid conjured a pack of
Durkwood boars, huge shaggy animals, gray-black
with silver fringes, and tusks so long and curled they
spiraled out from flaring snouts. The boars, dropped
into confusion, scrabbled, then charged the biggest
moving things around.

Black horses veered and slammed one another,
spilling riders. They reared and toppled back,
crushed humans in the saddle. Many riders, used to
hunting wild pigs, swooped and sliced at the animals
with their long scimitars, or spitted them with lances.
But their attack split down the middle, buying precious seconds for Greensleeves's troops.

The druid struck again. Touching a coiled green
shape at her hem, she called an ancient name almost
impossible to pronounce.

A long, long shape rippled around the boles of the
giant red oaks, rippled green and brown, retaining
those colors. Like some animated hedge, the shape
coalesced and gave a tremendous hiss like the sough
of a blast furnace. Not a dragon, but a craw wurm, a
legless lizard scores of feet long. A great maw, sharp-
edged as broken glass, gaped big enough to swallow
a horse. Greensleeves had tracked this great beast in
the far western forests, where it fed on deer and
goats, and had risked her life to get close enough to
tag it. That risk paid off now.

Any horses still under control panicked. Screams of terrified mounts ripped the air. The wurm's long alien undulating shape slithered into the open, the musty-dry snake smell of it setting the horses' nostrils flaring. So fast did horses twist and bolt they trampled a dozen soldiers under their iron hooves, for the soldiers, too, fled every which way from the skulking wurm. Even Greensleeves's own troops crept wide, bumping one another, but the druid told them to stay put, as the wurm would not attack them but veer around.

Her Greens and Blacks weren't convinced, but stood fast on quivering legs. They watched in horror as a horse, its leg dropped in a hole and broken, was bitten in half by powerful green-whiskered jaws. The rider had scrambled from the saddle, but the monstrous bloody snout mashed her against the horse's mangled carcass, and she was snuffed out like a candle.

A Black Dog shouted as a sudden light flared overhead. Karli of the Singing Moon, forgotten in the treetops with her flying boots, had conjured an efreet, a demon of the southern desert.

The being burned so bright the soldiers shielded their eyes. The efreet had the shape of a long-faced woman, naked and white-skinned as if dead, with flames at her hands and feet and head, twelve or fifteen feet tall. She swirled once in a circle of fire, then dove like a phoenix at Greensleeves's embattled troops. They smelled alien perfume, felt her heat on their upturned cheeks as the efreet rushed within a lance length.

Greensleeves didn't even pause. Sweeping one arm up, she magically lifted the babbling brook from its bed. Water and foam and fish and frogs arced through the sky like a blue rainbow and splashed the efreet. Her fire extinguished with a shriek; the demon spun three times and slammed into a tree trunk.

Greensleeves and others, already drenched, shook more water from their faces.

Greensleeves looked about. The efreet slumped limp and unconscious amidst tree roots. The craw wurm gobbled and scattered horses to the south. The shorn tree trunk smoldered. Fish flapped in pools at their feet.

Someone shouted. From behind charged a company of desert warriors with raised scimitars. From the left charged five fat tusked ogresses in garish parodies of dancing girl outfits, each with a long wavy-bladed knife.

Greensleeves stood her ground and raised both arms.

Instantly, the water from the brook that soaked the soil came to life. It rose like an ocean wave, studded with rocks and dirt and grass and leaves and twigs, then froze solid, a wall of ice, a dirty barricade ten feet high. Dumbfounded, the desert folk slid to a halt, while the ogresses stabbed the dirt and ice wall with their knives in frustrated rage.

Greensleeves looked for Karli and saw her flitting west, out of the grove. Fleeing.

And as she disappeared over the treetops, so too did her conjured minions. Desert warriors, riders, horses, ogresses—all vanished. With a flare, the fire efreet lifted from the branches like a smoke cloud and shot jets of flame that ignited treetops, setting leaves and branches crackling. Then she soared after her mistress.

Hands and eyes smoking, Greensleeves searched for more enemies to punish.

There were none to be seen.

The woods burned in spots, for it had been a dry summer, but Greensleeves snapped her fingers and summoned a downpour that doused the fires in minutes. She and her followers couldn't get any wetter. She snapped her fingers and the downpour quit. Gray clouds roiled overhead, their balance upset.

The craw wurm circled, missing the vanished horses; Greensleeves banished it with another touch to her cloak. The wall of ice she melted, turning the ground to mud. The air was thick with smog from doused fires and icy fog.

In the quiet that followed, the babble of the brook refilling its bed and the drip of water from trees was loud. People spoke in whispers. A shout sounded in the south as White reinforcements and camp followers and healers arrived. They paused at the scene of destruction and mayhem, but swiftly took charge of Gull and the other wounded. Despite the hustle and bustle, the heavy air seemed to muffle all noise.

Greensleeves looked at her grove. Most of the huts were ruined, smashed, vandalized, and burnt. The brook was soiled and muddy, flowers and grasses and mosses had been trampled underfoot, treetops were scorched and ugly, bark and broken wood lay everywhere. One giant oak was a splintered stump, a ghost of itself.

She rubbed her tired face with a dirty hand, then opened her eyes to find Kwam and the magic students standing before her. Other camp followers crept from the trees to join the reinforcements.

"At the first sign of magic, we grabbed everyone and hied for the woods," Kwam told her simply. "We had no way to fight these fiends."

Wearily, Greensleeves took his lean hand. "That was wise. I'm glad you're all safe."

Tybalt swung his head in a circle. He picked up the skull of Gurias, tossing it from hand to hand in his excitement. "My, Greensleeves! What a triumph! Something to inspire a dozen songs! You've bested—

how many?—six or seven powerful wizards all by
yourself!"

The druid nodded. "I did, yes."

Then, to everyone's horror, she began to cry.

CHAPTER
11

GREENSLEEVES SAT BY HER BROTHER'S SIDE and wanted to cry again.

Gull lay in a tent erected in what remained of Greensleeves's Grove. A steady rain fell, drumming on the tent canvas. Lily sat at her husband's side holding a squirming daughter. Yet Lily was reluctant to let her child stray, as if monsters and killers still lurked in their once-friendly woods. A healer named Prane had left to give the family privacy, but no one spoke much. Greensleeves looked out the tent flaps at the gray day, puffed a mosquito away from her face.

Gull could speak, just barely. He was still a wreck days after the battle with the warlord. For a time, concussed by the sword pommel, they'd feared he'd never wake again. Yet he had, to suffer pain from a smashed collarbone, dislocated shoulder, sprained neck, bruises to his breast and throat, a smashed kneecap, and other scrapes and bruises. Greensleeves and Amma, the chief healer, had regenerated the broken bones, though they ached as they knit. Yet Gull was almost as strong as the oaks he'd once felled, and a few more days of rest would see him walking again.

The forest recovered as slowly. Scouts had scoured the woods, reported all traces of wizards gone, vanished. Even Immugio, snared and staked, had escaped. They'd left behind only their destruction and dead.

"The thing I don't understand," Gull whispered through a bruised throat, "is why the warlord *hated* me so. He wasn't just doing his duty, he lusted to kill *me* personally."

Greensleeves nodded wearily. "Yes. He toyed with you, battered you for sheer joy. That's why you're so torn up, not just spitted and dead. He was so savage, so—"

"Eh?" Gull craned his head to peek at her through puffy eyelids, winced, then stayed still. "So—what?"

The druid shook her head. "So—familiar? I got close enough to hear his voice. It reminded me of someone, but not someone I know, if that makes sense."

"It doesn't," croaked her brother.

"No, I'm afraid not. Still, he had good teeth and red hair. I saw the stubble on his jaw. I wondered why a man, or woman, I suppose, would surrender their lives to become such a—beast."

"Power," said Gull. "As with wizards."

"Yes." They knew little of the Keldon warlords. The Kelds, it was said, were a warlike tribe from a hard land in the far north. They chose children of theirs and neighboring tribes to be made warlords through a secret ceremony where they swore total obedience for total power. Then they roamed south as mercenary captains and freebooters and pirates, and returned their fortunes home. "We have so many enemies now, it shouldn't surprise us if some seem familiar. We've probably accumulated more foes than friends."

"No," said Lily. "That's not true. We've many fine people here in camp, and thousands of others who praise your names daily in villages and cities and farms we've liberated from wizards' thralldom." She gave a start as her baby kicked inside and patted her belly. "Don't ever forget that. It's for those folks, and the souls of your dead family, that you fight this good fight."

"And cause our friends to die," replied the druid. "How many did we lose? How many more will breathe their last from infection in the next days? And how many more *want* to die? When Kuni asked for new Guardians, sixty-three women volunteered! *Sixty-three!* Yet every one knows she might be killed, *will* probably be killed! Horribly! Or worse, lost in the depths of hell like poor Petalia—"

"They love you, is all," said Lily. Hyacinth wriggled from her mother's arms and scampered out the door, heedless of the rain. Lily sighed. As quartermaster of the army, she knew the numbers too well. Over ninety had been killed or gravely wounded, mostly Black Dogs. The survivors had vowed to recruit and reform, but for now were dispersed to other centuries, so the proud Dogs existed only in memory. They'd lost almost twenty cavalry, a tenth of their number. And some campfollowers and healers had been killed in dustups. How many would survive amputations and sepsis remained to be seen. But Lily demurred, "Our losses are unimportant. What matters is we survived and can fight again, right now if we had to."

Greensleeves shook her head. She rose to stand by the tent flaps, staring out into the rain. Some folks scurrying by, cloaks over their heads, wondered why she let it rain: druids could control the weather, couldn't they? Why not make it rain at night?

But Greensleeves would let nature take its own course for a while. No more altering the groves or trees or herds for her, not even for healing nature's scars. She'd done too much damage to the forest and might only make it worse.

She said, "I don't know how to make this up. It was my fault the wizards slipped their leash. Had I conjured them more often, probed them for lies, I might—"

"Hush up, Greenie," scratched Gull. "You didn't let them loose. They used magic to wriggle free. Probably Towser's doing: he's the sneaking, back-stabbing kind. We never did enslave him, so he's been free to stir up other wizards against us."

Greensleeves turned. "But if I had—"

"Hush, sister," said Lily. "You're blaming yourself for naught. We agreed, long ago, that having you parole the wizards was an imperfect solution and we'd need to drum up something else. But we neglected to help you. It was too much for one person to manage, even one with powers such as yours."

The druid nodded, too weary to argue. She slumped on her stool and hitched one of Gull's bandages higher. "Perhaps. Their conspiracy was well planned. Someone stole into the magic hut and filched my nova pentacle and made copies to prevent me from conjuring them and prevent my shifting where they are. I tried and failed."

"I'm glad—" Gull hacked. The women looked curious. "Glad Towser didn't die in that tidal wave. I want to strangle him slowly with my—bare hands. For Father, and Mother, and Rainfall and Angelwing and Poppyseed and Lion and Cub and poor lost Sparrow Hawk. I want him to know who's killing him, so he can savor it as much as I—" His throat betrayed him, and he coughed so much he jerked half-upright, straining his wounds, leaking fresh blood. Lily used both hands to shove him onto the camp bed and pulled the blanket close when he began to shiver.

Prane came in with a warmed potion. It took all three to prop Gull so he could drink it. Soon he dozed. Greensleeves bent and kissed his purple-green forehead.

Sitting back, she told the quartermaster, "We shan't argue anymore, for it gets us nowhere. But we must face facts. The forest is hurting from our presence and no longer a safe haven. And camping here was only a temporary solution, anyway, for in between our campaigns. We must move on."

"Where?" Lily frowned, dark brows slanting. "We've argued about where to go at every officer's meeting forever, it seems. Do you have some destination in mind?"

"No. No." Greensleeves stood up, feeling old and worn out. "But I think I know where to find the answer."

Tybalt and Kwam had relocated to a smaller tree hut, farther removed from the center of the grove, formerly used as a guard post. The place was even smaller than the original magic hut, with huge branches bracketing the room on two sides and oddly shaped planks fit in between. But the students' faces were long as Greensleeves topped the ladder, bodyguards climbing behind.

"There's not much left to study. . . . " Tybalt pulled on his long nose and sadly held up a mechanical claw. "All that's left of that flying horseshoe crab. Too bad. I was close to figuring out what it did. . . . "

Despite the gloom, Kwam snorted quietly. Tybalt was always on the verge of discovering the meaning behind something.

Tybalt held up a parchment scrap that portrayed an angry crowd hanging a dog over a fire. "This one, I figured, was an animal control spell. But half-burned like this . . . "

Greensleeves shrugged rain off her cloak and tsked. The hut was so small her bodyguards stayed on the ladder. "Better we don't fathom that spell. Where's the helmet, please?"

Kwam moved a heap of charred remnants, opened a carved cedarwood box, and took out a greenish stone helmet. Its surface was crinkled, carved to resemble a human brain. "We found this buried in leaves below the balcony. I reckon Karli tried to snatch it again, and again it protected itself by slipping through her fingers. It just doesn't want to go with her."

Kwam held the stone helmet reverently. Plain it might be, but that only proved appearances were deceptive, Greensleeves thought. As with Kwam. "Still waters run deep," her mother Bittersweet had said, and it was certainly the case with her lover.

Gently, Greensleeves took the helm and contemplated it. "This helm . . . we might not know much, but one thing is clear. The only thing those dastardly wizards have in common is me and this helmet. I don't see how it's me, so it must be this thing."

Kwam blinked. Tybalt pulled on his nose. The hut swayed with the tree in a rain-borne breeze. Greensleeves realized that, since they offered no argument, they must have reached the same conclusion earlier. Was she the only dense one?

Tybalt offered, "We know a little. The Sages of Lat-Nam fashioned it, probably to stop the Brothers, Urza and Mishra, from conquering the Domains, or just each other. The legends tell how entire realms were stripped bare and processed into war materiél. Whole continents were blasted flat in battles that raged from horizon to horizon."

"But the Sages were wiped out, we think, and the Brothers triumphant," Kwam supplied. "Yet the helmet *does* work, because it enthralls anyone we fit it to."

Greensleeves nodded absently. "Yes, because in a way, the great wizards are still inside it. They pooled their minds to impress the commands into the helmet. But there has to be more—"

"*Ah!*" Everyone started as Tybalt shouted. He grabbed his purple hat as he hopped in place like a child. "That's it! The sages *connected* their minds to form the commands! So when *we* put the helmet on new wizards—nowaday wizards—*we* connected them with each other! Oh! What arrogant *fools* we've been not to see that!"

"S'true. It must be." Kwam wiped his forehead. "We've been digging our own graves for three years."

Greensleeves added, "My father, Cinnamon Bear, used to say 'Friends come and go, but enemies accumulate.' Yes, we've hauled wizards in like fish, tamed them, and let them go. But we left the lines in their mouths, and now they're all tangled in collusion against us."

The helmet felt heavy in her hands, or perhaps she was tired, so she sat on a stump. "We used the helmet to get ourselves into trouble, perhaps we can use it to bail ourselves out." To their puzzled stares, she added, "When I donned the helm, just that once, I found I could hear, or feel, or *see* into the minds of those ancient sages even while they screamed at you. All sorts of secrets lurk there: stories, songs, spells."

The two magic students were quiet. They knew well what the helmet could do. A non-wizard, Tybalt, had donned it first, experimenting, and almost lost his mind. Any wizards they put it on suffered, ranting, until they submitted. Only Greensleeves had ever resisted its demands and retained her sanity, and that only because she'd once been a simpleton and understood madness.

Now the druid talked as if alone. "But there's some secret I've missed. In here." She tapped the green dome with a small callused finger.

"How can we help?" asked Kwam, and Greensleeves turned a smile on him. This was why she loved him: he

let her be herself, helped when asked, respected her
judgment.

"Just watch me, please. If I seem to—suffer . . ."

She couldn't finish. For a long time after coming
into her mind and wizardry, Greensleeves had been
haunted by the fear of insanity, of her mind reverting
to a jumbled wilderness. Even now, sometimes, odd
thoughts gibbered at her from the dark, and she had
to work to banish them. But no one knew that, not
even her lover.

Then, before she could fret any longer, she pulled
the helmet on her head.

Voices like hammers in her skull. Howling like a
windstorm at sea. Blinding lights that silhouetted
creaking angular figures. Wizards arguing, arguing,
arguing.

Greensleeves fought to hang onto her mind. Her
thoughts were slapped and pushed and shoved aside.
A hundred wizards shouted at her, all at once, a
cacophony, yet each voice as clear as a church bell. A
soft voice like a butterfly's insisting she help, not hin-
der. A growling like rocks being chewed; an ogre
threatening to rip her brain from her skull and eat it
if she didn't submit. A young voice conniving,
promising, wheedling. An ancient voice droning
about the balance. A dry voice like a cold drill. And
more, and more.

And as they harangued the druid, the depths of
their minds lay revealed to Greensleeves, everything
every one had ever known.

Scraps of spells hurtled past like leaves in a hurricane. Snatches of songs cooed in the wind. Images
and beings she couldn't even comprehend spun
around her. A ghostly figure with a huge head like a
child's. Exploding mountains dotted with eyes. Fish
made of mana swimming in an ethereal sea. Faceless
skeletons building cromlechs dripping with honey. A
white jester dancing with a blind coyote. A riven

brain pouring forth light. Images that made her laugh, and cry, want to sing, or hide whimpering.

Peering into the minds of these great wizards, Greensleeves caught glimpses of gods at work, and she felt as tiny and insignificant as an ant. Yet she saw the people in them, too, and where they came from: mystic heights and lost valleys and shining waterfalls and haunted castles and windswept deserts. And homes like anyone else's, where mothers crocheted by the fire and children played pickup sticks.

And, too, she saw how these wizards were linked by the magic and this helmet, and so could talk through their minds, as Greensleeves's enemies could now contact one another. Mutually tagged, thrust into the same hunter's bag like wounded quail.

An oversight on her part, she knew. A fatal mistake to miss the connection.

But she had to see more.

Fighting, pushing, Greensleeves shoved the howlers aside, as if barging through a belligerent crowd. Because beyond, behind them, she sensed the cause of their fear, the reason they ordered submission.

Three years ago, she couldn't have shunted them aside, wouldn't have known how. Back then, it had taken all her strength to maintain her sanity under the mental assault. Now she bulled past these wizards like lambs in a pasture, for she was equal to even the greatest of them.

And she saw why they argued and worried.

Their world was besieged by war.

A clanking and thumping shook the earth. Outside, through stone-lined windows, she saw war machines filling the crumbled horizon, from the mountains to the stumps of a forest to a blighted seashore. Clockwork beasts by the hundreds, in all shapes and sizes, advanced across a ravaged plain. A bitter wind brought the sulfur stink of burning rock oil. Fire fell from the sky, and an acid rain seared flesh to the bone. Soldiers, not human, but giant mutants of animals and demons walking upright, screamed and snorted as they died attacking the battlements. An iron tower with eyes and three arms crushed catapults and siege towers and scurrying soldiers. Metal skeletons wielding swords were slagged by white-hot fireballs. Mechanical birds as big as sailing ships dropped eggs that exploded in black gouts and red smoke. Men and women with wings and swords died attacking the pilots. A tower made of ivory cracked and burned, the dusty stink making camels and elephants squeal. And all the time, a clock ticked on a shelf, counting down to doom.

Arguments flew within the college like stones outside. The plan would work. It wouldn't. It must or they would all die. They'd all die anyway. The helmet can control the Brothers. Not unless someone dons it, and who'll risk that? But the rest of the plan has a chance. Not just controlling wizards, but stopping them entirely. Who would submit to testing? No one, and now it was too late. Not if we hide the plan, bury it deep. But there was no time. The walls flamed inside and out. Blood bubbled and turned black as it ran out arrow slits.

It was too late, and here came the fireballs—

Greensleeves screamed and dove from the stump, covered her eyes and ears, begged for mercy.

Then the vision stopped, and the silence was deafening.

Her sweating brow was suddenly cool.

Kwam stood over her, the stone helmet in his hands. He'd plucked it off her head. He set it aside, took her shoulders gently, and stared at her with deep brown anxious eyes. "Are you all right?"

"Yes, yes," Greensleeves panted. She was wet from head to toe, her hands shook, her heart pounded as if she'd run ten miles. The rainy breeze through the hut door chilled her, and she shivered. She caught Kwam's hand for comfort. "Yes, yes. I think I know—the secret."

"What secret?" blurted Tybalt.

"Not the secret," Greensleeves corrected. She laid her head on Kwam's breast, drawing strength from him. "But where the secret might be. If only we can find it."

"As near as I can tell"—Greensleeves sat on the floor, hugging her knees, Kwam hugging her—"the Sages did create the helmet to stop the Brothers, Urza and Mishra. It would need a hundred wizards to conquer them, if it were even possible. They completed the first part, impressing commands to submit into the helmet—except they may not have perfected it, for I'm sure they didn't intend the recalcitrant wizards to be linked. But they never got to finish the second part, whatever it was. The Brothers got wind of the plan and attacked the college with armies and war machines. I sensed clockwork beasts by the hundreds, like Stiggur's construct. That's how old it is, I guess. . . ."

She took a deep breath. "But they said it. *Not just controlling wizards, but stopping them entirely.* And *hide the plan, bury it deep.*"

Tybalt paced the small stretch of plank floor. "So the secret is still there, buried under the college!" His eyes shone at the prospect of so much magic.

"If it exists," cautioned Greensleeves. "They had little time to work. None, at the end, I suspect."

Kwam murmured. "But . . . the site of the College of Sages, in Lat-Nam—no one knows where it is. Wizards have hunted for it for centuries."

Greensleeves nodded wearily and stared out the small doorway of the hut at the cool green whispering leaves of great red oaks, all misted with summer rain. "Then it's time someone found it."

That night, despite her exhaustion, Greensleeves could not sleep.

She'd finally figured out one thing. Chaney's shade did not join her the nights Greensleeves couldn't sleep. The shade woke her deliberately. Strange she hadn't realized it before. But why should the dead remember fatigue and the healing balm of sleep?

And so, if she lay awake, Chaney must be out there, waiting.

Sky-clad as usual, Greensleeves left the tiny hut, not her real home, for that had been ransacked, but one hastily rebuilt. She brushed past her bodyguard, another woman drawn from the White Bears. For a moment, Greensleeves was ashamed because she'd forgotten the guard's name.

A young pale shape perched in the branches of an oak, shimmering slightly in some unfelt wind. Greensleeves leaned on the railing and hailed her.

"I've news for you, child," said the dead druid.

"You're leaving," Greensleeves told her.

"Yes." The shade turned her head, moved her lips, speaking to someone else, perhaps asking them to wait. To her former student she said, "It's time. The woods need time to heal, more than any druid can aid, or druid's shade. And you are bound far away, so little keeps me. The arms of Gaea's Liege are wide, but were I to miss them, I'd be here forever. A long time."

Greensleeves only nodded. To wander the Whispering Woods forever seemed a kind enough fate. Yet the woods did need to heal, for their ancient whispering was almost stilled.

"I leave you these words," said the shade. She leaned forward but did not fall from the branch, only hovered in the air. "We can accomplish nothing important unless we give our all: every fiber, ever nerve, every drop of blood and sweat. Our souls, even. For what you hope to accomplish, be prepared to make the final sacrifice. Always, without holding back. Lack of heart will make you fail."

Again, Greensleeves nodded. She'd heard it before; the meaning was never clear, but questions were pointless. The shade was only partly thinking of her. When Chaney's body had departed this sphere, so had most of her thoughts.

The shade stood up and wafted backward, as it to fade into the tree like a dryad. "I'm off, child. Remember I love you, and watch you always. Good luck. And may the Spirit of the Forest breathe through you."

Then she was gone.

It was some moments before Greensleeves realized this time was for good. Chaney would not return. She felt a catch in her throat, a pang in her heart, but that was all. Chaney had died long ago, and Greensleeves had mourned her then. This shade was just the echo of her voice, if she were even real, and not a figment of Greensleeves's mind.

There was many things in her mind she knew nothing about. But perhaps everyone had that problem.

Wearily, she turned back to bed. As she passed the guard, who bid her goodnight, she asked, "I'm sorry, I've forgotten your name."

"Wichasta, milady." She was slim, tall, dark, straight-backed. "From Captain Dionne's White Bear Century."

Strange, thought Greensleeves, that I, a small nude druid, am deferred to by a husky bodyguard in white armor and steel weapons. "Yes, thank you, Wichasta. I appreciate your help, and won't forget again."

"It's nothing. Goodnight, milady."

Kwam was awake, having lit a candle. Propped up on one elbow, with the candlelight flickering across his brown skin and silky chest hair, Greensleeves marveled that he looked warm and sexy and loving and kind all at once.

She plunked down on their rope bed and combed her hair with her fingers for something to do.

"She's gone, isn't she?" Kwam asked quietly.

The druid nodded. "How did you know?"

"I saw it in your face."

Greensleeves lay back in the bed, scratched her stomach idly. "She talked again of making the 'final sacrifice.' What can it be? If it's my life, I'd willingly give it to stop all the fighting. I *hate* it so! Yet more and more folks are killed and the forest ravaged! I exploded that poor deluded boy Gurias, just an arrogant puppy, with lightning and blew up a tree besides. Where's the good in that? I'd give anything to stop all this fighting!"

"I believe you." Kwam kissed the side of her neck. "It's not in your nature to fight, any more than it is a willow tree's. You were meant to nurture life, both of people and the land, not foster death. And for that I love you. So please don't change. I love you just as you are."

But Greensleeves sighed. "I'd readily give my life to save others: I'm no more important that anyone else. But it's all as murky as a disturbed pond. What's my fate that Chaney can read in the future? What other sacrifices can I make, when I have no time for myself or you or the forest or even helping folk?"

Kwam brushed hair from her forehead. "Whatever your fate, we'll face it together. Be certain of that."

She smiled and caressed his brown cheek. "My sweet, gentle Kwam. You'd accept me as I am, quirks and foibles and insecurities and all?"

For an answer, he kissed her, and she kissed back.

CHAPTER
12

"I THOUGHT—CATTLE PREFERRED—LOW-lands," Gull puffed.

Greensleeves waved a hand, winded. "They're—*not*—cattle! Watch—what you say! Wait—let's rest."

The party slumped onto rocks along the worn and narrow path that wound up the mountain. Even Helki leaned against a rock wall and held her heaving chest. No one looked up to see how much farther they had to go, for the towering heights were lost in the clouds.

"Tell me again—" Gull panted "—why you can't just—shift us—up there."

"Because we'd be—killed instantly. Or so—they told me." Greensleeves unslung a wool-wrapped water bottle and took a sip, then passed it around.

Straggling along the trail were some thirty people. This small party had left the main army far to the west of the Whispering Woods, across the Ice Rime Hills, near a large seaport called Oyster Bay. There, under the command of Varrius and Quartermaster Lily, the army was to revictual, repair, reform, and

recruit. In the meantime, Gull and Greensleeves had
departed with this contingent, shifted to the land at
the base of these mountains, talked to the locals, and
begun their trek.

Wrapped in winter clothes to fight the keen, rar-
efied air, the party had wended through hills and up
the mountain for six days, trudging, sometimes
crawling hand over hand. The party contained
Greensleeves, with four bodyguards led by Kuni, and
Gull, also with four led by "Muley" Muliya, the bodyguards having refused to let their leaders go alone.
Holleb and Helki were in attendance, fitted with
cleated horseshoes, regretting they'd worn full armor
and tackle. Five of Hermine's D'Avenant archers had
proved handy: three times now, they'd shot goatlike
chamois from the uppermost crags to augment the
iron rations. Also along were Kamee and two librarians and one cartographer, laden with pack baskets
stuffed with parchments, books, and incomplete
maps. A healer, Prane, had come in case anyone
broke a leg or sustained a fall, but so far they'd been
lucky. Kwam was along to represent the magic students, or so people allowed. Also following was the
southern dwarf, Uxmal, and a companion Quexotl,
because they'd requested to see the mountains, which
reminded them of home. Somewhere up ahead was
"Jingling" Jayne and a trio of her drab-colored scouts.
And huddling near Gull was a lump like a diseased
raccoon: Egg Sucker bundled in ratty hides. Gull had
insisted he come because, without the general's protection, someone in camp would surely kill him.

"Perhaps it's a test," Greensleeves said once again.
"You'd have to be determined to come this far to get
a single question answered."

"It's a bloody test, all right," Gull puffed. Not only
was the mountain as steep as a staircase for miles, but
the higher they plodded the thinner the air grew. And
he was still stiff from his battle with the warlord. "A

test of how smart you are. If you climb this far, it says something."

His sister frowned. "That you're smart enough to scale this mountain unaided?"

"No," Gull groused, "that you're too addle-pated to stay on the flatlands—oh!"

He flinched as a scout appeared without a sound. Jingling Jayne's newest recruits were as quiet as ghosts and deadly as rattlesnakes, and Gull couldn't stand their sneaking to his side unseen. He swore they used magic, but Jayne denied it. But then, commanding these folk, she'd become quiet and deceptive herself.

This was a burly man with a blond beard and twin braids that bounced on his furred chest. His name was Percival. Rumors said he'd once killed three sailors who'd called him "Percy." "We've found their cave entrance."

Gull stared back into the man's ice-blue eyes, blinked first. "Do they know we're here?"

The man snorted. "No."

Gull struggled to his feet, levering himself up with his axe handle. "Perhaps we ought to make some noise to announce ourselves—"

But Percival was gone.

Jingling Jayne met them farther up, pointed out their destination. Even higher, cut into a sheer face of the mountain, was a long horizontal slit. Along the lip walked a guard with a huge war axe over one shoulder.

Not a human.

Jayne nodded obliquely. "This path leads to a flat stretch where that guard can study us. Then it enters a chimney with cut steps. There is no other way into their stronghold, not without ropes and hammers and pitons."

"This will do. We've nothing to hide. And if there's a flat stretch up there, I'll squat and kiss it." Gull

called back, "Soon there! Let's hope they've a hot
spring to soak our aching legs!"

Grunting, the party clambered up the chimney,
numb feet slipping on the chiseled steps. Gull had to
bend almost double. The only ones not entering were
the scouts, haunting the windswept crags to watch
the back trail, and Helki and Holleb, who would not
enter such a tight space.

Gull climbed first, axe clumsily held in one hand.
He doubted they would be repelled; if the Hurlooners
wished to kill them, they could have done it a dozen
times already. Yet it was a relief to finally stumble
into a stone chamber that rang with their footsteps.

And meet their first minotaurs.

The minotaurs of the Hurloon Mountains were
huge, monstrous, topping Gull by two feet or more.
They breathed heavily, their breath steaming in the
air, sweet as fresh grass. They had short muzzles and
horns capped with gold. All bore tattoos in squares
and whorls that infiltrated their shaggy, curly white
hair and even scrolled onto their horns. Their arms
had only four fat black-tipped fingers and no thumbs.
Their legs, thick and shaggy-stockinged, had the
backward crook of animal legs and polished black
hooves the size of steel helmets. All wore the same
garb, a red wool skirt or kilt, so it was impossible to
tell anyone's sex.

There were three minotaurs, all with gleaming war
axes as big as snow shovels.

More people clumped up the stairs, paused at the
top at sight of the strange beings, and were pushed
from below. Flanked by bodyguards, Greensleeves
moved in front of her brother.

The lead minotaur asked the traditional question,
"Why have you come?" in a gurgling timbre that
made their breastbones rattle.

Greensleeves gave the traditional answer. "To ask
a question."

The minotaur nodded. "Then receive an answer."

The weary travelers were shown to a large common room—originally herd creatures, the minotaurs didn't value privacy—where they could strip off their boots, soak their feet, and wash off sweat. But the chamber was cold—they were all cold—and there were no signs of fires. The only light came from two windows cut in a stone wall, and that light was gray and gloomy. They were served platters of food, mostly various mushrooms, and water so cold it made their teeth ache.

The party of humans, dwarves, and a lone goblin sat on skins on the floor. Gradually, as the cold penetrated, they edged together until they were one furry steaming lump.

"I hope we get your answer before we die of chills." Gull had to look around the cloud of his breath to see his sister.

His sister ate mushrooms without qualms, for she'd lived on them when a simpleton. "Don't complain. This will be a high mark in your life. The Hurloon minotaurs are known throughout the Domains as master storytellers. Their origins go back so far, folk claim they were the first race made by the gods, and real cattle were modeled after them. They know all the histories of all the speaking races."

Gull shook his head. "Then why don't these stupid cows know how to rub two sticks together?"

"Even I can do that!" piped a goblin voice from a heap of tattered furs. "Start a fire, roast a nice fat hen, or a juicy lizard—"

"Belt up, Egg. I suppose there's nothing to burn up here, and it's too far from the valleys to haul coal or wood, but Balls of Boris, it's cold! And we've no guarantee they'll tell us a thing!"

"Have faith, brother," said the druid. "And it's not that cold in here. Bracing air sharpens the brain."

But she pulled the blankets tighter around her and hunkered between Kwam and her Guardians.

After a cold night huddled in the stone room, Greensleeves was summoned to the council chamber.

This room had nothing in it but minotaurs. Cut ages ago from naked rock, open windows overlooked range after range of frosty mountain peaks. The minotaurs squatted on crooked legs, kilts brushing the floor, in a circle with nothing at the center. Her two bodyguards were told to remain at the door, while Greensleeves was invited to join the circle. At first she was puzzled by the lack of furniture and decoration, until she realized the storytellers lived mostly in their own imaginations. They lived for ceremony and song, too, and long introductions. It took hours for each member of the council to be presented, because each gave a brief story of his or her life and accomplishments. They had names such as Skywatcher, Thundersong, Snowbeast, and Moonbeam, yet they also called one another pet or joke names such as Little Flower Eater, Bean Nudger, Sleeps By Day, and Dropped Six Sticks. Once Greensleeves learned their names, she lost her grip on them. Much of her had gone numb, for the mountain winds whipped through this chamber with nothing to slow them.

Finally, the council got around to Greensleeves. A minotaur with a long chin beard, Thundersong, asked, "Pray, tell us of yourself."

The druid had thought a long time about what to say. She wished to make a favorable impression, not waste their time, but not appear brusque. Yet her father had always said, "Never mind the pickles and cheese—tell me what happened." So she plunged in.

"Well, Your Graces, we found among our possessions a stone helmet that is very old—"

Twenty pairs of dark brown eyes closed, so she stopped. Thundersong said, "So sorry if we confuse you, but we ask the background to your story, and yourself. Please, could you tell us of your parents?"

"Oh." Greensleeves blushed. She'd rushed in too fast, perhaps offended them by seeming greedy for information. Taking a deep—shuddering—breath, she began, "My father's name was Cinnamon Bear, my mother's Bittersweet. I had many brothers and sisters. . . . "

The minotaurs closed their eyes again. Greensleeves balked. Thundersong, infinitely patient, asked, "Please, we need the greater picture to grasp your account. Start with your father, if you will. What were his parents' names, and their parents, and their parents? Take your time. We have plenty."

Greensleeves's mind rang like a bell. *Uh, oh. . . .*

Hours later, the druid and bodyguards hobbled back to the common room.

Since it was dark outside anyway, the party had moved to a room without windows. In pitch blackness, everyone huddled under blankets like a nest of squirrels, but they jumped up, bumping one another, when Greensleeves returned.

"Finally!" Gull panted. "Finally you're back! We've been waiting hours with nothing to do but hear our teeth chatter! Did you get the answer? Did they tell where—"

Greensleeves couldn't speak. She shivered uncontrollably from sitting in the chill wind and talking the day long. Fumbling in the dark, Kwam wrapped her in his blanket, pulled her to his chest, gasped at how cold she was. "N-n-no. I d-didn't f-find out y-yet. They a-asked a few qu-questions f-first."

"Asked *you* questions?" yelped Gull. Other people groaned. "I thought *they* had all the answers!"

"Th-they m-might, b-but it will b-be a while b-before we know. I'm only up to t-telling about y-you."

"Me? *What?*" His voice was loud and brittle in the frosty room.

They had to feed her mushrooms and rub her shoulders and hands to get her warmed enough to talk. The minotaurs, it seemed, could never have too much information. So they asked about Greensleeves's parentage, and her home, her village of White Ridge. When she had explained, clumsily, that she didn't know much of her parents, for she'd been a simpleton when younger, they'd found that fascinating. So she'd talked about her life in the forest, among her animal friends, telling their names, and habits, and ways of living.

Gull exploded, "You talked for *nine hours* about badgers and rabbits? You never even told them about the battle of White Ridge, how it was destroyed?"

"W-we didn't get th-that f-far. I hope to in-introduce it in a c-couple of d-days."

"*Days?*" hissed through clenched teeth. Gull was stunned. "It'll be *months* before you can ask about the college!"

"N-no, it w-won't." Greensleeves huddled against Kwam's chest, trembling so hard she made him shiver. "I-I'll be d-dead from ch-ch-chills l-long before th-then . . ."

It was, in fact, only seven days before Greensleeves finished her story.

The minotaurs had been attentive all along, staring with big brown eyes, hanging on every word. But they'd asked questions—hundreds of them. Often the minotaurs would discuss Greensleeves's reply, each adding something, an old and similar event, a parable that illustrated a point, the whole group occasionally singing for the sheer joy of it. Greensleeves found it fascinating, for all she was freezing. She'd wished magic were allowed, for she could have conjured wood or coal or even fireballs or sprites. But they warned her against "finger sparkling" and she obeyed.

But finally the minotaurs had asked enough questions and fell quiet.

Nodding around to the rest, Thundersong asked, "And what is your question?"

Greensleeves jerked awake. The cold made her sleepy—she'd heard freezing to death was like nodding off. For a tick, she just stared stupidly, then realized the moment had come. She had to phrase it carefully, for legend said the minotaurs of the Hurloon Mountains, who knew everything, allowed only a single question.

Whether they would answer was not known.

She croaked, her throat raspy from days of nonstop talking. "Please, good lords, where lie the ruins of the ancient College of the Sages of Lat-Nam?"

A murmur circled the room. "A good question," mumbled one minotaur. But they gave no indication if they knew.

Thundersong asked, "Will you be so kind as to excuse us? We needs deliberate."

Deliberate what? she asked herself. But the archdruid nodded graciously, thanked them all for listening, and left the room.

Shuffling through the frigid halls, Greensleeves was hailed by a minotaur, a young one, to judge by the short chin beard. It carried a bundle of furs that kicked and gibbered. "Milady, perhaps you've lost something." It held the bundle by a skinny gray-green leg.

Greensleeves heard, "Leggo! I didn't take nothin'! It was rats I was after! They was eating the mushrooms, not me! And they was stale anyway! Leggo me leg!"

The minotaur asked, "Will you take responsibility for this, please?"

"That's asking a b-bit m-much," stammered the druid. "B-but yes. Micka, if you w-will?"

The burly bodyguard caught the bony leg, thumped

the bundled goblin on the stone floor to silence it. "P-permission to ch-chuck it out the w-window, m-milady?"

Greensleeves hobbled on, shivering. "N-no, b-better he s-suffers with the r-rest of us."

Egg Sucker's protests bounced off the icy walls. "Hey, leggo me leg! I didn't take nothing—much! Hey . . . !"

It took them a while to locate Gull and Kwam and the rest.

Since the second day, the party of twenty-plus had wandered the caves that riddled the heights and bellies of these mountains. Rather than sit in the darkness, or freezing in the light, they'd simply tramped—everywhere. Up and down staircases, along icy ridges, in and out of stone-framed doors, across peaks, down to black caves where they stumbled and cursed. Wrapped in every blanket and cloak they possessed, they tripped down the chimney twice a day to visit the centaurs and scouts, and fetch them water and mushrooms. Fueled by mushrooms, Gull and company walked till their legs ached. But they were warm, and slept well in the night-dark cubby.

The only ones happy were Kamee and her scholars. They had hoped the minotaurs had a library to visit, but found not a scrap of paper in all these lonesome caves. The library lived in the great craggy skulls of the beast-folk. So each scholar chose a minotaur to follow and pester with questions. They learned a lot, but had to stop scribbling often and suck on their frozen quills, despite having tucked the inkpots in their bosoms.

Greensleeves finally found the party in a gallery that split a spine of the mountain, with ragged windows on both sides. They gave a stunning view of clouds and mountaintops, until one's eyeballs glazed with ice.

Gull almost went berserk at this further delay.

"*What* in the name of Axelrod Gunnarson is there to *deliberate* on? These stupid cows"—he added more choice names—"either know where the (muleskinner's curses) ruins are or they *don't*! Why must we freeze off our balls and arses *waiting* to see whether—"

Huddled against Kwam's chest, Greensleeves let her brother wind down. At least his cursing warmed the air. With frayed patience, she told him, "It's not the *site* they deliberate, but *us*! They won't tell us where the site is if we're not worthy to know it. Don't forget that wizards have searched for the ruins for centuries. No doubt *hundreds* have come here asking the same question. And they've never told *anyone*!"

"How do we know that?" Gull had let his beard grow to keep warm, and he was scruffy and hollow-eyed and blue-lipped. "They might have spilled the secret to the last five wizards! Your ancient ruins might be a holiday resort, for all we know!"

Greensleeves only clung to Kwam and shivered.

"Roast oxen!" Gull muttered. "I'm going to have a *cord* of firewood hauled up this mountain, and I'm going to *butcher* some *steers*, and I'm going to eat hot dripping fatty charred-on-the-outside oozing-juice-on-the-inside roast oxen until I *puke*!"

Uxmal and Muley groaned at the idea of hot food, but most just shivered and suffered as the mountain winds sliced through the gallery and their clothes.

Gull wasn't finished. "We've got to get the answer and get off this damned mountaintop! I might be a father again by now! With a new son, or another daughter!"

"Daughter," blurted Greensleeves, then covered her mouth.

Gull jerked, leaned close to his little sister, and glared with red eyes at hers peeking above Kwam's blanket. "*What* did you say?"

"Nothing?"

"You did so!" He leaned closer. His breath stank: no one could wash here. "You said I'd have a daughter!"

Eventually Greensleeves tugged the blanket down to reveal a red dripping nose. "D-druids are in tune with their surroundings, remember? One day Lily was wondering what to name the baby, and I happened to sense that—it's a girl. A big one."

"Thank you," Gull growled, his voice icier than the walls. "Perhaps I'll name her Blabbermouth after her aunt!"

He wrapped his blanket tight. "Let's walk!"

But Micka first handed him Egg Sucker's scrawny leg. Flipping the squawking goblin over his shoulder like a dead chicken, the woodcutter stomped off.

The answer came quickly, in minotaur terms. After only five days of deliberation, Skywatcher found them on the lip of the great slash in the mountainside.

"We have news. The council has decided. Since your crusade seeks to mete out justice and advance knowledge, to construct rather than destroy, and improve rather than level . . . " She declaimed for some time as the humans waited, frozen breath bated. Finally she finished, "We will help you learn the site of the college. Have you the stone helmet?"

"*Help* us . . . ?" Greensleeves began. But with fumbling hands, Kwam dug the boxed artifact from a pack. The minotaur held the chilly helmet lightly in her great four-fingered hands, then pushed back Greensleeves's hood and set it gently on her greasy hair. The druid stiffened at the sudden onslaught of voices like a tornado in her skull. But the tattooed minotaur touched the helm and the voices quieted.

And over the background hum, like a hive of bees on late summer, Greensleeves saw where the college lay, as easily as if staring out a window. "Oh! *There!*"

As the druid doffed the helm, Skywatcher said, "Had you worn the helmet long enough, you would have seen the site. Everything leaves a trail as it moves through time and space, as the white-headed eagle leaves a trail in the sky. You should have recalled that."

"Oh, yes, of course. . . . " Greensleeves was careful not to look at her brother, but she felt his glare burning like a fire arrow.

Gull hissed under his breath, *"You could have figured it out all along?"*

Skywatcher watched both of them, nodding. Smiling? The humans couldn't tell. "So you may go. Thank you, and all your company, for coming. We enjoyed the tales of your exploits and hope to hear many more. And Sir Gull, I hope you find your feast of 'roast oxen' once you've left this vale of 'stupid cows.'"

Gull's brushy mouth fell open. "You can . . . read minds?"

The half-smile creased the cow muzzle. "How think you we collect so many stories? Now run along. Gather your retainers from here and the slopes below, and Lady Greensleeves can whisk you all away to your distant army."

Now Greensleeves gaped. "I thought magic was disallowed—" But the minotaur only waved a stumpy hand. Gull wrapped both hands around his axe handle and flexed it rather than scream.

The humans and dwarves wasted no more time. Within half an hour, they cowered on a whistling slope with the centaurs and scouts.

Greensleeves beamed despite her chapped cheeks and lips. "We're off for Lat-Nam and the College of the Sages! Think of what we'll find!"

"Food!" piped a bundle by Gull's leg.

"And warm feet!" growled the woodcutter. "Wave your hands, will you?"

Making sure she had everyone, Greensleeves swirled a circle with her hands and brought bright earth colors to the wind-scoured ledge.

Then they were gone.

CHAPTER
13

"THERE'S NOTHING HERE!" GULL BARKED.
"Ouch! Damn it!"

"More like, there's too much here!" Greensleeves shoved back branches and bracken at either side, only to be stung by brambles and nettles.

The advance party was mostly the same individuals who had suffered in the mountains of Hurloon: Gull and Greensleeves with their four bodyguards, Jingling Jayne and her broody scouts, the centaur lancers, five D'Avenant archers, Kamee and some cartographers, the healer, and the two dwarves. They'd returned briefly to the main army to revictual and refit. Recruiting was going well, Varrius reported, with more volunteers than they could use, so the army was almost up to snuff and training hard.

Lily, Gull discovered, had given him another daughter, a small red nubbin so fussy and squally they'd named her Bittersweet for now, partly in tribute to Gull's mother. Lily was fine but exhausted by the screaming, demanding child, glad to see her husband, sad to see him leave so soon. Most of the army was reluctant to see them go, but Greensleeves promised to shift in the main army once they'd reconnoitered the landscape of the fabled college.

So here they were, knee-deep in vicious tangled vines. The growth was all around, hardly a forest, for the biggest trees were no more than thirty feet high, brittle and pulpy. Tea trees, someone called them, salted with bushy hawthorn trees with finger-long needles. All the trees were choked with brambles, parasitic vines slowly killing the trees while climbing toward sunlight. Everything had thorns; even the crabgrass was smothered under dead spiked leaves. And spiraling up from the vicious brush were insects drilling for blood. Within seconds, the party was swearing, slapping themselves right and left, and roasting, for it was hot and close in the brush, as well.

Jingling Jayne's scouts had already disappeared. Gull barked, "Find some way out of here! Fan out!"

Everyone in the party drew a sword or knife and hacked at the tangle. "This way!" shouted a scout they couldn't see. Gull barked, people plied swords, and they cut a channel through the stinging, insect-plagued mess.

Then they stopped, stunned.

Before them, the forest broke off to reveal an expanse of blue as bright as any sapphire. They sighed as a cool sea breeze wafted in their faces, blowing back the insects. People squinted in the bright light.

The water was achingly blue, as if it would dye one's hand to touch it. A rocky bay with many fingers and peninsulas formed a rough half-circle. Off in the distance were islands, close enough to be seen as green and overgrown like this land. In the middle distance, black-and-white striped dolphins turned foaming somersaults. They stood on a cliff of white rock, a peninsula, some thirty feet above waves that churned and swirled on rocks.

"South," said Gull. "Far south, like where Morven

used to sail, though not as far south as that benighted tropical isle."

"This is what they call a scrub forest," said Kamee, the scholar. She scratched swollen insect bites on her lined face. "Just an overgrown scrublands, really. Trash trees and vines and buffalo grass, good for nothing."

"It's not the fault of the land," Greensleeves mused. She stooped, clawed some wiry grass aside, scooped a handful of soil, tasted it, spit it out. "The soil is sick. Poisoned."

"Poisoned?" asked her brother. "With what?"

"Everything." Greensleeves stirred the dusty soil with her finger. "Arsenic. Antimony. Quicksilver. We're in the right place, for there was powerful devastation here. Alchemy was visited on this land and blighted it."

Gull turned, looked at the scabby forest they'd hacked through and scowled. "But I don't see any ruins. It looks as if no one's ever set foot here."

Greensleeves said nothing, but beside her, Kwam pointed. "See there? Those rocks are square cut."

Greensleeves hung onto Kwam's sleeve and craned on tiptoes to see. It was true. A jumble of rocks at the bottom of the cliff, though cracked and chipped and covered with seaweed and driftwood, had clearly once been quarried and shaped by hammers and chisels. Kwam laid on his belly to peer over the broken cliff. "There's quarried stone under our feet, covered in dirt. It might be a road, or ramp to the sea."

"Look here," came the call of a scout. She'd chopped down some sea grapes that strangled a fig tree. Gull helped her rip them aside. Exposed was an old mossy wall, but the moss etched an ancient battle scene in three shades of green.

Greensleeves traced a design with her finger and looked at the choked forest, the irregular shore. "This is it, then. What's left of the college."

Percival, the hulking scout with blond pigtails, appeared like a shadow behind Jingling Jayne. "There's more. Come see."

Percival and Jayne slashed overhead and sideways to hack through clutching vines, thorny branches, and knee-high grass that cut at their clothes like a razor. The two centaurs, Helki and Holleb, suffered the worst, having more skin exposed along their long flanks. Everyone slapped and swore at midges and mosquitoes. Along the way, they had to circumvent many deadfalls where the pulpy trees had toppled in high winds, dragging the tangle with them, weaving it tighter. Occasionally they slopped through pools of fetid water from which arose more insects. They passed pillars of pitted rock snarled in vines, once columns to some building, and chopped along a double row of crumbling pillars. They knew it was some ancient hall, though there was no sign under the matted leaves and punky spiked plants of the original floor.

Once Holleb barked and pointed at the sky like a hunting dog. He half-reared, slicing a rotten seed pod out of his line of sight with his lance. He grunted, unsatisfied, to Helki.

"What is it?" asked Gull.

Holleb wouldn't answer, but his wife did. "Holleb thought he saw someone flying."

"Flying?" Gull spun at the word. "Like Towser? Is that bastard here?"

"No," grumbled Holleb. The centaur had the keenest eyesight in the entire army and was disgruntled by failing to see better. "No, was flying man. Woman, actually. With wings."

"Wings?" asked a dozen people.

"Folk with wings," Gull muttered. "There's a name for them, but I'll believe it when I see it."

Just behind him, Greensleeves was quiet, and he asked her why. Absentmindedly she reached out to touch a spiked century plant with fleshy leaves almost five feet long. "This forest grows twisted and unhealthy because of poisons in the soil. But there's more to it than that. There's something underneath us."

"I'll say," Gull groused. He batted a bloodsucking fly from his ear. "Even the dead leaves prick your hide."

"No," said his sister. She tugged her embroidered cloak free of some briars, tearing red and blue threads. "I mean, there's something *underneath*—"

"Look at that!" barked Kwam. And people fell silent.

A harsh winking light showed through the snarl, and when they broke free of the clutching forest, everyone stared.

The forest quit abruptly, ran out in little fingers of brush, dropped down a dusty slope, and struck a desert. A desert unlike any had ever seen before.

Surrounded by his four bodyguards, Gull pressed ahead when everyone else stopped. Scuffling in his heavy boots, he half-slid down the dusty slope to the desert floor. The ground under his feet crunched like broken glass. Wondering, he bent and picked up a fragment.

The chip was mostly black, with gray and yellow streaks, the size of Gull's palm. "It looks like obsidian, but it's not . . . "

"No," said his sister, who'd crunched out after him. "It *is* glass. Pure glass. Black glass."

Indeed, from the west where the desert met the forest, to the south and a scabby shoreline, extending east and north to a close horizon of gray hills, lay a desert of black glass chips. Here and there were spotted tufts of cactus or coarse yellow grass, the hardy plants having nudged the chips aside, but mostly there was only desolate hot glass. A scout had ventured deeper and gave a shout. Jingling Jayne came to

Gull to report a low wall of blue stone ran for a hundred feet, then petered out.

Gull turned the glass chip over and over his hand. He brushed his brow free of sweat, for the southern sun was hot reflecting from the bleak wastes. "I don't understand."

"You know how they make glass," his sister explained. "You've seen glass blowers making bottles in town. They heat sand and chemicals in a fire until it's molten, then blow through a tube to shape it."

Gull nodded absently. "Yes, but . . . those fires are *hot*. You need a blast furnace to melt sand to glass. . . ."

The druid only nodded. The party was quiet, for the ravaged wasteland was an eerie place that killed conversation.

The serious Kamee whispered, "So it is true. This land was blasted by fires hotter than Hell. The Brothers visited the land of the Sages and wiped them out of existence."

Gull tossed down the black chip, and it clattered on its neighbors. "There can't be much left. A column, a pillar or two, some square rocks—"

"And precious little magic." Greensleeves sighed. "The land's been stripped bare. My thumbs prick only a little. I'm afraid we'll get precious few answers to our questions—"

"Hola!" shouted Muley. She jumped in front of Gull and raised her long lance at a steep angle. "Back under the trees, milord! Quick!"

Everyone looked at the sky.

Flying at them were angels. With swords.

The angels sang as they soared into battle. Their song was wild and free, with a bone-rattling thrum, like the wind in the rigging of a ship being driven upon the rocks. The weird keen set the adventurers' hackles rising.

The angels carried bright silver swords and shields of polished bronze that gleamed like miniature suns.

There were more than a hundred angels, filling the bright sky with white wings and a thunderous flapping. Male and female alike were garbed in sheer wraps knotted at one hip to double as scabbards for their swords. They were all blondes, with skin tanned dark by this southern sun. Their feet were bare, their arms and legs muscular, their chests deep and broad from powerful wings that stretched more than twenty feet across. The air throbbed as the winged horde blacked out the sun to dive against the intruders.

Their fierce beauty had frozen the adventurers in their places. Then someone shouted a warning, and the seasoned warriors ran for safety even while drawing swords and nocking arrows to bowstrings. Yet many a doughty fighter, survivor of a hundred skirmishes, groaned at the thought of actually striking one of these flying beauties.

Even upon reaching the forest's edge, Gull didn't have time to take a stand, for Muley backed squarely into him, shoving with her broad rump, forcing him backward with sheer weight. "Go, milord! Move to the forest! Quickly! We'll form a rear guard!" Even in such a tense moment, Gull noted she never used the word "retreat."

Gull ran, blessing the dead Chaney for regenerating his knee, so that where once he'd limped, now he sprinted like a spring colt. He dashed amidst the trees, breaking bracken with his head and arms, his bodyguards dogging his heels. Bursting through to the trail they'd hacked, he found Greensleeves almost hidden behind a screen of broad-shouldered bodyguards. The other fighters had turned to draw their bows or ready lances. Far back, Kamee shooed her scholars, including Kwam, to hunker down. They knew to stay out of the way during action.

Gull glanced upward, trying to guess how to direct an aerial battle for the first time in his life. The tea trees were thirty feet high and festooned with vines, but in many spots near the edge the bracken was only shoulder high—leaving heads exposed to angelic swords. He tried to calculate whether they could run to deeper cover before the angels dove upon them.

And while he was calculating an attack, his sister was pushing down the bows and arrows lifted by her Guardians of the Grove and shouting at the D'Avenant archers and scouts and even the two black-bearded dwarves with their crossbows. "Don't shoot! I forbid it! No one is to shoot them! We'll talk instead!"

"Stop it, Greenie!" shouted her brother from behind a tree. "Don't interfere! You'll get us hurt—"

"Heads down!" roared Holleb, and took his own advice by side-swiping Helki into a thorn hedge.

With a ululating chorus, the angels sliced through the forest with sweeping swords.

Greensleeves wouldn't have believed they could maneuver amidst this scrub and overgrown monkey puzzle trees. Yet the angels folded their wings and dove like kestrels spinning through pines after sparrows, like ospreys skimming the water to catch fish. They were set upon before Greensleeves could conjure, or even imagine, a spell of protection.

And where these birds of prey struck, they drew blood.

The archdruid flinched as an angel folded her wings and shot directly overhead, close enough to touch. Dropping, losing altitude, in danger of crashing to earth, the winged being half-spun in the air and slashed. So fast did the attack come, and so unexpectedly amidst these trees, Miko got her shield up too late. Silver steel struck green-painted iron with a frightful *clang*, and the bodyguard's shoulder was sliced to the bone. Gasping, Miko tried to keep her shield up even as blood coursed down her white ox-hide armor.

Kuni chopped at another angel zipping overhead,

but misjudged its speed, so she only slashed the creature's foot, lopping toes. Even then it still struck at the bodyguard behind Greensleeves, banging a furrow in Wichasta's steel helmet.

"Take prisoners!" Gull shouted above the swish of swords and arrows and thunder of wings. "Take one alive!"

A dozen blows were struck in as few seconds. One of Gull's bodyguards was slashed in the face and dropped like a stone. Helki stabbed upward with her lance and had the broad steel head sheared off to clatter against Holleb's breastplate. Without flinching, the man-stallion dropped his lance, reared fifteen feet in the air, and snatched with huge hands at the angel's ankles. But he might as well have tried to salt a bird's tail, for the angel kicked as it spun and actually laughed at the big centaur.

Sword blows clanked and thunked amidst the adventurers' party like a stone rain. Uxmal's small crossbow was shattered by a well-aimed sword tip. An archer lost a hank of hair to another. A scout burrowing for cover was scored along his back, not three feet off the ground. One of Gull's bodyguards had her shield rim slammed backward into her forehead so she collapsed, stunned and bleeding.

Yet the party got in their own blows. Two archers held nocks so long their vision was filled with tanned skin and white wings. When they loosed, the slap of arrows into flesh was so loud, like a board hitting a fence, it made people wince. One of the angels died, shot through the chest, and slammed to the ground with a bone-breaking crunch. The other, crippled by a stomach wound, plowed full into his assailant. Both were bowled over, tumbling end over end, black clothes and white feathers and green leaves all in a jumble.

Percival, coldest of the dour scouts, swung his sword two-handed from the ground and cut an angel to the spine, so she folded over the blade, slewed sideways, and fetched into a tea tree in a .¸. ˙s of broken branches.

Then the angels were gone. Only a few dead and dying lay on the trampled foliage, and the odd white feather, longer and whiter than a swan's.

"Keep prisoners alive!" Gull shouted. His soldiers knew the most important thing the army gathered was information, but in the heat of battle, such niceties as sparing the wounded were often forgotten.

The army's general cast a quick look around, swore because the scrub blocked sight. Percival's angel was almost cut in half, white-skinned now, beautiful even in death. The first angel shot by an archer was also dead, its heart torn. But the one who'd bowled into the other archer was alive, though shot through the guts and in excruciating pain. Gull hopped and thrashed in that direction, and Greensleeves joined him, their bodyguards clambering behind.

The wounded angel tried to crawl away into the brush. One D'Avenant archer was out cold, but the others grabbed hold of the angel's twisted wings and hung on, though the wings flailed so violently they had to double feathers up in their fists.

Greensleeves took command. "Gently, gently! The poor thing's in pain! I think we've made some terrible mistake! Hold him, but gently—oh!"

The last was a bleat. Though bent double on his knees, hands clutching his bleeding stomach, the blond angel glared at her with deep brown eyes, and with such hatred and dark determination that Greensleeves recoiled in shock. But she was overwhelmed with pity also, for the angel would never fly again.

Kuni and two other guardians had left their wounded comrade behind. The captain leveled her sword and kept between the wounded angel and her mistress. Yet even the hard-headed Kuni gaped when the angel lunged.

For he didn't drive for Greensleeves, but rather for Kuni's weapon.

Stabbing out with a dirt-speckled hand, the angel grabbed Kuni's sword by the hilt and pulled it down to impale himself on the sharp blade. Both he and Kuni gasped as the steel bit deeply into his ribs and lungs.

Only then did the angel relax, the look of hatred leave his eyes, replaced by the vacant stare into eternity. He coughed once, blood on his lips, and crumpled to the forest floor.

"Oh, no . . . " said Greensleeves. And she cried, as did Kuni.

"I still don't see why they should attack us," Gull groused. He'd said it a dozen times, so no one answered.

"Or why they be so fierce," said Helki. "Like mountain eagles they are, eyes sharp and hard."

"Think what they've seen," murmured Kamee, always after knowledge. "Flying in the sun, looking down at the world . . . "

"We have birds of upper air," said Uxmal in his glottal accent. "Con-dors. Never touch ground, only circle always, hatch eggs on backs. Like these an-juls."

The adventurers sat crammed around a small fire in a clearing newly hacked from the scrub forest. The scouts had chosen a spot between four sturdy trees, then cut smaller trees and lashed them into a crude roof with slash piled on top. Any attacking angels would need to pass the pickets and trot up to the fire. Gull worried the fire would set the crude roof ablaze, but people were willing to chance it. They piled on green leaves to drive off the whining insects, and sat squinting and coughing in the smoke.

They'd discussed the angel's attack, and the survivor's suicide, for hours without reaching a consensus.

Some thought the angel had feared torture. Others that he'd refused to be sullied by ground-dwellers. Others that his cult worshiped death, and he was releasing his spirit to the sky again, for all could see he'd never have flown again.

Not everyone spoke, for half a dozen were wounded, either muzzy-headed from Prane's potion or teeth-gratingly awake with pain for having refused it. The party ate iron rations as well as the roasted meat of some large flightless birds the scouts had shot. The meat was more suited to shoe leather than food. They drank wine from botas.

The dead angels had been buried at the edge of the scrub forest. Shallow graves scraped in the black glass desert had revealed gray sand underneath. The graves were clearly marked with stakes and loose feathers stuck in the tops. Greensleeves hoped, by demonstrating concern for their dead, the living angels might be dissuaded from another attack.

The archdruid listened to folks argue and yet didn't agree. The angels were murderous, yes, but she'd seen something else in that brown-eyed glare, a fierce, keen intelligence, and she'd been trying to decipher its meaning all evening.

But she was chilled. She tried to imagine grabbing a sword and plunging it into her own bosom. To deliberately throw your life away for—what? What idea, what purpose, what devil or god drove these people? How could anything so beautiful be so savage?

Yet the druid knew beauty and savagery were not linked any more than truth and beauty. A tiger was beautiful, but so was a monarch butterfly. Beauty lay in the soul.

And that angel's soul had been driven by—she could scarce believe it—love. But love of what? This scabby forest? The blighted desert?

Lost in reverie, she jumped as someone shouted.

The brush around them exploded with a thrashing and crashing.

Strange dark men and women, scaled and wet, lunged at them with tridents.

CHAPTER
14

GREENSLEEVES DIDN'T SEE MUCH OF THE ensuing battle, for she was immediately thrown to the ground by the ever-ready Guardians.

It was discovered at dawn that the pickets had succumbed to a potion rubbed on leaves around the periphery of camp. Derived from a plant root that paralyzed fish, the drug had stunned the victims when they brushed against it, then they died from trident tines. Two scouts, including the savage Percival, and an archer had perished.

And by their deaths, let the attackers loose on the party.

Past a bodyguard's calves, Greensleeves glimpsed the assailants. They were lean and muscular and as iridescent as mackerels in the sparkling firelight. Merfolk, she thought, come to tread dry land. Yet she knew they were more. Their faces were lean and sharp-cut, like the shells of horseshoe crabs, their ears and eyebrows pointed: obviously elves returned to the sea. Their hair was long and black and silky in firelight, their scaled skin dappled as if with a thousand

tiny pearls. Greensleeves noted incongruously that
leaves stuck to their wet bodies. They were completely
naked and seemingly sexless, for the men's private
parts almost receded into their groins, and the women
had no breasts to speak of. Webbing showed between
their fingers and toes and under their arms. Their only
tools were slim tridents with triple tines fashioned
from some nonrusting metal.

They were silent and as deadly efficient as sharks.

Doubly stunned by the lack of the pickets' warning
and the swift attack by such alien folk, the adventurers barely had time to leap to their feet. Hands flew
to weapons too late.

Kuni was pierced by twin thrusts to the gut as three
merfolk rushed the druid's cluster. Greensleeves saw
the tines jut out her back. Wounded Miko was
snagged in the throat by a trident and died gargling
blood, yet she grabbed the shaft of the weapon to
prevent the merwoman going after Greensleeves.
Gull's captain of bodyguards, Muley, took a trident
thrust through the thigh and crowded her assailant,
pushing to get him off balance while she drew her
sword. Her desperate gamble worked, for tensing her
thigh muscles locked the cruel barb, and she slashed
her attacker across the face. Quetoxl, Uxmal's companion, was speared in the belly and hoisted off the
ground like a prize salmon. The dwarven captain
grabbed his friend's crossbow to shoot and kill his
opponent. Holleb, who'd started on all four hooved
feet, took a thrust in the flank as he spun, then
another in the opposite flank. Yet he teetered forward on forelegs and kicked back to smash the chests
of two merfolk and send them flying into brush.
Helki whinnied as she chopped another attacker
down with a lance, her taller reach outdistancing the
trident thrusts. Short and furious bouts flared all
around the circle of fire. Human shouts and screams
and gasps echoed in the night, scared sleeping birds

off their perches. The eerie merfolk fought without a sound.

Gull kept himself alive only because he'd been polishing his axe head, which rusted in the sea air, and so could unlimber and swing it quickly. His blow missed the first merman, who fell back, but thudded across the chest of another, skipped off him to fetch in the side of a merwoman. Yet she was so tough that, when she dropped, she plucked the axe handle from his sweaty grasp. The ex-muleskinner slapped a hand to his belt and snapped out his whip. It hissed in the air as he slung it behind his head, seeking a target.

But there were none.

There was no scrub forest, either.

Despite being crushed to earth and trampled by friend and foe, Greensleeves had rattled off a shifting spell.

She didn't shift far, only two miles or so. The party staggered when their feet grated on black glass and not crushed leaves.

Greensleeves's spell, conjured so quickly, had also shifted four merfolk with them. Confused, they were savagely cut down before they could react.

Mortally wounded, Kuni toppled backward onto Greensleeves. The druid caught her, but her armored weight dropped her to the desert glass. The dead Miko had been left behind. Others fell, and Uxmal wept as his friend Quetoxl died in his arms. Others swore bitterly, Jingling Jayne especially, because her scouts had failed to warn them. The healer, Prane, scurried from wounded to wounded, deciding whom to treat first.

Gull swore long and hard, his whip hanging limply from his hand.

"Who the *devil* were those bastards?" he finally gasped.

"Guards," panted his sister.

"Yes, mistress?" croaked Micka and Wichasta, her sole remaining Guardians.

But the druid only shook her head. "No. The angels, the seafolk. They're guards. I realized it just now, should have known from the look on that angel's face. His dying thoughts were of total devotion—like poor Kuni here. He and the rest are guardians of this land, this old ruin. And we've invaded their territory and brought all this death for nothing."

Then her voice broke, and she cradled the dead Kuni in her arms and wept like a little girl lost.

The adventurers had no wish to return to the forest and risk another attack by merfolk, but neither did they wish to remain in the desert subject to aerial assault by angels. Jayne reckoned the angels would not fly by night, and that merfolk would not venture into the desert, so they settled for huddling against the ancient crumbled walls of blue stone, wrapped in cloaks for lack of a fire.

It went unspoken, but everyone had the same thought: with a crook of her finger, Greensleeves could shift them half a world away, almost anywhere. But the druid didn't offer to move them, and most assumed she refused to flee an enemy. So they hunkered down and tried to sleep, and wondered what the dawn would bring.

Sunup brought a scream from Greensleeves's bodyguards and then her brother, for the archdruid was gone. Vanished.

Greensleeves had not vanished, but had merely spun a camouflage spell and walked away without leaving a trace.

She wandered deep into the desert toward the distant mountains, throwing a long dawn shadow on the crazed black glass. She carried only the green helmet in her hand and walked tall, squinting into the rising sun.

The night had been chill, but sunlight banished the cold, evaporating the dew instantly from flat rocks and hollows. Tendrils of mist wafted into the sky, and a strange bird, unseen in some rocky nest, called. As with everywhere she went, Greensleeves tuned herself to the land, and where others had seen only desolation, she sensed the thin tendrils of life that skittered through the desert. Close to the forest border, tussocks of grass took root amidst the black chips, and weeds sent up pink buds no bigger than a candlewick. Lizards like dusky rainbows scuttled in the shadow of rocks, hunting beetles as red-orange as ladybugs. Ants by the hundreds of millions burrowed and worked to feed their young, so many that Greensleeves felt as if her soles were tingling from their rapid manic industry. High overhead, a yellow-brown kestrel hunted pocket mice with long legs and tufted tails, and along the edge of the forest slunk a small cousin to a raccoon, sandy yellow like the ground she'd left behind. Greensleeves made the raccoon pause by snickering from the corner of her mouth, a familiar cry with a strange accent.

Yet Greensleeves grieved for the land, for it was poisoned like the soil under the forest and the murky pools. This place would be a long time healing, perhaps longer than men and women would be alive to see it.

The druid walked on, deeper into the desert, away from the forest and the thin life it offered. She carried no water, no food, no protection other than her embroidered cloak. She wouldn't need water if her plan worked right.

Or if it failed.

And if she died here, at least her body would feed the scalded land and help it heal.

Then, like a dark halo around the rising sun, she saw them.

Angels, a dozen or more, swooped toward the

intruder in the black desert, the land they were charged to protect. Greensleeves saw sunlight flash on their white wings, glint off their burnished weapons. Exposed out here, alone, they could chop her to mincemeat in seconds.

Unless . . .

Louder they were, now, like a windstorm over the desert; flapping their huge wings, soaring on thermals like eagles, dropping again. Soon they'd be close enough to touch her, and kill her.

Greensleeves waited.

And just before their final plunge with swords held high, she raised her hand.

Gull, as usual when his sister disappeared from camp, raged and stomped and harangued and sent scouts running in all directions. One came running back after two hours to report her tracks in the desert. The entire party, shrunken in size by death and wounding, stood at the edge of the desert and stared where another scout showed the start of Greensleeves's tracks, begun as if from thin air.

"Damn her," Gull huffed, icy calm as always when a decision was needed. "Even I can see she used a camouflage spell to sneak out past the sentries and into the desert. But, by the Arms of Axelrod, *why*?"

Holleb, with the sharpest eyes in the company, snapped up his head as if sniffing the wind. He raised his lance with one brawny arm to point. "The angels return!"

The scholars backed out of the way of the soldiers, who formed a shoulder-to-shoulder ring around Gull. Only the woodcutter was still, squinting at the hot sky. Something was fluttering, not flying. As if—

"What are they carrying?"

Holleb snorted again, and Helki made a gurgling sound, a question. "It is—Greensleeves!"

Then Gull was walking forward, and soldiers and bodyguards had to advance, too. The general slid

down the shingle to the hot desert floor and strode
out, his boots crunching on black glass. Then he
stopped, his axe dangling from his good right hand.

The horde of angels grew bigger against the white-
blue sky until they looked like a thunderhead block-
ing the sun. There were many more angels than
before: hundreds and hundreds. The humans could
distinguish younger angels, children, as well as feeble
elders propped on two sides by heartier helpers. Most
of the angels looked strong and powerful, yet like
birds, bore no fat, so what passed for a lean austere
beauty in the youngsters became a gaunt, starved
look in old age. The thrum of their wings was like an
approaching tornado, and the soldiers and scouts
raised their weapons in sweaty-handed anticipation.

But Gull stood still and waited, and by and by, the
foremost angels dropped to the ground outside bowshot and walked. None had swords drawn, and there
were no shields.

They carried only Greensleeves, ferried by two
lean, muscular angels who formed a cradle with their
arms. The archdruid's feet dangled like a child's on a
swing, and she giggled breathlessly as the two angels
alighted to the sand and set her gently down.

More and more angels touched down on laced sandals until, with the white wings and blond hair, the
desert looked like a field of sunflowers in bloom.
When the dust had settled, Gull pushed past his
bodyguards until he could address his sister.

His tone was a tired sigh, the voice of a big brother
charged with watching a troublesome sibling. "All
right, Greenie. What is it *this* time?"

The druid brushed hair out of her face and thanked
the two porters. She held up the green stone helmet.
"Well, brother, it was as I guessed.

"The angels and merfolk were appointed guardians
eons ago when the Sages of Lat-Nam ruled this land.
The Sages created them, gave mortal folk the power

of flight, and elves the gift of the sea. The two races protected the college for a long time. That time I donned the helmet and had the vision of the final destruction, I glimpsed angels with swords dying bravely to drive back monsters. But I forgot. They and the merfolk survived the destruction and have guarded ever since, driving away intruders. That's why they attacked."

Remembering the battle of the day before, and the dead companions, both sides stirred, but discipline kept them quiet. Greensleeves added, "They wish now they hadn't had to attack.

"Once I reasoned that out, I needed to prove it. So I snuck out of camp—I apologize to the pickets—and walked toward the mountains." She gestured vaguely over her shoulder. "The angels spotted me, of course, and came flying to—intercept me. But I held up this—the stone helmet. It was enough, and we talked, and they carried me to their home in the mountains. You must all see it sometime; it escaped the Brothers' devastation. It's lovely, with views for miles from more balconies than you can count, and fountains in pools. But anyway, I was taken to their scholars, who recognized the helmet. One of the elders even donned it to hear the chorus of shouts inside: he got quite a surprise."

"Greenie . . . " Gull spoke chidingly, as if they were the only two for miles and she had been caught stealing apples. "Why didn't you *tell* me? You could have been *killed*!"

His little sister nodded, contrite about his worry, but then shrugged. "Better I should be killed trying to make peace than more of us or them fighting unnecessary battles."

People shook their head, astonished and admiring, as did the angels. "Anyway, it's better now. The elders decided that, since I own the stone helmet and wish to carry on the learning of the Sages and oppose evil wizards, I'm their legitimate heir. So they'll aid our quest. And the merfolk will help, too, they reckon."

Gull—general, woodcutter, and brother—nodded, but that was all. He resisted glancing back at the edge of the desert, where lay fresh graves of humans and angels and now merfolk. Though they'd only been fulfilling their duty, as had he, Gull couldn't forgive them right away, and doubted his followers would. So the general said in a neutral tone, "Thank them, then, for flying you back. We've been talking, Kamee and the rest, and the only solution we see to find your Sages' buried secret is dig it up. That will be a dirty and tiresome job. If they wish to help, they're welcome. And that's all I'm going to say for now. Are they game?"

Greensleeves turned to an elder in the midst of the flock, an incredibly lean and wizened woman, more bird than human. She consulted the elder in a low voice, and the woman rasped back.

The druid turned. "They'll help. The sage who fathered them took inspiration from the legend of Serra angels. He named them Duler angels. The seafolk are the Copper Conch tribe, fashioned after the merfolk of the Pearl Trident, but with legs, not tails."

"That's nice." Gull was already turning away, his bodyguards backstepping after him. He thumped his axe head over his shoulder and marched for the scrub forest. "Let's get to work."

Before they could dig up the ruins, however, they needed to shift the bulk of the army to this tortured and convoluted landscape.

Greensleeves first fetched the dwarven sappers, who got to work readying the site. They cleared brush, laid out a camp, located a reservoir of water that Greensleeves purified, cut trails. Exploring, the scouts found the forest petered out some six miles to the west, giving way to savanna, as Kamee named the low hills of knee-high grass and tall trees with windswept tops. That was good news, for its fodder would support cavalry horses and livestock. A road was chopped to the savanna, and guard posts established. More posts were erected on the sea cliff and along the edge of the desert.

Everyone knew why. It was only a matter of time before Towser and Karli's congress of wizards found them and attacked.

Finally, Greensleeves deemed it safe enough and took four days to shift the army hither without exhausting herself. Camp was established, and the army, flexible and motivated, settled in to drilling the new recruits and exploring the new land.

When the actual excavating was to begin, Gull turned over all aspects to Uxmal and his dwarves. Using the advice of scouts and cartographers and librarians, Uxmal and his southern cohorts laid out stakes and strings in triangles, built scaffoldings of bamboo, thrashed in the brush, asked the blacksmiths to hammer out extra shovels and picks and crowbars, and finally announced that *here*, in a stretch of scrub that looked no different than any other spot, they would begin cutting and digging.

Within two hours, they uncovered a face.

The face was about four feet down through the dusty gray soil. It was a jolly fat-cheeked sun with curly rays radiating from its head. The whole was a mosaic, carefully fit tiles each no bigger than a thumb joint, in antique but lustrous colors fired centuries ago and laid in the sun to fade. Pale blues like a summer sky, reds like rust, deep ambers made up the sun. Uxmal, chief of the sappers, got down on his knees and carefully brushed the face clear, and it shone brighter every minute.

The dwarves slashed more brush, threw more dirt aside, jerked out roots, hefted stones. Surrounding

the sun were planets and the two moons of the
Domains, the Mist Moon and Glitter Moon. The circle was large, almost twenty feet across: big enough
to dance on, someone joked.

Around the outside of the planets ran a trough a
handspan deep for channeling rain. More dirt sailed
in the air. Past the trough lay more mosaics, more
detailed. Brought into daylight were legends and
myths and monsters from ancient times, all fashioned
of colored glazed chips. Some of the legends were
familiar: people recognized the saintly Jacques Le
Vert battling the Brute before the tree city of
Pendlehaven; Lady Evangela riding a rainbow to the
Mist Moon; Marhault crawling from the burned
wreckage of his ship and vowing revenge. But many
pictures were unfamiliar, a topic of debate, for everyone in the army studied the fantastic stories. A jeweled sword was shoved into the midst of a vast grassy
plain while a storm raged overhead. A carved pump-
kin rolled down a hill towards a pot billowing smoke.
A burning woman danced atop a stone plinth.

The dwarves continued to dig, and many people
joined in, even those not on duty. Men and women
and children dug with borrowed shovels and pails,
then spoons and knives when the tools were all
taken. Wider grew the circle. Artifacts were found: a
clockwork gear big as a wagon wheel, a melted
sword, clusters of teeth—all that remained of incinerated and crushed skeletons.

At noon, the angels arrived and offered to help,
and did, but with their huge wings, they were ill-
suited to digging or even passing baskets, so they
were shunted aside, still unforgiven. Eventually they
flew off without a word, and the army was glad to
see them go.

Volunteers worked on their hands and knees with
brushes and buckets to scrub the tiles clean, and they
shone as if in gratitude. Fountains were discovered,

their statues snapped off and tumbled, then the underground pipes that had fed them. Circular stone curbs came to light, with only dirt inside, and finally confirmed what Greensleeves had suspected all along.

The face was the centerpiece of a huge ornamental garden, a showpiece to the world. The scrub that had sprung up on its bones was composed of the hardiest members of that ancient garden. Originally, she supposed, most of this land to the horizons had been savanna wending to the low blue mountains. The Sages had built the college here—no one knew why this spot was favored—and introduced many alien plants and creatures. And, of course, constructed their own, including the angels and merfolk.

By dark, the dwarves had uncovered the sloped opening to a tunnel large enough to take a span of oxen. Investigating, they found a matching tunnel opposite across the circle, for the garden was laid out symmetrically.

By the light of bonfires of slash, Gull and Uxmal, Kamee and Greensleeves consulted over the tunnel entrance, which was packed solidly with dirt.

"What do you think, Greenie?" asked Gull. "Is your secret of the helmet or whatever it is down there?"

The druid demurred. "Under a garden? I have no way of knowing."

"What we do wid de dirt?" asked the ever-practical dwarf.

"How big is this garden thing?" countered Gull.

The dwarf consulted the librarian, paced off a while, came back. "We reckon is one hundred, mebbe one hundred five paces across. Human paces. Big circle."

Gull craned around in the near-tropical darkness. The main camp was a quarter-mile north, the low ocean cliff a quarter-mile south. Around them loomed the bug-infested forest slashed back in a ragged circle.

"What say—" Gull mused, "we move camp onto this garden? We could fortify the rim, make it safe."

"Why?" asked Uxmal. "Is dumb. We haf to mag camp on top of work site, move here and dere and bag again for noddin'."

Gull shrugged, suddenly embarrassed. "It would make for, I don't know, a goal, a good story, to live atop these ancient legends and secrets. Gardens are just as important to morale as weapons and food and songs."

Greensleeves squinted at her hardheaded brother. "Why, Gull, that's positively poetic."

Her brother rolled his eyes. "It's just a good idea to be close to—whatever we're after." And he walked off, trailed by bodyguards.

Greensleeves looked down at the close-packed dirt. The dwarf said to her, "Tomorrow we dig, find much."

"What? I wonder."

Two days later, a monster erupted from the hole.

CHAPTER
15

TEAMS OF HUMANS AND DWARVES WORKED
steadily to clear the garden, while others excavated
the tunnels, and still others worked on the perimeter
fortifications.

The new-dug soil and rocks were put to use. Uxmal
supervised the ramping of bulwarks of gray earth and
stones all around the circle, with ditches outside. Cut
tea trees were built into the ramparts as a palisade,
taller than Gull, lashed and pegged, and every thirty
feet a watch tower was erected. Two entrances bol-
stered with strong doors faced east and west. It made
a strange picture, a tall dirt wall and towers of peeled
poles and split-shingle roofs surrounding a fresh-
washed circle of sparkling mosaics telling of ancient
glories, and spotted in the empty flowerbeds, a camp
of tents and cookfires and lines of drying laundry. As
the forest was dug away and more garden exposed,
people spread out. The land was not completely
denuded: some flowerbeds were left with their tea
trees or bamboo patches for shade. Folks worked at
their usual tasks, others scrubbed and polished tiles,

and sang while doing so, for the army was inspired—
they, too, they felt, were performing great works that
would be recorded in legends someday. Scruffy children bearing wooden swords made imaginary war
and acted out the scenes and spun themselves dizzy
tracing the mazelike designs with their feet.

There was no sign of the angels or merfolk, and
gradually people stopped talking about their fickle
allies.

Then came the first disaster.

By all accounts, told later, the sappers aided by
humans had been making good time excavating the
twin tunnels. By the light of candles stuck to helmets,
they labored sweating to chip the hard-packed earth
with pickaxes and mattocks and shovels, and filled
basket after basket with detritus. The tunnels sloped
first downward for thirty feet, away from the center,
then flattened into ancient corridors that promised
still more mysteries.

Then one dwarf spotted gold. Instantly shouts
welled up and the digging increased frantically. Soon
they uncovered a bulging gold orb on a stick.

Then a dwarf touched it with her bare hand, and
the object exploded into life.

It was not an orb, but a cantilevered knee.

With a rumble that shook the earth, a gush of
steam and belch of gas, a gold-plated monster tore
loose from the packed dirt and thundered into the
open tunnel. The dwarf before it was crushed
instantly. Others further back, with room to dodge,
suffered only broken limbs.

The camp panicked when the monster roared out
of the tunnel, as fast as a horse could run, hissing
and steaming and clattering like a crate of dishes
falling down stairs.

Someone shouted its name. A dragon engine.

Gull was on the ramparts, supervising the fortifications, visiting with Lily and the children, when the

thing burst into the midst of camp. To him it looked like a dragon's golden skeleton. It was clearly a clock-work contraption of brass or gold-plated steel. A head like a bird's sported flaring green jewels for eyes, and a spout on its skull belched steam. Gears and camshafts pumped and whirled, driving articu-lated legs and clawed feet so sharp they shredded tents, cordwood, dirt, and tiles.

Belching, hissing, rattling, swiveling its head like a snake, it shed dirt from its tarnished frame—splashed with blood across its metal breast—as it clanked and careened around the camp. The two front claws see-sawed, whipping in the air and slashing down, shred-ding whatever came to hand. With some aggressive sense, it aimed for the largest knots of people, scurry-ing after them like mice. One old man, too slow, was pinned under a mighty claw and neatly sliced into three pieces.

Spinning its head completely around, the dragon spotted another clutch of people and crabbed after them. Only by diving through a hole in the unfinished palisade did they escape. The dragon's long skeletal tail whipped freely, its end as sharp as a scorpion's sting, and lopped the tops from a stand of bamboo.

Gull grabbed Lily's shoulder, tossed Hyacinth to a nurse, and pushed both women and the child through the palisade gap. "Get under cover, far away!" Then he barked at a cluster of gaping soldiers, "Grab your lances and stop it!" Startled, the men and women scrambled for lances, poles, halberds, anything lengthy. But up on the ramparts, Gull asked Jingling Jayne, "What the hell do we do about *that*? Where's Greenie? She can shift—" But his sister was away from camp, off in the forest somewhere.

The chief of scouts shook her head. "Arrow and spears are useless. The dwarves are supposed to know machines . . . "

"Box it, maybe," Gull thought aloud. "Get ropes,

or chains, and tangle it, lash it to a tree, until someone can crush its metal guts. Maybe Stiggur's clockwork beast, or Liko, can thump it—"

Most everyone had scurried out of the dragon's
path, either through the gaps in the palisade or
behind trees or into the tunnel entrance itself. No one
was in immediate danger, because it seemed reluctant
to climb the earthen ramparts, but Gull knew he had
to evacuate the camp.

All along the dragon engine had been hissing, as a
living creature might gasp for breath. It now faced a
section of palisade where folks peered around the
edge at the monster. Suddenly the engine shoved its
head forward and snapped open its jaws as if choking
on something stuck in its throat. People crept closer
out of curiosity.

Some dreadful premonition made Gull shout, "Get
away! Get down!" Spooked, people obeyed instantly,
scurrying for protection behind dirt and the palisade.

Hissed and clicking, the engine suddenly dislodged
the obstacle. A small tube showed at the back of the
dragon's throat. More clicks sounded. A shower of
sparks glittered behind its gold fangs.

Another click, a spark—and *whoosh*!

A jet of flame shot from the dragon's maw a full
thirty feet. People diving for cover had their hems
and hose set afire.

"Gas!" shouted Jayne. "Swamp gas!"

"Stangg's Stones! No hope for capturing it now!"
Gull bellowed across the camp, *"Run!"*

The dragon wheeled. Its gas jet, finally unclogged
of dirt, belched hellfire, igniting walls, tents, gear.
Everywhere people scrambled to get out of camp.

Gull dove behind the palisade and swore uselessly.
Damn all magic and magical geegaws! was all he
could think. People were burned, the camp was being
destroyed, and all he could do—

—was look to the sky.

A thrum of wings sounded overhead. Gusts of wind set the foliage tossing across the forest. The sky filled with lithe brown bodies and wide white wings.

Angels had come to their rescue.

With a flurry of wings and graceful arcing loops, angels swirled through black smoke and swooped into camp.

Canny and quick as sparrows, half a dozen fliers banked and soared not twelve feet above the marauding engine's head. The mechanical maw snapped at them, the head crooked back and belched fire, but always the angels winged aside at the last second, impossible to swat.

The dragon churned steely claws, swiveled its head, lunged and fired at a flitting form here, there, elsewhere, always missing. Then the angels sang to one another and together zoomed toward the east gateway. Rattling, the engine clanked after them, sure as a mule after a carrot.

Flying like that was a risk, and deadly. One angel, young and inexperienced, or just unlucky, missed a loop. The dragon's maw, devilishly hot, snapped shut on the angel's legs. Bones crunched and broke, then wings. When the dragon snapped open red-rimmed jaws, the crumpled body fell to be crushed underfoot.

Yet the remaining angels never let up in their teasing, but swirled like autumn leaves before the monster's snapping head. Rapidly the dragon engine followed, until it ground out the eastern gate. From there, with sandaled feet almost touching its gold fangs, the angels banked south.

The dragon raced after them. The angels followed a wide trail hacked through the forest, but the machine was wider. It bashed through tea trees and bamboo and monkey puzzle trees, shredded bark and leaves, smashing foliage flat. Gull grabbed his axe and loped after them, as did dozens of others. The spectators could see the angels tiring from their swooping and soaring, all while dodging tree trunks and the deadly snapping jaws of the metal beast.

Yet soon they flashed into the clear, for the forest abruptly ended.

The mindless dragon engine didn't notice.

Angels put on a last burst of speed, straining wings until they were close to dropping, and soared into a bright white-blue sky.

The dragon engine charged after them.

Right off the broken cliff.

In the last seconds, the beast tried to halt. Its rear claws gave a teeth-grating *screek!* as they ripped through soil and scraped on quarried stones. Its tail twisted downward like a fishhook to brake its rush, yet tons of metal worked against it, and it stumbled over the cliff edge. The saw-whip tail struck chips of marble from the edge, then it was gone.

By the time Gull arrived, puffing, the frightful crash and smash and clatter was over. A hollow boom sounded, and a whiff of swamp gas wafted up the cliff face. Thirty feet below, the woodcutter saw the dragon engine shattered on the rocks. Tidal water hissed around the hot muzzle.

Gull shook his head. "Stiggur will be sad to miss another clockwork toy."

A heavy fluttering overhead sounded like an oncoming storm. A dozen angels landed on the cliff, winded, chests heaving. They couldn't speak, but didn't need to.

Gull shifted his axe to his maimed left hand, and with his good right, shook the hand of each exhausted angel, saying, "Thank you! Thank you!"

At the forest's edge, people cheered.

Greensleeves arrived with her bodyguards from her sojourn in the forest and was told the news.

She found Gull standing at the gaping mouth of a tunnel. "Brother, you must stop the digging! What if they uncover another monster?"

"What of it?" Gull gave her a strange, faraway look, one she'd never seen before.

"What of it?" The druid waved her hands in the air, searching for words. "People were hurt, killed! That was some old war engine reactivated by the light or air or someone's touch! It might have been set deliberately as a trap! The Sages might have retreated to these tunnels in the last days of the apocalypse! There might be a hundred more traps down there!"

"True, true." Her brother nodded. "I told them that. But they said if that's so, your secret of how to control wizards must be down here. And other secrets that will benefit all of us. A map of the Domains, perhaps, showing everyone's homeland. Maybe treasure, too. So they've got a bone in their teeth, and mysteries to solve, and they're going to dig them up."

"What?" For the first time, Greensleeves looked around the camp, saw a few people cleaning up, comforting the wounded, toting the dead. But not many. "Where *is* everyone?"

Gull only pointed down the tunnel. "Digging."

Greensleeves just stared into the darkness.

As the army dug, they found more monsters, more close escapes, more deaths.

An angel was incinerated to ashes when he brushed against a silver ball lodged in a dirt wall. Comrades recounted that his tightly folded wing brushed a silver protuberance. There was a tremendous flash and bang, and all that remained was a few scorched feathers and the stink of burnt flesh. People in the vicinity were blinded for two days by the silver flare.

Still, they dug.

A dwarf had his head broken when he stepped on a slimy rubbery mat only to have the mat rear up and slam him against the low ceiling. A slug as big as an ox came alive, flailed at them with sticky pods, and humped after them on one giant foot. It took three soldiers with lances to kill the pulpy thing, and five with iron hooks to drag it out of the tunnels and dump it over the cliff onto seaweedy rocks. Seabirds feasted for three days.

Still, the army dug. Day and night, now.

Two sappers fainted when a vile gray gas gushed from under a flagstone, and it took hours of hurling in torches to purify the poisonous air. One team was driven screaming from a tunnel when they burst open a colony of fire ants the size of a house. It took fire and burning pitch to kill all the ants, and their metallic stink made folks retch for days.

Still, they dug.

Soldiers insisted they alone should be allowed to dig. It was too dangerous for sappers and camp followers, they argued. The soldiers just wanted to hog the glory, others retorted, and suddenly a hundred and fifty dirty workers were brawling in the tunnel and up in the sunlight. Gull stepped in and declared that anyone who wished may dig. That brought more trouble, for now cooks and nurses and leatherworkers wanted to join in. But there weren't enough tools, so finally folks drew lots, and men and women cursed when they were stuck aboveground.

A woman died from inhaling dust trapped in one pocket, a virulent poison left by the warfare. Many fell sick, coughing blood, or were burned by touching the soil, lesions erupting on their hands so they couldn't hold tools. No sooner did they trudge to the healers than someone else caught up their shovels and picks.

And dug.

"They're mad!" Greensleeves wailed one night at supper around the campfire. "Mad to want to risk their lives!"

"No, they're challenged," Gull replied. "This ruin, this lost city, is trying to shake them off, scare them away, and they're determined to beat it."

"I don't understand!" Now the druid was crying. "They shouldn't be sacrificing themselves like this! What if there *is* no secret? What if we don't find any control for wizards or anything else? What if people are dying on *my word* for nothing?"

Gull frowned, but shook his head. "It's not you they sacrifice for, Greenie. It's something larger."

"What?" She sniffled, and Wichasta handed her a handkerchief. "By the gods, all we ever do is fight, and now we're fighting the land and ancient magic itself! What are we dying for?"

Gull only shook his head. "I can't really say. We've banded together to fight wizards, and come here for knowledge, and have to fight tooth and claw to get it, and . . . We're caught up in a legend, Greenie, an epic as big as any story about Tobias Andrion or Lady Caleria. A story that will live forever, something to tell our grandchildren we were part of."

"Those who survive," the druid whimpered.

"We'll survive," said her brother.

So the army dug, and suffered crippling and maiming, and dug harder, and refused to quit at the end of their shifts, and had to be prodded out with spears, and dug, and dug.

At the end of two weeks, Uxmal brought Gull and Greensleeves into the tunnels for a tour.

Although soldiers and sappers and campfollowers faced danger daily, none of them would allow their beloved leaders to enter underground until Uxmal, with a smile, assured their bodyguards the way was safe.

The leaders were fascinated. The walls were of cut stone, marble or something harder, polished satin smooth in the old days. At one point, the dwarven chief showed Gull his reflection in an unscorched

span of stone. The walls were a soft brown with gold
flecks, the floor white with gray streaks, but all were
filthy. Many of the walls were cracked, and large gaps
showed between blocks in the walls and ceiling.

The tunnels branched, giving way to rooms and
halls and passages in all directions, winding well past
the boundaries of the mosaic-laden garden overhead.
Gull with his axe, and Greensleeves with her embroidered cloak of many colors, were quiet as they followed the dwarf down staircases thirty feet wide,
passed through torchlit corridors that would allow
six cavalry to ride abreast, crossed atriums with dry
pools in their floors, walked up ramps and past
carved columns and arches. And there was more,
Uxmal guessed: up above, under the dense wrack of
the forest, were probably sprinkled further pathways
and gazebos and ornate walls.

Torches in ancient sconces lit the leaders' way, yet
Uxmal wore a mining helmet with a candle that
dripped wax onto his fat nose. He talked as they
walked. It was his guess the dirt they'd excavated had
been deliberately funneled into the tunnels. Given the
bones they'd found, someone must have sent down
an avalanche of scalding mud. Leaks between the
ceiling blocks had trickled over centuries to fill any
spaces. Consulting with the magic students, the sappers agreed the menaces dispersed throughout the
dirt were deliberate death traps. Even the slug had
been in magical hibernation, they guessed, and fresh
air had revived it.

"Yes," Greensleeves told them. "I saw the destruction in the helm. The Brothers' agents must have
wanted this place buried from sight of humankind."

The dwarven chief reported that, as each room had
been unearthed, they searched but found little.
Occasionally they turned up a charred or cracked
skull—many not human—or a broken sword or
lance. Once a splintered chest bound with silver

bands revealed a cache of gold. Many more silver bombs had exploded, though with shielding no one was harmed. The curious dwarves had tried to pry some loose to study, but they always exploded with a flash and bang.

Gull and Greensleeves had walked around and about, tramping over dirt-streaked marble floors until they were dizzy, when Uxmal turned down a wide corridor. Bright sunlight poured along smudged walls.

They heard the surf pounding, and smelled salt air. The end of a corridor overlooked the sea: a hole in the cliff, perhaps twenty feet above the water, with the cliff lip ten feet above. The passage had been plugged with stone, Uxmal explained.

The tunnel simply stopped. Gray marble floor tiles ended, gap-toothed where other tiles had cascaded into the surf.

Trailed by bodyguards, the three looked at the impossibly blue water. Far out, a whale spouted, its plume blowing away on the sea wind. In the choppy bay framed by ragged peninsulas, a gull dropped from a nest in the cliff's edge and crashed like a dart into the water after a silver fish.

Gull looked around at the square hole and frowned. "Where did this lead?"

The dwarf spread stubby callused hands at the yawning space and ocean below.

"Out dere."

"We're finished," said Greensleeves.

She'd brought the army officers from camp to the cliff's edge. It was late evening, but the sky was pink and purple in the west. The druid's tousled brown hair snapped in the wind, and her embroidered cloak billowed behind like angel wings.

"All this excavation has done no good. According to guesses by Uxmal and Kamee, the college was built with five arms like a starfish. This was one arm.

Some central structure lay in the center, where the bay is now. Those broken islands are what's left of the other arms."

The officers were glum. Gull muttered, "I'm glad the Brothers died long ago. If they could summon power to send miles of stone tunnels and a castle crashing into the sea, I'm glad we never need face them."

"I'd risk it, for knowledge," said the archdruid. "It's the only thing I hold precious beyond my friends. But what I wanted to know, the remaining secret of the helmet, what they couldn't enchant for lack of time, lies out there. Forever lost."

Late that night, Gull returned to his tent and heard young Bittersweet bawling. By candlelight, Lily sat in her nightdress on their cot, jostling, jiggling, tickling the baby, but Bittersweet only screamed, red face contorted. Trying to hush her, Lily finally broke into tears.

Gull propped his axe against a tent pole, took the screeching infant, and tried the same. But the child would not hush at his cooing, so he finally asked a bodyguard to fetch a nurse, who took the child away, still screaming.

Lily wiped tears with the heel of her hand. "I'm sorry, Gull. I'm a bad mother."

"Hush." Gull sat down and cradled her head against his chest, patted her. "That's not true. You're a fine mother. Look, Hyacinth is turning out fine." Indeed, their elder daughter was asleep on a small cot, mouth open, hair frowzy around her small head.

"Oh, I'm tired, Gull!" She hugged him tight, but had little strength. "The child screams all the time, I'm still weak from childbirth, you're never around . . ."

"I know, I know," he crooned.

"I wish I were an angel," Lily murmured.

Gull craned back, squinted in the dim light. "A what?"

"Oh, Gull . . . " Lily breathed. "Have you watched them? *Really* watched them? They're so beautiful, swooping and soaring on the wind, free as can be. How I envy them. They have no responsibilities, can do as they please."

"They have responsibilities. They're charged with protecting this land, or what's left of it." Gull gently eased his wife onto her cot and drew up a blanket. "Now hush, Lily. You're just tired. You don't know what you're saying."

"But I do." She sighed, half asleep. "It would be so beautiful to fly like them. I could fly once, remember? I made others fly, too. It felt wonderful! I've forgotten how, but perhaps I could learn again. But I couldn't leave the children, or my responsibilities. . . . " She nodded off.

Gull wiped his brow and slowly undressed. "My wife wants to fly, my sister wants secrets no one knows, my army is without a goal again, and I don't know what to do next. Maybe we should all just fly away and leave our responsibilities behind. . . . "

He plumped down on his cot, jumped as something squawled underneath him.

Ripping back a quilt, he found Egg Sucker clutching the corner of a blanket. "Y' almost squashed me! Gimme that back! It's cold!"

"Cold, is it?" Gull growled. "You little sneak, I'll give you *cold*!"

Gull grabbed the goblin by one leg and charged out of the tent. Startled lancers stepped back as Gull took a running start, then hurled the goblin by his leg like a stick of cordwood.

The goblin pinwheeled clear over the nearest palisade wall, screaming all the way.

CHAPTER
16

CURLED UP WITH KWAM IN A DOUBLE CAMP
bed, Greensleeves woke to a stealthy tussle outside
her tent: feet slapping, quiet grunting, a muffled
curse. Someone stumbled against the tent pole and
shook the fabric. The archdruid rose and pulled a
gown over her head.

Outside was blackness save for the odd torch and
picket fires glinting on mosaics. Two Guardians of
the Grove scuffled with a half dozen merfolk, naked
and dripping and slippery skinned. The seafolk tried
to shove past the guards; the Guardians blocked with
their lances. The merfolk didn't speak, and the
guards argued in harsh whispers lest they wake their
mistress.

Everyone jumped as Greensleeves asked, "What's
this about, please?"

Micka, the new captain, answered while keeping an
eye on the gleaming fish-folk. "They insist on seeing
you, milady, and won't leave. I'm afraid we'll have to
use violence—"

The druid shook her tousled head. "No, they

must have a good reason. How may I help you, good people?"

The sea dwellers, they'd learned, communicated with their minds, so couldn't talk to land dwellers. Above the waves, they mimed. A black-haired mer-woman, naked and scaly as a mackerel, simply crooked a hand. Greensleeves must come.

Greensleeves mimed questions, but the answer was the same. *Come now.*

Finally Greensleeves raised a finger to wait, turned inside, and donned her best gown. She sensed this was a formal occasion, for the merfolk mostly kept to them-selves. Pulling on low boots and hanging her cloak around her shoulders, she turned to kiss Kwam, but the magic student was up, dressing to join her. Combing callused fingers through her hair, Greensleeves stepped out to follow the merfolk—to the shore, presumably. Kwam trailed her, rubbing his eyes and yawning, hard to see in his black clothes, along with six guards, the day shift having been roused.

They walked, not to the cliff edge, but into the scrub forest, along a trail wide enough for two abreast. This stretch of forest was untouched, for the trail pitched down staggered natural stairs and patches of ancient carved steps, much overgrown with roots and brush and dead leaves. The smell of rot was heavy in Greensleeves's nose, but mingled with the crisp sea air. Despite the heat of the previ-ous day, the night breeze swirling around her bare ankles was chilly, and she was glad for her cloak. She had to be aware of her footing, for they crept by torchlight borne by her bodyguards. Merfolk, used to the ocean depths, could see in the dark like cats.

Finally they left the overhang of scruffy trees to a shallow rocky beach in a tiny cove. The rocks were varied, from boulders to egg-shaped pebbles. The surf was quiet, lapping lazily, straining through seaweed with a hiss.

Greensleeves gazed around. The night was bright
with stars, and she ordered the torches extinguished
to allow night vision. Soon she made out the silvery
outline of surf, the forest above, the merfolk. All six
stood at the shore, presenting lean naked backs
sporting tiny frills and tight buttocks. None moved.
They just stood, waiting.

The Guardians, used to long night duty, fell into
their semitorpor, half-resting, half-alert. Kwam
perched on a rock and dozed, despite his native
curiosity.

They waited a long time while stars whirled overhead, only the tide talking. Greensleeves stifled a
yawn, thought of her bed. Then one of the merfolk
stirred, and then all did.

Something rose from the surf.

The Guardians snapped awake, clustered around
Greensleeves, leveled spears like a ring of pointed
steel. Micka ordered them to back into the forest, but
Greensleeves countermanded her. For some reason,
she trusted these merfolk would not harm her. And
curiosity drove her to see what was arriving.

Whatever it was, it was big.

The first thing Greensleeves saw, hundreds of feet
out, was a huge fin like a shark's cutting the water.
Immediately there followed, far behind, a softer fin
with a gentle curve like a fan's.

Before Greensleeves could assemble the picture of
this great fish in her mind—she knew much of land
creatures, but almost nothing of the sea—her vision
shattered. For the great fin parted the soughing
waves to reveal the face of a man.

As if lifted on a hoist, the man rose above the
waves until he towered over them, though he was
still a hundred feet out. A giant, Greensleeves knew.

Or a god.

The master of the waves was revealed in his full
splendor, and everyone caught their breath.

The sea god brought his own spectral light, like a comet in the sky, so many details were lit as if by fire. His skin was a deep purple, his belly a pale green like a fish's. He was so imposing, and so ornate, it was hard to tell what was decoration and what natural flesh. The great fin jutted from his bald head and curled halfway down his back. Above his ears sprouted more fins, and from his ears dangled earrings cut from circles of mother-of-pearl. Fins like wings sprouted from his shoulders like a billowing cape, and mighty gold bands encircled his bulging arms. He wore gauntlets of brass or bronze set with huge jewels like the eyes of a whale. His body, thicker around than two people could encompass with their arms, tapered at the waist to a serpent's, and this long articulated snake's body trailed down into the water and far out behind to grow into an enormous and gently curved fin. In his hands, he carried a spear branched like a tree, the ends doubly barbed and folded back.

Almost silently, the sea god rolled in with the tide and poised upright, bobbing slowly to the pulse of the waves. When he was within spear's length, he spoke.

With his mind.

You are Greensleeves. He sent the message straight to the brain, so it echoed in her skull as if shouted in a canyon. Yet it was a gentle and tolerant voice for its immense power.

Yes, she answered without speaking. *And you are . . . ?*

A suggestion of a chuckle rippled through her mind. Greensleeves recalled her brother's words, that the gods must have a great sense of humor to set people at their silly travails.

The answer stunned her nonetheless.

I am the Lord of Atlantis. You shall come with me.

Yes, she answered automatically.

Micka sensed something passing between her mistress and the sea god, saw Greensleeves take a step forward, and dropped her spear across the druid's path. Half-begging, half-ordering, she shouted, "Milady, no! He's bewitched you! You can't—you'll drown—"

Micka froze. So did the rest, merfolk included. The lord had halted them in their tracks. Only Greensleeves could move, and she walked forward as if in a dream—a pleasant one—until her boots sloshed in chill seawater.

When she was knee-deep, the Lord of Atlantis touched her shoulder with his spear. He backed away, she walked, and together they moved into the surf, past it to deep water.

When the water rose to Greensleeves's chin, the sea god flicked his tail, mighty as a whale's. Encircling Greensleeves, he caught her in his coils, and together they plunged under the waves.

Out of sight of the stars.

At first, Greensleeves thought she was drowning.

When the water closed over her head, she woke to the danger as if she'd been sleepwalking. Panic made her start, doubly so, for the mammoth coils of the Lord of Atlantis enwrapped her. Desperately she held her breath.

But the sea god touched her lips with a thick purple finger, and she could breathe. Whether she inhaled water like a fish, or was suspended in some air pocket, she could not tell. Surely she was wet all over, but not cold, and when she lifted a hand, it drifted lazily downward like milkweed fluff. She must be floating, she thought. Or sinking.

Yet she had little time to think. The Lord of Atlantis, bathed in the green-white light of his own making, lit the water around for a dozen feet. The sea god moved her easily with great purple hands, propped her on his back, coaxed her hands onto his shoulder frills for support. Then, with scarcely a flicker, he kicked his tail and propelled them into the depths.

A pair of dolphins swam close to investigate and were left behind. More fish flitted by: a school of yellow butterfish, sleek white-silver bonito pursuing them; a sunfish big and flat as a barrel top; many more fish Greensleeves didn't know, including a huge shark with its skull jutting in two directions like a cobbler's hammer. Yet even it made way for the Lord of Atlantis.

Clinging to the stiff rubbery frills, with the feel of water rippling past her feet but not her face, questions came to Greensleeves's mind. She was unsure if she should speak—it might break some spell—but the questions remained.

And was answered.

You seek the Sages of Lat-Nam, their secrets, came the reply like a great booming bell in her mind.

How did you know? she framed automatically. Then realized, Of course, he can read my thoughts.

I remember them, rang the bell.

She was startled. *You do? But that would be—*

Ages ago. Yes, for one such as you. Not so long for the sea. They were good men and women, if too introspective.

Introspective? she asked. What an odd word. Greensleeves found it odd, too, to converse with the back of someone's head, especially a frilled purple head underwater.

Too caught up in pursuit of magic. Their glory and their undoing.

For all the ancient wisdom this sea god represented, Greensleeves found herself thinking he was no older than someone's father: patient and wise, and a little tired, perhaps. Yet the conversation took place in seconds, so quickly did her thoughts flicker and receive answer.

The voice thrummed in her mind as they sank

deeper, farther out to sea. Greensleeves reflected it could be day or night up above, stormy or calm, summer or winter. But down here it would never change much. A world of infinite peace.

The sea lord spoke. *The Sages toyed with magic, fed on it, moved it, believed in it and little else. They were blind to the wishes of others. They intruded on my realm by fashioning the Copper Conch tribe of merfolk. I let them remain, but warned the Sages to never again tamper with my sea and shore and subjects. They saw the threat of the Brothers too late. Machines and plague and fire and mud engulfed them. The sea still suffers today, for many subjects are born sick or twisted and die before their time.*

Greensleeves thought of many questions, but the Lord of Atlantis told her, *It is wrong to dwell too much in magic, too much in anything. A being in balance questions all, learns from all, loves all. Do you comprehend?*

Yes, replied the archdruid, for it was the only answer. It was something she knew. Too much magic, or of anything, put a body and mind out of balance. It was good to be reminded. *Yes, I promise to keep life—and magic—in perspective.*

As I thought, came the reply, and a hint of dry chuckle. *Now come and learn.*

Greensleeves blinked. By the body-light of the sea god, she glimpsed the sea floor. Below was a forest of coral as large as the Whispering Woods, fantastically diverse. Mossy fish and shelled creatures walked and swam and flew through trees and flowers and plants and animals of every color and size and description. Streamers of kelp soared into the sky, and jellyfish like clouds rippled along, while squids jetted after flickering fish as bright as birds. A whole world, perhaps never seen by a human before, creeped and crawled and spun and thrilled and lived and died just under Greensleeves's feet, stretching in every direction.

She blinked and gasped as suddenly a cliff, an undersea mountain, loomed. A large sea cave gaped. With a single churn of his tail, the sea god propelled them inside.

There was no air in the chamber. It was a tunnel, or corridor, such as the army had excavated above ground, perhaps two dozen feet across and half that high. They skimmed down the corridor, the Lord of Atlantis swimming almost straight out, so his massive size might pass. The place was wholly black, had been for centuries, she guessed. But once it had been dry, for iron sconces decorated the walls. Most of the walls were covered with a fine fuzz of sea moss, and the floor was thick with lumpy half-formed coral that sported whitish crabs scuttling after pale fish.

Then she saw light ahead.

Familiar light.

The Lord of Atlantis swirled to a halt, setting scores of plants and animals aquiver in his undersea wind. Greensleeves felt a bump as his thick body touched the uneven floor, and she climbed down from his back carefully, as if dismounting a mad stallion.

She turned in a slow circle, staring. The ancient mossy walls glowed, so infused with mana were they.

The room was familiar, though she'd never seen it before.

Not with her eyes.

Unconsciously, Greensleeves touched her head, found her tousled hair floating gently like a halo. Her head was bare, yet felt covered. As if by a helmet.

The green stone helmet fashioned by the Sages ages ago.

It was here, in this room, they had made it, empowered it. She pictured them now, screaming at one another as devastation overtook them, and fire and stone and monsters smashed the tower down around their ears.

And later, some unimaginable force destroyed the

center of the college, sank its starfish arms to the sea bed. Dropped this entire wing, somehow intact, magically preserved, into the realm of the fishes.

Behind her, in the tunnel, the Lord of Atlantis watched her patiently. She wondered what she must find. At a step, something nudged her foot and she bent to pick it up slowly in the thick cool water.

It was a fragment of skull, only half the face. Barnacles and coral had encrusted it completely, like a living mask of stone and moss. As she watched, a tiny pink shrimp came questing out of the single eye-hole, feelers twitching on the undersea breeze.

"Who were you?" she wondered aloud. Her voice was loud in her ears because of water encasing her.

Then she remembered something Chaney had taught her long ago.

Sleep on a skull to commune with the dead.

Gently, fearful it might crumble, Greensleeves touched the coral fragment to her brow. It was rough with stony sea growth, yet she felt the kiss of wet moss, too.

"What was it?" she whispered to the ancient, dead Sage. "What was the secret of the stone helm? How did you intend to control evil wizards? Can you tell me? For I and my brother have sworn to stop evil magic where we may. We'll carry on your work, good master or mistress, but please—please—tell me the secret."

Deep inside her mind squeaked a raspy, scratchy voice almost stilled by age and encrustings.

Greensleeves listened hard.

And the skull told her.

A huge wave rolled into shore just as the sun was rising. In the trough of the wave rode the Lord of Atlantis. With a flick of his tail, he gently shrugged Greensleeves toward shore. She leaped into the breast-high water, turned to thank him again, but he was gone, only the churning waves to be seen.

Someone shouted.

Greensleeves struck out with an arm, caught her footing on the shifting pebble bottom, burst through the foam of the wave. Already she felt the spell, protection from water, dissipating. Yet when she stepped ashore, no more than her boots and hem were wet.

Along with the six bodyguards, Kwam had waited on the beach, and he ran into the swirling surf to embrace her.

"I found it!" Greensleeves spoke into his shoulder, as he hugged her tightly. "I found it, Kwam! I know the secret of the helmet! We can—"

But he was speaking at the same time, murmuring over and over. "—glad, I'm so glad! We couldn't move when you were pulled under! The merfolk told us nothing, only slipped into the waves after you! We feared sharks! I thought—"

Greensleeves stopped chattering, surprised by the fright in his voice. She hadn't thought of anyone worrying: she'd felt safe every minute under the protection of the Lord of Atlantis. But despite his panic, she was thrilled someone cared about her so, loved her so—

She was distracted. Up the hillside, above the forest, danced red-yellow light. Not the dawn. Fires: huge ones, out of control. And a roaring even the surf couldn't drown. Her Guardians glanced that way anxiously.

"Why, what's happening?"

The magic student touched the top of her head and kissed her there. "Another reason I worried about you. We're under attack again. The combined wizards have found us."

Flanked by six women with spears and swords, Greensleeves and Kwam stumbled in the smoky light up the trail toward the forest, only to find a pack of saber-toothed cats screeching at squealing mammoths along the forest's edge. A group of pale-skinned cave

folk spotted them, grunted wildly, and made as if to
hurl stone-tipped spears. Her bodyguards shouted
and raised their shields, but Greensleeves merely
sliced her hand in the air and shifted herself and her
companions to the camp.

Madness reigned. By the light of roaring campfires,
Greensleeves saw soldiers and sappers manned the
earthworks all around the huge mosaic, fighting bitterly against waves of shrilling marauders and monsters. Many soldiers were without boots or helmets,
so suddenly had they been roused from their
bedrolls. One woman named Hannah, who normally
sported four neat pigtails, had wild hair fluttering
around her head like streamers. Soldiers stabbed
with lances and spears to keep the mob from climbing over the palisade or chopping through it. Blue
barbarians, cave folk, and swarthy pirates screamed
and swung and swore and died. A number had
already wormed inside, and their bodies slumped on
the ramparts. At the rear, shouting them on, rang the
harsh bellow of the Keldon warlord.

Nor was this the only battle. Beyond in the scrub
forest, Greensleeves heard mammoths trumpet in triumph, horses scream in terror. The cavalry must be
fighting out there.

Surrounded by only six Green Lancers—the others
plugged gaps in the walls—Gull shouted orders and
encouragement that no one heard. He wore only his
kilt and toted his huge axe. In the yellow flickering
light his skin gleamed with sweat and other peoples'
blood.

He left off shouting orders to a sapper to bark at
his sister, "Where the hell have you been?"

"Under the sea. Where did they come from?"

"Who knows?" he shouted over the clash of battle
and windy howling. "Can you push 'em back?"

For answer, Greensleeves touched a spot on her
embroidered cloak, twirled her hand in the air, and

uttered a high keening spell like wind in the treetops.

Instantly smoke and ash whipped around her; her hair flew snapping and tangling. Wind spun all over the camp, a solid wall of it, shrieked like the tormented damned.

Plucked from some storm-tossed sea, the hurricane smelled of burned air and cool rain and sea salt. Greensleeves glimpsed an albatross and flying fish caught in its folds. Fitful, the storm blew in gusts and puffs capable of snatching a sailor overboard or snapping stout masts.

When the storm landed among the invaders, it hurled them sprawling into one another, blinded them, sucked the air from their lungs, battered their minds numb.

Yet even as it punished the foe, it avoided Greensleeves's followers, for a protection spell extended outward to the rim of the earthworks. She was the eye of the hurricane. Greens and Reds and Whites staggered as the curtain of rain and wind thrashed at arm's length. With their captains shrieking to fall back, men and women and dwarves tumbled from the ramparts, gazing in wonder at the circular wall like the inside of a giant's well.

"Don't spread the storm too far!" Gull warned. "Our cavalry and others are out there!"

His sister ignored him. Both hands clenched, Greensleeves maintained the protection sphere even as she increased the intensity of the storm. Above the shrieking wind they heard the crashing and smashing of branches in the forest, the screams of enemy wounded being crushed and bludgeoned by whirling debris.

Harder blew the storm, until rain and thundering billows began to leak through the curtain of protection, spilling water in muddy cataracts down the ramparts. People cupped hands to their mouths, for it grew hard to breathe. Many peeked uneasily at the archdruid, afraid of her power, afraid it ran out of control.

But Greensleeves held the storm intact, bottled on two sides, until her fists began to tremble, her arms ache, her body quiver. She bit her lip to hang on, but it felt as if wild horses were tearing her apart.

When she felt the danger of losing control, she muttered an unsummoning spell quickly.

In an instant, the storm was gone.

And Greensleeves collapsed like a split sail.

CHAPTER
17

PEOPLE BLINKED, QUIET, STUNNED.
One second the storm raged at hand like some
quivering cliff of granite, the next the sky was clear,
and by misty dawn light they could see the forest.
Branches drooped, wet leaves hung limply, and pools
of salty water steamed on the warm earth. Tumbled
amidst the mud and leaves were dozens of felled
invaders: tusked barbarians with their blue war paint
scoured off, pirates in sodden clothes, cave folk who
covered their heads to shield against sky gods. Slowly
the enemy force clambered to its feet, sunk half to
the knees in mud and leaves, stared dazedly around,
then skulked into the forest. Many never rose, beaten
senseless by the storm or else drowned in muddy
pools.

Equally senseless was Greensleeves, collapsed on
the mosaic tiles and surrounded by six flustered
bodyguards. The druid opened her eyes, head swimming. "The fighting's just started, and already I'm
more casualty than help. . . ."

"You've had a long night, mistress." Micka, the

brawny farm girl, carried the small druid to her tent
and lovingly laid her in bed.

Outside, as the rising sun burned seawater into
steam, captains and sergeants chivvied their forces
into order, saw the wounded toted to the hospital,
guards reappointed, gear fetched and weapons sharpened. Dionne of the Scorpions and Neith of the Seals
asked permission to slay stragglers, but Gull
declined, arguing it would serve little good to slog
through mud and a hostile forest. "Besides, those
troops aren't the real enemy. It's wizards and that
damned warlord we want. Better we see our people
get breakfast and harness. We've got a long day of
fighting ahead."

He rapped out more orders, then noticed his sister
was missing. When he found her in the musty tent,
he remarked, "Gad, you're handy!"

Greensleeves sat up and sipped honeyed tea. She
ignored the contradiction in his words: Gull hated
magic and wizards, yet praised his sister's wizardry.

A pair of lancers had fetched Gull's clothes. He
pulled on his leather tunic and boots and steel helmet. Handed dried meat and bread, he wolfed it as
he scanned the camp and surrounding woods. "We
should have cut the damned forest back farther. They
could shelter a herd of mammoths in there. But fine
time to think of it."

Greensleeves shook her head. Between lack of
sleep, meeting a god, visiting the sea bed, and con-
taining a hurricane, she could scarce remember her
name. But curiosity won out. "I wonder how Towser
and the bound wizards found us?"

"*Unbound* wizards. That magic failed, too."

Greensleeves's frayed temper flared. "I *told* you,
I'm a druid, not a jailer! I *don't* want to be responsible for them!"

Gull squinted at her, chewed, slurped warm beer
from a leather jack. "I'm not blaming you, Greenie.

These bastards are everyone's problem, one we've never solved properly. I'd just cut off their heads and been done with it, but that's the eternal argument." He shrugged it away. "And I don't know how they tracked us down. They might have sniffed out some of those glowing artifacts your students play with. Or there might be a spy in our ranks who signaled them. Maybe the minotaurs told them, or birds. I don't know. They're here and we must fight them, by the will of the gods. But, Balls of Boris, I hate magic!"

Greensleeves stifled a sigh. "Me, too, sometimes. But this gets us nowhere. What do we do now?"

It was Gull's turn to sigh. "The other old argument. We fight. Some of us die."

Greensleeves heard feet shuffle outside the tent. Her Guardians of the Grove knew about dying: they'd lost six of their number in three months. The only original member left was Caltha, who'd had her collarbone smashed.

The thought of more fighting and dying made Greensleeves slump. Arguments came and went with only one constant: the army's major goal was to stop wizards in their tracks, usually by fighting. Still, she offered, "We could shift elsewhere. Anywhere in the Domains." Her tone was plaintive and she hated it, but she didn't want to see anyone else hurt. And their problems seemed insolvable.

Her big brother shook his head. He hefted his axe, absently drew a sharpening stone from a pouch, and touched up the edge. "No. We've argued that topic too many times, too. They'd just find us again. And I'm not running anymore. We're fated by the gods to fight Towser's thralls to the death. So be it."

Greensleeves pushed herself off the cot, came to lean on the tent pole. As the camp was straightened, bodies were lugged past: men and women hacked to death by swords, pierced by spears, blinded by clubs and whips. Greensleeves suddenly wanted to cry. "I wish we didn't have to fight at all."

"I wish I were still a woodcutter," Gull muttered. "Lily wishes she could fly. Men wish for gold, women for love, children for sweets. Wishes mean naught—What did you say earlier, you'd been *under the water*?"

"Aye." She waved a dismissive hand. "I learned the secret of the helm, but it's nothing to help us now. I have to think what it means. I don't know what to do."

Gull grunted. "When you figure it out, let us know." He scanned the forest, fresh-washed and sparkling in the sun, and thumped his axe handle on the mosaic tiles underfoot. "One thing is clear. We've got to gather information, find out who's out there, then map a strategy so we don't get chopped to bits—eh?"

Someone shouted and pointed overhead. People shielded their eyes to squint into the eastern sky. High up, dozens of shapes flitted and flapped, soared and swooped, like swallows playing in updrafts. But sunlight winked on long shining steel and polished helmets.

"The angels carry swords, but not helmets," Gull mused. "Who do they battle? Who else flies?"

Greensleeves peered. The angels sailed amidst other winged folk in blue robes and golden armor. Sword strokes from the angels failed to slow the golden ones, but returning strokes wounded angels. As everyone watched, one angel plummeted in a trail of shorn bloody feathers toward the desert.

"Phantasms," Greensleeves murmured. "I think they fight phantasms. Shapes like ghosts you cannot touch, but can touch you. Kill you."

Gull swore. "More bloody backstabbing magic . . . Where the hell are my cavalry and scouts? They should have sent word by now!" He called for his horse and tromped off.

Greensleeves was left with her Guardians, yet felt alone. "Sometimes I wish I'd never heard of magic. . . . "

Surrounded by thirty Green Lancers, Gull galloped through the forest on the western trail to learn the fate of his cavalry bivouacked on the savanna. Small pockets of enemy troops tried charges, but the force brushed them aside and thundered on. Soon the scruffy trees thinned to copses and knee-high grass took over.

A picket sounded her trumpet and a squad, all centaurs of the Rose Company, charged to meet Gull's troop. By the bandages and tatters, Gull knew they'd been bloodied, too. The centaurs steered him toward Captain Helki's command post.

The she-mare and her staff were backed against a thick copse of fluffy-topped trees. They pored over a map. Nearby, human nurses tended the wounded, centaurs and cavalrymen and horses, all together.

"Helki!" Gull reined close enough to smell her, that odd mix of human and horse sweat, sweet grass, leather, and metal polish. Her breastplate had been scored by a sharp blade. Some of her messengers sported bandages, and one lacked a helmet. "How goes it?"

Helki's face was flushed inside the frowning helmet. "Squads of riders in blue slash our flanks. We try to guess how many, but they change so, we wonder if they shift in and out. We fight them as may. Infantry on flying carpets, too, come and go. Also, orcs hide in these groves, run out to stab our wounded, cowards be damned." Raiding her flanks she could forgive, for that was war. But killing the wounded angered her.

Gull scanned the grassy horizon, but too many copses and groves blocked the view. Occasionally a flock of large running birds galloped by like living bushes. In the distance he saw blue-robed cavalry—Karli's desert riders—pursued by a mixed human-centaur force. They ran, but dashed behind yet another copse, probably to circle and attack anew.

"You're too far out," Gull told his captain. "They're toying with us, slashing and running, just like the war in the Whispering Woods, trying to wear us down. They didn't resume their attack on camp this morning. They're hiding and regrouping, probably to pick off stragglers by day and raid us by night. Towser knows he might lose a head-to-head battle, because we're volunteers and he's got thralls. So he's using sneak attacks."

He craned in the saddle, waved back toward the scrub forest, a mile or more distant. "Pull your troops back to the edge, but leave some running room. Their cavalry won't venture into the forest to get behind you because it's too thick. And if you must, you can retreat down the trail to the camp. I think that will prevent their hamstringing you. And we'll find out who's actually opposing us."

"Yes." The she-mare nodded so her helmet bobbled. "Is good, will work, if that is truly their plan." She whirled to bray orders to the messengers, but a picket off to their left shouted. Curious, Helki and Gull spurred that way to better see.

At two bowshots' range, a large phalanx of desert riders, thirty or more, had formed a line abreast. At their center was a now familiar figure. The Keldon warlord.

The giant man wore his iron-fanged helmet and a flowing red cape, and carried in a stirrup cup a tall lance with a bloodred pennant. The beast he rode was some mutant, incredibly huge and burly, for no normal horse could carry him. The beast was a deep roan color, like dried blood, with a stiff scraggly mane and forward-jutting horns like a wild bull's.

At sight of the warlord, Helki shrilled. Centaurs and cavalry cantered to her side and formed their own line abreast. It was clear the centaur captain intended to charge. Gull's lancers, thirty of them, looked at him, eager to join the charge. Gull only raised a hand, thinking fast.

Helki shrieked another war cry, and her troops echoed it. Hooves chopped yellow grass, anxious to be off.

"*Hold!*" Gull hollered. All turned, puzzled.

His lancers scrambling to keep up with him, and Gull wheeled around the line, between Helki and the warlord. "I told you to fall back to the forest and I meant it!"

Within her shuttered helm, Helki frowned, unhappy with the orders. But, disciplined, she ordered her troops to break formation and retreat.

From afar came a harsh cry. "Cowards! Cowards led by a sniveling puling jellyfish! A *woodcutter* who plays at war!"

Gull whirled. The warlord taunted as his line walked steadily forward.

"Who *is* that bastard that he *hounds* me so?" Gull raised in his stirrups to shout back, "Not a fool, for sure! I won't play your game—I'll set the rules! Now find some helpless prisoners to torture, you—" and muleskinner's curses rang across the prairie.

For answer, the warlord laughed aloud, lowered his lance, and bellowed, "*Charge!*"

Before Gull knew what was happening, his cavalry troop shouted back. Someone, not Helki, yelled "Charge!" A trumpeter called the attack, and the line roared and kicked their mounts' flanks—

—and halted, milling and confused, as Gull blocked their path. "*I said no!*" He waved his axe by the head, swept the long handle back toward the forest. "Get back, the lot of you! That's an order!"

Helki, trained as a soldier since she could stand,

was aghast at her troop's breach of discipline. With real anger, she barked and snarled and sent her cavalry scything through the tall grass toward the forest, with the warlord's horsemen not a hundred feet behind.

Muley called the Green Lancers into position around Gull, and they followed, riding hard for the forest. The plain drummed to hundreds of hoofbeats.

Behind came a jeering shout and the bellowing of the warlord for Gull to stand and fight.

Wind in his face, Gull swore bitterly. He hated to run, but he had to protect Helki's troops, fewer in number. He couldn't let them sacrifice their lives in foolish charges. Watching the contour of the forest ahead, he bellowed, "Left oblique!" and horses and centaurs angled left.

"I don't like runnin'!" Muley panted as she galloped alongside. Her green pennant fluttered in the wind. "I'd rather fight!"

"You'll have a belly full of fighting before it's over!" Gull raised his voice. "Wheel here! Wheel and spread out!"

Trained to perfection, Helki's command spurred in a circle, tight as a flock of sparrows. Gull had aimed them to shoot a gap twenty feet wide between two brambly groves: straight into a pocket two hundred feet across. A narrow trail beckoned into the forest. Watching everywhere at once, Gull urged his lancers back against the forest, out of the cavalry's path. Waving his axe handle, he yelled for Helki to spread her force right and left. The she-mare caught his intent.

Within seconds, the cavalry was out of sight behind high brambles. Gull sat foursquare in the center of the pocket, in full sight, surrounded by bodyguards. The warlord's cavalry laughed to see him without true cavalry, thinking Helki's force had deserted their leader, fled down the forest trail.

Shouting death threats, they chopped up the earth with their mounts hooves and squeezed their line four abreast to shoot the gap.

And died.

Helki's cavalry ripped the enemy from two sides with lance and saber. Desert riders were torn from the saddle by long lances with rose pennants. Others were hacked from the saddle and crushed under sharp hooves.

Shouts of triumph turned to howls of outrage. Helki's centaurs and cavalry worked together, slid past one another, plunged long steel into enemy ranks and danced aside nimbly as deer. The desert riders' headlong charge ended only when, bodies of horses and men and women clogging the gap between brambles, the rearmost horses balked to enter the grove.

But the Keldon warlord, who'd hung back and watched his troops die, expressed neither rage nor remorse. He reared atop his war beast and shook a clenched fist. "Coward, Gull! You hide behind lesser mortals, behind this riffraff that strike from ambush! You're no leader! You're a coward and I'll rip out your liver with my bare hands!"

Still as a bronze statue, Gull sat his horse, axe across the pommel. The warlord's riders backed away, unable to drive their horses forward. Helki's troops waited, lances tilted skyward so blood ran down the shafts, or else with cavalry sabers hanging limp and dripping. They looked at Gull and wondered how he'd answer this abuse.

Gull did nothing, said nothing. He was puzzled.

Why, tolled in his brain, did the warlord hate him so? So intensely, so personally?

And why, for love of the gods, did his voice sound *familiar?* Gull had never seen this man, or anyone so huge, in his life. So why did this man's voice ring a bell?

After more cursing and ranting, the Keldon war-lord growled at his troops, yanked the reins of his queer monster-horse, and turned to leave. The thunder of their passage faded; dust settled.

When birdsong had returned to the glades, Gull barked, too loudly, "Helki, attend me!"

Gull stared at the gap where the warlord had departed as he spoke. "Helki, I want you to address your troops, make them understand. We're under attack as never before, with hundreds of foemen after our hides. And this time, we won't run, but fight to the death."

The Rose Cavalry and Green Lancers glanced at each other as Gull went on, "This army is all volunteers, not thralls conjured by a wizard. But our people joined to fight, not to throw their lives away. So I'm telling you and all the other captains to spread the word. Our cause might be hopeless. Therefore—"

The general, tall and straight on his dapple-gray horse, sucked in a deep breath, steadied his angry breathing. "Therefore, I'm calling *again* for volunteers, not to fight, but to die. Anyone wishing to live—anyone with sense—will not be condemned if they withdraw. Anyone wishing to leave should assemble on the mosaic sun at sundown. Greensleeves will shift them elsewhere. Most of the camp followers and children will go first, then anyone else. Is that understood?"

"Perfectly," said the centaur captain. Her back was straight, her lance unwavering. The rose pennant at the end fluttered in the breeze.

"Good. Any troops who opt to stay—and the gods have mercy on their souls—will remain at the edge of the forest and keep guard. Don't let anyone get sucked into traps: we'll need everyone who doesn't shift out. Understood? Good. I'm off to tell the other captains."

Wheeling, he and his bodyguards entered the forest by the narrow trail.

When the sound of their drumming hooves had faded, Helki raised her voice, pointed her lance at the trail. "You heard our general. Anyone wishing to leave, go."

Over a fast meal taken in a dusty hand, brother and sister talked outside their tents. The sun was low, and long shadows stippled the meandering mosaic stories and legends picked out in gay faded colors.

" . . . Gold Cavalry in the glass desert fight warriors in brown armor on scorpions and even half-scorpion folks. And big black birds like vultures that can rip a man's arm off. And in the forest, mammoths crush friend and foe alike. We've skirmishes all around us. Our scouts are ambushing barbarians with nothing but knives. And a librarian reported the merfolk battle charmed sharks as smart and deadly as wolves, but they've got these white-striped whales to help them. And . . . " He ran out of breath, gulped a mouthful of red wine. "And I don't know what all. I see no end to the fighting. If anything, it's intensifying. We won't get much sleep."

He stood and dusted off his clothes, tottering with weariness, and leaned a hand on Muley's wide shoulder to steady himself.

Greensleeves got up, too. She'd spent the afternoon conjuring walls of brambles and light, conjuring seawater and waterspouts to extinguish fires, causing small quakes that cracked the earth to separate warring factions, summoning wolf and wolverine packs to harry raiders. She was so tired she could cry.

But more, she dreaded what her brother prophesied would be the final battle, and either their deaths or the wizards'. In a large way, she couldn't help but think it her fault. If she didn't have magic-making, none of this chaos would be happening. People assured her that was nonsense, but deep down she felt it was true. And she had no idea how to stop the madness.

Gull squinted into the setting sun. "Come, Greenie. You need shift away the nonfighters and children."

Greensleeves wasn't even sure she could conjure any more today. Her arms ached and fingers burned. Her head throbbed from fretting and concentrating. She looked toward the central mosaic, where a crowd had been gathering for an hour. A lot of people to shift, she groaned.

But she hooked Kwam's elbow—patient Kwam, always ready and willing to help—and walked that way with her brother.

The crowd watched their two leaders thread past campfires and tents and piles of gear and cordwood and horse pickets. On the outskirts of the crowd, Gull noted Helki and Holleb, the tall centaurs, had ridden in, as had other cavalry troops who'd picketed their horses. But the crowd was eerily silent, where Gull had expected lame jokes and tearful good-byes. No one spoke, and a child who wailed was immediately shushed and hugged tightly.

The Green Lancers, as always, surrounded and preceded Gull, while the Guardians of the Grove trailed Greensleeves. As they approached, Muley barked, "Make way for the general and Greensleeves!"

The crowd parted.

Gull and Greensleeves stopped dead.

The center was empty.

Gull and Greensleeves failed to notice that their bodyguards—for once—didn't dog their heels. Kwam slipped loose of Greensleeves's hand. Brother and sister walked to the middle alone. Their entourage toed the lip of the sun circle, but came no closer.

Gull turned in bewilderment. Greensleeves looked down at the fat-cheeked smiling face with its frizzy rays, as if the sun could answer. "I don't understand. . . . "

Gull looked at the crowd around the sun circle. People were packed ten and fifteen deep, waiting and watching. But no one would set a toe over the line. He asked, "What's the meaning of this? Who's going to shift out?"

Silence, deep and warm from the packed bodies.

"Are you afraid to come forward? I said no one would be chastised for saving their lives, or their children's. Step forward, those who are going."

No one moved. Some stared the general in the face, and some looked away or down, but no one spoke.

Greensleeves felt a queer sensation in the pit of her stomach, as if she were falling.

Gull *tsk*ed. "Enough foolishness. We're wasting time." He singled out a man in a smudged apron, a blacksmith and armorer who carried a peeping child in a sack over his shoulder. "Ezno, your work is done here. Fetch your sons and daughters and—"

The smith licked his lips and slowly shook his head. "The cavalry need me to shoe horses, Gull. They can't fight otherwise."

Puzzled, Gull frowned. "Well, then, hand your baby there—Carine, didn't you name her?—to a nurse. They'll be shifting out." He pointed to a nurse, a fat woman with a wimple wound tight around her head and an apron of many pockets. Half a dozen children clung to her skirts. "Dasha, you've sense. Bring them forward—"

But Dasha, too, shook her head. "I'm a bad nurse, general. The children won't obey. And I can't leave them behind."

Greensleeves tried gentle persuasion. "Dasha, surely you understand it's not safe for the children. They'll be hurt, killed if we don't—"

"They want to fight," said the nurse. Beside her, a boy knee-high lifted a grubby hand to show off his toy bow and arrow.

Greensleeves's words died on her lips.

Gull shook his head and marched across the circle.

For the first time ever, he saw his followers shrink back as if he were a monster. Amidst them, Lily held Bittersweet, and a nurse held Hyacinth. Kwam stood alongside, looking pensive. Gull pointed. "Helki, help me here! Send in the troops who are departing—"

"There are none, my general!" called the centaur loud and clear. "Not one wishes to go!"

"But that's—" Gull reached for a cook with steam-straggly hair and only one hand. "Amissa, get out here! We'll be on cold rations—"

The cook pulled back as Gull grabbed her burn-scarred hand. She was too frightened to speak but, to the general's amazement, dozens of hands latched onto her shoulders and skirts. Stunned, Gull let her go.

Anger rose within him. "You can't all stay! It's stupid! We'll keep a core of fighters, folks with nothing to lose, and that's all! Amissa, you lost that hand when camp was overrun! A desert raider cut it off! You almost died! And you will die—Lily, help me!" In desperation, he turned to his sensible wife, but she only shook her head, eyes bright with tears.

Gull gave up. "Muley! Bring your lancers and we'll separate these fools! We can't spend all night—"

His jaw dropped as Muley pronounced, "No, General Gull. I'm sorry, but no. We won't enter this circle. Not now, not ever."

"Nor I," pronounced Ezno, the smith.

"Nor I," snapped Dasha, the nurse.

"Nor I," squeaked Amissa, the cook.

"Nor I!" called someone in back. "Nor I!" a voice echoed. "Nor I! Nor I! Nor I!"

The chorus went round and round the circle like a song. Gull could only shake his head. He raised his hands, the good right and the maimed left with only two fingers. "But—don't you see—it's death to stay behind! The wizards are sworn to destroy us, or enslave us, or worse! They won't—"

Louder, the army chanted, *"Nor I! Nor I! Nor I!"*

Gull tried to yell above them, but finally quit and just stood and wondered. "I thought I was the only stubborn damned fool in this army. . . . "

And Greensleeves, alone by his side, without even her beloved Kwam, cried.

CHAPTER
18

"WHY DO THEY DO IT, HELKI?"

Forgetting her manners, that centaurs hated to be treated as beasts of burden, Greensleeves slumped against her friend's warm flank. The centaur didn't protest. "Why do they work so hard, fight and die for me and my brother?"

"They don't," replied the centaur. "They do for themselves."

"Eh?"

Night had fallen, and bonfires lit the camp. Larger fires than usual. There was singing throughout camp, and roars of laughter, and toasting with mugs, and gay dancing. After Gull had given up trying to convince people to shift away, the camp had fallen to dinner. But gradually, as people savored their moral victory, a festival atmosphere sprang up, though pickets still manned the palisades.

Greensleeves found it horrible and confusing. She and Kwam had walked the camp and been greeted happily by many folk, until the druid encountered her centaur friends, still in armor and tackle, gossiping

with other cavalry. Greensleeves had tried to formu-
late coherent questions and had finally blurted out, "I
don't understand! They're going to die, probably, yet
they're happy to make the sacrifice! Gull and I aren't
worth that kind of devotion!"

"It is not for Gull and you." From her great height,
the centaur stroked the woman's tousled head where
she leaned against her flank; Kwam stood silently a
few feet away, listening. "People sacrifice for themselves. For their families, and their dreams to go
home. But mostly they sacrifice for cause."

"What is our cause?" Greensleeves stared at the
brilliant fires. "I've forgotten."

"They have not. Every day, with every task, people
work for the good cause you and Gull started. It
makes them bigger."

"What? How?"

Helki struggled to find the right words in a foreign
tongue. "Is not war, not army. Is crusade to stop wizards. It is—idea. Glorious idea. People attach themselves to idea, make it their own. They grow bigger to
match new idea in head."

"I—I don't understand."

Helki huffed, stamped. Her tail swished as she
thought. "I will tell you story. From time we traveled
in far west forest. Holleb then not as friendly as now.
But he changed." The man-stallion, standing nearby,
grunted, but Helki went on. "Listen, I tell. . . . "

The bandits were canny, and made no sound as they
leaped from the trees, long knives ready to slash and
stab.

But their prey, which crept along the densely
wooded trail, were not ordinary humans.

Holleb and Helki, centaur lancers, were scouting
for the army. They wore helmets and breastplates of
painted fluted steel, with war harness and gear

strapped along their powerful and glossy roan flanks. They carried lances as long as their bodies, decorated with bright feathers. The man-stallion, Holleb, stood almost nine feet tall, with arms like tree trunks and feathery white stockings above his massive hooves. Helki, his mate, almost as large, moved with no more noise than a wildcat.

As the two bandits, clad in rags and scraps of stolen armor and dirt, dropped from the trees, each centaur snorted a warning to the other.

Holleb's lance flashed and caught the first bandit, a young man, square in the belly. The razor steel head, a full handspan wide, sliced through the youth's liver and kidneys and ripped out through his back. As the dying youth slid bloodily along the shaft, the centaur coolly tipped the lance to slide him back off. With powerful red-hairy hands, Holleb twisted the lance at the last moment to further shred the man's guts, then flicked him away so his head smashed the bole of a tree. The robber was dead three times before he hit the ground.

Helki faced a woman trying to leap upon her wide horse back. Kicking with her back legs, the she-mare skipped to one side so the woman sprawled on the forest floor. The force of landing drove the wind from her lungs. Inverting her lance, Helki took aim and popped the iron-shod butt against the bandit's skull, stunning her. She gave another rap to the woman's jaw. The bandit flopped still.

Gazing down at her captive from her great height, Helki smiled with satisfaction.

But she bleated as Holleb slid alongside her and lanced the bandit in the belly. The woman jerked like a fish on a hook. Dropping his end, Holleb thrust upward to pierce her heart. The woman spasmed, spit bright blood, and died.

"Why do you kill her?" Helki spoke in the common language of humans, though barely above a whisper, since they were on scout. "Gull would have us capture our enemies if possible!"

Holleb's harsh growl came in the snorting, whinnying language of the centaurs of the steppes. He spoke thus whenever they were alone. "Gull is a fool. If you fling a rat from a grain bin, does it never return? These bandits raid our food wagons, steal and despoil, so we track them down. And stop them."

Gull the Woodcutter had asked the two to find the sneak thieves because none of his human trackers could follow their trail. With eyes that could see to the horizon, the centaurs could "track a bug across the face of the moon."

Helki inspected the buttcap of her lance to make sure it was tight. She flicked her lance tip across the woman's tattered clothing, found nothing but a knife scabbard and fleas. "We are not in the steppelands. Things are different now. We work *with* the two-legs. We must respect their ways."

Holleb caught yellow leaves from a bittersweet vine and carefully wiped the blood from his lance. He inspected the razor edge for nicks. "We work *for* the two-legs, as our people have always. But we must not become *like* the two-legs. They will never be half what we are. Things are *not* different. Do not forget that."

Helki shook her head. With one hand, she caught the dead woman by the hair, hoisted her, and stuffed her carcass through the bittersweet behind a stone wall, hiding the bodies in case more bandits came this way. "We cannot erase the blood."

"No matter. If they come through, they will be running with us in pursuit. And humans are blind, could trip over a buffalo. These hiding in the trees thought we could not see them."

He scanned the woods ahead and behind. Late autumn was trending toward winter. It had rained this morning, would rain again before early nightfall.

Yet the woods were still clad in brilliant colors. Leaves of yellow beech, orange pin oaks, and buff black oaks still formed a canopy like inverted sunlight in the forest. The air was musty-tangy from the perfume of red bittersweet berries and teaberries and tannin from oak bark. Flickering movements from the drop-spinning of leaves was distracting, but the centaurs adjusted their vision to screen out anything smaller than a human face.

With no more talk, they leveled their lances, spaced themselves two body-lengths apart, and resumed the hunt. The trail was level under their feet, almost flat. After another two hundred feet, it split abruptly, exactly left and right. Both avenues were marked by looming maple trees, their trunks so thick they'd tumbled sections of stone walls by pushing sideways.

Helki circled slowly. Centaurs liked to spin in circles, ready for any danger, rather than turn their heads—a habit they knew made humans nervous, who feared having their feet crushed under massive iron-shod hooves. Her tackle, a bronze sword, coils of rope, haversacks for food, chinked and rustled softly.

"Main street. Maples were ornamental trees."

Holleb grunted assent. They'd known ruins lay ahead when they struck the road, albeit inches thick with loam. Holleb tripped down one avenue, ducked and craned to see what lay beyond the stone walls and tree trunks, but the land was stacked in terraces and mazes and stone outbuildings. He returned to his mate. "Big gardens gone wild. Many pockets to search."

Helki had scouted the other avenue. "Old mansions. Is dry lake on that side, and old boathouse. But this must be back side of estates. A large city, there must be, off to west, to support this much big houses. All ruined, it would be, yet we should tell Greensleeves for searching of artifacts, and cartographers and librarians to put on maps."

Holleb snorted. Human history did not interest him.

The man-stallion peeked through leaves at the lowering sky, bringing rain and early evening, and made up his mind, though he disliked splitting their team. "We have not enough time to search everywhere. You go north, I south. If road is symmetrical, will meet before houses in west. If find trail, call like long-eared owl. Wait for me—do not go after them alone."

Helki hid a smile as she nodded. She knew all this, but liked to have her husband fuss over her. Centaurs, mated for life, cared for each other deeply, more deeply than humans could comprehend, Helki suspected. And despite his gruff exterior, Holleb was the sloppiest sentimentalist she knew. Holleb couldn't sing the old war songs, or recite love sagas, without breaking into tears. Yet it was these strong emotions, never far from the surface, that made him project such a crusty appearance, such ferocity in war and the cold dispatching of prisoners. And Holleb was sometimes wracked so badly by homesickness for their lost land Helki could barely drag him out of a funk. So she'd welcomed this scouting detail. Busy, Holleb was happy.

"Is good we work together. Like old times." He gave her a rare smile, a salute of his lance, and the oldest joke known. "Watch your tail!" Then, serious again, he trotted down the avenue, eyes scanning everywhere.

Helki sighed from deep in her bosom, then turned back to the road. They had enemies to track, somewhere in this overgrown maze. And not far off.

Peering from under the jutting brow of her painted helmet, Helki scanned the road for signs of disturbance. These bandits, she decided, were clever. They wore shoes of raw deerhide with the hair left on, and scuffed their feet as they walked, so they blurred the trail even as they laid it.

Turning a square corner, circling west, something flickered in her side vision, and she tensed. Crouching, down a dark tunnel she spotted a bruised aspen leaf twisted on its stem. Someone had brushed it, turned it bottom-side up, so the white veins glowed. Helki checked her back trail, lowered her front legs, and peered down the tunnel, an old cut through a stone wall. Yes, there were footprints made by at least three humans, probably two males and a woman with a narrower foot. But they were days old, long enough for ants to rebuild their crushed hill in the hollow of a heel. No tracks came out, so she decided to leave the trail alone and find its exit somewhere to the northwest.

The only disadvantage to centaur scouts, she knew, was their great size and fear of tight places, which made them reluctant to crawl down holes and tunnels.

A thrumming under her hooves warned someone approached on four sturdy legs. Whirling, she instinctively leveled her lance, made sure there were open reaches to run if necessary. But at the same time, she knew who it was.

Holleb tripped around the corner, knees high, feathery stockings fluttering. Muscles rippled under his glossy hide. His stockings were speckled with fallen beech leaves. Whispering, growling, he called in centaur, "I have found a trail!"

"Is so? Show me," said his mate. She waited until he came within a lance-length.

Then she thrust, straight and true, aiming for the spot above his breastplate and below his jutting chin. Muscles in her arms bunched and knotted as she slammed the shaft like a giant arrow launched from a ballista.

Before Holleb could lift his lance, the wide steel head pierced his throat, severed his windpipe and blood vessels, parted his spine. As Helki whipped back her lance, the wound sprayed bright blood in a gushing fan. The man-stallion barely blinked before his half-lopped head tilted and he crashed to the roadway. A beetle, awash in blood, climbed out of the sticky pool and up his long bronzed nose, across the unmoving eyeball.

"Fool!" spat the she-mare. She swiped her lance on the centaur's roan hide. It was no longer glossy, but fading like the fallen leaves. Before a minute had passed, the centaur had turned into a curled leathery thing like some big cracked seed pod.

Dancing with eagerness, Helki made sure the steel lance head was still fixed tightly to the shaft, and still sharp.

Then she dug in her hooves and galloped down the avenue.

Holleb saw the first threat, but not the second.

He'd traced the stone walls, found a trail similar to Helki's discovery. But this trail was fresh, only a day old to judge by the sharp damp edges to a footprint. This tunnel was high enough to accommodate even him, if he stooped, for it passed through a stone archway not ten feet into the brambles.

Lifting hanging branches with his lance, the centaur tripped silently under the archway. The briars were old ancient roses, he noted, as thick as ropes, studded with spikes, with tiny white buds clinging here and there. The space was a stone-lined courtyard, though only handspans of stone showed, the garden was so dense. A monstrous mountain ash had buckled flagstones from underneath, as if the tree had shuffled its roots. Saw-edged leaves and clusters of dark yellow berries filled the sky above his head.

Ducking under the branches, disliking the close quarters, Holleb scanned the mixed foliage underfoot for crushed leaves that marked the passage of people. But no sooner did he enter than something filled the opposite archway and made him snap up his lance.

His mate. "Helki! What—"

From behind the stone walls, taller than his head, leaped four ragged shapes obscured by gray clouds.

Nets.

Holleb jerked up the butt of one lance and caught a bandit in the gut. The filthy ratty-haired girl whooped and folded around the wood. Not bothering to shake her off, Holleb whipped the lance the opposite direction and ripped a bandit through the thigh. But another thief thumped onto his wide back. He felt a burning pinprick as a short knife sank into his ribs. He jerked back an elbow to brush the assailant off, but the man ducked and the centaur missed. Holleb felt another jab, gritted his teeth and ignored it. As long as the thief didn't saw at his spine, he'd probably be shaken off soon. A net tangled his right arm and lance butt, and another whapped into his helmet, obscuring his vision.

Helki rushed to aid her mate. Screaming a war cry, she clubbed aside a woman who scuffled with a net, knocking her into a tall clump of rhododendron that clicked and chittered. Helki's intervention gave the man-stallion time to dislodge the nets. One net he shrugged off his helmet and flicked it behind to entangle the man with the knife. The other he stamped underfoot, then bunched his arm to shred it. It was woven of hemp, strong enough to tether an ox, but Holleb was stronger than any ox.

There were no more attacks, for two bandits scuttled through the archways, and the one trapped in the bush scaled the wall like a squirrel and dove over, white rump showing under her torn tunic. The last one wheezed on the ground, rolled and tried to crawl away. Helki banged the butt of her lance on the bandit's neck to shock her into stillness.

"We do well together, like old times!" she crowed.

"No," intoned Holleb. "Things are different."

From three feet away, he drove the lance into her

side just behind the breastplate. Helki shrilled, shied away from the awful pain, but Holleb stepped in closer, twisted to grind the barbed head through her liver and guts, to tear her apart inside.

Yet the she-mare only stared with wide brown eyes full of sorrow. When she opened her mouth, blood splashed from her lips onto Holleb's face. She begged, "Why—"

And Holleb had a horrible thought. That he'd been overconfident, had struck too quickly.

That he'd made a mistake and killed his mate.

Horror gripped him, froze him. Visions of Helki flashed through his mind: her running wild and free and unclothed along the rocky steppes, sunlight glinting on her flanks, taunting him to catch her; grinning fiercely at him as they galloped into their first battle, making him laugh to overcome the fear; currying his flanks as they frolicked in a waterfall pool miles from the tribe. . . .

Mesmerized by horror, Holleb failed to see one of Helki's hands transform into a jagged scaly hook like a mantis's claw. The hook curled upward, slashed for his throat—

—and flopped to the leaf-strewn floor, sheared off neatly at the wrist. Blood spurted onto Holleb's breastplate, but this blood was brown.

Helki—the real Helki—had leaped in one bound through the archway, scythed down with her razor-sharp lance, and lopped off the monster's hand before it could tear out her husband's throat.

The she-centaur swiped sideways with her lance and slit the back of the monster-Helki's neck as if slicing a melon. Eyes rolling, the phantom crumpled to the garden floor. Within minutes, it curdled to a brown lump cloaked in baggy brown leather, like some giant discarded cocoon. The creature's face was long and angular, tight-strung with muscle, dry as a mummy's.

Holleb groaned with relief to see his mate alive, to realize he hadn't killed her. "But what is—"

Helki nudged the dead leather bundle with her lance. "Doppleganger or clone. I know not which. A thing that mimics, is all. Perhaps smart enough to fool human, half-blind as they are, but not eyes of centaur. One came to me, spoke in your voice. But it had leaves in stockings, did not know real Holleb would remove them lest they scuff and make noise. And had not the pucker in your right haunch where arrow long time ago struck." She looked up at her mate and grinned. "Mostly did not have smile hiding behind eyes."

Holleb chuckled, a raspy rumbly sound. "That was what I missed. Its eyes were dead, while yours are like sunlight through waterfall. But I was frightened because it did not change when I stabbed it."

With an expert twist, Helki hooked the doppleganger's shoulder with a barb of her lance and flipped it over. The stab wound Holleb had made was low on the creature's withered brown body. "You struck where liver and lungs would be on centaur. Yet only bowels there on this thing. Not killing blow, so it hung on, kept my shape to strike you with claw. Perhaps could heal self quickly."

Holleb nodded sagely. But he pulled off his helmet and mopped his sweaty brow. His mohawk hair was plastered to his skull. "I worried, thought I struck too fast, without thinking. . . ."

Helki smiled, tripped forward and kissed him on the chin, nuzzled his long nose with hers. "You are too smart to be fooled for long, my proud warrior."

The centaur only looked sheepish as he resettled his helmet. "Let us gather the bandits. It will not take long."

It didn't. Within an hour they had rounded up the four remaining bandits and trussed them in the garden courtyard. Dazed from blows to the head and body, the ragged scoundrels sat on the flowerbeds and stared straight ahead, shivering, awaiting death.

Helki propped her lance butt on the ground, half-leaned on it, and asked her mate too casually, "What we do with them?"

He pointed to his ear, indicating he was ready to listen, and pointed at the bandits. "Talk."

Startled, the bandits glanced at each other. Finally, the eldest female, dirty-faced and snarly-haired, whimpered, "We didn't mean any harm! We only stole food! We didn't have any choice! Those things made us do it! They were ancient, hiding here since these were settled homes, living like vampires. They could look like anyone. Your mother, your best friend . . . They lured us here and we had to steal to feed 'em! Some tried to run away, but it killed them—"

Holleb raised a hand and the woman flinched. He reached behind, scratched where a bandage covered two pinpricks in his back. The woman rolled her eyes, expecting torture.

Finally the man-stallion spoke. "We should kill you for crimes. Is sensible. But . . . " He glanced at Helki and muttered, "But Gull believes should turn enemies into friends. Such he did with us, took us into his army when we were abandoned far from home. Our army needs scouts. If you can steal food so clever and leave no trail, would make good scouts. Will you accept?"

It took a moment for his words to sink in, then came relief. The woman babbled, "Yes, yes! We'll join! We'll do whatever you say! Gladly! Anything to get out of these ruins!"

Holleb raised a hand to shush her. He couldn't abide the way humans chattered. With a flick of a mighty wrist, the lance licked out and severed their bonds. Warily, the ex-bandits scrambled to their feet. Holleb nodded his head toward the archway and the road to camp. He rumbled, "Know you the way?" It was a full minute before the new scouts realized he'd joked, and laughed nervously.

As the party tripped through the autumn woods, Helki asked Holleb in the language of centaurs, "You change your mind these days, my husband?"

"No," he pronounced, but grinned. "But things are different, whether I like or not. And Gull will be pleased."

His mate snickered and bumped his rump with her own. "So will Helki. . . . "

"So," Helki finished telling Greensleeves the story, "Holleb found big idea, accepted it as his own. But because idea is bigger than him, he grows to match it.

"See?" The centaur trotted in a small circle to face her gloomy friend. "Think how far you have come. You were halfwit, simplemind. Gull cut trees, could have stayed woodcutter forever. Lily was whore, could have pleasured men till old and ugly and tossed into street. Liko simple giant who catch fish. Stiggur cook's boy. Egg Sucker thief. Holleb and me mercenaries, fight whoever pay us. But all these folk accept idea of crusade, grow bigger, accomplish great things together.

"Gull becomes wise general, far-sighted and strong but fair. Lily is good mother and quartermaster. You are mighty wizard, help many many people. Stiggur learn to work engines, very smart. Even Liko helps us. Even Egg Sucker, perhaps. Kwam, your friend, learns much and tells us. And Holleb, as shows my story, accepts two-legs as friends.

"*That* is why we fight and work and dig and sacrifice and maybe die! Not for no reason, but for goodness of crusade! Idea makes people strong, and they give back to idea."

"But all the fighting, the dying! If I'd never learned magic—"

Helki shook her helmeted head, mane wagging behind. "As long as army exists, seeks out wizards to battle, will be a target to attack. But what else? Disband army and go home? Leave wizards to rule range, tyrannize folks as they wish? This army is hope for all common folk in Domains!"

Greensleeves digested the new thoughts. "But Gull and I—"

"You and Gull are symbols, like king and queen, or gods, or flag, or homeland. You are leaders of idea."

"Leading to fighting and dying."

"If need be. But work, too, turn land from bad to good. Help villages. Make friends of new races. Learn history. Draw maps. Collect magic things. And teach wizards lesson."

Greensleeves sighed. "I wish the idea was as clear to me as it is to everyone else."

Helki patted the archdruid's tousled head. "In time. All things in time." Linking arms with Holleb, the two trotted off into the night, tails swishing, leaving Greensleeves and Kwam alone in the darkness.

"We don't *have* time. None at all," Greensleeves grumbled. She stared at the winking stars overhead. "Yet if all these folk will fight to the death, fight to *stay* and fight for what they believe in . . . how can I not?"

"How not indeed?" said Kwam. And he kissed her.

But she clung to his neck, weeping. "Oh, Kwam! I don't want you to die!"

The magic student kissed the top of her head. "I don't want to die, either, or for you to die. But what else should we do, shift away somewhere? Go hide in the Whispering Woods?"

"Of course not," Greensleeves sniffled. "I couldn't leave . . . these loyal folk . . . behind . . . "

Kwam smiled and wiped away her tears with his finger. "Ah, for the beginning of wisdom . . ."

CHAPTER
19

THE FIGHTING RAGED ON, EVERYWHERE throughout the land, day and night.

A goblin balloon brigade was pierced by angel swords and drowned in the ocean. Uthden trolls erupted from tunnels only to be knocked silly by dwarven hammers and mattocks. Sedge trolls lurking in the forest were lanced by scouts with boar spears, until nettling imps striking at the scouts' eyes with thorns drove them back. A horde of white-haired, tall-tusked, blue-painted barbarians were tumbled and routed by a craw wurm, then ridden under the hooves of a centaur company. But a wall of tombstones diverted the horsefolk into a field of caltrops, where many were crippled. Elven archers killed orcs by the score, but in their battle hysteria, pursued their ancient enemy into a trap and were mauled by Red soldiers with locked shields. Merfolk with dolphin allies fought charmed sharks and folk who were half killer whale. Archers shot wyverns from the sky, yet died from the poisonous blood sprayed upon them. Black-bearded men with scorpion bodies and bronze armor slashed and stung cavalry in the desert of crazed black glass.

Battles were huge, spread for miles over plains, or small and personal, with the fighters gasping and grappling in the dark. Immugio, the ogre-giant, and his orcs met in the forest with two-headed Liko and his twin clubs and Stiggur's clockwork beast, as well as a dozen camp followers toting hammers and cleavers and makeshift weapons. The two giants shook the earth as they slammed into one another, rocking back and forth, trampling friend and foe, breaking branches and uprooting trunks, all while Stiggur shot his two-yard crossbow bolts and orcs screamed and gibbered and died. Only a forest fire engendered by Immugio broke off the combat, but Liko suffered a broken arm and a shorn ear. The clockwork beast was heaped with wounded and dying as it stumped back to camp.

Always the main camp was attacked, and time and again the attacks repulsed. Greensleeves stayed close to home, conjuring defensive spells. She summoned zephyrs to blow away clouds of yellow gas that withered flowers on the vine and caused people to fall retching, their mouths and throats burned. She summoned walls of brambles, red earth, fire, stone, and light to drive back screaming hordes. Fire sprites rose in smoking clouds to beat back rapacious vultures that clawed at soldiers' faces. She called up dryads to entwine in vines a basilisk that turned a child catatonic with its vicious bite. She conjured a pack of wolverines to gobble up a storm of rats that dropped from the trees.

When able, she shifted with her bodyguards to other arenas to help as she might. A timber-wolf pack scared away phalanxes of cavalry. She visited upon a clutch of disheveled berserkers a wanderlust spell, so they gave up their fight and ran off into the desert, following some vision. She cracked the earth into gullies and toppled trees for barricades and diverted streams to turn dirt into quagmire. She conjured until she was dizzy and made mistakes. Once she shifted around the campfire of some cave folk roasting a horse. Immediately they seized their weapons and fell upon her party, and brawny Micka was brained saving her mistress's life before Greensleeves could shift away.

At that point, she was too weary even to cry.

"What infuriates me," Gull rasped, "is that we see so little of the damned wizards themselves! They hide back there—way back from the lines—and hurl wave after wave of thralls at us, and none of them bruise so much as a finger!"

The general slumped against an earthen rampart and gnawed a haunch of salt pork. Gull was hollow-eyed, unshaven, and shaky-handed from days of fighting. He'd gone without food and sleep until even his great strength flagged.

They talked by flickering firelight, a fire made of a smashed barrel. No one could gather proper firewood, and the camp was dark. Greensleeves's Guardians and Gull's Green Lancers, their numbers halved, stood watch in a rough circle, most asleep on their feet. The rest of camp was quiet as soldiers and camp followers patched gear and bandaged limbs and brewed tea and shifted barricades and waited for the next assault. Through their soles they felt the chink of dwarves at work in the tunnels.

Gull ate as he talked half to himself. "The elitist bastards sit back there, probably sipping red wine and eating honey cakes, while their pawns make suicide attacks and their horses founder and fold up and die. I saw Immugio come to grips with Liko, and Ludoc urging his cave folk forward, or perhaps those are Dwen's. That cursed Keldon warlord strides like a god and pushes fighters into the jaws of death. Haakon no longer summons demons, I know. Dacian

is dead; she was falling-down drunk and botched a
spell, and one Hermine's archers pegged her.
Leechnip is supposed to be dead, but something gobbled up all the corpses back there in the sedge. Fabia
was driving a gold chariot pulled by four white
horses until the angels dispatched them and she disappeared. And Queen Thunderhead of the goblins
has run off, someone thought. But of Towser and
Karli I've seen no sign.

"But I'm just as good at killing troops. We had
over a thousand when this campaign began. Now
we're lucky if we've six hundred still on their feet. I
can barely walk without tripping over our dead and
wounded."

Greensleeves nodded wearily. Too tired to eat, she
lay with her head against a saddle and sipped spring
water from a silver chalice. "I know well our losses.
I've shifted more corpses than I can count—ours and
theirs—deep into the desert. Vultures are thick as a
thunderhead. And the sneak attacks . . . Today one of
my bodyguards insisted on tasting my food and came
down sick as a dog, though how the poison was
introduced is beyond me. And I'd have taken a dag-
ger in the back from an invisible intruder if Nashira
hadn't accidentally bumped her and clubbed her
down. It's horrible to find oneself so hated."

Gull growled, "I can't even remember what we're
fighting about. Towser and his toadies are out to kill
us is all I remember, and we're out to keep them
from killing us, and hundreds of innocents are caught
in a meat grinder between us."

Greensleeves jerked awake, for Gull's words
reminded her of the laments she'd made to Helki the
other night. But Lily answered for her. "I remember."

Gull's wife was almost invisible with a dark cloak
around her shoulders. She sat on dirty tiles nursing
Bittersweet while a nurse cradled a sleeping
Hyacinth. Lily was glad to be near her husband,

whom she'd only seen intermittently for days now. As quartermaster, she'd coordinated efforts to keep food and water and supplies flowing through camp and out to the scattered forces, all the while disposing of sewage and garbage from the camp to hold down infection and plague. Her hands trembled from exhaustion as she stroked her baby's dark curly hair.

"The purpose of our crusade is, and always has been, to stop the predations of wizards upon innocent folk. We came here, to these ruins, to gather knowledge for stopping wizards, and they've come to defeat us. But we'll find the knowledge, brush them back, chain them, and see they never harm anyone again. I know this, and so do you, and everyone in the army. Don't lose sight of the goal."

Gull grunted, but he nodded. Greensleeves sighed. A quest for knowledge, she recalled. She'd descended the sea with the Lord of Atlantis after a secret for controlling wizards. She'd asked a skull and gotten answers, or more questions, for the whole trip was a jumble in her head, like a shattered dream.

A Green Lancer called a challenge, then let pass Stiggur and Dela and Egg Sucker. The boy limped with a bandage around his calf, a thin scruffy copy of his hero, Gull. Egg Sucker, with his skunk-striped hair and ragged rabbit skins, looked like something from a garbage heap. The goblin eyed Gull's leg of salt pork hungrily, and Gull sighed and flipped it to him.

Stiggur reported, "Another attack masses to the north. Perhaps a hundred or more blue barbarians and cave-folk. I saw them from atop Knothead." He'd named the ancient clockwork horse after Gull's long-dead mule.

With a groan, the general rose. He slugged a mug of water, for they had nothing else to drink, signaled a cook's helper for food to take with him. A boy brought a basket of dried herring, curled brown chips salt-rank and musty. Gull picked up his nicked woodcutting axe and reached for a handful of flakes. "Stiggur, run around the palisade and notify the captains. I'll see—*what the hell?*"

With a bound like a hare, Egg Sucker leaped at Gull's hand and snatched away the dried fish. The basket tumbled, spilling brown chips on the ground and into the campfire.

Weary unto death, Gull's temper exploded. He grabbed the goblin by the scruff and shook him hard enough to snap his neck. "Bells of Kormus! You filthy little scut! Can't you get your own food for once without stealing—"

He stopped as Lily screamed.

Scattered in the murky firelight lay dried herring like brown bark. But a dozen chips writhed.

Cursing, Gull raised his big boots and stamped and stamped on the crawling curls. Stiggur joined him, as did many of the bodyguards; the circle looked like a manic dance.

When nothing moved on the ancient tiles, Stiggur squatted beside the fire and poked at the broken chips with the end of his knife. "Scorpions! The whole basket was crawling with scorpions hidden in the fish!"

The cook's boy stood horror-struck at the edge of the crowd. "It was just on the table in plain sight, was all! Jotham told me to fetch them to the general! But I didn't—"

Someone shushed him, patted his shoulder. Gull rasped, "T'wasn't your fault, boy. We've had assassins in camp before—eh?"

In the excitement, Gull had retained his grip on Egg Sucker. He set him on his feet, but the goblin collapsed. Shocked, Gull knelt by the tiny thief's side.

Egg Sucker writhed as if from chills or fever. His gappy yellow teeth chattered. The goblin clutched his own wrist; his right hand was swollen three times normal size.

"What . . . ?" Gull grabbed the goblin's hand. "You were stung! Love of the gods, Egg! You shouldn't have stolen my—"

But Lily interrupted him. She stood with her baby folded in the cloak against her breast. "Hush, Gull. Egg Sucker didn't try to steal your food. He saw the scorpions in your hand and knocked them away."

"What?" Fuddled, Gull looked from his wife to the shivering goblin. Clumsily he accepted a cloak from a lancer and wrapped the small frame. Egg Sucker's eyes started from his head, his breath hissing as poison coursed through him. "Egg, that doesn't make sense! You—you saved my life! Why?"

Looming above him, Muley, captain of the Green Lancers answered, "Any of us would do the same."

Gull clutched Egg Sucker to his breast, as if he could infuse the creature with his own life force. "Greenie, can't you do something?"

Greensleeves shook her head as tears ran down her cheeks. "Not against poison. No."

Gull rocked Egg Sucker like his own child. "Why did you do it, Egg? You've always been—you never— you could have gone back to your own people at any time, you know. There were goblins fighting against us. You could have joined them."

Egg Sucker's shivering suddenly stopped. His voice creaked like a hinge, already distant. "I—I just—likes being with—you lot—" The voice dried up, and he was gone.

People rubbed noses and eyes, snuffled against their cuffs. Gull rocked the dead goblin. "It's foolish to mourn him. He was a useless wretch, stealing and mucking about, causing us grief. He didn't have to give his life to save mine. . . ."

Then he cried quietly, his cheek against the lank skunk-striped hair.

"It's true what they say," Lily pronounced quietly. "Love conquers all. And it's for love of others we fight."

The dam broke that night, and the exhausted defenders could no longer stem the flood.

Stretched thin, slowed by fatigue, one wall of the White Century gave way before the howling horde. Gull barked to his Green Lancers to follow, and outran them to the breach, but swarthy pirates had uprooted the stakes of the palisade and broken through, already leaping over the bodies of the dead and stampeding onto the mosaic sun circle. With sword and club and cutlass and spear they carved into the defenders—men and women, soldiers and campfollowers, elders and children. Roaring defiance, swinging his double-headed woodcutting axe so fast it whistled, Gull smashed into a knot of pirates like an avalanche, with his bodyguards crowding behind. Stamping and shouting and swinging by the red smoky light of guttering campfires, they slew the pirates, only to find blue barbarians and cave folk and more pirates ravaging the rest of the camp.

Propped up by Kwam, Greensleeves fought to muster the mana necessary for conjuring. Spells fizzled at her fingertips. Neither rain nor wind nor quake could she drag along her ethereal tags, nor even seawater, which lay only a quarter-mile away. She gave a gasp, raised her hands, and pitched backward in a faint. Only Kwam prevented her smashing her skull against the ancient tiles, while Guardians fended off fiends with their long wicked spears.

Gull saw his sister, their last hope for defense, collapse. He shouted to Muley, "We've lost this place! Form a ring and fall back to the shafts! We'll make a stand in the tunnels! Trumpeter!"

A peal cut through the shouting and clash of arms: the call to retreat. As planned, men and women grabbed weapons and children and scampered toward the twin ramps to the tunnels. Soldiers ringed the entrances and shouted, urging them down. Gull ran hither and thither with his lancers, slashing viciously to drive back knots of foemen so his people could escape. In the milling chaos and smoke and fire and darkness, he couldn't be sure everyone was rescued, but Muley yanked on his tunic, begging him to fall back. They did, stabbing and swinging, losing a lancer every minute as the frustrated marauders found fewer enemies and concentrated on the famous General Gull.

By the time Gull reached the ramp, he had a dozen lancers left. Muley bled from cuts on her arm and face, and others were similarly hurt. Though he didn't know it, Gull was bleeding down his neck, his calf, his ribs. But he shouted everyone into the tunnels and was almost the last to enter.

As he fell back, lancers pressing against his ribs, the mob came after him into the shaft, howling for blood. Only when Gull passed the doughty Uxmal did the dwarves spring their last defense.

Shouting in their guttural foreign tongue, they knocked away wooden supports and shoved on a hinged stone two feet thick. Cantilevered by weights, the huge door slammed shut across the entrance to the tunnel. A hand and foot, lopped off, fell to the floor of the tunnel. Three barbarians were trapped inside and were quickly cut down.

In the sudden quiet and close darkness, Gull slumped against the wall and wiped his forehead, found it sticky with blood. To his wounded followers and the dwarves, he croaked only, "Good work."

Then he fumbled through the darkness to find his family.

Greensleeves revived to find Kwam looming over her in semidarkness. Smoky torches lined the ancient painted walls. Gradually she understood she was in the tunnels, safe for the moment. But when she sought to summon something, anything along the invisible tags that surrounded her like spiderwebs, she found only emptiness.

"Kwam, I've lost my conjuring ability! I can't summon!" Then she was crying, for fear, for loneliness, for worry, for sheer exhaustion. Kwam held her as she sobbed, but she soon gave it up. Crying was too tiring, and they had no time for it.

Gull joined them, cradling his daughters in both arms with Lily following behind, a hand on his belt. No other officers were present, for they were scurrying through the halls and corridors rounding up their followers, seeing their defenses were not breached. Uxmal and his dwarves were off at the ends of the various boltholes, paving the way for escape up to the forest and out along the sea cliff.

Gull didn't waste time. Juggling his children, he asked, "Greenie, can you shift us out of here?"

Greensleeves laid her head against cool stone, accepted a water bottle from Kwam and sipped from it. She was sorrowful no longer, just resigned and trying to make the best of it. "No, not tonight. Maybe never. I'm as bereft of magic as a candle with no wick. I've squandered it over too many days. I don't even know if my conjuring will come back."

Strangely calm, Gull nodded. "Oh, well. This last stand has been a disaster all around. It's appropriate we can't flee by magic. I never liked it anyway."

Around them, soldiers stropped weapons and tightened belts, shuffled into squads as their captains ordered. Everywhere lay the wounded, groaning or grinding their teeth in anguish; healers moved among them, helping as they could. Torches came and went, odd shadows creeping along the walls, masking the fatigue and resignation in peoples' faces. A sergeant bound Muley's head where she'd been clipped below the helmet, then reached toward Gull. Gull waved the healer away, ordering him to tend the others.

Greensleeves said, "We're trapped down here. Until the dwarves break out our boltholes."

Gull sat down heavily, shot his legs, winced as dirt

ground into a calf wound. "That won't be much help.
Some might escape only to be cut down by desert riders or barbarians or trolls or whatnot. Unless Liko
and Stiggur and our cavalry are still alive to help
defend. But it's not much of an answer: I ran out of
answers long ago. I wish now I'd insisted some folks
shift away, but no one would leave, so they've none
to blame but themselves. Though they can blame me
if they wish. I don't mind."

Lily put her hand on her husband's. "They'll sing
songs and spin legends about you forever, Gull, and
you, too, Greensleeves. Wherever people are oppressed
by wizards, some storyteller will say, 'Let me tell you of
Gull and Greensleeves and how they fought wizardry
with their last breath.'"

Gull actually chuckled. He chucked his big-eyed
daughter under the chin. "When they smash down
those stone doors, some of us will defend the tunnels
while the rest flee. That will be me and my lancers.
You'll have to take our daughters and go, Lily."

Lily didn't argue. Her eyes were moist in the torchlit darkness.

Kwam passed around his water bottle until it was
it dry. Greensleeves held her lover's hand. She wondered if she asked him to go, would he? Probably
not. He loved her too much. More than she deserved.

She tried to think constructively. "What else can
we do? Could we negotiate with Towser and Karli?
Offer ourselves as hostages to let the others go free?
Sacrifice ourselves? Would they honor that?"

And she thought again of Chaney's talk of the
"final sacrifice" and wondered if the dead druid
watched her student now. Greensleeves was willing
to give her life to save her followers, but was it
enough? Would it even help? She squeezed Kwam's
strong hand.

Gull clucked his tongue, as he'd clucked to his
mule team long ago, and shook his tousled head.

"Perhaps. They want us body and soul, it's true. But they wouldn't let our army escape and reform."

"It couldn't reform without you, General. And Greensleeves," said Muley in the darkness.

White teeth showed as Gull grinned. "Yes, it would. It must. We're not important. Helki could lead the army, or Varrius, if he's still alive. Lily could. Or you, Muley. No, we're too dangerous to wizards. They'll throw monsters and murderers at us till we're just a memory. So I really don't know . . . what . . . "

People craned to hear, heard only silence, and saw Gull was asleep, his head against the stone wall, his daughter Hyacinth curled on his chest under his maimed hand, thumb in her mouth.

They sat quietly, each alone, and thought.

Gull dreamt.

He'd had many dreams lately, when he could snatch sleep, his mind ajumble from visions and reality mixed together.

This time he was back in White Ridge, the village where he'd been born, but it was ruined, rent and burnt by an earthquake, the houses fallen, the riverbed dry.

Yet there were no enemies about, only his family.

He stood alone in the middle of the village, cool under a hot sun. Far off, on the next ridge, stood his family, those who'd died from stone rain and weakness and plague. His father, Cinnamon Bear, was no longer bent at the waist from a broken back, but upright and whole, looking much like Gull except grayer. His mother, Bittersweet, blocky and broad, stood smiling, her hair as golden as corn under the sun. Beside them were his brothers and sisters, Rainfall, Angelwing, Poppyseed, Lion, and Cub, so small he didn't even have a proper name yet, just a nickname from following his older brother about. The only one missing, he realized, was Sparrow

Hawk, his younger brother of the red hair and freckles, impulsive and mischievous, last seen running around a barn to battle red soldiers three times his size.

Gull wondered idly, If he were viewing the dead, why was Sparrow Hawk not among them? If dreams meant anything (for he knew he dreamt), did it mean Hawk was alive somewhere?

Gull wanted to run to his family. It was wonderful to see them, but heartbreaking to be so near and come no closer. He wanted to hold them and hug them and pull Poppyseed's pigtails once more, but his feet were rooted to the spot. And that was right, part of him knew, for he was alive and they dead, and should not mix, though they could communicate in dreams.

Gull called across the distance. "I'm sorry! I'm sorry I've failed to bring these wizards to justice! I've tried my best, but it wasn't enough!"

Yet his family wasn't listening. They pointed, all of them, behind Gull's shoulder.

Unsticking his feet, Gull turned in the fog-dampened slow-motion of dreams, and saw Sparrow Hawk grinning at him from the next ridge. His brother held up a rusty spike for a sword and waved toward something over the next ridge. In the mistiness of dreamstuff, Gull could not see what it was. Wondering where this dream led, he shuffled after Sparrow Hawk, obeying his parents, leaving them behind once more. . . .

Why should he follow Sparrow Hawk? Where might the boy lead? And what . . . ?

Suddenly Gull woke. And understood.

"Gull!" Lily shook him. Groggily, he unstuck his eyes, scuffed his feet to get his neck off the wall. "Gull! There's a boat out on the water, and Towser's in it!"

Muzzy-headed, still exhausted, Gull crawled to his feet. He handed his great axe to a nurse for caretaking, shifted his sleeping daughter to his right hand like a weapon, had both taken away and switched. He told Lily, "I'm awake. Show me. But what the hell can he want? C'mon, Greenie." With his good hand, he hoisted his sister.

Stumbling over wounded and supplies and lost gear, haunted by wisps of his strange dream of family, Gull with his bodyguards and Lily and Greensleeves threaded through the dimness until a pair of dwarves took them in hand. Down more tunnels they went, until Gull felt he was dreaming again and would never leave these close, moist, confusing walls. But finally he smelled salt air ahead.

It was the end of the tunnel, where the cliff dropped two dozen feet to the surf. The dwarves had fortified the hole, mortaring stone into a waist-high barricade. Gull squinted around for danger, signs of ambush, found none, and leaned on the barricade.

Down in nighttime dark bobbed a fishing boat holding Towser and the dark-skinned Karli. A glow around them gleamed like lamplight, so they looked like ghosts adrift in a black starless night. They floated within easy bowshot, but seemed not to fear. Probably they were shielded. Six pirates backed oars to hold the boat against the waves that beat on the cliff.

Over the boom of surf, Gull glared at his old enemy, still dressed in a gown of rainbow stripes, with stiff-washed hair and a walrus mustache. Though he'd fought the wizard's minions for months now, Gull hadn't actually laid eyes on Towser since the day a tidal wave wiped out his forces and wagon train. At sight of him, Gull's teeth ground.

"I see you! What do you want?"

He barked in surprise as a pirate lifted an oar. From it fluttered a white rag. Towser struggled to balance in the pitching boat, cupped his hands, and yelled, "I propose a truce! We should talk!"

"Talk?" Gull said aloud to those around him. "What is there to talk about? All I want is to grab Towser by the neck and smash his skull!"

Greensleeves caught his thick wrist. "We have others to think of, brother. We should talk."

The woodcutter ground his teeth in helpless rage, then grunted. "Why not?"

He shouted into the night wind. "All right! Let's talk!"

CHAPTER
20

THEY MET ON THE DESERT OF BLACK GLASS.

Flanked by their surviving bodyguards, Gull and Greensleeves marched from the scrub forest toward the colorful gathering a quarter-mile out. Brother and sister were dirty and disheveled, worn to a nub from days of endless fighting, Gull's great axe a heavy weight in his belt. But they held their heads high as they crunched across the plain.

The wizards were all there. Immugio the ogre-giant carried an arm in a sling from his battle with Liko. Dwen the ocean wizard clenched her fake Lance of the Sea and glared hatred at them. Fabia, resplendent in gauzy red, sat in her chariot of now-mismatched horses, surrounded by handsome and beautiful followers in red tunics. Despite rumor, Queen Thunderhead of the goblins was there, with goblins gibbering. Grizzled Ludoc, in furs, stroked his falcon and wolf's neck. Haakon, self-proclaimed King of the Badlands, looked kingly, for he'd collected a full suit of armor and painted the whole silver and red, and a long red cape hung behind. He'd even fitted a ruby into his helmet over his empty eye socket. As if taunting, each wizard sported the nova pentacle that prevented them being shifted by Greensleeves.

Missing, Gull noted wryly, were Gurias of Tolaria, exploded by his sister in the Whispering Woods. Leechnip the sedge troll, rumored to be dead, wasn't to be seen, but might be lurking in the scrub forest, unwilling to enter the desert. Also gone was Dacian the Red, she who had called down a stone rain on White Ridge and felled his father and others. So they'd reduced the enemy by two or three wizards: that was something.

But Gull's worst enemy, Towser of the silver tongue and back-stabbing ways, was alive and well and smirking in his triumph. Beside him was the dark-skinned, white-haired Karli in her jacket festooned with buttons and medallions, as treacherous as a cobra.

The wizard conclave was flanked by dozens of blue-robed desert warriors, loyal to Karli, curved scimitars bright in the sun. At the rear capered desert cavalry on brightly caparisoned horses hung with tingling bells.

And directly behind Towser, as big as a sphinx on this scalded desert, stood the Keldon warlord. He gleamed with sweat despite the gentle breeze. His powerful arms, as thick as Gull's thighs, were folded across his chest. The tip of his two-handed sword brushed the black glass underfoot.

Yesterday Gull would have hated the warlord, but not now.

Towser and Karli stood behind a plain wooden table with a sheet of parchment and a quill pen in a stone inkpot. Gull and Greensleeves halted within arm's reach. Their bodyguards stiffened, held lances upright, tense as bowstrings. Everyone expected treachery except Gull and Greensleeves. Oddly, they believed Towser would keep his word—his own word—and merely talk.

The wizard raised both hands as if in friendship, his rainbow sleeves drooping. His robe of many colors was as shiny iridescent as ever, like an insect's wing, his hair stiffened with limewash, his mustache proud. But his face no longer looked young. He could have been a grandfather for the crow's feet around his eyes and mouth. Yet he smiled as if greeting old friends.

"Gull, Greensleeves, we're so glad you'll talk like sensible folk. Surely we all agree there's been enough mayhem and killing—"

"No," Gull interjected. "Not enough, for you're still alive."

Towser blinked, and his face hardened, but he mustered his false joviality again. "You know, after all . . . it's never been right that Greensleeves kept these other wizards"—he waved a hand at the hate-stamped faces—"in her thrall, that she forced them to her beck and call. If, Greensleeves, you keep wizards as pawns, how are you any better than us, eh?"

Gull growled, "My sister is better than you as a lion is better than a leech. But you're right. We never should have kept you as thralls: I would have chopped your heads off. But my sister insists there's good in everyone, even bastard grasping wizards, so you've been left alive."

"It's you tall ones been left alive!" shrilled the wizened Queen Thunderhead with her rags and crown of bent nails. "It's us who'll feast on your bones around your campfires!"

Gull jerked his head at her. "Know you, hag, my sister was proved aright and I wrong, for a *goblin* gave his life to save mine! I've ordered all in my army never again to malign goblins in my hearing."

This confusing news caused a stir. Towser, who seemed tired, waved a hand. "Well, never mind the pleasantries. Let's get on with it, shall we? I have a document here for your perusal."

He handed the single sheet of parchment to Gull, but the woodcutter didn't even look at it. He simply handed it to Greensleeves, who could read. The druid peered at the calligraphed hand, beautifully rendered, her small finger tracing the letters, but only for a few lines.

"These are terms of surrender." She kited the parchment back onto the table. The errant breeze blew it off, and no one stooped to retrieve it.

Towser lifted his thin shoulders and sighed dramatically. Karli rubbed her nose to cover a smirk. She seemed glad to see Towser put out, and obviously relished more combat; if Towser had aged these past months, Karli had grown younger, more kittenish. But she had fangs.

The striped wizard said, "You've just suffered a reversal of fortune, as happens to everyone eventually. You can't win here. We'll drive your army from this place and take control. The secrets of the ancient Sages will be ours—"

"There are no secrets," Greensleeves interrupted. Her voice sounded small in the desert air. "We found a portion of tunnels, but they're empty. I visited the seabed and found only ghosts. There are no artifacts, no sources of power. And this land is sick and poisoned. There's nothing worth fighting or dying for."

Now Towser was confused. It was a mark of Greensleeves's sincerity that he believed her. "But . . . if you're not fighting to hang onto the Sages' secrets, then what . . . ?"

"We're fighting to fight you," said Gull. "That's what we do. Oppose wizards who use power to oppress pawns, as you call them. We're staying put until you're crushed and scattered to the winds."

"If anyone is to surrender," Greensleeves added, "it should be you. You can kill us, but never defeat us."

Towser's mouth worked. A greedy man, he'd naturally assumed the army fought for riches and power. Now he didn't know what to say.

Karli did. With her husky desert accent, she pronounced, "Then we'll kill you! You'll be gone and crushed and not even a memory in a few years! And we'll have our forces and march forward unopposed!"

"Perhaps," Greensleeves returned mildly, "but we will continue as a memory. Lily said so. Everywhere in the Domains, in time, all common people will know other commoners fought wizards and sometimes won. That will be our legacy, and enough."

Towser rolled his eyes and ran a hand down his face. Behind him, the ranks of the desert soldiers and cavalry stirred, a whisper running among them, and he barked them quiet. "So this war is to continue? You'll fight until every man, woman, and child is gutted and left for vultures? You'd drive your army over a cliff like lemmings? Is that what you want?"

"No," said Gull again. "And to that end, *I* have a proposal. A counterproposal. A fight to the finish."

Towser glanced at Karli, who glanced back. Gull's followers looked around in confusion.

Gull raised a brawny arm and pointed squarely at the Keldon warlord. "I, as general of the army, challenge your warlord to personal combat. If I'm killed, Greensleeves takes the army and shifts out of here, and you get these empty ruins. But if I win, you leave this land and never return."

Greensleeves and Muley both cried, "No, wait!" People buzzed all around.

But Towser grinned and barked, "Done!" He chuckled for sheer delight, unable to believe his luck. "Done! We accept!"

For anyone could see that Gull, strong and able, was no match for the mighty warlord. The Keldon man would crush Gull as a hawk breaks a pigeon.

But the woodcutter only rested his maimed hand on the axe in his belt. "Tomorrow, then. Noon. Here."

"Perfect!" Towser crowed. "We'll hold off all attacks in the meantime! And if you win, we'll withdraw and ne'er return!" But he laughed, for he tasted victory and was already planning how to exploit it.

Gull turned on his heel and strode off toward the forest so quickly Greensleeves had to trot to catch up to him.

"G-Gull! Br-brother!" Upset, Greensleeves stuttered, a habit she'd lost years ago. "Y-you can't fight him! He's too big! Too strong! He'll k-kill you!"

"Perhaps," Gull replied without looking. "Perhaps not."

"But, G-Gull!" Greensleeves tripped over the hem of her tattered skirt as they entered the trail through the scrub forest. "It wasn't necessary! We could have f-fought all together—"

But her brother marched on ahead. Greensleeves dropped back and watched him go, tears on her cheeks.

"I still don't understand, brother," said Greensleeves for the dozenth time.

The druid sat with Gull and Lily at a small campfire on the sun circle. Towser had kept his word and pulled back his barbarian army. Gull and Greensleeves's people again camped aboveground, having reinforced the palisade and earthworks. But everyone was quiet, as if already mourning the death of their leader. A child that shrilled with laughter was shushed by a dozen adults. In a ring of bodyguards, the family sat alone, left in peace by common consent.

Gull was marvelously calm for someone facing certain death on the morrow. He rocked a sleeping Hyacinth in the crook of one brawny arm, held his sister's slim hand with the other craggy paw. "Dueling him gives our army time to rest and plan. If I'm right and win, you'll need to watch for treachery. If I'm wrong and lose . . . maybe you can strike a better bargain. Either way, it might save lives all around."

"Nonsense!" Greensleeves sniffled. "None of that makes sense! You'll be dead and we'll be in the same fix! Only worse, because I won't know what to do without you!"

Gull squeezed her hand, but she snatched it away, half in fear, half in anger. He said, "You fight wizards any way you can. There's no avoiding it. And plenty of folks in this army can tell you how. You've got some of the finest minds in the Domains here: life-long soldiers and healers and scholars and clerks. I'm almost unnecessary, for I'm only a woodcutter."

The druid refused to be comforted. "You know that's not true, but I won't argue. If you must fight this warlord—and I don't see why—may I at least empower you with some spells? Don't worry—" she added hurriedly "—sleep did my magic-making a world of good. I can augment your strength and speed, give you keen vision. And Kwam has all sorts of artifac's: breastplates that magically turn a blade, helmets—"

"No, Greenie. I've never liked magic and won't use it now. And it won't help if I'm wrong."

"What does *that* mean?" Greensleeves's sorrow gave way to anger. Hyacinth jerked awake at her tone, but then murmured and nestled against her father's chest. The druid whispered, "If you're wrong in *what*? What's in your mind?"

"I had a dream," Gull mused, "a dream of our family. Bittersweet and Cinnamon Bear, our brothers and sisters . . . But I won't say more, lest I lose the magic of it." He grinned at his own contradictions. "Will you excuse us, please, Greenie? We want to be alone."

"Oh!" Greensleeves's emotions wobbled as if in a high wind, and she couldn't speak. She clambered up in a flurry of skirts, tripped, was caught by Gull. She whirled to storm off, but changed her mind and kissed her brother on the top of the head. Then she broke free of the ring of bodyguards and ran to Kwam, weeping.

With only the sound of the campfire snapping, Lily said quietly, "She worries about you. She'll miss you."

Gull teased, "And you won't?"

Lily smiled sadly, eyes glistening. "You don't do things by half, Gull. I've known all along I might become a widow. The idea frightens me, but at least I'm accustomed to it. I trust your judgment, my husband."

"I've always admired your strength, Lily." He hugged her shoulder and pulled her close. "You've a core of steel."

Lily bent over her sleeping baby and tucked the blanket closer around the pink face. "And you've a head of wood, you're so stubborn. But what can I expect from a woodcutter?"

Gull sighed. "That's all I ever wanted to be, strange as it seems. I would have been content to marry a good woman and cut trees and teach my children to shape wood and grow fat and gray by the fireside. But all these mad adventures have been worth it, because I met you."

Now Lily sighed, but for pure pleasure as she slumped against her solid husband. "At least we've a common goal. All I ever wanted was to be a good man's wife."

"Not an angel?" he teased.

Lily shook her head, her brown hair brushing his bare arm. "I don't know what I was thinking, imagining I'd leave this world behind. Why would I need to fly when a man as wonderful and loving and decent as you walks the earth?"

Gull stroked her hair and kissed it. "If you're happy, I'm happy."

"Oh, husband . . . " Then she sighed, thinking of the morrow, and how this love of theirs would end. "But, Gull, what's this dream you mentioned?"

"Oh, yes. My plan, such as it is. I dreamed of my family. . . . "

And he told his dream. And its message.

Came the dawn, with more preparations and fortifications, and finally, a time close to noon.

On the sun circle, Gull let himself be fussed over. Unbeknownst, his Green Lancers had spent the night cleaning his equipment. He was surprised at a fresh leather kilt and tunic as glossy as a horse's coat. His helmet and breastplate, dinged and scratched before, now gleamed. Muley held his mighty double-headed axe, the handle freshly smoothed and the steel head polished as bright as a mirror. Stiggur had braided a new mulewhip. Gratefully, Gull was dressed: steel helmet, leather clothes and tall boots, wide belt with the whip tucked in, steel breastplate, and a blue cape that fluttered in the breeze. Finally, Gull accepted his fearsome axe, and people oohed and ahhed.

But there was little talk. Only Hyacinth, at her mother's skirts, spoke up to ask, "Where Papa go?"

Lily sniffed back tears as she proudly watched her calm husband. "Papa's going to work with his axe, dear. He'll be back soon."

Gull squinted up at the sun. "It's time."

He set out on the trail through the scrub forest, half of his bodyguards in front and half behind. Most of the army trailed in their wake. Liko stumped along, and Stiggur's clockwork beast pounded iron-shod feet through bracken, the boy driver crying openly. Cavalry, humans and centaurs alike, tripped through the brush and threaded among the spindly trees to keep their general in sight. And behind, with a nurse carrying Hyacinth, came Lily and Greensleeves and Kwam and the others.

Passage through the forest was quick, and they stepped into blinding sun that beat on the black glass desert. Angels had flown from their distant mountain and lined the forest's edge, white wings gleaming.

Out on the desert was a long half-circle: Towser and the wizards and many thralls in colorful garments. And foremost, alone, waited the Keldon warlord.

Between forest and desert, Gull stopped. He spoke loudly that his words might carry to the back of the crowd, which now numbered in the hundreds.

"This is where I leave you! I thank you all for your help and friendship! Remember we fight for right and justice and freedom, and never let that hope—die." Choked up, faced by scores of weeping followers, he could say no more. He took Lily's hand and kissed it as if she were a queen.

Beside him, Muley could not restrain herself. "Please, General! Gull! Let us go with you!" Folks were embarrassed, for it was clear Lily was not the only woman who loved Gull. But he only shook his head, and bent and kissed Muley's hard flat cheek.

He turned to say something to Greensleeves, but couldn't think of a thing. Neither could she, though her eyes shone with love and stubborn pride. So Gull simply mussed her hair, as he'd done in simpler times, and turned.

And marched into the desert. Alone.

The Keldon warlord looked bigger than ever, a mountain of muscle, glistening with sweat, breath rushing like a great bellows, limbs quivering with power. Set for killing, he'd left behind his red cape and reindeer antlers, and wore only a black kilt and war harness and the closed iron helmet with fanged teeth and glowing red eyepieces. Seeing Gull approach with his gleaming axe, the warlord slowly drew his two-handed sword, a weapon as tall as Gull himself, and held it poised in the air.

Gull stopped twelve feet from the giant man, planted his feet, and tilted his chin upward. The breeze over the desert flicked the corners of his blue cape.

The warlord sniffed, as if so puny an opponent

were beneath his dignity. He rumbled like thunder over the mountains. "Gull, called the Woodcutter. Are you ready to die?"

Gull lifted his chin higher. Far behind, he felt the rustle and stir of many people watching. Past the warlord were scores more, enemies eager for his death. And foremost, Towser.

But the woodcutter shook his head. "No. Not yet."

And he hurled his axe to the ground.

A gasp rose at the forest behind him, but he ignored it.

Gull tugged off his gleaming helmet and threw it atop his fallen axe. He tore off his blue cape and let it drop, wrenched at his breastplate to break the straps, threw it down with a clank. Gull plucked his mule-whip from his belt and threw it atop the pile, grabbed his leather tunic and shredded it from his chest.

He was done, standing in only his leather kilt and boots, half-naked and unarmed.

If the Keldon warlord was confused, he didn't show it. Gull supposed he'd slain many victims, and some had gone mad at the end. The behemoth raised his sword, took a step, and growled, "You'd die without a weapon in your hands?"

"There's little point in my fighting," said Gull. He crossed his arms over his bare chest. Behind the warlord, he saw Towser and company leaning forward to catch their words, so he spoke loudly. "I can't defeat you in a duel. But if I'm to die, I have a last request."

The warlord stopped, the sword bobbing like a snake's tongue. "If 'tis within my power."

Gull waved a hand across his face. "Remove your iron helmet that I might see the face of my executioner."

In the background, Towser yelled, "No! Don't do it!"

But Gull shouted over the wizard's orders. "It's a simple request, and 'twill do no harm! If you have any *honor*, if Keldon warlords have *pride*, and *no fear* of showing their faces to the gods, you'll grant my wish! Well?"

Slowly, the warlord lowered his sword a little, still ready for combat. With his free hand, he plucked at the iron fangs hanging over his mouth.

Towser shouted again and raised his hands as if spelling. "No! That's not part of the contract—"

But the helmet clanked to the crazed black glass of the desert.

The warlord looked startlingly normal without his hideous headgear. His face was craggy, knotted with muscle, scarred from many battles or cruel training, his skin pale from wearing the helmet the day long. His hair was cropped short and red, like the stubble on his jaws.

"As I thought," said Gull. His voice trembled. "Sparrow Hawk."

"*Hawk!*"

The shriek came from the edge of the forest. Gull turned and saw Greensleeves stumble forward, trailed by Kwam and her Guardians. The druid had a hand to her mouth. She'd recognized her long-lost brother.

Gull relaxed his arms and made fists at his side. He talked, the warlord listened. "I suspected as much, Hawk, but without knowing it consciously, and it's haunted me. I noticed your beard was red in our first battle, and I wondered who you might be. I found your voice familiar: it sounds like our father's with you grown up. But it wasn't until I had the dream, the dream of our family, that I understood. Our parents were on the side of the dead, but you were behind me, in the land of the living, and they urged I follow you. Cinnamon Bear, and Bittersweet, our brothers and sisters, wherever they are, knew who you were, and finally communicated it to me.

"Or else *you* caused my dream. You have power to rule men's minds, cloud their thoughts, churn their emotions, make them obedient and battle-mad. Such strong thoughts may have carried to my mind as I slept and provided me clues. I think *you* sent me those thoughts deliberately, that I might know you."

The warlord only shook his craggy head. "N-no . . . "

Gull stood amazed at the transformation in his "little brother," last seen when he was eleven summers old. Sparrow Hawk was the spitting image of their father, Cinnamon Bear, in his prime.

"I'll guess further!" Gull raised his voice, that it might carry on the breeze to the edge of the forest. "I'll guess you were taken prisoner at the Battle of White Ridge. A company of soldiers always needs bright boys to fetch and carry and learn the ropes of soldiering. We took Stiggur on that way. But I'll guess further. I'll bet *Towser*"—Gull pointed at the striped wizard—"I'll bet *Towser*, with his treacherous double-dealing, seeking a way to destroy Greensleeves and me, learned who you were. I'll bet he bought your servitude, sent you to the Kelds, had you trained in a collapsed-time spell, infused with magic, and enchanted into the form of a mighty warlord. And Towser used his mind-control spells to twist love for your family into hatred. Why else would you hate me so, having never met me? Towser convinced you we abandoned you, didn't he? Do I guess aright?"

"Abandoned . . . " mused the warlord. "Deserted . . . "

"*Aye!*" shouted Gull, and heat came into his voice. "That's *Towser's* ways, he who recruited me so he could keep Greensleeves close for a *sacrifice*, who hired Lily to sacrifice *her* when the time came right! He must have thought it a rare good *joke* to sic my own kin, my own *brother,* on me!"

"Kill him!" Towser shouted. "Don't listen! Kill him now!"

"Yes!" Gull challenged, arms flung wide to bare his chest. "Kill me and lose yourself! Deny what you are! My *brother*! *Brother* to Greensleeves up there, scion of Cinnamon Bear and Bittersweet, a son of White Ridge! Raise your sword and deny yourself! Accept that they've made you a beast, a killing machine with no soul!

"Or," he dropped his voice, and everyone strained to hear. "Find your soul within that shell. Return as our brother, Sparrow Hawk, once lost, found again."

Gull then extended both empty arms.

The warlord raised his sword, stared at it as if he'd never seen it before. He looked at Gull again and dropped the weapon.

And stumbled forward, clumsy, tripping over his own feet, not a giant man, or warlord, but an eleven-year-old boy who'd found his way back from the wilderness.

Grinning widely, Gull caught the monster-man in his arms and hugged him close. "Welcome home, Sparrow Hawk."

Up by the tree line, Greensleeves clutched her friends' hands and wept for joy. "Oh, Kwam! Did you see? Did you see them, Lily? I can scarce believe it! Here Gull's said we must fight to the death, fight all the time, and *not* fighting defeated Towser and returned us our brother! Oh, the bravery of them both—*what*?"

The two brothers broke apart as Towser howled in outrage. Beside him was Haakon, the wizard-king in silver armor. The striped wizard shouted. Riders vaulted to the saddle, soldiers whipped forth scimitars—all urged to the attack by a screaming-mad Towser and shrilling Karli.

Gull and Hawk, seeing the new activity, moved back. Gull was urging his brother to run for the ridge, and Hawk was arguing, when Haakon struck on Towser's command.

A fireball as large as the desert sun sizzled in Haakon's hands. Soldiers and wizards and even

Towser fell back from the heat of the blazing sphere. Horses screamed. Greensleeves could barely see the enemy for the white-hot light.

Then Haakon launched the fireball.

Hawk wrapped his arms around Gull.

And Greensleeves screamed as her two brothers were engulfed in flame.

CHAPTER
21

GREENSLEEVES STOOD SHOCKED AND horrified.

Where her two brothers had been was only a hole, a shallow scorched pit, with charred humps at the bottom.

Things were moving too fast. She couldn't comprehend what she saw. Emotions boiled within her, making her mind a maelstrom. Surprise at Gull's brilliance and her brother's identity. Joy at seeing her brother returned to the fold. Fright as the two were attacked. Sorrow at the scorching fireball that consumed them. Condemnation of her own foolishness and gullibility, that she'd trusted Towser to uphold his end of the bargain.

And with that, rising above all, burning them away like a fireball in her mind, came anger. A deep flaming resentment such as she'd never known.

All around her, fragments of the army burst into action. Captains shouted soldiers into ranks. Trumpeters pealed, drums rumbled. Outraged soldiers roared a challenge as they trotted double-quick onto the black glass desert. Muley screamed and her Green Lancers set out at a run, a suicide charge, pennants flying. Stiggur hollered at Dela as they struggled to arm the giant ballista on the clockwork beast. Liko pounded the earth with his twin clubs, eager to join the charge. Angels drew swords, sang a battle cry, and soared into the air in a flurry of mighty wings. Ravens and D'Avenant archers snatched arrows to their bows and skipped after the centuries: Red, Blue, and White. At either end of the army, Holleb and Helki shrilled their battle cry, stamped their thunderous feet, leveled their lances, and charged. Camp followers, even the magic students, set out after the army to help or destroy as they might.

Out in the desert, amid whirling sand and flashing horse tails, Towser shouted the attack. Dwen swiped her lance in the air and conjured pale-skinned cave folk by the dozens. Ludoc launched his flaming eagle to conjure cave bears and stampeding red bulls. Queen Thunderhead jabbered to her goblins. Other wizards conjured beasts and foemen. Thousands of enemies were being summoned, hot to destroy the few hundreds of Greensleeves's followers. And foremost of the enemy, shrilling, was Towser of the brushy mustache and striped robe, urging them on, demanding all they could give for this final battle, final slaughter.

Only one person stood still: Greensleeves. Overwhelmed by emotion. Because, for the first time in her life, she wanted to kill someone.

Then, as chaos and madness crashed around her, she was frozen, stunned by a new insight.

In a flash, as if Chaney's ghost appeared before her, Greensleeves understood what was meant by "the final sacrifice."

She *had* been willing to sacrifice her life to stop these wizards.

She had *even* been willing to sacrifice her friends and followers to halt their depredations.

But deep down, she *hadn't* been willing to sacrifice her principles.

Trained in the ways of the druids, Greensleeves had continually sought to maintain the balances: between humans and nature, between chaos and order, between life and death, between good and evil. In striving to keep that balance, she'd always held back her power. She'd applied only minimal force to stop wizards, used only a fraction of her power to change the woods, given only a tiny push here and there, used force to counter force, and no more.

But not those around her. Her followers, bodyguards and soldiers and camp followers, had given their all in every battle, fighting for their lives and homes and freedom. Guardians of the Grove had time and again hurled themselves between danger and their mistress: Bly and Alina had been crushed by a monster, Petalia pitched into the abyss, Doris crisped by lightning. The army, and sappers, and camp followers had dug and dug in the deadly tunnels to find a secret for Greensleeves and themselves. Her friends had nearly frozen to learn what they could from the minotaurs. Angels and merfolk had fought to protect their sacred land. Gull had sacrificed his life to save Sparrow Hawk's. Even the goblin Egg Sucker had given his life to save a human's.

And all this time, Greensleeves had held back.

But now she'd reached the brink, the edge, the final sacrifice. She must use *all* her power, *all* her will, *all* her abilities to stop the wizards, for nothing less would deter their greed, hatred, and envy.

Greensleeves had to sacrifice not only her life, and the lives of her family and lover and friends, she had to sacrifice *everything* she believed in.

And she would.

Brushing back tousled hair, shrugging back her embroidered cloak, shooting up her sleeves,

Greensleeves flexed her fingers and pointed at Towser's army of enemies.

"Towser!" she shouted. *"Prepare for war!"*

No one heard her battle cry, for the desert was a sea of noise: shouting, screaming, clashing of swords on shields, the drumming of hooves, the blare of trumpets and riffle of drums.

But with one stroke, Greensleeves put an end to it.

Snapping her arms wide, she conjured a shield spell that extended for hundreds of feet in both directions. And like the sweeping arms of a giant, or the gush of a mighty sea wave, the invisible wall fanned out and halted everyone in its path—all her followers of every stripe.

Horses shrilled and balked as they struck the invisible barrier, many pitching their riders over their heads to thud against the spongy solidness and slide to the ground. Men and women running, with lances down and swords outthrust, felt their weapons bump and rammed into nothingness as solid as a brick wall. As more and more struck the barrier, shouts died, the trumpets wailed to silence, and folks milled about, confused.

And with another shrug, Greensleeves removed them from danger. She did not push them, but lifted one and all bodily and swept them backward, hundreds of people and horses, behind her, up to the edge of the forest where they'd started. Set lightly on their feet by magic, soldiers and camp followers could only gape and shout in consternation. And look to their mistress, who, with Gull's death, now controlled the army.

Yet Greensleeves did not look at her followers. Fifty feet into the desert, she stood alone and faced the enemy. A breeze moved through her tousled brown hair, played with the hem of her cloak.

Greensleeves's bodyguards wailed but could not pass the wall. Stiggur shouted something from atop his clockwork beast. Lily cried her name. Others shouted to be released, to stand with her, to fight.

Greensleeves, Archdruid of the Whispering Woods, ignored them.

Like her brother before, she was responsible for their lives. And as her brother had gone forth, so would she.

This was her fight.

Against the combined wizards.

Karli's desert riders, sweeping in from the west, caromed off the invisible wall, saw a single target they could strike, and thundered toward the druid.

They were the first to feel her wrath. Four hundred strong, they chorused and yipped and waved curved scimitars over their heads, only to shriek as the desert floor before them cracked like a darkglass window and shot walls of brambles into the sky.

But these were not the rambling twisted hedges of thorns Greensleeves had conjured in the past. Giant brown-green stalks exploded, dozens of feet high, their trunks thicker than a horse's body. Huge branches laced with fanglike thorns uncoiled like snakes, rustled across the ground so hard and fast they scratched furrows in the black glass to reveal gray sand underneath. Saw-toothed stalks whipped in an invisible wind. Quicker riders turned their mounts, even dumped them grunting to the glassy ground, but many were caught in the brambles. Riders and mounts were hoisted off the ground, riven by still-growing thorns, twisted in their embrace, crushed between slithering stalks. Panicked, most riders reared their horses and spun around to pelt blindly toward open desert, yet the writhing vines chased them almost as fast as a horse could run. The air was full of creaking and groaning and snapping, a thorny jungle created in minutes. On a breeze came the sharp bitter tang of thorn sap and leaves.

But the druid barely noticed her miracle. Hot for revenge, she turned to a new attack. And found it.

Haakon the First, King of the Badlands, leveled his arm and launched a blazing fireball at Greensleeves. The druid didn't even flinch as the comet was spanked into the air by the invisible wall, bounced and lobbed overhead to plunge deep into the scrub forest.

Greensleeves saw Haakon's hands glow with a second fireball and didn't hesitate. Slashing her hand in the air, she summoned forked lightning that split the cloudless sky and brought thunder crashing.

The bolt lit the armored Haakon like a skyrocket. He was flung six feet into the air. His limbs pinwheeled, his head flopped, smoke billowed from fissures in his charred silver-and-red armor. He landed limp as a rag doll, arms and legs crooked, nothing inside his armor but burnt gristle and bone.

Wizards, conjuring still, gaped. Fabia looked to Dwen, who looked to Ludoc, who looked to Queen Thunderhead. All looked to Karli and Towser, but both were summoning anew. The striped wizard screeched, "Strike her, you fools! Smash her!"

Karli touched gold buttons on her short jacket and summoned half a dozen red-skinned, black-haired ogresses with thick lips and snarling fangs. With a wave of her hand, Karli sent the ogresses charging toward the druid. But Greensleeves touched her temple, pointed, and instantly the monster-women forgot their purpose. Stupefied, they cast about like lost children for orders and succor.

Ludoc steered his red bulls, a herd of them, across the splintered desert, but Greensleeves flicked her fingers and lighted fire sprites on their tender noses. When the panicked bulls roared toward a chasm, the druid spirited up a craw wurm, suddenly filling the desert floor like a moving green hill, and the beast swallowed a bellowing bull whole. More threats came flying from the half-dozen wizards, a panoply of colors and feathers and fur and clouds and screams, too

many creatures and monsters appearing too fast for
the spectators at the forest's edge to even count, but
Greensleeves brushed them back one by one with her
own conjurings, even shouting one spell and unsummoning half a dozen creatures at once.

Holding aloft a stoneware jar, Towser called his
blue cloud djinn, vague and ghostly in the blinding
sun. From the djinn's fingertips puffed streams of
blue smoke. Where they struck sprang up white-
haired, blue-skinned, tusked barbarians, male and
female, with bronze swords and obsidian-studded
clubs. When a hundred or more had arrived, the
djinn clapped his hands. The warriors gave a collective shout and charged the ragtag army on the hill
and the druid who stood before them.

For a count of five.

Greensleeves pushed both small hands down by
her side, as if digging fingers into the earth, muttered
one of the oldest spells known to druidism, and spat
at the barbarians.

The desert trembled. Cracked glass flew in all directions like hail. Gray sand spouted higher than a man
could reach, and geysers erupted in a hundred places.
Though the ocean was not a mile away, it was fresh
water Greensleeves hurled, summoned by her will
alone from the depths of the land, water laid down
eons ago and trapped from the light. Fresh, sweet,
and pure, it exploded upward, a reverse storm, and
splashed and bashed and flushed and knocked barbarians sprawling, killing dozens with its force and
power as they were tossed into the air like flotsam.

Flustered by the fury of the attack, doused by cas-
cades of water, Towser dropped the stone jar so it
smashed into splinters. He cast about for his desert
soldiers, the blue-clad men and women who rode carpets and horses, and demanded protection, but even
these doughty warriors drew back from the onslaught.
Towser barked at Karli, "Do something!"

"She was your thrall!" retorted the desert woman, flustered and fatigued from spelling. "You control her!"

"I'll stop her!" shouted the feisty Dwen. Hoisting her fake Lance of the Sea, she hollered in an ancient tongue, waved the spear back and forth. "I'm lord of the oceans! I'll blast her into the forest!"

The myriad geysers, still shooting straight and true a hundred feet high, bent before the ocean wizard's spelling. The waterspouts crooked like wheat before a windstorm, until the tops began to blow into spume and a fine mist rolled toward Greensleeves on the ridge. Dwen bit her lip as she struggled to control that vast volume of water, bend it to her will.

Greensleeves bared her teeth in a snarl, growled like her badger of old, and flicked her finger.

The waterspouts instantly laid down in the opposite direction, jets of water like giant arrows hurled from ballistas. Dwen's magic was swept aside like the rantings of a spoiled child. The spouts sliced through more sand and glass, blew them in a deadly hail at Towser's army, doused them with sandy mud, and soused them off their feet. Tusked blue-dyed barbarians, bruised and half-drowned, scurried away or dragged comrades from amidst the deadly waterjets.

Greensleeves brought her hands together as if grasping a bottle. When they touched, half a dozen waterspouts cut through the earth again, carving new channels in a second, and formed one jet a dozen feet across.

The vast funnel of water smashed into Dwen's position. Her fake lance snapped as both wrists broke. One splintered end stabbed her chest, ripping her gold-embroidered blue tunic to rags; the other end tangled her legs and wrenched a knee. Under the force of the water avalanche, the ocean wizard was knocked cold and flung off her feet into Immugio, the ogre-giant. Even his great bulk was bowled over, and hampered by one arm in a sling, he killed two horses and their riders stumbling and crashing backward. Dwen, broken, slumped into a muddy puddle and bled into the streaming water.

All this mad activity occurred in seconds, faster than anyone but Greensleeves could take it in. Green Lancers, Guardians of the Grove, Lily grieving over a dead husband, Greensleeves's officers Varrius and Dionne and Neith and Jingling Jayne and others, even Kwam, locked out by her shield, tried to get through to her, tried to comprehend what she was doing.

Towser's army was a shambles. Fabia of the Golden Throat had had enough. Shouting to her followers, she whipped her horses around. Queen Thunderhead simply turned and ran shrieking, a hundred goblins scampering after her. Ludoc's eagle banked and keened in the sky, still aflame, afraid to return to her master. Ludoc's wolf loped away across the crazed dunes.

Towser shouted at Karli to do something, and the desert wizard grabbed buttons on her gay jacket. But their thralls backed away steadily from the mad druid on the ridge, she who could call lightning from a clear sky, waterspouts from a desert, hundreds of creatures from field and forest.

Someone called, "Greensleeves! Milady! They're done! They'll surrender!"

But Greensleeves didn't hear. The druid was raging mad. She clenched her small fists and growled like her dead brother. "They want power? I'll show them *power*! I'll show them the greatest force of all!"

With one hand, and no effort, she sliced a circle in the air, aiming the cut at her enemies.

Instantly the ground cracked in two places, the cracks radiating outward in seconds.

Like a giant invisible knife, the crack rippled away from the ridge, slicing the desert, to encircle the wizards and thralls in the distance. Within seconds they were cut off by a chasm so deep none could see the bottom, and the chasm widened until it was half a bowshot across. Fabia only saved her life by leaping from her chariot, spraining her hands, bruising her fair face against jagged rocks. Her team of four horses sailed off the precipice, tangled and scream-ing. Queen Thunderhead went over the cliff along with a dozen of her goblins, squealing as they plum-meted into silence.

"Now you'll pay!" With her enemy trapped on an artificial plateau, Greensleeves threw back her head and sang, a weird wild cry that echoed across the desert.

Greensleeves's own followers fell back from the invisible shield, even Kwam, for they'd never heard her sing a spell before. Old Chaney the archdruid had reduced every spell to a song, but no one knew this one: a strange haunting sound, soaring and dipping, the notes clashing and grating, chilling their blood.

Then a scout pointed north, toward the mountain of the angels. She howled with fright, no words, only sounds.

For there a green form, a green monster, loomed larger than the mountains.

Tall as a thundercloud, the green monster stepped over the mountains and entered the desert, blotting out the sun. Only the vaguest shape of a man or woman, it had a wide and deep chest, long sloping arms, huge legs, a round head with a muzzle, and suggestion of eyes. It was green all over, the color of deep rich grass in brightest summer. It seemed not solid, nor did the earth shake under its broad flat feet, rather it was as filmy as cloud stuff. The sky behind it seemed to trail in its wake like smoke, until the northern sky and then all the heavens were so thick with clouds the sun disappeared, and the desert was suddenly chilly.

And as the monster approached, it grew taller.

"The Force of Nature!" Greensleeves crowed. Her

words were hurled at Towser and the surviving shivering wizards, but no one could hear for the howling, rising wind. The druid cried, "The most powerful force in the Domains! A part of every living thing, controlling everything! This will be your reward, Towser, and you, Karli! You'll be crushed underfoot by the might of the natural world, your mana sucked into its being to become a force for good!"

Panicking, Towser stopped giving orders and making threats and concentrated on conjuring himself away, anywhere. Beside him, Karli did the same, as did a bleeding Fabia, while the wizards who could not shift and all their followers shrieked with fright.

Yet nothing came of their spells. Towser's fingertips sparkled blue and then sputtered. Karli's magic buttons and medallions went dark. Fabia felt herself aging scores of years, for magic had kept her young and beautiful. Ludoc's falcon, flaming in the sky, shut off like a spigot and became a normal bird.

"It's taken your magic, stolen your mana, absorbed it from every source at hand!" Greensleeves laughed aloud to see their astonishment.

But she failed to notice her own followers shying away, some running pell-mell through the forest for shelter. Even Kwam backed off, for this was no Greensleeves he'd ever seen before.

She was laughing hysterically, drunk with mana, mad with power. And growing more powerful by the minute.

Out in the desert, in a scorched hollow full of noise and shifting sand and drying puddles, Gull the Woodcutter plucked his face from crazed glass and felt pain.

His legs, his arm, his side were afire as if he'd been roasted alive. His scalp was cold where his hair had burned off. And something crushed him against the ground, something huge and heavy, warm and wet.

He shifted, scrabbled to sit upright, heard a groan

and smelled blood and scorched flesh. Then he remembered.

"Hawk!" Gull squinted, but couldn't see very well. The desert sky had gone dark and cloudy. He tried to roll over, hissed as sand ground into his singed sap-sticky flesh, cried with pain as he crawled from underneath his brother.

He remembered now. As the flare and flash of the fireball had rocketed at them, Sparrow Hawk had wrapped his arms around Gull, saved his life shield-ing him with his own massive body.

"Why?" Gull found himself crying. "Why does— argh!—everyone sacrifice for—aggh!—me? I never did anything—Gods! It hurts—special! Hawk! Can you hear me?"

He shouted though his brother's scorched head wasn't ten inches away. Gull cried again as he saw the damage Hawk had taken. Huge amounts of flesh had been burned away, and he leaked fluids and blood from cracked burns in a hundred places. Yet he was alive, for dead men don't bleed, Gull knew. Perhaps the Kelds' enchantments protected a warlord from wounds, though these were no ordinary wounds.

Hawk groaned again as Gull crawled free. The woodcutter was confused by the water, by the bram-bles, by broken bodies, by the darkness. Towser's army was in disarray, and up on the ridge most of his own army was gone. Only Greensleeves stood there, silhouetted against the dark forest like some white and green star. She looked toward the north, where the forefront of a storm blew in, driving a sandstorm or tornado before it. Or so Gull thought. His eyes were blistered and gritty with sand.

But he knew what to do.

"Come on, Hawk!" Gull grabbed his brother's massive arm, but skin sloughed off, slippery with blood. "Come on! Get up! We've got to get out of here! Something's brewing and it looks bad!"

Gull's brother only groaned. His entire back, down his flanks, and the backs of his legs were scorched bloody. Gull could see ribs under a film of dusty blood. "Go—brother. Leave—me."

"No!" Gull gave up pulling, tried instead to crawl back underneath the giant man. "I lost you—once! I won't—uh!—lose you again!"

Stumbling, gasping from the pain of his own wounds, Gull scrambled for purchase and balance, hoisted his brother across his singed shoulders, though pain ripped through him and brought tears to his eyes. "Come—on! Gods, but you're—heavy!"

"Please—Gull . . . " Hawk drooled down Gull's back and waved his arms feebly. Both men were dusted with sand now, itching and burning in their wounds. "You saved me from—slavery. That's enough. . . . "

Gull planted one foot, shifted and cried again, got to his feet. Sand whirled all around, and he couldn't be sure of his destination. He was babbling, too, but couldn't stop. "Listen to your—ugh!—big brother! We go together—or not—at all! Besides, you're an—uncle! Two nieces! And my wife—what did they feed you?—you needs meet her—"

But he had no more breath for talking and struggled to stay upright as he stumbled toward what he thought was the forest.

"Love of the Gods," he whispered, "if this—storm is—Greenie's doing, she must be—powerful mad. Mother had a—temper, too. . . . "

Half-blind, staggering, grunting, he tottered off into the dark swirling waste with his dying brother.

Unable to see, he plodded straight for a bottomless chasm.

CHAPTER
22

PEOPLE SCATTERED AS THE FORCE OF
Nature strode onto the plain of black glass.

Greensleeves's followers ran into the woods, or
spurred their horses down the tree line to find shelter
in distance. Lacking cover, many of Towser's followers also hied for the woods, running wide to circle
gaping crevices and the invisible shield wall. Before
long, former enemies were milling and dodging
beside Gull's army, comrades in blind panic. Yet few
could see their way and went by the feel of the
ground and instinct. The sky was a turmoil of low
boiling clouds, and winds whipped in every direction,
hurling sand and glass chips and leaves and bracken,
until no one could tell direction or neighbor. The
mortals were united in one objective: getting out of
the sight of the angry godlike being that strode
toward them.

All except Greensleeves, and hunkering far behind,
her Guardians and lover Kwam.

Yet as the Force of Nature approached, still far off
but miles high, it grew more insubstantial, more

ethereal, like an oncoming fog bank that never came
to hand.

Because as it approached, Greensleeves absorbed
its energy.

The archdruid knew of the power of the Force of
Nature, for her mentor, the archdruid Chaney, had
mentioned it in whispers, stories, hints, and warnings
that it was not to be trifled with unless it meant the
end of a world.

Not a true being or god, the force was rather a
manifestation of the mana contained in a land, a
shape to contain the power, a vessel. It could only be
summoned in any land once in a few centuries, for
nature gave up energy and life stubbornly. This land
where Greensleeves stood had been sucked dry of
magic long ago, its very essence consumed by the
Sages of Lat-Nam and then the blistering attack that
destroyed them. But there was far more of this continent to the north, land unsoiled and untouched, land
that had been a long time growing, and it was this
source that the force tapped now.

And having been tapped, it conveyed its mana, so
the power of a continent surged through Greensleeves.

She tingled in every fiber. Energy coursed through
her veins and pulsed in her mind. She hadn't felt
power like this but once, when she inhaled the dying
Chaney's last breath and became an archdruid. And
that power had been one wizard's, while this was the
life force of a continent. Her mind swam in a sea of
fire.

And for the first time in her life, Greensleeves
knew what it was to become a great wizard—a
planeswalker.

She could see the path now: how to lift herself up,
how to take the next step, how to leave humanity
behind.

This land, these Domains, she saw, were but a single plane in an infinite number of planes. There was

so much more out there even her enhanced mind couldn't encompass it all.

With one leap, she could move between the spheres. She could stride the starways, warm her hands over blazing suns. She could make herself a goddess and cut a swathe through the universe, gather whole planets and stars and galaxies into her arms, draw forth their energy, empower herself even more. She could pull down planets and break them over her knee like melons. She could drink of the cool ether of the skyways. She could eat stars.

With power drawn from this land, with the Force of Nature channeling into her, she could become a god.

She could conquer other gods, steal their mana, build thrones of their bones, use their flesh to fertilize her dreams. And it was so easy. The power was there to be used, waiting, singing to her like a siren's song.

With power like this . . .

But something interrupted her reverie. Something, something small, buzzed. Called her name . . .

"Greensleeves! *Greensleeves!*"

Slowly, Greensleeves searched around. Her feet were planted in the Domains still, but her head was amidst clouds where the air crackled in her nostrils. Slowly she blinked. The Force of Nature was gone, nothing but a gray-green cloud on the far horizon. The energy of it, the power, the mana, lived in her now. She contained it, could channel it, could launch herself into the stars, planeswalking.

But for that nagging voice . . .

From her great height—was she as tall as the Force of Nature, or was this an illusion of the power?—she looked down and saw, like an ant at her feet, Kwam in his black clothes and long solemn face and long black hair. Both hands were raised as if in supplication—a mortal pestering a god for favors. Blinking,

Greensleeves tried to remember this mortal, and why
he worshiped her. . . .

Other sounds huffed in her ears. A grunting, panting.

Far below scurried more ants. One, scorched and
bleeding, crawled on bleeding hands and knees
across shards of black glass. On the ant's back it carried another charred lump: food, something to eat
back in the nest. But no . . . this other shape had
meant something to her long ago. As had the ant.
The white-black-red ant crawled with its heavy burden through whirling sand, headed for a crevasse
deep as the earth itself. For the life of her,
Greensleeves couldn't remember why the ant bothered, or why she even thought about it.

But there was more. Ants everywhere. If she
weren't careful in her new role as goddess, she might
shuffle her feet and crush them. Not that it would
matter. Ants must learn not to trifle with gods. Gods
had concerns mortals could not grasp, just as
Chaney, when she had passed beyond, had too many
concerns to properly help Greensleeves anymore.

Chaney, Greensleeves thought. Where exactly had
she gone? What was it she'd done for Greensleeves?

And all these ants, so bothersome. Below her was a
toy clockwork animal, and on its back a boy and girl
struggled to pull others up onto the beast, away from
the thrashing trees and falling branches. Women
dressed in green formed a ring of steel around her, to
keep worshipers at bay, she assumed, and that was
good. But others milled everywhere. A woman in
white with blue and yellow and red flowers hunkered
down with a nurse and sheltered children, and
Greensleeves could not understand that, for the
zephyrs that howled around her knees seemed only
the gentlest breeze. Yet everywhere people cowered
from them. At the edge of the desert, soldiers of the
White Century worked with axes to chop branches
off a fallen tree, and blue-streaked barbarians helped

them so dozens of strangers could hide amidst the tumbled barricade. A two-headed giant crouched on all fours and made a canopy of his body, though he was pounded fiercely by stones and flung branches and even loose weapons, and under him cowered scores of gibbering goblins who clutched one another in fright. Farther away, dwarves fought to keep tunnel walls from collapsing as dozens of blue-clad soldiers helped. Yet encroaching waves from a storm-tossed sea sent long coamers smashing into cliffsides and boiling into tunnels and overlapping the forest in a hundred places. Angels struggled against the wind and spume of sea-spray to help desert riders and centaurs form a ring of living horseflesh.

Greensleeves felt the power sing in her soul and thought this was all good. Nature should act this way, for humans and other thinking beings had despoiled this land, long ago and more recently, and now nature would sweep them away.

For nature needed to cleanse the land periodically. A forest fire burned away chaff that the soil might feel the sun and grow anew. Floods washed from the hillsides, scouring the land to the sea. Tidal waves could sweep away the tawdry workings of humans and animals, erode the garbage, restore the balance. Earthquakes stirred the soil, storms flattened the forest, blight withered crops to make way for new. Such was the way of nature, destroying and cleansing and growing anew. Insignificant people, ants, might perish, but the balance would settle and reemerge.

And once this land was purged, Greensleeves would step to the stars and take her place among the gods . . .

"Greensleeves! Help us!"

Again that annoying buzz. Searching, she spotted the black-clad man. He was cut and bleeding on the face and hands because he didn't shrink away, like any sensible creature, but held up his hands to call to

her. He'd be killed by wind and whirling shards of
black glass soon . . .

Why call?

Who was he?

Something tickled the back of her mind, occluded
thoughts of stars and moons and skyways and her
new life. The man had often spoken of what? His
own power? No, another power.

Love. That was it.

Vaguely she recalled the notion of love. A feeling
between two humans, a passing fancy.

That was it. Kwam had loved her.

And she him.

Now she recalled. She'd been a human, a woman,
and known a man's love. Not like the worship of a
goddess, but a close tight-holding love that had
warmed her in a different way, different than this
power that surged through her.

That was it. She'd loved Kwam, too.

But if that were true, why was she here, head in
the clouds?

Gull, too, she remembered. Her brother, when she'd
been mortal. And Lily, Gull's own love. And two children named for flowers and vines. And Sparrow
Hawk, a brother she'd loved and lost and regained.
And her Guardians, who protected her from harm, as
if a goddess needed protection. But she'd been mortal
then, needed love and care. And dozens, no, hundreds
of others had loved her, and she them: soldiers and
camp followers and cooks and cartographers and
smiths and children.

Now she recalled them all. She'd almost forgotten.

And Kwam wanted help. From her. Because the
army, friends and foe, were under assault from
nature gone mad.

And that—she realized now—was her doing.

With a start, Greensleeves, half-god, half-mortal,
came to her senses. She raised her hands, saw them

crackle with energy as lightning lanced between clouds, saw the clouds swirl as she breathed. Oh, yes, she'd summoned the Force of Nature, and it was purging the land.

And all her friends with it.

They'd be dead, swept away, buried under flying soil, blown or sucked into the ocean, dropped in crevices that closed like coffins.

No, she couldn't allow that.

Because people, she recalled now, were important, too. They were part of the land, part of the scheme of things. And it was her task to see they lived with the land and not off it.

But the mana, the power, the energy and life force of a continent lived within her, boiled inside, ready to explode.

She had to give up the power, let it go.

But how? If she loosed the power at once, it would devastate this land, blast it to bedrock, obliterate it fully as if the moons crashed from the sky.

What to do?

If she were to remain in these Domains, remain human, rooted to the earth, she'd have to diffuse the colossal power, channel it slowly, carefully. But soon, or she'd go blazing into the sky like a rocket.

Channel it, then, she would.

For nature was not only a destroyer, a cleansing force, the source of death, but the source of rebirth and life, too. Yet destruction was easier than construction. Greensleeves, archdruid or goddess or mere mortal, could channel the mana, but it was like diverting a raging river with her bare hands. Powerful though she was, she might be swept away and crushed.

But she must try. Even if it killed her.

Delaying, just thinking and studying, hurt, for the energies began to consume her. They roiled within her like lava in a volcano, like a boiling hot spring.

Her beautiful embroidered cloak, her hand-wrought grimoire of spells about her shoulders, began to smolder, the threads to unravel, until a thousand shimmering filaments blew away in the wind.

This was the hardest fight she'd ever fought, Greensleeves knew, for she had to fight herself.

But she ignored the danger to herself and concentrated. Below was the desert of black glass, an ancient blighted place underlaid with a thousand poisons. Nothing but the hardiest weeds could grow there, and their lives were short. If she must rid herself of some power, this was the place to start.

From her great height, she pointed crackling hands and let go rivers of energy at the blasted plain. And as the mana flowed from her, she pictured in her mind what the land had been long ago and might be again.

And all across the black desert, from forest to mountain to sea, chips of fused glass began to shift, to work, to grind together.

The noise was horrendous, like the rattle of pebbles in surf magnified a million times. People covered their ears at the roar. Some had been trapped out on the desert floor, but these Greensleeves shielded in cocoons of mana, so they weren't harmed. The chasms splitting the earth sealed, the giant brambles were ground to powder, the geyser holes filled in. Within minutes, the thunderous grinding slowed and stopped. And left behind, smooth as a baby's blanket, was a wilderness of soft fine sand as black as the night sky.

But the energy within Greensleeves still ran wild. Her hair stood on end. She watched her sleeves catch fire, her flesh smoke, yet she felt more amazement than pain. She couldn't release all the mana yet.

Under the sand were poisons, Greensleeves knew, laid down long ago, saturating the once-living soil. With smoking fingers that shot sparks, the young goddess aimed her thoughts deep. Curling thousands of invisible fingers, she worked the poisons against one another, blending and mixing, canceling one another out, breaking toxins down into original harmless elements. Vapors gushed from the sand, green and red and yellow, and strange odors whipped away on howling winds. Within minutes, the soil was clean again, rich and hearty and ready for growth.

Greensleeves burned now. She'd contained the power for too long. Her guts churned, bubbling like a witch's cauldron. But she thought of Chaney, and sacrifice, and knew what to do.

Growth needed water. Lower to the ground now, Greensleeves felt out the water she'd brought forth previously and summoned it again, not in exploding cataracts and geysers, but in a thousand tiny springs and freshets that bubbled from the black rich soil and spilled in every direction, watering the land.

The storm was calming, the skies overhead no longer boiled. Lightning ceased, and the waters seeping throughout the land kept sand from blowing off. Still Greensleeves crackled with energy. Her vision was blurry, as if her eyes cooked in their sockets and her blood boiled. She needed to be rid of more mana.

Reaching out, she found every seed, every grain of pollen, every spore hidden in the land or blown on the winds, and she weighted each, bore them down to the soil, poured mana into them, asked they take root and prosper. And such was the wealth of power that grass sprang up like wildfire across the erstwhile desert, and trees of many kinds unfolded and sank roots deep and drank the water and tasted the soil: red pines and larches and pepper trees and palms and oaks and eucalyptus and poplars. A thousand kinds of flowers and herbs—hyacinths and roses and thyme and daisies and clover and bluebells and lilies and rosemary—bloomed in minutes, and nodded their heads in the sighing wind.

Groaning with fiery pain, Greensleeves worked

more miracles. Sweeping humans hither and thither
without harm, like mice before a giant broom, she
rooted out the poisons in the scrub forest and broke
them down also. Ancient curses and threats were rendered harmless, and natural life could stretch without
bounds once more. She rooted in her mind as far as
the savanna and the seabed, and deep into them, to
scour out all toxins, enemies of life, until the land
was pure and sweet in every direction and down
under the rolling waves.

Vying for balance, Greensleeves stretched invisible
arms of mana in all directions, into the revitalized
scrub forest and far over the mountains, conjured
handfuls and then hundreds of animals and birds.
Hares and bluebirds and cranes and possums and
squirrels and deer and spiders and badgers and ants
and bears and roaches and snakes and worms and
tapirs and owls fluttered through the new groves and
copses and banks of flowing flowers.

But the archdruid, the almost-goddess, wasn't
done. With a shrug of her shoulders and stir of her
hands, she split open the tunnels fashioned by
ancient hands, evicted the human occupants to safety
in the woods, uprooted the ancient blocks and tunnels and statues and frescoes, and crumbled them to
powder till not a trace stood. Reaching out with her
mind, she groped along the seabed where she'd traveled, brushed aside seaweed and fish and crabs and
sea serpents, and pulverized the sunken works of
men until only crumbs were left.

Only then, after moving heaven and earth, did
Greensleeves finish. With a puff at the sky, she blew
away the last shreds of dark clouds, sucked in the last
vagary winds. Only then did she feel the awesome
energies quelling, dissipating like fog in sunshine,
leaving her wracked body shuddering. And finally,
the magic was under control, humming quietly in her
veins, mana she could handle safely.

She grabbed her throbbing head, reeled and almost fell. But someone caught her, as always. Kwam.

Blinking, peering about, Greensleeves felt sun on her bare head and shoulders, gentle breezes kiss her flushed cheeks.

The storm was over.

And people cheered.

Curiously, Greensleeves peered at her hands and found them blackened as if by soot. Her fingers were numb while the bones in her arms tingled. Her clothes were smoke-stained, the ends of her hair crispy, singed. Her shoes had been cooked off her feet, so she kicked away charred scraps. Her green sleeves were burned off clear to her bony shoulders. She'd come close, she thought. Close to consuming herself and this end of the continent in a fireball like the sun striking earth.

Yet her efforts, risky and death-defying, had been worthwhile, for she was rewarded by a vision of beauty. The sun shone on a land restored. Before her were trees and flowers and rocky brooks and bright glades filled with animals and singing birds as far as the eye could see, from the edge of the reborn scrub forest across sweeping meadows to the far mountains of the Duler angels, down to a sharp clean shoreline where fish leaped for pure joy.

And people all around cheered, friends and followers and many former enemies, too, come out of hiding to marvel at the druid's miracle. Striding amidst them was Gull, unloading the behemoth Sparrow Hawk to the healers, and grabbing his wife Lily and his children and hugging them tightly.

Her faithful bodyguards wept openly for their mistress. And beside her stood Kwam with his gentle smile and a battered, bruised, bloody face.

"Welcome back," he croaked. "We feared you'd— leave us."

"And walk with the gods?" Her own voice sounded

like bird song on the glowing air. "No. I'll remain here with my friends. That's one sacrifice I'll gladly make."

Kwam hugged her tightly, and everyone cheered and sang themselves hoarse.

CHAPTER
23

IN THE AFTERMATH, CLEANING UP TOOK some time. People were scattered throughout forest and field. Many had lost their direction in the new terrain and had to be found by angels. Some units of the armies on both sides had unsettled grudges which had to be quashed. Gradually an uneasy truce prevailed, with everyone watching everyone else.

Gull and Greensleeves set up camp in the new rolling meadow at the edge of the forest, the once blasted desert, now a soft, warm, rolling expanse of grass and gorse and flowers and trees. They'd found their tents and gear standing on the sun circle, the only ancient artifact left intact after the resurrection of the forest and purging of the tunnels underneath. Gull and his commander Varrius wanted to fortify the meadow camp, erect ditches and earthworks and a palisade in case of sneak attack, but Greensleeves overruled the men and they didn't argue. They were heartily sick of fighting and welcomed an excuse to be lazy.

Not that there wasn't work. There were wounded

by the hundreds to tend, supply lines to reestablish, rules of sanitation to enforce, companies to refit and reform, guard details to scour the woods and meadows for stragglers, delegations to send to the merfolk and angels. Yet amidst this work rose celebration, singing and dancing and toasting with flagons of wine and ale, and plenty of time to fun. The children ran wild, picked flowers, played hide-and-seek in the new woods, splashed in the surf. Many adults slipped away from chores to join them.

And one by one, the offending wizards were rounded up.

The wizards had been drained of all mana by the Force of Nature and were only now recouping. The survivors tried to conjure themselves away, or else escape overland, but were easily caught and prodded into camp at spearpoint.

Immugio still had one arm in a sling. Dwen had splints on both wrists, a bandaged hole in her chest, and a scalp wound. The once-glorious Fabia trudged with her head down, her beauty marred by scrapes and bruises, two teeth lost colliding with a rock. She'd also aged decades, hair streaked with gray, fair skin withered. Old Ludoc, hard and grizzled as his mountains, was unharmed, but his eagle and wolf had deserted him for freedom and he seemed lost without them. The wizards were herded into a pen, given food and blankets, and warned to stay put.

Still, they were the lucky ones. Queen Thunderhead had disappeared down a crevice, Leechnip had been hacked to pieces in the forest, Dacian pierced by an arrow, Haakon blasted to fragments. His bones and armor had been turned into soil in the great transformation, and only a poplar tree marked his grave.

Interestingly, the twin perpetrators of the attack, Towser and Karli, came through unharmed. But their faces were hard and bitter, their manner sullen. Towser especially looked afraid of dying.

Well he might. For when he was finally prodded into camp by a patrol of White Bears, Gull gave a shout. "There's the bastard! Fetch my axe!"

Grabbing up his woodcutting axe from a Green Lancer, Gull ran toward the prisoners. Ignoring Karli and the others, Gull yanked Towser by the sagging hem of his rainbow gown and shook him like a puppy.

"Towser!" he growled, "I've waited a long time for this day! More than three years, since you destroyed my village and family and lied about it, since you hired me only to capture my sister for sacrifice, since you banished me that you might kill her—"

The striped wizard took the abuse without protest. Evidently he'd feared this day. His once-boyish face was aged years by worry, his fine robes soiled and worn, and broken brass chains at his belt showed he'd lost his grimoire. His hands hung slackly as Gull stoked his anger by reciting Towser's crimes.

Finally the woodcutter shut up. "We'll make this short!"

Dragging the unresisting wizard, Gull clumped to the nearest woodpile, to a big stump used for splitting logs. He slammed Towser over the stump, chest down. Gull spit on his hands and shifted his axe. Towser lay unmoving, trembling, eyes closed, passive as an old rooster who knew his time had run out.

Without another word, Gull hoisted his axe high to behead the wizard.

The haft of his axe exploded.

Gull yelled and flapped hands riven by hickory splinters. The eight-pound axe head thudded onto kindling behind him. Towser lay unmoving, shivering. Gull cursed.

"Greenie!"

Gull glared at his small sister. For a moment, time turned back to a simpler time.

His sister's fine clothes had been destroyed when

she wielded her great power, right down to her shoes. Now she wore a simple white woolen gown with green knitted sleeves borrowed from a Guardian. Barefoot and bareheaded, her hair needed combing. Standing at a woodpile with his axe (or what was left of it), as in days of old, Gull was transported to when he was a simple village woodcutter and his sister a troublesome simpleton.

But her voice and manner were composed, serene, years wiser than Gull. At her quiet insistence, "No, Gull, don't hurt him," he found himself obeying.

He'd seen some odd changes in these years, but those in his little sister were the greatest.

Still, he tried to protest. "It won't hurt! I'll chop his head off quick, it won't hurt a bit! And it's better than he deserves for what he did to our family and White Ridge and us! We should hang him in a gibbet and let him die slowly, with crows picking out his eyes—"

"Stop." The small druid laid a hand on her brother's knotty arm. "It's not Towser I care about, brother, but you."

"Me?" Gull saw Lily approach with nurses and children in tow. He groaned inwardly. He wouldn't win this argument, not against the two women in his life. He tried not to whine, "What have *I* got to do with it?"

Greensleeves smiled to draw the sting of disappointment. "Towser is an enemy, true. But he's evil and you're not. I can't let you sacrifice your humanity by punishing him when helpless. I can't let you kill in cold blood, no matter what he deserves."

"Nor I," echoed Lily. She bounced Hyacinth on her hip. "After all, he offended me, too, but I don't want him punished this way."

Sulky, Gull pulled splinters out of his callused palm with his teeth. "I shouldn't sacrifice my humanity, eh? Or Towser's either? Fine. If you won't punish him like this—and I think sticking his head on a spike would cure his evil ways—then what?"

Greensleeves lost her smile and bit her lip, her decision was so solemn. "I've a way to stop him. It involves the secret of the Sages of Lat-Nam, and the stone helmet. . . . "

In a while, most of the army had gathered around the pen where the wizards were corralled.

Gull waited with his arms crossed over his chest, Lily hanging onto his elbow, Bittersweet balanced on her hip. Sparrow Hawk joined them, or "Hawk" as he was now called in manhood. He stood stooped, his back from neck to ankles a mass of enflamed weeping skin the healers had worked night and day to reconstruct and regenerate. Lumpy-faced Hawk would be crippled for life, stiff with scar tissue, but he was alive and reunited with his family and not complaining. Still, it was odd to Gull that his "little sister" seemed years more mature than he, and his "little brother" towered over him like some war machine. Gull was head of his family only by tradition. Yet he smiled as Hyacinth tried to climb "Uncle Hawk's" massive leg, and the giant man lifted her giggling with one thick hand.

More of the camp came trotting over to see the wizards punished, and Greensleeves waited patiently while the wizards fidgeted in their pen. Close at hand were Gull's Green Lancers, pennants snapping, and Greensleeves's own Guardians of the Grove. Liko stumped alongside the whirring clockwork beast with Stiggur atop, where he could see over the crowd. Captains and sergeants barked at their surviving troops, formed them into neat ranks, the Red Scorpions, the White Bears, the Blue Seals, and one or two black armbands to mark the decimated Black Dogs. Proud camp followers of every color and stripe stood close by. The Ravens and D'Avenant archers waited solemnly, bows canted at their shoulders.

Behind them, taller, were ranks of centaurs and cavalry, the horses twitching their flanks and tails at newborn flies. Eventually all the army waited on the rippling sweet-smelling sward of grass rife with flowers, in sight of the angels' mountain and the renewed forest, with the hint of the sea lapping rocks in the distance.

Upon Greensleeves's command, the six wizards were herded out of their pen and lined up to face her, albeit inside a ring of spears leveled by bodyguards. Greensleeves knew this was an epic moment, the culmination of the army's work, and she let them savor the victory. But inside she was sad.

Finally she lifted her voice, and a hush fell so that only birds could be heard trilling and keening. "Friends, we are gathered to see the final judgment laid on these wizards, who have profited by the sweat and tears of others, who have abused their magical abilities to lord wizardry over common folk, whom they call pawns.

"But rather than punish them outright, let us pity them. For theirs is not a happy lot, despite their great powers. They won magic and authority and a fistful of geegaws, and then lost it, and now have nothing, while we have friendship and companionship, hard work and steady goals, and most importantly, love. With such good things have we battled these and other wizards, and always won."

Immugio, the huge ogre-giant, shifted from one broad foot to another. Dwen, the ocean wizard, seething with hatred still, grimaced through the pain of her broken wrists. Fabia looked at the ground: with her youth and beauty had gone her arrogance and purpose in life. Old Ludoc glared, unafraid to die. Karli of the dark skin and white hair sneered openly rather than admit defeat. Towser just looked dazed, thinking perhaps of that axe looming over his head.

"We won," Greensleeves turned and addressed the army, sketching with her hands in the air, "because we understand the need for sacrifice. All of us surrendered our autonomy to work together. Each of us, from oldest veteran to smallest child, has been willing to give his or her life for the cause of good. And too many have, even a wretched goblin who saw the light of love. And that is the difference between us and them, and always will be. Love and sacrifice triumphed over selfishness. It's an old moral, but a true one.

"And yet," Greensleeves turned again to the wizards, "we remain burdened with these wizards. We dislike to execute them, no matter what they deserve, for killing in cold blood cheapens us and besmirches our crusade. Yet we can no longer turn them loose, for we know their selfishness will thirst for revenge. This has been our ongoing problem, and we've handled it badly. *I've* handled it badly. Had I done better, many of our comrades would be alive today. . . . "

She finished quietly, "But now, may the gods forgive us, I have a solution."

People buzzed, and the wizards looked more nervous than ever. Gull muttered to Lily, "That's right. She found the secret of something-or-other at the bottom of the sea. We've been too busy to learn what it was."

Solemnly, Greensleeves turned to Kwam, who stood with Tybalt and the other magic students. Without a word, they opened a wooden box and took out the ancient helmet of pale green stone, crinkled to resemble a human brain. Everyone remembered that helmet had been fashioned centuries ago close to this spot, empowered to bring errant wizards to heel.

Greensleeves settled the helmet on her head. "Magic, I've learned in my travels, is a way of seeing. Just as a blind person cannot imagine the colors of the rainbow, so a commoner cannot imagine the colors of magic. There comes a time to a very few when they can suddenly perceive magic, and thus bend it to their will. No one knows how or why some folk can suddenly 'see' and become wizards. But a conclave of wizards fashioned this helmet"—she tapped it with gentle fingertips—"to counter that phenomenon. The ancient Sages were obliterated by the Brothers before they could finish the helmet, but their ghosts and bones told me their intent. Today, you will all bear witness to what I do. Hold him, please."

Prepared for the order, Greensleeves's Guardians of the Grove grabbed Towser, dragged him forward, and shoved him to his knees. The dazed wizard came alert at that and protested, but was pinned fast.

Without a word, Greensleeves touched her left hand to the helmet on her brow. The other hand she pressed hard onto Towser's stiff yellow hair. Onlookers gasped as her hand sank bloodlessly to the wrist.

Towser shrieked, screamed, champed his teeth. But he couldn't move, and Greensleeves's psychic touch to his mind lasted only a second. She stood back, her hand clean, and doffed the helmet. "Release him."

Stunned, outraged, Towser scrambled to his feet, felt his skull as if he'd been scalped. Confused, he hunted in his mind, finally realized the truth.

"It's gone! It's gone! My wizardry! You've stolen it!"

Greensleeves nodded, her voice sad. "Yes. I've unhinged your power, broken the thread, reversed your seeing. You won't conjure ever again. You're a pawn now, like so many you've hurt in the past."

"No!" The ex-wizard clutched his head in both hands. "No! *Nooooooo!!!*"

He bowled past the Guardians, burst through the crowd. When soldiers made to grab him, Greensleeves shook her head. "Let him go. We're done with him."

The army watched as the ex-wizard ran blindly over the meadow, his flying feet shredding daisies and clover and bluebells, until he ran into a low rill and was lost to sight.

With a sigh, Greensleeves redonned the helmet and turned to the remaining wizards. All were cowed now. Even Dwen and Karli had lost their sneers and stared with terror in their eyes.

Greensleeves looked them over. "As for you lot . . . "

"No, please! Please, milady!" They all gibbered, even Ludoc. "Please don't take our magic!"

Greensleeves shook her head sadly and pointed at Karli, who was grabbed by the Guardians and slammed to her knees. The dark woman with white hair began to wail.

Greensleeves stretched out a hand, then stopped. Someone had grabbed her shoulder.

Gull. "Greenie, is this really necessary?"

A curious look crossed her face. "Gull, you've said all along we need a way to stop these wizards—"

"Well . . . " Gull looked at the path Towser had cut through the meadow, then looked at the blue sky above, the warm sun. "It seems a little drastic, is all."

"It *is* drastic," replied the druid. "It's horrid. What I did to Towser is merciless. Like gouging out the eyes of a seeing man, making him blind. But it's necessary to stop him. He's played with power and been sacrificed to it."

"But we'll be good, milady!" Karli pleaded, looking more a girl than ever. "We won't hurt anyone again! Only don't blind us! Please!"

A buzzing went through the army, an instant argument on whether to proceed. Stepping forward, Lily shifted her child and wet her lips. "We have argued, Greenie, there's much good these wizards can do if motivated. We can use their knowledge and shifting skills to extend our maps, find the lost homelands of our army."

"And they can heal," rumbled the huge stooped Hawk. "I've seen it. Many of us still suffer."

"Yes," said Gull. "And they can be put to work, rebuilding villages and homes and castles they've wrecked. You said so yourself."

Greensleeves shook her head, fuddled. Here the most bloodthirsty advocates of punishing the wizards pleaded for clemency, while she, charged with minding them and hating it, had finally faced up to the job. It was a strange world, she thought, and magic just made it stranger. She listened to the crowd and heard forgiveness in their murmurings.

She shrugged back tousled hair that flickered in the flower-scented breeze. "Very well. If we agree to control them, I'll let them keep their sight. I dislike tearing power from anyone. It's too cruel."

"Good," said Gull, and he smiled. "Good. That's my smart little sister."

Greensleeves laughed, and everyone laughed with her.

Yet as the army and captive wizards relaxed, and jokes went around, Greensleeves watched a flight of ducks fly overhead and sighed silently. For there was more to the truth than she'd told.

She had lied that Towser's magical abilities were expunged forever. At any time, she could reach into his mind and reconnect the bridge, the link, the thread, and restore his wizardry.

In fact, she could make *anyone* a wizard by touching their mind and connecting that thread. Anyone. Even her lover, Kwam, who, like all students of magic, wanted more than anything the ability to conjure.

Yet she couldn't tell them, not now. If word got out Greensleeves could make anyone a wizard, madness and chaos would result, wars would split the world, and she'd be hounded to an early grave. The Domains, the times, weren't ready for that.

So for now, she'd hold the secret tight in her bosom. And if it burned her within, she was willing to make that sacrifice.

Captains shouted their troops at ease, and the army began to break into a crowd eager for the midday meal. But Gull had been thinking, and raised his voice. "Hold! Hold fast, all of you! We're not done!"

"We're not?" asked Lily and Greensleeves. Everyone else looked on curiously. What other wonders might they see today?

Gull waved a two-fingered hand. "No. We need something else. . . . A pledge, I think."

"Pledge?" asked a couple of dozen.

Gull scratched his chin as he idly picked up his elder daughter. "Just something . . . Ah, I know!"

He groped beneath his daughter on his belt, missed something, called atop the clockwork beast. "Stiggur, your whip, please!"

Puzzled, the young man tugged out his own mule-whip, fashioned after his hero's, and tossed it down. Gull flicked the whip along the grass as people shuffled away. Still juggling his daughter, the woodcutter whisked the blacksnake leather forward and popped it over the heads of the five captive wizards.

"Kneel!" he bellowed. *Crack!* went the whip, lopping off a lock of Karli's white hair. "Kneel, you scurvy scuts!"

Hurriedly, awkwardly with their wounds and bruises and splints, Immugio and Fabia and Karli and Dwen and Ludoc knelt. The ogre-giant was as tall as a man even kneeling, so Gull popped the whip again, and the ogre mashed his nose to earth.

As everyone gaped, Gull shouted, "That's better! Greenie, stand front and center before them! Now, you lot, I want you to repeat after me! Um . . . 'I, and state your name, hereby swear undying allegiance to my mistress Greensleeves . . .'"

The wizards murmured the pledge, adding the babel of their names, hesitated as Gull paused to think. Finally he said, "Greensleeves, who shall henceforth be called High Wizard of the Domains!"

"'High Wizard of the Domains'" mumbled the wizards.

Greensleeves started to protest, "Gull, I don't want—"

"Louder!" barked the general. He popped the whip so hard his daughter Bittersweet began to cry. "Hail, Greensleeves, High Wizard of the Domains! Shout it!"

They did. Together, first mumbling, but then finding the rhythm, the prisoners chanted, "Hail, Greensleeves, High Wizard of the Domains! Hail, Greensleeves . . ."

Everyone was surprised when Liko, the simple giant, chanted along. Up on the clockwork beast, Stiggur shouted it with a laugh. Then Helki and Holleb joined in. And Gull and his wife and children, and Hawk. Varrius raised his hands and signaled the soldiers to join in, and soon everyone was chanting, "Hail, Greensleeves, High Wizard of the Domains! Hail, Greensleeves . . ." Even Kwam yelled it as he stood by her side, laughing.

Greensleeves's protests were lost in the uproar. "Really, I don't! But it's not true! We—there are still *hundreds* of wizards out there! Every shape and kind, thousands who never heard of me and won't obey! We must—Can you *stop*?"

But no one listened, except Kwam, and he only hugged her close. After a while, Greensleeves just laughed. "Oh, well, if that's what everyone wants. I can give up that much . . ."

And she kissed her lover on the ear and reached out to hug her family close.

CLAYTON EMERY is the author of *Magic: The Gathering: Whispering Woods* and *Shattered Chains; Tales of Robin Hood; Shadow World Book One: The Burning Goddess* and *Book Three: City of Assassins*; an American Revolution novel, *Marines to the Tops!* and the "Robin & Marian" stories in *Ellery Queen's Mystery Magazine*. He lives in Rye, New Hampshire. His 1767 house continues to need a *lot* of care, but the gardens are coming in nicely.

FREE

UNIQUE CARD OFFER

To celebrate the launch of America's hottest new gaming fiction series, Wizards of the Coast, Inc., and HarperPrism are making available, for a limited time only, one new Magic: The Gathering™ card not for sale in any store.

Send a **stamped self-addressed envelope** and **proof of purchase** (cash register receipt attached to this coupon) to HarperPrism, Dept. FS, 10 East 53rd Street, New York, NY 10022. **Absolutely no phone queries accepted.** Mail fulfillment questions to Dept. Q. at above address.

No photocopies of this page will be accepted.

- -

Offer good in U.S. and Canada only. Please allow 10–12 weeks for delivery.

Name: _____

Address: _____

City: _____ State: _____ Zip: _____

Age: _____ Sex: (M / F)

Store where book was purchased: _____

_____

Offer expires 3/96.

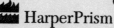 HarperPrism

FS